As he mused █████████████ **became aware** █████████████ **past the edge of his booth.**

A human male, dressed in the jumpsuit and gear vest of a dock worker, slid into the seat opposite him. Only the lower half of his face was visible, the rest hidden behind dark pilot's eyeshades and a grimy gray ushanka hat. Tuvok's immediate sense was that this was a disguise of some sort; it did not match the man who wore it. He had an ill-trimmed beard that split into a smile that Tuvok found immediately familiar. "Mind if I join you?"

"I am waiting for a friend," Tuvok said automatically, appending the code phrase he had been given. "From the barge."

"The barge sank," came the correct counter. "What a shame." The man reached up to remove his hat and glasses, and what Tuvok had taken at first glance to be a mistaken observation on his part was revealed as quite the opposite.

"Sir?" he whispered.

William Riker's face looked back at him, a humorless twist to his lips. "Yeah," said the newcomer with a shrug. "I get that a lot."

Don't miss these other exciting novels in

THE FALL

STAR TREK®
THE FALL

THE POISONED CHALICE

JAMES SWALLOW

Based upon *Star Trek* and
Star Trek: The Next Generation®
created by Gene Roddenberry
and
Star Trek: Deep Space Nine®
created by Rick Berman & Michael Piller

POCKET BOOKS
New York   London   Toronto   Sydney   New Delhi   Coranum

Pocket Books
A Division of Simon & Schuster, Inc.
1230 Avenue of the Americas
New York, NY 10020

This book is a work of fiction. Any references to historical events, real people, or real places are used fictitiously. Other names, characters, places, and events are products of the author's imagination, and any resemblance to actual events or places or persons, living or dead, is entirely coincidental.

First Pocket Books paperback edition December 2013

POCKET and colophon are registered trademarks of Simon & Schuster, Inc.

For information about special discounts for bulk purchases, please contact Simon & Schuster Special Sales at 1-866-506-1949 or business@simonandschuster.com.

The Simon & Schuster Speakers Bureau can bring authors to your live event. For more information or to book an event, contact the Simon & Schuster Speakers Bureau at 1-866-248-3049 or visit our website at www.simonspeakers.com.

Cover design by Alan Dingman; cover art by Tobias Richter

Manufactured in the United States of America

10 9 8 7 6 5 4 3 2 1

ISBN 978-1-4767-2222-1
ISBN 978-1-4767-2227-6 (ebook)

Historian's Note

On August 27, 2385, the new Deep Space 9 was dedicated (*Star Trek: The Fall—Revelation and Dust*). The tragic event that occurred during the ceremony and the chaos that followed created ripples across the quadrants, including the election of a new castellan to the Cardassian Union. Starfleet vessels have been deployed to bolster the Federation's security and ensure the safety of its allies (*Star Trek: The Fall—The Crimson Shadow*).

The stunning announcement that a rogue ex–Starfleet officer, Doctor Julian Bashir, solved the Andorian reproduction crisis has stunned the Federation Council, and within the corridors of power there is a disquieting scramble for power (*Star Trek: The Fall—A Ceremony of Losses*).

This story takes place just after the arrest of Bashir, between September 20 and October 12, 2385.

But in these cases
We still have judgment here; that we but teach
Bloody instructions, which, being taught, return
To plague the inventor: this even-handed justice
Commends the ingredients of our poison'd
 chalice
To our own lips.

—*Macbeth,*
Act I, Scene VII

One

The blackness rippled with the faint onset of precursor radiation, and from a velocity-distorted glimmer, a vessel emerged, falling under the light of familiar stars.

Sleek and uncluttered, the Starfleet-clean lines of the *U.S.S. Titan*'s ice-gray hull and warp engine outriggers caught the distant luminosity of Earth's sun as she turned inward, from the egress point past the orbit of Mars. Impulse grids flared with orange fire as *Titan* moved on to a speed course, cutting across the commercial civilian shipping lanes on a high-priority path in toward the third planet.

At another time, under other circumstances, the return of one of the fleet's most advanced explorer ships to home base would have been met with some measure of celebration; but not on this day. A long shadow had fallen over the United Federation of Planets, and every citizen of that great coalition seemed to be holding his or her breath, uncertain of what would come next.

Captain William Riker folded his arms across his chest, his expression grim and distant as he watched the motion of the stars on the bridge's main viewscreen. The circumstances of *Titan*'s expedited return to the Sol system troubled him greatly. Not for the first time, his ship's grand mission to explore the unknown territories of the Beta Quadrant's vast Gum Nebula had been interrupted by an urgent recall order from Starfleet Command. Before, it had been the herald to invasion by a massed Borg armada. And now, much to Riker's dismay, once again *Titan* was called away from her core purpose because of an act of brutal violence.

He turned the moment over in his mind, as he had done time and time again in the last few days, examining it from each angle, trying to make sense of it.

Nanietta Bacco is dead. The president of the United Federation of Planets, the woman who had guided the Federation through some of its most challenging, most harrowing trials of recent times lay murdered at the hand of an assassin, shot while aboard the newly constructed Deep Space 9 space station at Bajor. The images of the assassination, captured as they happened by reporters present for the dedication ceremony, still burned hard in Riker's thoughts. *The Shot Heard Round the Galaxy,* they were calling it. One simple act, the mere pressure of a finger upon a trigger, and the troubles of the UFP had grown darker and more ominous overnight.

Riker never had the honor of meeting Bacco in person, although she had personally contacted the *Titan* in the wake of the Borg crisis in order to bestow a presidential unit citation upon the vessel; the ceremonial pennant for that award hung belowdecks on the wall of the main crew lounge. Will's admiration for the no-nonsense, hard-stock colonial woman had risen greatly when she had gruffly dispensed with "all the formal crap" and told him with clear-eyed honesty that every serving crewman on his ship had an open invite to have a drink with her at the presidential office in Paris.

"Just don't all come at once," Bacco had said and smiled. Riker regretted that he would never get that chance now.

"Earth Space Central signals we're clear for approach." Seated to his left, Riker's first officer, Commander Christine Vale, glanced up from the panel beside her, reading off the message. "McKinley's ready for us, sir."

Riker acknowledged the report with a terse nod, letting Vale relay orders to Lieutenants Aili Lavena and Sariel Rager at the conn and ops consoles. For the first time, he noticed that his second-in-command had dyed a streak of her hair white, something he recalled was a traditional color of mourning among the people of the Izar colonies.

The bridge was uncharacteristically silent. Along with Rager and Lavena at the forward stations and Vale at his right, Riker's second officer Commander Tuvok stood behind him at the tactical console, with ship's security chief Ranul Keru nearby. Tuvok's composed Vulcan manner was as stoic as ever, but Keru, along with *Titan*'s Cardassian science officer Zurin Dakal and Karen McCreedy, one of the engineering team, seemed to have lost themselves in their work.

Titan's captain kept a loose rein on officer discipline and his crew was professional enough to know that didn't imply any lack of restraint, only a relaxed informality. That openness was seemingly absent now. No one was in the mood to talk.

Riker tensed in his command chair. He resisted the urge to rise to his feet, as if the action of physical movement would somehow shake off the bleak mood clouding him and his crew. The fact was, he had as many questions as his officers did, and it gnawed at Riker that he could not give his people something to hold on to.

Bacco's death and the storm of half-truths and unknowns that surrounded it were in danger of doing more damage to the morale of the Federation than the horror of the act itself. Even as *Titan* had been recalled to Earth, new reports were coming in, fractured and contradictory stories about an incident in the Andor system. All Riker knew for certain was that serving members of Starfleet had been detained—including people he considered friends—pending an investigation at the highest levels.

Some rumors said that the ongoing genetic problem regarding the Andorians and their complex reproductive processes had been solved, others said that it had passed a catastrophic tipping point and triggered anarchy. *Titan*'s own Andorian crewmembers, who so recently had faced jeopardy from their own kind after the incident with the *Starship Therin,* now waited fearfully for news of their planet and the fate of their people. Andor's succession from the Federation was still an open wound for many; a decision motivated by Starfleet's unwillingness to pass on classified data that could have been used in finding a resolution to the fertility crisis.

What concerned Riker the most were the allegations of armed intervention by the Federation. The old adage was true: the only thing that traveled faster than warp speed was scuttlebutt—and there was talk about Starfleet firing on Starfleet. As Earth grew into definition on the viewscreen, the captain hoped that here, in the nerve center of the United Federation of Planets, some kind of truth would make itself clear.

"Approaching McKinley Station," said Rager, as the iron-red space platform rose over the curve of the planet. Illuminated from behind by the glow of a rising sun, the station's curved frame resembled a great metallic claw reaching out to snare the *Titan*.

Riker shook off the forbidding portent of the image and cleared his throat. "Maneuvering thrusters, Lieutenant. Bring us in."

"Thrusters, aye." Rager's careful focus led the ship into the dock and there was a slight bump as tractor beams took hold to guide *Titan* to a safe berth.

"*We have you,* Titan," said the dock controller's voice over the hailing channel. "*Welcome back to the barn. Wish it could be under better circumstances.*"

"*Titan* concurs, McKinley, and thank you," said Riker, nodding to himself. He turned from the screen and found Vale watching him intently.

"So here we are," she began. "You think we'll get some answers now?"

Riker hesitated before speaking. The orders that had cut short their mission in the Gum Nebula had been curt, to say the least. The answers Vale wanted were as much to questions of those orders as they were about the presidential assassination and the Andor confrontation. Finally, he said what had been on his mind since the command had come in. "I wish I knew, Chris. All I'm certain of is that an expedited return to Starfleet Command does not bode well."

A chime from one of the consoles sounded before Vale could respond. "Incoming signal," reported Tuvok. The Vulcan glanced up from his tactical station over Riker's shoulder. "A priority one message from the office of the commander of Starfleet. Admiral Leonard Akaar requires the immediate presence of Captain William T. Riker at Starfleet Command, San Francisco."

"That was fast," Vale said dryly.

The captain got to his feet and his executive officer followed suit. "You know Akaar," said Riker. "Never a man to let the grass grow under his feet. The ship is yours, Commander. Let Lieutenant Radowski know I'm on my way down to transporter room three."

He tugged his uniform tunic straight and walked toward the turbolift. Vale followed for a couple of steps, speaking in a voice that only Riker would hear. "Word of advice? Try not to look like you're marching to the gallows."

Riker stopped on the threshold of the lift and shot her a look. "Tell my wife . . . I have a feeling I may very likely miss dinner."

The high, curved ceiling of Starfleet Command's transporter station sketched itself in around Riker. As the humming chorus of rematerialization faded, he took his first breath of Earth air in years and stepped off the pad.

Gangly arms folded around a padd, a thin and dark-furred felineoid stood waiting for him off to one side; a mustard-yellow collar denoting assignment to operations was visible at his neck, along with the rank pips of a junior grade lieutenant. "Captain Riker, sir. I am Ssura, assigned to you by Admiral Akaar." He extended a paw and blinked nervously. "If you would accompany me?"

"Lead on." Riker studied Ssura's gait as he walked and noted the patches of white on the back of his head that broke up the otherwise night-dark tone of his fur. The young officer was a Caitian, and like those of his species who served on *Titan,* Ssura went barefoot and barely made a sound as he moved.

"If it is not an imposition, I will say I am honored to meet you," Ssura said over his shoulder. "Your mission logs, the voyages of *Enterprise.* I studied them at the Academy. Inspiring."

"It's the job we do, Mister Ssura. I just happened to be there on the right days."

The Caitian cocked his head. "How can you determine which day is the right day?"

"You don't," Riker replied. "That's the rub." He frowned; he was in no mood to discuss the finer details of missions past. "Lieutenant, let's cut to the chase. Am I going to be wasting my time if I ask you exactly why I was summoned?"

"Yes, Captain, you are," Ssura said with a nod. "Are there any other questions you have that I cannot answer?"

"A ship-ful," Riker replied, the frown deepening.

They entered a turbolift and the slight junior officer tapped in a destination code with a clawed finger before looking up at him, his green eyes wide. "Sir, you are possibly thinking I am being obstructive. That is not my intent. May I speak freely?"

Riker gave a wary nod. "Until I say otherwise, you can consider that a standing order."

"My colleagues . . . fellow officers of junior rank . . . they sought to compel me to ask you as to what you may have heard out in the greater quadrant about . . . events at hand."

Despite himself, Riker gave a bitter chuckle. "I was going to ask you the same thing."

Ssura gave a shrug. "Again, another waste of your time, sir. There have been few official statements in the immediate aftermath of President Bacco's death. The Federation Council speaks of it as required for issues of security."

Riker raised an eyebrow. "And yet there are unconfirmed reports and gossip on every media channel in the quadrant."

"Indeed so. Who can tell what is true, and what is supposition?" said the lieutenant. The turbolift halted and the doors opened. "Here we are." Ssura led Riker along a corridor lined with conference chambers and briefing rooms.

Riker's first clue that this would be no ordinary meeting had been when Ssura ordered the lift to go to the conference levels of the complex instead of directly to Akaar's office on the upper floors. Now as they approached one of the doorways, he saw four men in the dark, nondescript suits that were the typical uniform of the Federation Council's security detail.

Each of the Protection Detail operatives wore optical-aural comm devices that looped over one ear, suspending a small holographic lens over their eyes. One of them made no attempt to hide the fact he was scanning Riker and Ssura with a military-specification tricorder, but they all stepped aside as the doors opened.

Riker's lips thinned as he heard the echo of Vale's words about a gallows march, and he entered.

It was a tribunal chamber, and Riker was standing on the wrong side of it. This wasn't the first time he had been in places like this, a curved raised bench ahead of him and a panel of unsmiling senior officers arrayed behind it. But in the past, each time he had known what he was walking into. Here and now, Riker came up short, suddenly wondering.

Had he done something wrong? In the midst of all the concerns washing over the Federation at this moment, had something important slipped past his notice? Suddenly, Will felt like a midshipman again, about to be called on the carpet for some infraction of regulations.

Ssura halted at a respectful distance behind him as Riker walked to the podium. Directly in front of the captain sat Fleet Admiral Leonard James Akaar, his hard-eyed and craggy face framed by shoulder-length hair the shade of gunmetal. The Capellan, tall and broad like all the males of his species, was a head higher than the olive-skinned Vulcan woman to his right and the Benzite male to his left—even while Akaar was seated. The other two admirals shared Akaar's steady, unwavering focus.

"Captain William T. Riker, commander *Starship Titan*," he announced formally, "reporting as ordered." As the words left his mouth, Riker noticed another group in the chamber. Seated off to one side were figures in civilian garb, and by their manner he immediately pegged them as staff of the Federation Council. He made a point of memorizing their faces for later review. Among them sat a Tellarite with heavily braided hair and a shaggy beard; a deep, disdainful scowl showed across his face.

"Riker," began Akaar, his voice a low rumble of thunder. "You are fully aware of our current situation?"

He decided to risk being completely candid with the superior officer. "In all honesty? Not *fully* aware, Admiral."

"That will be rectified in due course," said the Benzite.

Akaar went on. "Unfolding circumstances require an immediate reorganization of certain Starfleet assets and personnel." Riker caught the momentary flicker of the admiral's gaze toward the civilians. "Despite concerns from some quarters, I have deemed it necessary to issue a series of priority commands and re-tasking orders. You are subject to such an order, and so is the *Titan* and her crew."

Riker felt the blood drain from his face. *My ship.* His first thought was of his command, suddenly slipping from his grasp. *He's going to take away my ship.* He swallowed hard, feeling the metaphorical noose tightening around his career. *No,* he told himself. *Not possible. Not after all we've done.* Titan *has earned her place!*

The Vulcan officer read from a padd on the desk in front of her. "As of this stardate, the *U.S.S. Titan*'s mission of exploration is hereby suspended and her primary area of operations redesignated to Sector 001 and surrounding zones. The *Starship Ganymede* will extend her mission profile in the Gum Nebula in the *Titan*'s stead."

"You are hereby relieved of your post as commanding officer," Akaar went on, and the words landed like a punch in the gut. "New tasking to commence simultaneously." He stood up and beckoned Riker. "Step forward."

Riker did as he was told, his legs leaden and heavy. As Akaar approached, he found his voice again. "Sir, what is—?"

Akaar didn't give him the chance to finish the question. Instead, he reached up to Riker's throat and with remarkable dexterity, tugged at the side of his collar. Akaar's hand came away and in his fingers were four gold pips; the signifiers of a captain's rank.

Riker met Akaar's gaze, but the stern Capellan gave him nothing in return. With his other hand, the commander of the fleet pressed something into Riker's grip and stepped back.

Will looked down, outwardly rigid, inwardly in shock. There, in the palm of his hand, was a new rank sigil, a two-gold pip inside a gold rectangle. *What the hell?*

"William T. Riker, you are summarily promoted to the rank of rear admiral, with all the requirements and responsibilities thereof." The Vulcan officer said the words, but Riker was still trying to keep up.

"Your assignment is here at Starfleet Command," Akaar told him briskly. "Your designation will be 'flag officer without portfolio,' but you will report directly to me. Your mission is to act in support of my command in the current time of crisis."

"And . . . my crew?"

"For now, you have leave to retain the *Titan* as your flagship, if that is what you wish."

Riker took a deep breath, his fist tightening around the rank pin. He spoke quietly. "Admiral Akaar, sir, I don't think that I can accept this."

Akaar's dark eyes flashed. "Put it on, man," he growled, low and angry. "Or you'll leave this room with your discharge papers. Clear?"

Refusal, it seemed, was not an option. Riker glanced at the Tellarite and the other civilians, who were already gathering themselves to leave, as if they had dismissed the entire discussion. He had the sudden, damning sense that he was being used as a proxy in this arena, pulled without justification into a game where he didn't know the rules or the players.

A flare of anger lit inside him, a resentment at being treated like a dupe. He wanted to demand an explanation, to force it from Akaar then and there, but he knew that would never happen. What choice did he have to find the answers he wanted unless he accepted? More was going on in the Federation's corridors of power than he could guess at, that much was certain.

Riker felt as if he had been pushed to the edge of a cliff. He could fall . . . or he could stand fast.

Slowly and carefully, he reached up to his collar and snapped the sigil into place.

Feathery flakes of toxin-laden snow fell from a sky that resembled a sheet of beaten lead. The lower-than-standard gravity of the frigid little world encouraged the lazy blizzards that constantly washed across its surface, a far-off and feeble sun doing little more than warming the landscape to somewhere just below freezing point. Rounded towers of greenish ice, polluted by heavy metals in the soil, reached for the low clouds, occasionally backlit by flashes of lightning from over the line of the near horizon.

The planet was an unwelcoming place, barely capable of holding on to a thin and unforgiving biosphere. What life existed here was ugly and full of fury, rapacious beasts that preyed on each other in bursts of brutal savagery.

Some of the warriors expressed the desire to sharpen their skills with an impromptu hunt of the larger ursine forms, but their leader put down any such thoughts with an angry snarl. This was not a huntsman's retreat, not some game for youths. They had been called here for a mission, a deed that involved a weight of blood spilled and blood yet to be spilled.

The leader was the only one of them who knew the full dimension of the sortie. She alone knew why they were on this nameless, ice-rimed rock, and she had seen fit not to impart it to her men. She required only their obedience.

Some of them, the ones too quick to act and too slow to consider, would not have shown the correct dedication to the deed had they known its origins. No matter. All that they needed to know they had been told. This mission was about revenge, and that emotion sang to the heart of every Klingon.

Commander Ga'trk rolled back the hood of the gray battle cloak from her head and allowed the burning cold to sear her face. Ice crystals had already turned her brows a muddy white, and she brushed them away, taking care not to let the toxic snow anywhere near her eyes or lips. She peered owlishly through the storm, surveying the shapes of the prefabricated buildings below her. At her side, her subaltern Koir was using a periscope sight to do the same, running a passive scan for sensor beams or cloaked guardians.

From the top of the ridge where they crouched, Ga'trk could count six distinct dome-tents, common structures of Ferengi manufacture built for temporary colonies and used on a thousand different frontier worlds. Flexible tube corridors connected some of them, and dim illuminators picked out the shapes of heat-lock doors.

"No detections," reported Koir. "Transport inhibitor remains active." His words were as much for her ears as they were for those observing the unfolding events through the monitor device clipped to the warrior's shoulder. Through its omni-directional eye, a real-time holographic relay of the mission was being beamed back to their support ship and on to some nameless place where Ga'trk's masters watched and waited.

The commander accepted Koir's report without comment. Somewhere in the camp, a dispersal field generator was throwing out enough ionic distortion to render a direct beam-in impossible, but that did not deter the Klingon. To teleport in at point-blank range, to appear standing over an enemy as he rested and gut him before he could rise? Where was the challenge in that? Similarly, they could have bombarded the site from low orbit with a stun blast or erased it completely with a photon torpedo, but such tactics were the tools of weaklings.

No. The work of Ga'trk and her unit was to be the silent, lethal hand of the Empire. They had no formal designation within the ranks of the imperial military; they eschewed the gaudy trappings of honor and tribute that so many of their kinsmen counted as measure of their worth. Their trophies were in darkness and silence, in the unseen footprint and the vanishing of a foe.

Commander Ga'trk and her warriors had no medals and chains of status. The only thing they bore with pride was a brand—a single word, written across their chest beneath an Imperial trefoil.

The word was *qa'*; some translated it in the tongues of other races as if it meant *ghost,* but that did not plumb the full depths of the name. These were soldiers whose duty was to move like the breath of wind and leave no trace they had ever been there. No trace, that is, but the erasure of their chosen targets.

Ga'trk drew her *mek'leth* from the scabbard beneath her cloak with one hand and with the other hand, she drew a shrouded disruptor pistol. It was the signal Koir and the five other Klingons had been waiting for.

Like stalking wolves, they swept fast and silent over the lip of the ice ridge. Keeping low, the warriors fanned out into three smaller groups, approaching the encampment in a pincer formation.

The orders from the general had been direct and gave no room for interpretation. The terrorists hiding in this place were to be captured alive for forcible after-action interrogation. Terminations would be seen as failures and punished as such; Ga'trk's warriors were as skilled as surgeons with their blades, and they were expected to be precise.

It had been in a mission under similar parameters that intelligence had come to light, the same intelligence that had led them to this ice world. In that instance, the boarding of a gunrunner ship and the execution of a crew of Orions had given up this locale. Ga'trk frowned at the thought of that operation; compared to this sortie, it had been undisciplined, all noise and brute force. In the aftermath, mistakes made had required her to discharge two errant soldiers with her own *bat'leth*.

She hoped the data they had compelled from the Orions before they died had been worthwhile. Up until the moment she laid eyes on the camp, the commander had thought this to be a fool's errand.

The cowards in those domes, hiding in the snows and unaware of the killers that stalked them, had murdered an empress, and they were soon to pay for it. Not Ga'trk's queen, of course, but still the leader of an honored ally and thus undeserving of a wastrel's fate.

They reached the nearest dome and Koir's hands rose up, a pair of razor-sharp daggers glinting dully in each fist. He pierced the fabric skin of the building and cut open an entrance with two downward slashes. A tongue of thick material lolled out, and a gust of warm interior air blew across their faces.

Koir took a step closer, but Ga'trk hesitated, gripping her *mek'leth* tightly. The inside of the dome-tent was completely empty.

A new chill ran through her, something ingrained in her marrow from years of walking a warrior's path. The commander spun in place, drawing in a lungful of acrid air for a shout.

Not fast enough.

Buried in the snow, deep enough that they were lost to Koir's sensor scans, a dozen spherical pods now blinked into life and shot up through the slush to waist height, buoyed by antigravity generators. Each silvery globe was split around its equator by a glowing orange line; the emitter band for a multidirectional phaser discharge.

They fired as one, each pod releasing a ring of fire that expanded outward in a blazing sweep. Those caught in the path of the beam—and there were none who avoided that fate—were cut through. Some bisected like herd beasts at slaughter, others rendered without limbs or heads.

Ga'trk saw her *mek'leth,* her hand still gripping it tightly, forearm up to the elbow neatly severed, fall away in a jet of purple blood to the dirty snow at her feet. Agony poured into her, and she howled into the blizzard as the domes caught light. Plasma charges hidden beneath the floors turned them all into crackling bonfires, and the churn of flames briefly set the blizzard to a hissing, poisonous rain.

She staggered a short distance before the pressure wave from the plasma detonations knocked her off her feet and face-first into the snow. The ache of the cut limb was nothing to what came next; the unspeakable pain as her cloak burned, the armor plates on her back slagging and melting into her flesh.

Commander Ga'trk died cursing a foe that had never even shown her a face, an enemy who would lay a trap so craven. She died there, on that nameless ball of ice and rock, she and her men now ghosts in more than name.

Light-years away, on a military base on the planet Archanis, in a bunker that showed on no maps and behind a door that bore no detail, an aging warrior took up his *d'k tahg* and cut a wound along his forearm. The fresh mark made by the general's honor blade joined other long-healed white scars that webbed his flesh.

He let blood drip from the knife to the floor and grimaced at the other senior warriors in the command chamber. The glassy artificiality of the ice world faded around them, and they were once more standing upon the grid of a holodeck. Behind them, the technicians and operations crew said nothing, waiting.

The general began; first a low growl in the deepest register, held in the pit of his chest. Building and building until he gave it voice, made it a roar. He threw back his head and bellowed defiance, the echo of his cry calling from the lips of every Klingon in the room.

When the death shout faded, the old soldier sheathed his blade, considering his self-inflicted wound. It was his way to do this, to remember each and every death that came from his command. Each cut was a warrior, a ship, a battle squad lost to Sto-Vo-Kor, a blood cost that he had been responsible for.

"Enough," he muttered, turning to his adjutant. "This is the end to it."

The adjutant exchanged a wary glance with the other officers. "General. This endeavor stems from a request of great import. From the highest levels."

"I know that, whelp." The general ran a hand through his thinning beard, his forehead ridges thickening as he grimaced. "And we have done as the alliance demands of us. But enough now. No more Klingon blood will be spilled in the name of this."

"Honorless dogs," muttered another of the warriors. "They knew we were coming. Perhaps the Orions managed to warn them. . . ."

"What shall we tell our ally?" demanded the adjutant. "We were asked this favor because we were capable of it! Now we taste blood and we halt in our tracks?"

The general's blow came out of nowhere, a sweeping backhand that shattered the adjutant's nose and turned his face into a blood-streaked mess. He had the strength not to fall, but only barely, staggering back and clutching at the injury.

"Never dare to lecture me on *the taste of blood,*" said the old warrior, pausing to lick a little of the purple fluid that had gathered over the studs of his gauntlet. "We were asked to perform this deed, flattered by praise of our martial prowess! But it is hollow. See the truth, fool. The ally asks this of us not because we are capable of it, but because he considers our warriors *disposable.* He does not wish to sully himself with acts of murder, even in righteous vengeance. Better he uses the Klingons to be his wolves." He eyed the others in the room, daring them to speak against him. "He has us do what he will not." He shook his head. "But we have done enough already."

The general stalked forward and set his burning gaze on the adjutant. "Heed me," he told the other Klingon. "This is the message you will pass on. Say it to him, word for word, so there is no error." The old warrior switched from his native tongue to the human language of Federation Standard. "Tell him that the Bajoran will have to do his own dirty work from now on."

Vale became aware that she was pacing the captain's ready room in a slow, continuous orbit, and she sighed, pausing before she sat down on the edge of Riker's desk. The padd in her hand was filled with pages of regulation-issue Starfleet paperwork, docking protocols and the like transmitted over from McKinley Station after *Titan* had berthed at the platform; essentially it was boilerplate documentation, but it still needed the authorization of a ship's commanding officer—and as Riker had been summoned away before *Titan*'s impulse grids had a chance to cool, right now that was her.

She stared at the page without really seeing it, and she blew out a breath. Looking away, Christine glanced out the ready room's window to where the curve of the Earth's surface caught the glow of a sunrise. It looked the same as it ever had, she thought. From up here, peaceful and quiet.

Down there, it had to be a careful, civil chaos. In the entire history of the United Federation of Planets, from its formation more than two centuries ago, no serving president had ever been assassinated in office.

Not that there hadn't been attempts, of course. Ra-Ghoratreii of Efros had come the closest to taking that dubious honor, after the whole Gorkon conspiracy business, and it was barely a year ago that Nan Bacco herself had been the target of a failed effort on the Orion homeworld.

But now it had actually *happened*. Bacco's death was something new and terrible. The people of the Federation had never lost a leader like this, and no one knew where to start to process it. Candlelight vigils and memorial ceremonies were already being held on member-worlds across the quadrant, and the scenes of public despair from the late president's home Cestus III were harrowing.

The timing of it couldn't have been worse. The wounds of a Federation bloodied by the Borg Invasion were finally healing, and concerns over the rise of the Typhon Pact, the newest power in the galactic arena, had found some measure of stability. Olive branches had been extended to the Gorn and the Romulans. There was a sense of moving forward, that perhaps the quadrant was past the most terrible, that there was hope again.

But now this brutal attack on someone respected across the galaxy had shaken the people of the UFP once more. Add to that the uncertainty surrounding the relationship between the Federation and Andor, one of its founding members, and the ramifications of Bacco's death went far beyond Vale's ability to grasp.

She lost herself in the view from the window, measuring her own thoughts. In a way, she felt a little cold-blooded about it all. At first, Vale had experienced the same hard jolt of shock and anger that many of her crewmates did, the moment of breathless astonishment at the scenes of the assassination. But then, like a switch flipping inside her mind, all that emotion had been buried.

She looked at the news footage of the incident light-years distant on DS9, and she was analyzing it, calculating the clinical facts of the killing. Before *Titan,* before Starfleet, Christine Vale had been a peace officer in the Pibroch City Police Department on Izar, and somewhere underneath the arrowhead combadge and black uniform tunic, she was still a cop at heart. She looked at Bacco's death and saw a crime scene, disconnecting herself from the emotional content of the offense and asking the dispassionate questions. *Who was the shooter? How did they get a weapon through station security? What was the motive?*

On one level, she knew that the best investigative minds in the UFP were already finding answers to those questions and many more, but right at that moment, Vale wanted to be there with them, working the case. If for no other reason than to be able to begin to make sense of the brutality of the act, to feel as if she were doing something about it.

A sigh escaped her lips and she looked back to the padd, tapping the authorization tab, reluctantly returning to the matter at hand. When the intercom chimed in the quiet of the ready room, she almost jumped.

"Commander Vale?" Out on the bridge, Tuvok was keeping a watch on things. *"Incoming message for your attention."*

Despite the fact that she was alone in the room, Vale drew up and straightened. "Pipe it in here, will you?"

A moment later, Will Riker's voice issued out of

the air. *"Christine? Do we have privacy?"* She could hear
the faint sound of wind noise in the background, as if
he was up on a roof somewhere.

"It's just me. Go ahead, sir."

"I have had . . . a very interesting morning."

"Let me guess. The brass decided to give you early
retirement, Captain?" It was a weak attempt to lighten
her tone, and it fell flat.

"Worse than that," said Riker. *"As of now, I am the
brass. It's not 'Captain' anymore. Akaar just promoted me
to rear admiral."*

She was genuinely speechless for a long moment
before finding her voice again. "Does it make me a bad
person that the first thought I have is, 'Do I get the
ship now?'"

Vale heard the brief smile in his voice. *"Don't push
your luck, Commander. I've got you right where I need
you."*

It was tough to frame her next question, so in the
end she gave up. "Look, I'm just going to put this out
there; what the hell is going on, sir?"

*"Damned if I know. Apparently I get an office and
an aide, but so far this promotion doesn't appear to come
with any explanations. But there's more going on down
here than just the fallout from the shooting. I'm going to
need your steady hand up there, Chris."*

She nodded. "Aye, sir. The crew should be told.
And they'll have questions."

"They can take a number and get in line behind me."
He hesitated. *"Here's the thing. We don't know how long
Titan is going to be here, so my first order with this new
rank is to run up a shore leave schedule, grant liberty
to whomever needs it. I think our people could use some
air and open sky. And McKinley's tech staff can take the*

opportunity to give the ship a tune-up. Make that happen. In the meantime . . ." He drifted off for a second. *"I'll try to figure out how to explain this to Deanna. It's a lot to process."*

A grim certainty settled on Vale. "Captain . . . I mean, *Admiral* . . . don't get me wrong, it's not that I don't think you deserve the laurels and all . . . but this has come from out of nowhere. Especially now, after the assassination."

"You're not saying anything I'm not already thinking, believe me. I'm sure Admiral Akaar has his reasons. Maybe he'll see fit to share them with me, hopefully sooner rather than later. Carry on, Commander."

"Aye, sir," she added. "And, uh, congratulations."

"Thanks," said Riker. *"I hope."*

TWO

It was a good view, Riker reflected.

Out across the bay, looking in the direction of the great spans of the Golden Gate Bridge and beyond them the towers of San Francisco, there were only clear blue skies and the occasional puff of white cloud on the coastal breezes. Silver dots—flyers and air trams—caught blinks of sunshine as they moved through the city's aerial lanes. San Francisco was waking up, going to work, but Riker had been in the office since before dawn.

He hardly felt like his feet had touched the ground since the brisk promotion ceremony a day earlier. Lieutenant Ssura, now permanently assigned as his adjutant, had taken him to his new base of operations in the south tower of the Starfleet Command complex and spent the rest of the day acclimating the new admiral on the details of his posting. By the time they were done, it was ship's night up on *Titan,* and Riker wearily chose to snatch some sleep in the transient officers' barracks rather than beam back into orbit and wake his wife and daughter.

Deanna seemed to be taking the news a lot better than he did. She immediately dropped into what he had come to consider "counselor mode" and said all the right things to set his mind at ease . . . for the moment. Talking to her, he found all the trivia of a hundred minor decisions welling up in his thoughts. *Would they need to find a home on Earth now? A new school for Tasha?* Will Riker hadn't lived anywhere other than in the cabins of a starship for almost three decades, and the notion of suddenly finding a home back here on Earth was strangely banal and alien all at once. He'd been away for so long, back when escape from his youth in Alaska had been the only thing he wanted. It seemed odd coming home like this, the opportunity to think on it robbed from him.

He turned from the window to look at the wide desk where dozens of padds of varying sizes were neatly stacked. The room was sparse, lacking any touches of individuality save for a couple of generic-looking potted Aldebaran ferns and a painting on one wall of an old *Mann*-class starship chasing the wake of a comet.

Suddenly the office felt very small, despite the fact that it was almost twice the size of his ready room back on the *Titan*. Riker sat in the chair behind the desk and surveyed the piles of files Ssura had dutifully prepared for him.

"Is this going to be my center seat from now on?" he said to the air. An ember of resentment stirred in his chest, and with a grimace, Riker snatched the first padd off the top of the pile, resolving that he would get back to his ship in the shortest possible order, even if that meant docking *Titan* permanently in geostationary orbit.

When he looked up at the chronograph on the wall, two hours had passed and the pile of padds hadn't dwindled, only moved into smaller groupings spread out over the desktop. Tasking orders for ships and crews, re-supply authorizations, mission logs for review, transfer requests, scientific reports . . . The list went on and on. A landslide of paperwork threatened to bury Riker on his first day on the job, and if anything, that frustrated him even more.

Akaar pulled me out of the captain's chair to be his damned file clerk? He thought back to his earlier fears that he had been called back to Starfleet Command to be reprimanded for something, and for a moment, Riker wondered if that was in fact what had happened. The promotion to admiral wasn't a reward, it was a punishment. *I still have more to do out there,* he told himself, his gaze slipping back toward the painting of the starship.

A ping from the intercom on his desk interrupted Riker's morose train of thought, and Ssura's voice issued out, even as the door to the office was opening. *"Sir, I'm sorry, but he insisted on coming straight in—"*

The grim-faced Tellarite who had been at the promotion ceremony filled the doorway, and over his shoulder Riker saw Ssura bobbing up from his desk in the anteroom beyond, eyes wide.

"It's okay, Lieutenant. Carry on."

The door slid shut behind the Tellarite, and he cocked his porcine head, his dark, deep-set eyes studying the office. "Don't get up," he said, walking slowly across the room. "I can see you are busy."

"Mister Velk, isn't it?" Riker knew exactly who the civilian was. In a moment snatched between his endless briefings, he had searched the public databases for information on the men and women who had watched Akaar give him the new rank. Galif jav Velk had been hard to miss.

He didn't grace Riker with a reply as he helped

himself to a glass of water from a carafe on a nearby side table. According to the sparse biography that was a matter of public record, Velk had originally been a representative for one of Tellar's largest mining and mercantile concerns before a transition into the political arena in the 2360s. At some point in the last decade or so, Velk had come into alignment with Ishan Anjar, an ambitious councillor from post-occupation Bajor— the very man who now held the transitory office of president pro tempore following Nan Bacco's death. According to the Federation charter, Ishan would maintain the role as interim president for sixty days, until a special election could be called to determine who would take the office on a permanent basis.

Both Ishan and Velk were unabashed hawks, champions of a strong and well-armed Starfleet and a proactive military stance; but while the Bajoran leavened his views with a good amount of fatherly charisma, Velk was simply blunt and forthright. A hard-eyed and uncompromising figure from a race of beings who practically made stubbornness a virtue, Velk now served at Ishan's pleasure as his chief of staff.

There were other, less flattering names for him, however. The more vociferous political commentators in the Federation news media spoke about Velk as a "hatchet man," and it was true that in his corporate career as well as his political one, the Tellarite often made decisions that some might have called callous, even ruthless.

"How can I help you?" Riker asked, tamping down his irritation at the Tellarite's uninvited intrusion.

"The role you are going to fill," Velk began, his gaze still ranging around the room, "it is fluid. You'll come to understand that quickly enough . . . Admiral."

He lingered on the cityscape across the bay, adding the rank as if it was an afterthought.

"Doesn't look that way from this side of the desk," Riker replied, waving a hand at the padds. "But I'm a quick study."

"So I've heard." Velk put down the glass and at last he looked directly at Riker. "I have a lot to occupy my time at the moment. The Federation's resolve is being tested, and it is imperative that we do not buckle under the pressure. As such, when outside elements are introduced that cause additional concerns, I am greatly perturbed."

"I don't follow you." But he had an idea of what the Tellarite was implying.

"I opposed your recall and promotion." Velk said it without any shade of emotion to the statement. "I felt you were unsuitable, a view shared by many members of the cabinet. You're not a diplomat. You have little experience of . . . what is that human word? *Realpolitik*."

Riker's lips thinned. He hadn't even moved in and already he was being challenged. "Your candor is quite refreshing, Mister Velk, and I appreciate it. But as you can see, I've got a fair bit of reading to catch up on. So do you have a point to make, or did you just come up here to enjoy the view?"

"Akaar promoted you; that's done." Velk continued as if Riker hadn't spoken. "So now you'll be working with the members of the cabinet, and we have to make the best of it. I wanted you to understand my outlook at the earliest opportunity, so that there is no room for misinterpretation. I don't have time for such things."

"We agree on that, at least. So let me show you

the same courtesy." Riker leaned forward. "I'm sure there're a dozen other officers who would be better suited to wearing this." He tapped at the rank pin on his collar. "Frankly, I'm a little surprised Akaar didn't give it to Jean-Luc Picard—"

"Picard?" Velk said the name with cold disdain. "In my opinion, a man unable to follow orders. But the president pro tem is more tolerant than I. He has ordered Picard and the *Enterprise* on a mission to Ferenginar to deal with a developing diplomatic situation there."

This was the first Riker had heard of it; the day's intelligence reports were the first documents he had read, and nothing had been mentioned about problems with the Ferengi Alliance. "What situation would that be?"

"There is a possibility that the Typhon Pact may be making overtures to the Ferengi, regardless of their membership in the Khitomer Accords. Picard is there to keep them from accepting the offer. I would hope he's capable of accomplishing that, at least."

Riker ignored the jibe about his former captain and went on. "Mister Velk, you might have a negative opinion about me and my fellow officers, but let me make this clear. If Starfleet calls me to duty—*any* duty—I will serve to the best of my abilities and in the best interests of the United Federation of Planets. Do *you* understand *me*?"

"I believe so." Velk turned to leave, but Riker rose from his chair. He wasn't willing to end this confrontation just yet.

"As you made the trip, Mister Velk, perhaps you can explain something to me before you leave."

The Tellarite halted. "What is it?" he asked, frowning.

"Doctor Julian Bashir. Captain Ezri Dax." Riker saw Velk stiffen. "Doctor Tovak. Doctor Elizabeth Lense. Doctor Katherine Pulaski. Doctor Lemdock." He held up the padd containing the report that mentioned the names.

"The disposition of those individuals is not a matter for your concern."

"I don't agree." Riker folded his arms. "I owe my life to one of them. But according to the Federation Security Agency, under a special executive directive they are being held pending court martial charges. I want to know the reasons why."

Velk turned back to face him. "This is a very delicate matter. The Andorian problem . . ." He paused, a momentary look of distaste crossing his expression. "Bashir and the others violated their oath of service in a misguided attempt to take matters into their own hands."

What Velk dismissed as "the Andorian problem" had been a biological time bomb for that species. A race with four genders required for procreation, issues of falling birthrate, and infant mortality had finally brought Andor to the brink of global crisis—and the eventual result was the succession of a founder species from the very Federation they had helped to create. Velk was right when he said Bashir and the others had taken it upon themselves to aid the Andorians, but they had only apparently done so in reaction to the Federation Council's unwillingness to intervene. Whatever had happened out there in Epsilon Indi, Andor was now petitioning to return to the fold, but actual facts were thin on the ground.

"It is my understanding that the medical officers remain under house arrest while their involvement in the incident is fully determined. I am aware that the Pulaski woman served directly under you, but I would advise you not to allow your past associations to cloud the facts." Velk's expression became unreadable, with the steady focus of someone repeating a prepared statement. "Captain Dax disobeyed a direct order from Starfleet Command and she has been relieved of her position and placed under guard at the Jaros II penal colony. As for the ringleader, Bashir . . ." The Tellarite paused, framing his words. "You are familiar with the Shedai Meta-Genome?"

Riker gave a slow nod. "A storehouse of sensitive alien genetic data recovered in the twenty-third century. Highly classified." Even knowing that was at the very limits of his security clearance.

"Through means we have yet to determine, Bashir illegally accessed elements of that data and gave it to a non-aligned power . . . namely, the Andorians. He is being held at an undisclosed secure location, for his own protection. Once the present crisis has been dealt with, both he and Captain Dax will face a full military tribunal."

For now, Riker didn't argue over Dax's fate; but Julian Bashir's wasn't so clear-cut. His illegal actions were not in question, but his status was. He had officially resigned his commission as a Starfleet officer before he fled the Bajor system for Andoria, and he had apparently been granted political asylum on his arrival. Riker said so to Velk, trying to gauge any reaction. "He can't be held off the grid under such vague circumstances. Bashir has to be brought back to Earth for a full and transparent trial. The Andorians consider him a hero and under the protection of their planet, with all the rights and privileges of a resident of a non-aligned world. He should have his day in court, in the public eye."

Velk gave a curt shake of the head. "I don't agree. These are extraordinary circumstances, Riker. The presence of the Meta-Genome data makes this a national security issue, and the Federation Council deems Bashir to be a flight risk. You do realize he is a genetically manipulated human?"

"I don't see how that has any bearing on this," Riker began, but Velk was already raising a hand to stop him.

"Let me make you aware of something now, so you will no longer have any need to waste my time with such inquiries. I have already ordered the Security Agency to launch an investigation into the incident at Andor. This will be conducted independent of Starfleet Command, as so many of those involved or implicated in illegal activities are, as you put it, your fellow officers. In the meantime, the cabinet will continue to offer any and all assistance to the Andorian government."

"The Federation Security Agency answers to the office of the president," said Riker.

"Of course," Velk replied, as if that was blindingly obvious. "As such, I would advise you, Admiral, that rather than put effort into an endeavor that others will attend to, you should instead set to work on the most important job at hand. Assisting in locating the Tzenkethi terrorists responsible for the murder of the late president Bacco."

Riker's eyes narrowed at the statement. "There's no hard evidence that the killer was Tzenkethi. . . ." In the immediate aftermath of the Bacco shooting, a Bajoran named Enkar Sirsy had been discovered with the murder weapon and held for questioning. But Sirsy had later been released, cleared of all suspicion, and the only statement from the Federation Council had been that the investigation "was ongoing." In the information vacuum that followed, several media networks had claimed that credible sources inside the government considered the Tzenkethi Coalition as the likely instigator of the assassination.

It was an alarmist, if plausible, possibility. A founding member of the Typhon Pact along with the Romulans, Breen, Tholians, and other adversary states, the Tzenkethi were well known to manipulate other galactic powers for their own ends.

"The rumors are true," Velk replied, his words clipped and dismissive. "Tzenkethi DNA traces were found on evidence connected to the assassination. Leads are being followed as we speak." He glowered at Riker, as if he was offended that the admiral was daring to question him. "The Typhon Pact has the most to gain from chaos in the Federation," Velk insisted. "It was so-called 'rogue elements' from the Pact who were responsible for the destruction of the original Deep Space Nine space station, and while we could not prove conclusively that it was the Breen Intelligence Directorate who tried to assassinate President Bacco on Orion last year, I now believe that the Tzenkethi have done what the Breen could not. Mark my words, they *are* behind this."

Velk's parting words hung in the air after he was gone, and presently Lieutenant Ssura entered the office, his ears sloped forward forlornly. "Sir? Apologies. I was not correct on the protocols, and the chief of staff—"

"It's fine," Riker told him. "I think I've just learned more in one conversation than hours of reading those files would get me." He paused, thinking, then shot his aide a glance. "Contact my wife on the *Titan*. Tell her to make a dinner reservation."

Entering the main engineering compartment, Tuvok was not surprised when the first sound he heard was the strident voice of Doctor Xin Ra-Havreii, the *Titan*'s chief engineer.

"No," he was saying, "you don't just walk in here and start taking things to pieces. I don't care who gave you permission." The Efrosian had a tendency to talk loudly and slowly when confronted with someone intent on contradicting him, as if he were condescending to converse with a life-form of subnormal intelligence. Tuvok saw Ra-Havreii standing in front of the starship's dual warp core, bathed in the glow of the matter-antimatter stream as it pulsed at idle. He had his hands on his hips, his narrow chin jutting forward, and he was blocking the path of a group of other Starfleet officers and noncoms, all in engineering coveralls.

The new arrivals were an overhaul crew from McKinley Station, and some of them were guiding antigravity trolleys loaded with components and equipment cases. The officer at the focus of Ra-Havreii's invective was a lieutenant commander, a Deltan, and his face was tight with annoyance. "Sir, if you will just—"

"Just what?" Ra-Havreii snapped. "Just let you start banging on things like a troupe of primates? I know every bolt and weld in this ship, lad, and if you think for one second I am going to let some greasy-fingered yard-bound *stranger* poke and prod my vessel, you're gravely mistaken."

Tuvok's arrival caught the gaze of Ensign Crandall, one of Ra-Havreii's staff, and he rolled his eyes in a silent plea for help. "Chief Engineer," Tuvok began, stopping the other officer before he could continue his tirade, "why are you obstructing these people in their duties?"

Ra-Havreii rounded on him, brandishing a padd. "Have you seen this? Have you?" Tuvok barely got a look at the screen before the engineer waved it away. "The captain gets a promotion and the first thing he does is have the ship dismantled? I always thought those stories were a joke, but it seems it is true; the moment any officer in Starfleet gets kicked up to the admiralty they automatically become unbalanced!"

"Ordering an overhaul of the *Titan* is in no way a sign of impaired judgment," Tuvok replied coolly. "In point of fact, Doctor, one might argue that it is your present behavior that is indicative of such a bias."

"My point exactly," muttered the Deltan, earning him a sharp look from the chief engineer. "We're not here to *dismantle* anything, Commander. Admiral Riker ordered us to expedite a number of hardware and repair requests in *Titan*'s maintenance queue, and so we have. We're here to help." He gestured around.

It was evident that *Titan*'s engine room was more sparsely populated than usual; in fact, like much of the ship, crew numbers had already thinned considerably thanks to a generous shore leave schedule posted by Commander Vale. Tuvok declined the offer to partake in any planetside liberty. His wife, T'Pel, was on *Titan* and he had no emotional need to "stretch his legs," as Vale had put it. The same did not seem so for many of the other crewmembers, however. The Vulcan noted that a significant proportion of the ship's complement had either elected to visit or otherwise communicate with their family units in the days after the assassination on Deep Space 9. The reflection of an emotional need, he surmised, to reinforce the connection with loved ones in the face of a greater crisis.

"I don't know you," Ra-Havreii was saying to the Deltan. "And any one of my team can tell you, people I don't know don't get to touch my engines."

"He is pretty anal about it," offered Crandall wearily, and Ra-Havreii shot him an acidic glare.

"I'm not being obstructive," the engineer insisted, "just *careful*."

The Deltan threw up his hands. "Fine, sir. We'll just leave these components here on the deck. You can have your own people fit them and take twice as long about it, while we put our feet up and drink *raktajino* back on the station."

But Tuvok noted that Ra-Havreii had stopped listening to the junior officer after he said the word "components." He pushed past him to the nearest antigrav and peered at one of the new modules. "This is one of the new covariant field modulator pods. The Type Seventeen. I requested one of these six months ago." The Efrosian's manner shifted, his annoyance melting away. "I've been wanting to get my hands on this for a while. . . ."

"As I said," replied the Deltan, "the admiral said—"

Ra-Havreii gave an airy wave. "All right, all right, I didn't ask for your life story. Get to work, then. Let's see how efficient you spacedock types are." He turned to Crandall. "You, make sure they don't break anything."

Tuvok raised an eyebrow. "May I assume the maintenance will now proceed without issue?"

"Of course," said Ra-Havreii, waving him away. He was already moving down the line of new items of hardware, a low smile on his face.

The commander didn't believe that for a moment, of course. In his service aboard the *Titan,* Tuvok had come to understand that the ship's chief engineer was, to be certain, *idiosyncratic.*

He turned away to return to his other duties and almost collided with an ambulatory tower of equipment boxes. Tuvok nimbly sidestepped, but the diminutive figure carrying the cases still staggered. The uppermost box shifted and fell, revealing a deer-like head and wide, augmetic eyes. The Vulcan caught the container easily before it struck the ground.

"Oh. Sir!" piped Ensign Torvig Bu-Kar-Nguv, a slightly startled tone in his voice. "I didn't sense you there." The Choblik cocked his head, shifting the weight of the other boxes in between the two cybernetic manipulator arms extending from his torso.

"A smaller load for someone of your physical dimensions would be more logical, Ensign," Tuvok noted. "Continue. I will assist you."

"My thanks, Commander." Torvig's metal-toed feet clacked over the deck and Tuvok followed him, carrying the errant container in both hands. He expected the ensign to join the maintenance team from McKinley, but instead the Choblik used the artificial claw-like appendage on the end of his prehensile tail to open a hatch into another annex of the engineering deck, one of the auxiliary support bays.

Torvig made quick work of stacking his containers and took the last one from Tuvok with a bob of his head. "Thank you again, sir. I can take it from here."

However, Tuvok made no move to leave, instead

looking around the bay. "Were you not among the crew granted opportunity for shore leave, Ensign?"

"I was," Torvig replied, opening the cases. "I chose to refuse. As we are in stand-down mode for the next few days, I hoped to use the time to work on a . . . lower-priority project."

Tuvok noticed a mechanical shape suspended in a work frame nearby, draped in shadows where the lamps surrounding it were inactive. It was immediately familiar to him: two almost spherical pods of dull metals, a cluster of stocky manipulator limbs hanging loosely below the main body. A spider-like form, inert and silent.

"Lights," he ordered, and the lamps snapped on, revealing the shape of the alien mechanoid known as SecondGen White-Blue. When Tuvok had first encountered this machine-creature, it had moved with life and intent and ready intelligence; but now it was nothing but dead metal.

"I kept him in storage for a while," Torvig explained, almost guiltily. "Down on cargo deck three. But it didn't feel right." Tuvok said nothing as the ensign nervously fiddled with a photonic probe. "Commander Ra-Havreii talked about dismantling him, but I am uncertain if he was making an exaggerated statement for comedic effect. . . ."

"Anything is possible." On an impulse he couldn't immediately quantify, Tuvok reached out a hand and placed it on the motionless form of the machine. White-Blue was an artificial intelligence, the product of a synthetic species from the Beta Quadrant known as the Sentries. Created long ago by a now-deceased race of organic beings, the Sentry Coalition had made first contact with the *Titan* out past Canis Major; in the aftermath of that event, the being White-Blue had been granted permission to remain on board the starship as a guest. The AI had later assisted the *Titan* crew during their encounter with the alien terraforming construct known as Brahma-Shiva, at great personal risk; but it had been at the planet Ta'ith near the Vela Pulsar that Tuvok had truly come to know the mind of the mechanoid. Together, one organic brain and one synthetic, they had briefly shared consciousness with a machine known as One One Six in a risky attempt to prevent the destruction of the planet. White-Blue had sacrificed its core intellect, transferring itself into One One Six in order to save Ta'ith from destruction. All that remained of the machine-form now was its physical "droneframe," the databanks and positronic mind within it apparently empty.

Tuvok drew back his hand from the cold metal. "Ensign, what do you hope to achieve here?"

Torvig blinked, taken aback by the question. "I considered White-Blue to be a friend, sir. I feel it is only right to attempt to reconstruct his consciousness." He nodded to a portable computer core. "A backup version of his core processes exists in this device. In time I hope to restore him to an active state."

"Curious," Tuvok continued. "Mister Torvig, if an organic being you considered a friend was also lost in such a manner, would you also try to reconstruct him?"

"I know what you're saying," Torvig replied. "That White-Blue has . . . *died* and that I should accept it. But I see no reason to. He is a synthetic intellect, sir. He doesn't adhere to the same laws of existence as we organics. He's *software*, not *hardware*. And I think I can reboot him."

"Have you considered what you will have if you succeed?" Tuvok glanced back at the silent machine. "The being that we knew has gone. Any new version will be only a facsimile, without the experiences that shaped the original White-Blue."

Torvig was silent for a long moment. "You may be right, Commander. But I owe it to him to make the attempt."

Tuvok wondered how much of the Choblik's desire to follow this path stemmed from his own needs rather than any altruistic desire to reanimate the Sentry; Torvig's people were a species of demi-intelligent arboreal life that had been cybernetically enhanced to the level of true sentience, and it was fair to say that his origins made it difficult for him to connect with other beings. In White-Blue, a fully engineered life-form, Torvig had found something of a kindred spirit, and he had difficulty letting that go.

"I wish you success, Mister Torvig," Tuvok said. "But I caution you; we must all eventually live with the losses of those close to us. It is the nature of all existence, organic or synthetic."

In the corridor beyond, Tuvok turned toward the turbolift to find the hulking, muscular form of Chief Petty Officer Dennisar approaching him. The big Orion nodded as he saw him. "Sir? A moment?" He offered the Vulcan a padd.

"Is there a problem, Chief?"

Dennisar shook his head. "I'm just the messenger, Commander. A signal came in for you from Starfleet, priority one, personal and urgent."

Tuvok raised an eyebrow. "You could have relayed it to me from the bridge."

"No, sir," said the Orion. "It's encrypted, a text file. For your eyes only. Commander Vale asked me to bring it to you personally."

He took the padd and saw the warning flash displayed on the screen. As Dennisar had stated, the message required Tuvok's thumbprint on a reader plate and his personal security authorization.

His task complete, the Orion gave a nod and returned to a waiting turbolift.

Tuvok glanced around; he was now alone in the corridor. He tapped the reader and spoke quietly. "Authorization: Tuvok-Pi-Alpha. Decrypt."

The padd chimed, and the lines of the message spooled out across the screen, dense strings of nonsense text re-forming into readable words. The Vulcan was no stranger to such coded messages; in earlier years, he had received communications in such a fashion during his missions while undercover in the Maquis. But those days were long behind him.

He was looking at new orders from the highest levels of Starfleet Command, a covert mandate that required his immediate acceptance, no questions asked. He was to depart the *U.S.S. Titan* in less than two hours, then to report to Starbase One in civilian attire to board a transport heading out of the Sol system. The orders concluded with a set of rendezvous coordinates in the Alpha Centauri system and a warning to reveal nothing of the message's contents to anyone.

Tuvok read the text a second time, committing it to memory, and then activated the padd's erase function.

It was a long moment before he turned away and set off.

*   *   *

Velk was only aware that the airtram had lifted off by the motion of the shaft of sunlight through the portal in the hull. The flyer's inertial compensators kept everything within it perfectly stable; he refused to travel any other way.

The Tellarite didn't like matter transporters. The concept of being discorporated and shot through the ether to be rebuilt somewhere else sat poorly with him. Galif jav Velk was reluctant to give up that degree of control over himself, to rely on someone else to take brief ownership of his molecules. Unless it was absolutely unavoidable, Velk traveled by shuttle or flyer, and he cared little for those he might inconvenience because of it.

San Francisco was already falling away, the aircraft moving into a priority suborbital sky lane that would take it up over North America and down over the Atlantic Ocean in a steep, swift arc. He would be back in Paris in less than fifty minutes, and the journey time could be put to better use than dealing with the minutiae that would await him at the council chambers.

Velk was the airtram's only passenger; the rear compartment was empty. The only crew were the pilot and co-pilot in the cockpit; Velk rejected the need for any support staff or assistants. A secretary program was all he required, a semi-intelligent software engine networked from his actual office in Europe.

He spoke to the cabin, his voice picked up by a communicator button on his jacket. "Computer."

"Working." The reply was bland and genderless.

"Security sweep."

After a moment's pause, the voice returned. *"Airtram security remains uncompromised."*

Velk nodded to himself, reaching for an attaché case at his side. "Screen all my calls until further notice."

"Do you wish me to dismiss any presidential override of that order?"

"I said *all*," Velk repeated irritably. "That includes Ishan." He opened the case and removed a metallic, ovoid-shaped device. "Cross-link subspace communications relay to me. Maximum signal encryption."

"Working. Link established, proceed when ready."

A train of cold blue indicator lights around the equator of the capsule glowed, and Velk sat it on the table in front of him. An ephemeral wave of light expanded out of the device, scanning the dimensions of the room, the objects within it, and washing over Velk himself. He allowed it to happen, waiting.

After a moment, planes of ghostly holographic light sketched in around him. Suddenly the walls of the cabin were lost, and he appeared to be sitting in a natural cavern of some kind. It was difficult to be certain; the holofield was deliberately vague, so as not to give too much away about the location of the transceiver at the other end of the communication.

A time-code imprint floated over the holomodule, ticking down to zero. The instant the numbers halted, a humanoid shape melted into view. Taller than Velk, and at a guess, more narrow in build, any other definition of the figure was lost. Like the ghostly image of the cave, the identity of the being was impossible to determine. Species, gender, age . . . these things were lost beneath a masking subroutine that made both Velk and his distant operative blank and featureless avatars to each other. In the highly unlikely event that someone was able to capture this signal, it would be almost meaningless to them.

"I'm here," said the hologram, the voice toneless and scrubbed of identity. "I wasn't expecting contact again so soon. What's wrong?"

"There have been some developments." Velk considered what the operative would be seeing at this same moment, a similar holographic shadow play beamed from an identical projector device. He imagined his own indistinct avatar gesturing with a hand from the faint sketch of a chair. "The Orion lead was worthless. They were not there."

The ghost figure did something that could have been a shrug, and even through the emotion-deadening subroutines in the transmission, Velk was certain he could detect a note of reproach. "Klingons. They were killed."

It took a moment for him to realize that had been a question. "Yes. The targets left traps behind for any pursuers."

"Of course they did. They're not fools." The operative walked slowly around the phantom cavern. "With respect, sir . . . I warned you this would happen. The Klingons are brute-force weapons, not suitable for this kind of mission. All the noise they made with the Orions, they let the targets know they were coming."

"That is clear now," Velk replied, his jaw stiffening. It galled him to have a subordinate point out his mistakes, but there was little he could say to deny them. The operative was correct. The initial plan to maintain a distance between the act and the intention behind it had gone awry, and now they were in danger of losing momentum. "As such," he went on, "we must address the problem and move forward. I recall an aphorism used by the Earthers: 'If you want a job done right, you must do it yourself.' This is how we will proceed from this point forward."

"I'm familiar with the phrase. We will need time to assemble a team."

He shook his head. "That work has already begun. Resources are being redirected as we speak."

"I'll be part of the action."

"Yes. Data will be streamed to you, coordinates and so on. Proceed at your own discretion, but keep me advised. Isolation of the targets is your only priority, is that clear?"

"Fully." The figure was silent for a moment. "What are my rules of engagement here?"

Velk leaned forward to reach for the holomodule. "No rules," he said irritably, assuming that the implication was apparent enough. "I am authorizing you to use any means necessary to progress your mission to the required conclusion." He paused, thinking. "I remember another Terran phrase. *No loose ends.*"

Velk tapped the device and the ghost light faded away, the cabin walls reappearing. He secured the module in his case once more and then sat silently, his dark eyes locked on some impossibly distant point, his thoughts turning inward.

Three

A light rain was falling over the city, but there was no evidence of it in the courtyard of the La Sorrento restaurant. Up above the heads of the diners, a discreet and transparent force field kept the drizzle from reaching the ground, and the carefully concealed environmental controls in the planters and stonework made sure that the outdoor portion of the bistro remained at a pleasant ambient temperature, despite the chill of the evening.

San Francisco's fashionable Nob Hill district had become the city's nexus for fine dining right around the time that Starfleet Command had moved in across the bay; all these years later the area was constantly busy with restaurants serving every variety of Terran food and offerings from dozens of Federation memberworlds.

Most of them, anyway. Deanna had been disappointed to see that the Andorian sushi bar on Taylor Street where she had eaten many times was now gone, replaced by an austere Vulcan café.

In the end, she had chosen Italian, and after calling in a favor with Chief Bolaji to babysit Tasha, it had been a relatively painless endeavor getting a reservation for that evening. She was still wondering how she had swung it; La Sorrento was a popular place, and the waiting list for a decent table was long.

As if he was reading her mind, her husband sipped a little wine from his glass to wash down his tortellini, and then he leaned forward. "Good choice. I'm surprised you got us in here. Did you slip the maître d' a bribe?"

She smiled slightly, brushing a curl of dark hair back over her ear. "Hardly. They were a little sniffy at first, until I told them my name. Things got a lot smoother after that."

"Oh?" Outwardly, Will seemed to take that in stride. To someone who didn't know him as intimately as his wife did—Betazoid empathy or not—he might have seemed almost indifferent. Deanna knew better. Beneath the surface, her husband was on edge. "I guess news travels fast in this town, especially fleet gossip. Doesn't hurt to score some points with the new admiral."

"Who says it was *your* name that got us a table?" She tried to lighten the mood. "You're not the only one with new responsibilities, dear." Deanna had already been approached by the Federation diplomatic corp with a request to make herself available for the rounds of ambassadorial functions that were an integral part of life in what was Earth's foremost interstellar town.

Will didn't smile in return, only nodding, his gaze lost in the straw-colored fluid in his glass. "How is that going?" he asked, at length.

"Togren from the diplomatic corps has asked me to provide some support. You remember him? From Denobula?" Will nodded and she went on. "A new ambassadorial party is arriving in the next few days, and he wanted my expertise on hand to act as a liaison."

"Who is the ambassador? Someone we used to shoot at?"

She shook her head. "Not exactly, but there's still going to be a strong chill in the room. We'll be meeting with Envoy Ramasanar ch'Nuillen."

Will raised an eyebrow. "The Andorian?"

Deanna nodded. "Presider zh'Felleth wants Andor to return to the fold, and the envoy is here to lead that venture." She frowned. "It seems like it was only yesterday the Andorians were seceding, and now they want to put that behind them. It's not going to be an easy road. . . . There is still plenty of ill feeling on both sides."

"The Federation Council won't just let them back in," Will mused grimly. "The Andorians have to know that. And the president pro tem has made no secret of his animosity about the whole secession business."

She nodded again. Ishan Anjar had put himself forward for the presidential office, and he had been campaigning hard, but one of Andor's most progressive politicians, the outspoken Kellessar zh'Tarash, had already publicly stated her desire to seek the same office. Of course, there was the minor impediment of needing Andor to officially rejoin the United Federation of Planets first, and while public sentiment seemed to be behind the idea, nothing was certain. The politics of the moment were complex and ever shifting, and not for the first time, Deanna wished that *Titan* could have stayed out in deep space to meet the kind of challenges she felt better equipped to deal with.

Will pushed his food around the plate, lost in thought. "Tell me what you're thinking," she said. "Let's not both sit here and pretend like this is another ordinary day."

You always know what I'm thinking, Imzadi. She heard the words in her mind, sensing the shades of his mood clinging to them, smoky and dark. He forced a smile, but he knew she wasn't going to be deflected.

Finally, her husband put down his fork and frowned. "What the hell just happened?" he asked, frustration simmering in his tone. "A week ago we're in deep space cataloging supernova remnants and looking for new species of cosmozoans. Now we're here, eating pasta while the Federation reels like it's been gut punched." He flicked at his collar, where rank pins would have sat; while they were both dressed in civilian clothes tonight, she knew what he meant. "I never asked for this. Hell, I'm still trying to get a grip on what it is I'm *actually* supposed to be doing here." Will paused, moderating his tone. "Deanna, someone is making me play catch-up, and I don't like it."

"You want to help," she said, nodding. "We all do. But this promotion . . . you're afraid it's the opposite of that."

"Why would Akaar sideline me and haul *Titan* back in? It doesn't make any sense, not with everything that's going on. . . . Bacco, the Andorians, and these arrests . . ."

"Have you talked to him since the ceremony?"

Her husband shook his head. "All of a sudden he's like a ghost. His staff take my messages, but he doesn't return them. And meanwhile I'm chained to a damn desk."

Deanna put a hand on Will's arm. "You know Admiral Akaar. You know he doesn't do anything without a good reason. You may just have to be patient."

"I've never been good with that," he admitted. "I

just don't want to get caught in the undertow here. I'm not a political animal; I never have been."

"Maybe that's the reason why Akaar pulled you in." She smiled again. "It's all right for you to have doubts, Will. Change does that to you. Some times we don't get to choose when and where it happens."

"Thank you, Counselor Troi," he replied, not unkindly. "But this time around it's not just my immediate future that's in the wind. There's you and Tasha . . . Are we going to be Earthbound from now on? And what about Christine and Tuvok and the rest of our crew? *Titan* can't be tied to a base, that's not what she was built for. . . ." He met her gaze. "I'm wondering what the hell I have let myself in for."

She paused. "I think you're where you need to be. I think we both are."

"How so?"

"Have you seen the news broadcasts since we made port? The network is full of tirades and counterarguments. Every pundit on the planet and off it has something to say. People are afraid, Will, and they're angry. Bacco was respected by millions, even by those who were her political opponents, and now that she's been taken from them, they have nowhere to direct their grief."

"That's not exactly true," noted Will. "There's more than enough blame to go around, deserved or not. And every day there seems to be a new nugget of information conveniently leaked to the media from some 'credible source' or other. . . ."

"What troubles me," Deanna began, "are the public reactions being fomented by the rhetoric coming from the Federation Council." She noted that the kind of language being used by politicians across the UFP reflected a troubling rise in sentiments directed against the newest player on the galactic stage, the Typhon Pact.

"Meet the new enemy," said Will. "Same as the old enemy."

Some more hyperbolic commentators described the Typhon Pact as a dark mirror of the Federation, a coalition of agitator member-states that had gathered behind a united front in the wake of the Borg crisis. It couldn't be denied that the Pact was a force to be reckoned with; the mere fact of its existence had irrevocably altered the geopolitical map of the Alpha and Beta Quadrants.

"They're the perfect monster-under-the-bed for alarmists," said Deanna. "A gathering of old Federation foes, drawing their plans against us."

Her husband nodded. "They fit the bill all right. The Holy Order of the Kinshaya, the Breen Confederacy, the Romulan Star Empire all making treaty with the Gorn, the Tholians, and the Tzenkethi. . . . There's not a single member of the Pact that hasn't at one time been a player in an armed conflict with us."

Deanna nodded. The Typhon Pact was difficult to anticipate and cunning in its affairs of state, and while there was weakness in the places where the Pact's members worked at cross purposes, it could not be denied that they represented the gravest military threat to the Federation's borders. "All that is true, but still they've shown no intent to invade. They've made plenty of attempts at subterfuge, some successful and some not, but that's to be expected. They're pushing at their boundaries and measuring the response, but Bacco herself was reaching out to some of them. . . . Hopefully that opportunity won't be lost now."

"We can hope. Any intent for war is absent, or so

it appears," Will concluded, finishing the thought for her. "That was well enough and good for the previous administration. Starfleet's job was to carry on, project quiet and steady strength while we kept the chance of some kind of friendship on the table."

"I remember Ishan Anjar being quite vocal about how much he disagreed with that. And he hasn't changed his mind," said Deanna. "Now his calls for a harder line against the Pact are in the ascendant." It seemed to her that anti–Typhon Pact sentiments were growing by the day, led in part by the belligerent stance of the president pro tem. Although he had yet to openly say the words in any public forum, it was the worst-kept secret on Earth that Ishan considered the Typhon Pact to be the prime suspect in the killing of Nan Bacco.

"If the Pact *is* going to be our enemy," Will said quietly, "then it's the Tzenkethi driving them to it. That's how the wind is blowing."

The cunning Tzenkethi had waged war on the Federation many times, and the recent battles still lived in the memories of many senior Starfleet officers and older civilians alike; it was this faction of the Typhon Pact that rhetoric targeted, despite the fact that nothing beyond circumstantial evidence connecting them to the DS9 incident had been revealed. Means and motive were not enough on their own, Deanna reflected, but in desperate times such things could slip away beneath the tide of public opinion.

"Do you believe that?" she asked him. "Do you think they are responsible?"

"History is full of wars that have started with a single assassin's bullet," Will told her. "If somebody took Bacco's life in order to cause turmoil in the Federation, then they've already succeeded." He paused, then shook his head. "She stood for something, Deanna. For the best of us. The Federation she wanted was one built on a foundation of honesty and reason. We can't let the last of her be the echo of a shot."

The machine drifted there, some three hundred meters up above the city of San Francisco, floating on a stiff breeze. If one could have seen it clearly, the device might have been described as resembling an avian form rendered by an avant-garde sculptor. It was slightly smaller than the common gulls that wheeled and turned over the water's edge down by the bay, metallic wings canted to ride the thermals over the cityscape.

Its skin was a composite of near-weightless aerogel compounds, built around a core of advanced micro-duotronic circuits. It could mimic the flight patterns and some behaviors of a real bird if required, but tonight that functionality was inactive. Its skin tone was matched to the shaded, cloudy sky above. For all intents and purposes, the little drone was invisible.

Bobbing on a compact antigravity motor no bigger than a pencil, the device held its station directly over the open courtyard of the La Sorrento restaurant. Sensor pits along the length of its body continually mapped the target zone beneath it, and the memory center of the unit monitored the ambient environment. It had only one target, and with a machine's faultless patience, the drone watched Admiral William Riker in everything he said and did.

The bistro's weather-shield had caused a minor issue at first, necessitating the need to recalibrate the audio scanners in order to isolate Riker's conversation from the ambient noise surrounding him, but that had been dealt with in short order.

The drone continued to loiter as it had for the past hour. Capable of solar charging or even wireless energy induction, it could remain on station indefinitely. Silent. Unseen. Watchful.

Meet the new enemy. Same as the old enemy.

Riker's words were gathered up by the synthetic ear of the device before being shot in microsecond bursts of data to a receiver in the top floor of a nondescript office building several blocks west, near Alamo Square.

On paper, the office was the server hub for a networking concern, a largely unmanned facility populated by rows of data cores and communication routers. In reality, the center of the space was a set of isolated cubicles, each sound shielded from the others by baffle fields. Each cubicle contained a monitor and an operator who worked shifts gathering surveillance data on a dozen different subjects. Some were scrutinized through drones similar to the one shadowing Riker; others through the monitoring of personal communications or data traffic patterns. The facility was known as Active Two.

The operators were trained to show no interest in the identity of their subjects, to treat them with dispassion and clinical regard. They were simply there to provide an observer's oversight to the mechanical recovery of intelligence material—because no matter what the era, or where the act took place, it remained a truism that even the most clever thinking machine could not spy on someone so well as another living being.

The Vulcan watching the live feed from the drone continued to listen to the admiral conversing with his wife. There were several of her species assigned to this posting; Vulcan physiology and mental acuity were particularly well suited to the lengthy, concentration-intensive and frequently tedious work of monitoring.

She glanced briefly at a tertiary display that indicated the passage of the recovered data. Typically, surveillance intelligence was parsed and then sifted for usable data on site at this location, before a digest version of the sensor recording was passed on to a higher level; but in this case, it appeared that someone at a more senior security clearance was already tapped into the direct feed, watching it unfold live just as she was. She paused, musing. This was highly irregular, and she considered alerting her superior, who sat several cubicles away at another station.

The Vulcan briefly allowed herself to wonder what it was about Admiral William T. Riker that required such scrutiny, then dismissed her own question as irrelevant. That was not a matter for her to dwell upon. She had her orders. She would carry them out.

We can't let the last of her be the echo of a shot, Riker was saying. A moment after the words were relayed back from the drone, the indicator showing the outside connection winked out, the feed to the higher clearance source abruptly terminated.

On the screen, the admiral refused a dessert in favor of a coffee while his wife indulged. Riker glanced up briefly, and his watcher noted he was frowning.

Despite the lateness of the hour—or perhaps because of it—the streets of the portside district were busy with ship crews on liberty and the occasional group of adventurous tourists. The Centauri sun had set just as Tuvok's transport had made landfall, and in the hours that had passed since then he had followed a circuitous path around the port city, taking maglev trams up and down the lines around the industrial zones to ensure he had not been followed. It was a standard espionage tradecraft technique and as automatic to the Vulcan as breathing. Even here, in the heart of the Federation's member-worlds, he did not lower his guard. The secret orders had set him on alert for even the smallest sign of something awry. He drew into the depths of his hooded jacket, his dark face lost in shadow.

A cold wind pushed down the streets as Tuvok arrived at the location designated for his rendezvous. A generous critic might have been willing to call the place a "tavern," but it barely qualified as such. Built into the side of a decaying hangar complex, a handful of merchant marine cargo modules had been welded together around a rig that appeared to be made of surplus parts from an old *Ptolemy*-class tug.

He entered through a tall steel door and a wave of distasteful odors washed over him. The sour organic smell of stale sweat from a dozen humanoid species, the tang of fermented alcoholic beverages, all mixed with ozone from what was likely a poorly shielded electrical system. Tuvok had to step aside as a pair of tall, reedy Xelatians ambled past him on the way out, their movements stiff and jerky. One of them bumped into the Vulcan and glared blankly from behind a rectangular brass breather mask before going on its way.

The tavern was divided into booths cut from hull metal. A long, curving bar that had once been part of a warp nacelle dominated one side of the establishment. Here and there, jury-rigged gaming tables hosted dom-jot or kella, although the surly manner of the players did not invite any casual approach.

Tuvok took in the room, looking for the best

vantage point, as a humanoid female resembling a Betazoid walked swiftly toward him. She appeared to flicker, her aspect shifting slightly. *A hologram, then,* he decided, *doubtless projected by a computer system behind the bar.* It had to have been scanning him as he entered, measuring what kind of server would be most enticing to a new customer.

The device was poorly calibrated and lagged, however. The faux-Betazoid first became a Terran woman of Asian extraction. "Hey, honey! What can I get—" The holographic waitress flickered again and transformed into a demure Vulcan female, her expression snapping from slyly welcoming to serious and thoughtful. "Greetings, traveler," she began again, with a poor imitation of a Shir'Kar accent. "How may I provide for you this night?"

"Altair water," he replied, moving past her toward a vacant booth.

Tuvok sat and nursed his drink for a while, feigning interest in a wall screen display showing an ice hockey game in progress elsewhere on the planet. Under cover of this, he cast a practiced eye over the rest of the tavern's clientele and noted several other patrons acting in a manner that could have been described as suspicious. None of them, however, seemed to be interested in him. He had no doubt that this place was the nexus for one or more criminal enterprises of minor scale, but his purpose here was not to interfere with such minutiae.

The fact remained that Tuvok was uncertain as to exactly what his purpose here *was*. Again he went over the orders in his mind, sifting the terse language for any deeper meaning. He recalled the words of his former commander Kathryn Janeway when confronted with similar directives in the past; "cloak and dagger," she had called it, an apt—if somewhat theatrical—description that illustrated not only the inherent obfuscation, but also the potential for danger.

As he mused on this, the Vulcan became aware of someone moving past the edge of his booth. A human male, dressed in the jumpsuit and gear vest of a dock worker, slid into the seat opposite him. Only the lower half of his face was visible, the rest hidden behind dark pilot's eyeshades and a grimy gray ushanka hat. Tuvok's immediate sense was that this was a disguise of some sort; it did not match the man who wore it. He had an ill-trimmed beard that split into a smile that Tuvok found immediately familiar. "Mind if I join you?"

"I am waiting for a friend," Tuvok said automatically, appending the code phrase he had been given. "From the barge."

"The barge sank," came the correct counter. "What a shame." The man reached up to remove his hat and glasses, and what Tuvok had taken at first glance to be a mistaken observation on his part was revealed as quite the opposite.

"Sir?" he whispered.

William Riker's face looked back at him, a humorless twist to his lips. "Yeah," said the newcomer with a shrug. "I get that a lot."

Tuvok's eyes narrowed as the moment of surprise faded. It was almost impossible that this man could be *Titan*'s commander, and equally there were myriad explanations for who or what else he *might* be. Anything from an android simulacrum to another hologram or a Changeling. . . . There were many possibilities, all of them troubling.

"Come on, Tuvok, let's cut to the chase," said the other man. "You remember me, don't you? Think back. We met on the *Spartacus,* you and me and your Maquis friends. That whole incident with the plague outbreak at the Helena colony? Of course, at the time I didn't know you were with Starfleet Intelligence."

"You are Thomas Riker," said the Vulcan, with a sudden rush of insight.

"Most people just call me Tom, for simplicity's sake."

For all intents and purposes, Tuvok was looking at William Riker's identical twin, but the circumstances that surrounded the two men did not stem from something as natural as sharing a mother's womb.

Tuvok had first encountered this man while under deep cover with a cell of Maquis renegades, later learning the full details of the incident that had led to Tom Riker's "birth" through mission reports from the *Enterprise*-D, under Jean-Luc Picard.

In 2369, the *Enterprise* had returned to the planet Nervala IV after a science team that included William Riker had been forced to evacuate eight years earlier; there, Picard's crew encountered a duplicate of the *Enterprise*'s first officer, created by a freak combination of atmospheric effects and a transporter malfunction. That duplicate—the very man who sat across from him now—had eventually taken Riker's middle name and set out to live a life of his own. But he had become disenchanted with life in Starfleet and thus was prime material for recruitment into the Maquis resistance movement.

"You left after Helena," Tuvok noted. "You abandoned the Federation for the Maquis."

"Yes. But that didn't work out so well for me in the

long run." The other Riker's approximation of events was somewhat understated; he had gone on to impersonate his so-called "brother" in an effort to steal the *U.S.S. Defiant* from Deep Space 9, an endeavor that ultimately failed and left Tom a prisoner of the Cardassian Union. He looked away. "I eventually got out, but I did some things I'm not proud of along the way."

"Curious," Tuvok allowed, measuring him intently. "The surface similarity is remarkable."

Tom's brow furrowed. "Surface similarity?" He reached up and traced the thin line of a scar that was almost hidden by the beard. "This give it away? It was a present from my Cardassian jailers."

"Indeed, but the scar is not the larger tell." Tuvok cocked his head. "As I observe you, I note several points of dissimilarity. Your body kinetics differ in several subtle but noticeable ways from those of Admiral Riker."

"*Admiral?*" Tom's eyes widened at the mention of the rank. "Well, how about that? It seems my brother is doing pretty well for himself these days. I heard he got his own ship. . . ."

"The *Titan*," noted Tuvok.

"About damn time." A shadow passed over Tom's face. "And he and Deanna . . . they finally got together, had a kid? Is that right?"

"A daughter. Her name is Natasha."

"Huh. What's she like?"

"A pleasant child of above-average intelligence for a human."

Tom gave a brief, brittle smile. "That's great. I . . . I'm happy for them." The tone of the man's voice suggested otherwise, but the Vulcan chose not to draw attention to it.

Instead, Tuvok raised an eyebrow. "Mister Riker, you will pardon me if my next question is indelicate . . . but it was my understanding that you had perished during the Dominion War."

He chuckled. "What's that Mark Twain quote? 'The reports of my death have been greatly exaggerated.' It's not like the Jem'Hadar didn't try their damnedest to make it happen, though. The fact is, it gave me a chance to drop out of sight and put my life back together. Since the war, I've been keeping off the grid as much as possible, maintaining a low profile. I guess you could say I'm an 'independent contractor' now."

"A mercenary."

Tom's smile cooled. "I do what I have to. You may have noticed that it's not so easy a galaxy out there these days. Not all of us have a family we get to go home to."

"That is so," Tuvok said, keeping his tone neutral. "And now you are here."

"For the same reason as you," Tom replied. "I was chosen to be your contact because they thought a familiar face would make it easier."

"*They*?" asked the Vulcan.

"You're the last recruit. The rest of the team is waiting for us on the ship." The other man stood, replacing his hat and glasses. "Come with me. I'll introduce you."

The chilling wind had brought black clouds with it, and as Tuvok followed Tom Riker across the thermoconcrete apron, rain began to fall, hissing off the surface of the port's wide landing platform.

He pulled the hood tighter over his head and peered at their destination. There, hazed by the glow of running lights, sat an ungainly cargo ship on four heavy support skids, streamers of water running off the hull.

Tuvok did not recognize the model or make of the vessel, but it was of a common enough configuration, and it bore baseline similarities with many ships of similar tonnage. He estimated the hull to be approximately 275 meters in length, almost comparable to the size of the saucer segment of the *Titan*. The freighter was rectangular in section, with rounded surfaces on the dorsal and ventral hulls. He saw the lines of large cargo hatches along the aft quarter and amidships. A short distance from the blunt bow of the ship, stubby pylons protruded from the sides of the fuselage at ninety-degree angles, and connected to each was an angular warp drive nacelle, similar to the ones in use across Starfleet in the 2270s. Rising from the upper surface of the hull, offset from the centerline toward the port side, was a large conning tower. An orchard of sensor masts extended upward around it, some of them flexing in the stiff breeze. A registration code—NAR-1337—was visible in large white letters across the tower.

Tom gestured up at the ship as they approached it. "Say hello to the *S.S. Snipe*. She may not look like much, but I'm told she's got it where it counts."

Tuvok didn't reply, his gaze running over the hull of the craft, looking for anything that seemed anomalous. He noted the nubs of military-surplus shield emitters and the shuttered mouth of a photon torpedo launcher. Both were prohibited by Federation shipping regulations on a civilian craft with an NAR registry, but he kept the observation to himself for the moment. Overall, the ship seemed spaceworthy, but her outward appearance had been poorly maintained. Cosmetic damage from micrometeorites and radiation scarred the hull. In many places the *Snipe* was patched with mismatched sheets of tritanium and ugly retrofits.

They passed under the starboard warp nacelle and a platform came away from the hull over their heads, dropping like an elevator to the rain-slick ground. A large humanoid male rode the platform down, leaning on a support rod, scowling at the inclement weather as if it were somehow personally spiting him.

Tom raised a hand and nodded a greeting. "You came to meet us, Khob. I'm touched."

The other being snorted. Dappled skin the color of sand pulled tight around his broad face. Tuvok saw his glittering eyes and recognized his species as Suliban. Much taller than the Vulcan and broader across the chest, Khob had an endomorphic physique more suited to manual labor on some heavy-gravity world than to a clandestine mission. He was doubtless some kind of aberration among his race; Suliban were more typically of slighter build.

He stepped off the elevator and waved a tricorder over Tuvok. "Hold still," he rumbled. "Won't take a second."

"I am carrying no weapons or concealed devices," Tuvok told him.

Khob's face shifted, showing disappointment. "Not looking for guns. Making sure you're not sick. Not carrying any viral vectors."

"This big fellow is our medic," Tom explained. "Another contractor, like me."

"Clean," Khob reported, as the tricorder beeped. He stepped back onto the elevator, beckoning them after him. "Time to go. Place is too damp for me."

"We've only been here a day," noted Tom.

"Day too long," corrected Khob. "Ferengi may like it. I don't."

"There are Ferengi on this ship?" asked Tuvok.

Tom nodded. "Just the one. Another one of yours, actually."

Tuvok didn't immediately follow the other Riker's meaning at first, but then the platform rose back into the *Snipe*'s cavernous cargo bay and the first face he saw had the distinctive ridged nose, pronounced forehead, and wide ears of a Ferenginar native.

"Commander Tuvok?" The Ferengi offered a handshake, then seemed to realize that was incorrect protocol for greeting a Vulcan. He gave a crooked smile. "Oh. Hello there, sir. I'm Nog." He tapped at the civilian jacket he was wearing, at the spot where a Starfleet combadge would have sat on a uniform tunic. "Lieutenant Commander Nog from Deep Space Nine."

"Indeed?" Tuvok considered this. "You were also summoned for this operation?"

"I was pulled from my engineering posting a few days after . . . after the incident." His smile faded as he remembered the moment, and Tuvok guessed that the young officer must have been there to witness the shooting of President Bacco in person. Nog seemed to push that thought away and nodded. "We're not the only Starfleet officers here, sir."

"Speaking of which," said Tom, "I'm going to check in with Ixxen, let her know we're good to go." He gave Tuvok a sideways look as he walked away. "Nog here will get you settled." Khob had already drifted off, his attention focused on his tricorder.

"He means Lieutenant Yal Ixxen," Nog explained. "She's our pilot. A Bolian ops specialist off the *U.S.S. Blake*. She was assigned just before I came on board." He inclined his head and bid the Vulcan to follow him.

Tuvok gave a nod, and they crossed the largely

vacant cargo bay, both of them ducking to pass through a steel hatchway into a long, narrow corridor.

The interior of the cargo ship was as unkempt as its exterior. There were no panels covering the walls to hide away the power conduits, EPS taps, and cable bundles, such as one might find on a Starfleet ship. Instead, pipes and thick trunks of wiring snaked along the walls, vivid hazard labels warning of live plasma streams or energy feeds. Gridded deck plates rang beneath their footfalls as they worked their way aft. Tuvok smelled machine lubricant and rust.

"Mister Nog, how many so-called 'recruits' are there aboard the *Snipe*?"

"Ten of us, along with a small crew for the ship," said the Ferengi. "Didn't they tell you that?"

"*They* have not imparted much information to me, Lieutenant Commander," he noted.

Nog gave him a look. "Ah. Because we were sort of hoping you would have some idea as to what this is all about, sir. As you're the last to arrive, and all."

"Your assumption is incorrect," he replied. "As, clearly, was mine that *you* would have that information to impart to *me*."

"So you're as clueless as the rest of us?" Nog gave a brief, cynical chuckle. "Well, in a way, I feel better." He paused, thinking about it. "No, actually, I feel worse."

A dull rumble sounded through the hull and the *Snipe* groaned as its thrusters powered up. A speaker horn overhead crackled, and a woman's voice spoke. "*Secure for lift-off. We'll be going to warp as soon as we break orbit.*"

Tuvok sensed the subtle shift in gravity as the *Snipe* left the surface of the planet and rose into the stormy sky.

Nog led him past a set of compartments, each one

a cramped crew cabin with a pair of bunks and fresher unit in one corner. He indicated one as they approached. "This is us. We're, uh, sharing. I hope that's okay?"

"I will make an effort to adapt," Tuvok replied. His attention was on the open hatch directly opposite; inside one of the other compartments a pair of diminutive Bynars were engaged in a conversation in their native language. A stream of high-speed data code raced back and forth between them, atonal and irregular in pitch.

"They've got really long name-designations," Nog noted, seeing his interest. "We're just calling them One-One and Zero-Zero for now. They're specialists in communications and information security." He pointed ahead. "The mess hall is up here."

The *Snipe* creaked around them as pressure changes exerted themselves on the hull, and the gravity gradient shifted once again as Tuvok followed the Ferengi into an open area that was part crew lounge, part dining hall. Metal benches and tables were bolted to the deck, and along one wall were a series of food dispensers that had seen better days.

At one of the tables, a tawny-skinned Elloran female gave him a quick, measuring look, the bony crest extending from the back of her skull bobbing as she turned back to her conversation with a pale human man of stocky build. Tuvok noted that the human had a series of tattoos about his neck; he recognized the glyphs depicted there as part of devotional texts from the planet Zeon. Neither of them seemed particularly interested in the new arrival.

A human female rose to greet them from another table, her flame-red hair cut close to her head and her eyes intent. She wore a tan ship-suit covered in pockets and gear clips, and Tuvok could not miss the holstered phaser at her hip.

"Commander," she began, with the brisk manner of someone used to the intricacies of rank and military service. "Lieutenant Colonel Jan Kincade, Starfleet ground forces. I'm what passes for in charge around here. Welcome aboard."

Tuvok inclined his head in return, considering her words. Technically, his rank was directly equal to Kincade's, but there had been no mention in his orders of assuming command of this mission over her, and at present, he had no inclination to pursue any question of seniority. "Colonel. May I inquire as to our destination?"

"Straight to business, eh? I heard that about Vulcans." She folded her arms. Kincade was slightly taller than he, but she had a whipcord build to her, an athlete's physique. "We're heading to coordinates out past Beta Rigel. My guess is we'll get a target then."

"A target?" echoed Tuvok.

Kincade snorted. "You're a tactical officer. Nog here has extensive battlefield experience. So do Khob, Ixxen, the Bynars. . . ." She indicated the Elloran and the Zeon. "Sahde and Ashur were private military contractors in the Triangle. You met Tom, someone you could call a 'jack-of-all-trades,' I guess. . . . And then there's me, trained by Starfleet to shoot at people on those occasions when all the 'we come in peace' stuff doesn't work. So you tell me, Commander Tuvok. What reason is there to gather a group of people with our unique combination of skills if not for a combat mission?"

He considered her words. "We are not currently in a state of war, Colonel."

"Maybe so." Her lips thinned. "But given current events, I wouldn't exactly say we're at peace either."

Four

Coastal weather in California was a mercurial thing, so Christine Vale had learned when she first came to Earth from Izar to enroll in Starfleet Academy. Those days were a good way behind her, but she still remembered clearly how the skies over San Francisco Bay could be filled with thick clouds one minute and blow clear to show perfect blue the next.

The cowl of rain that had recently swept over the city and the surrounding environs was gone today, and a bright sun beat down. The only signs of the previous night's precipitation were the fading puddles that grouped in the lee of paving stones and the damp patches on the concrete.

Still, the morning air was chilly, and as she stepped out of the Sausalito public transporter station, Christine caught a breath of the briny scent of the ocean. Even after all this time, it still seemed a little alien to her. Izar had only small inland seas, which she'd barely seen growing up in cities, and the expanse of Earth's oceans made the planet as unusual to her as waterworlds like Pacifica or Droplet, the world the *Titan* had discovered a few years back.

The Cetacean Institute was already open by the time she arrived, but there wasn't a lot of tourist traffic—a shuttle bus of schoolchildren up from Mexico, a few knots of early-bird sightseers. It was a weekday, and the place would be quiet.

She passed through the entrance atrium, under the shadow of a bronze statue that depicted a pair of humpback whales breaching the surface of the ocean. The memorial commemorated an event that had taken place decades before Christine's birth, something to do with the repopulation of that species coinciding with an attack on Earth by an alien invader. She half remembered something about it from her Federation history classes and resolved to refresh her memory at a later date.

The *Titan*'s first officer wandered into the lower levels of the institute's main complex, a building that had stood on this site for more than four centuries. Great glass panels rising high over her head held back thousands of gallons of seawater, and beyond them she could see humans in wetsuits and one native Arcadian drifting back and forth. Amid the divers were a pod of dolphins, some of them wearing manipulator waldoes in order to operate a waterproof data console.

"I have no idea what they're all working on," said Will Riker, "but it's fascinating to watch." He was sitting on an observation bench, an overcoat folded across his lap.

"Never been much of a swimmer myself," Vale noted, glancing around as she approached.

"You should try it," Riker told her. "It's liberating, in a way. Like being in zero-gee, but . . . different somehow." He glanced up. "Did you know we had cetaceans on board *Enterprise* for a while?"

"You mean, like them?" Vale pointed at the dolphins.

Riker nodded. "The thing I remember the most? They love bad jokes."

She sat. "So. Did you ask me here to make small talk about fish, or was there another reason, sir?"

"Mammals, not fish," Riker corrected. "We need to have a conversation," he went on.

"Here?" Vale asked. "I was kind of hoping I'd get to see your new office."

"I wanted a more relaxed location." He glanced away, and for the first time, Vale noticed a nervous-looking Caitian in a lieutenant's uniform loitering some distance away. He was eyeing the glass barrier with what looked like both suspicion and curiosity. "Mister Ssura's my new aide-de-camp," explained Riker. "Comes with the job."

"How's that going?"

"We'll see," Riker muttered. "Look, Chris, you know I trust my instincts. I'm only just starting to find the edges of this, but I'm certain that *Titan*'s return home and my sudden promotion are more than just a reaction to the turmoil of recent days. Right now, I'm trying to put the pieces together, but I can't be sure that what's happened has been because someone wants me here, or because someone *doesn't* want me somewhere else."

"The Andorian situation." Vale weighed the words as she said them. "Even before the shooting, that was a mess. If *Titan* has been called home because of that—"

"You think we would have been told right off the bat," Riker finished. "For now, the fallout from the president's assassination is casting a pall over everything. And you know me. I can't stand idly by, warming a chair with my backside while things go to hell." He sighed. "Nobody is giving me answers, so I'm going to get them myself." He tapped the rank tab on his collar. "I have this. I see no better reason to start using it."

"Oh, I know that look," she said, brushing back a stray white thread of her hair with a finger.

"What look?"

"The 'I'm gonna put my shoulder to this and push it out of the damn way' look. Ask Deanna. She knows the one. 'The Full Riker,' that's what the rest of the officers call it."

"So noted." He leaned back and gave her a nod. "I'm cutting you new orders, Number One." Riker pulled a padd from a pocket in the coat and handed it to her. On the device's small screen, Vale saw the image of a Starfleet *Nova*-class science vessel. "This is the *U.S.S. Lionheart*, a medical cruiser. Your new command, as of thirteen hundred hours today. You'll keep your rank but serve as brevet captain for the duration of the assignment."

A hundred different responses flashed through her mind at once, but all she said was "Oh."

Riker gave her a quizzical look. "*Oh*? I give you a starship command and that's what you have to say?"

"So not the *Titan,* then?"

He grinned. "Wait your turn, Chris. I'm not done with her yet. And not with you, either. This isn't permanent. You're going to be a caretaker CO. *Lionheart* has already been assigned to a new commander, Captain Ainsworth. But he's out at Starbase 47. You're going to take his new ship to him."

She frowned at the padd. "Permission to speak freely, Admiral?"

"When have you ever done otherwise, Commander Vale?" Riker's response was wry.

"If this is some kind of attempt to keep me out of harm's way, you can forget it."

"Perish the thought," he retorted. "You're doing this for me because it's a long way from Sol to Starbase 47. And along the way . . ." He let the sentence hang.

"I take it back," she said quickly. "So what am I really looking for?"

When Riker spoke again, his voice was low and firm. "I want to know *exactly* what happened on Andor. I don't want the paper-thin explanations that are circulating around Starfleet Command and not the slant on things that Velk is putting out into the media. You're going to find out for me." He paused. "I'm putting you on the *Lionheart* because that's not going to draw too much attention. Once you're out there, I want you to look into this situation with Julian Bashir. Find out where he's being held, if you can. The longer this goes on, the more I want to hear Bashir's side of the story. Something isn't right here. This goes beyond issues of Starfleet protocol and Federation security."

Vale nodded. She felt the same way, but she couldn't accept this without voicing her own misgivings. "Admiral . . . Will. You know I'd follow you to Hades and back if you gave the word. I trust you."

"But . . . ?"

"Shady orders? Doing an end-run around Admiral Akaar and the rest of the admiralty board? You've been in that nice office less than a week and already you're bending the rules. I'm not saying you're wrong, but I am saying you'd better be right."

"My name is on the authorization for those orders, Chris. No one else's."

She shook her head, staring into the depths of the tank. "That's not what I mean. Just think about this; if someone inside the fleet or the council is manipulating things, using you and the *Titan* as game pieces . . ." Vale gestured with the padd. "Maybe what you're doing right here is what they want you to do."

Riker was silent for a long time. Then abruptly he stood up, pulling on the coat. "I guess we'll find out soon enough," he said, beckoning to Lieutenant Ssura as he prepared to leave.

"First Tuvok and now me, huh?" she asked as an aside, getting up from the bench. "I should have guessed."

Riker's hand went out to halt her before she could turn away. "What about Tuvok?"

"He was given detachment orders yesterday, took off without a word. High-security stuff, way above my clearance level. I thought it was from you. . . ."

"No." He looked troubled. "This is the first I've heard of it."

Christine felt that chill again. "Okay, now I'm starting to think you might be right about someone pulling strings."

He paused. "I'll look into it. In the meantime, proceed as ordered. Clear skies and good hunting, Commander."

"Thank you, sir. And watch your back, Admiral." Vale tapped her combadge. "One to beam up."

Her last image of her captain and her friend was of his face, set in a grim and uncertain cast; then a humming white light whisked her away.

Nog prowled the corridors of the *Snipe* like a caged treni cat, uncomfortable with his new surroundings and skittish into the bargain. He kept fidgeting, and it had taken a while for him to figure out why.

It was the uniform—or rather, it was the lack of it.

In its own way, his reaction was ironic. Back when he had first followed his ambitions to the Academy, the awkward cut of Starfleet cadet grays had not hung well on his small frame, and he remembered constantly fiddling with the cuffs, the collar, the itchy head skirt. Always ill at ease being the one Ferengi among countless aliens.

But somewhere along the line that had changed, and no matter how hard he tried to pin down exactly when, Nog couldn't remember when being in uniform had gone from feeling odd to feeling *normal*. So much now that it dismayed him to be wandering the decks of a starship in anything other than the mustard undershirt, black tunic, and trousers. It just wasn't right to be on duty and out of colors. In the end, he had made do by replicating a slate-gray freight crew jumpsuit that vaguely resembled his old cadet's gear. The *Snipe*'s name and registration were emblazoned across his back, and wearing it Nog felt like he could blend in. Almost.

The collar was scratchy, though.

He wanted to pretend that he was just wandering aimlessly, but that was a lie. There was another thing that was bothering him, another itch he couldn't scratch. The *Snipe* didn't ring true to him.

It was hard to put it into words. Nog had no doubt that if he'd been here with, say, Chief O'Brien, the other engineer would have understood what he was getting at immediately. The *flow* of the ship was off.

Without being too metaphysical about the whole thing, Nog was someone who believed that a vessel, an engine, a machine of any kind, had a sort of rhythm to it. Not like music exactly, not even like mathematics, but just a sense of action and motion that—when it was working right—was close to perfection. He'd heard Montgomery Scott say something similar back on board the *Challenger* before everything that had happened there. It was the same kind of sense that allowed an engineer to sense the subtle vibrations in a ship's systems, sometimes before the dials and gauges showed anything awry; an affinity for technology, perhaps.

And Nog's affinity had been telling him *Snipe* was out of balance since the moment he had boarded her. Finally, he couldn't ignore the nagging sensation anymore and slipped away into the lower decks to sniff around. He let his ears catch the oscillations of the freighter's subsystems, mapping their patterns in his mind's eye.

In short order, he found himself at the point where the starboard engine pylon connected the main hull and the number two warp nacelle. More than anything, he wanted to climb in there and take a look around at the innards of the faster-than-light drive, but it was a risky thing to do while at warp speed, and picking the locks on the access hatches was likely to raise red flags on the *Snipe*'s bridge. Instead he peered at the screens of untended system monitors, watching the pulsing of the warp bubble insulating the ship from normal space-time.

It wasn't long before he found something odd. The engines were being throttled; rather than operating at their peak efficiency, their function was being deliberately retarded by a series of restrictor subroutines built into the system. That in itself was unusual enough, until Nog asked himself *why*. A ship of this class and tonnage typically topped out with engines capable of a warp-six cruising speed, maybe with enough power to make a short sprint to warp seven if they were pushed hard. But *Snipe*'s engines were currently running at a steady six-point-two, and the power curve showed that they were almost idling. The Ferengi ran the numbers in his head and estimated that in the speed stakes, the freighter was probably capable of giving a *Defiant*-class starship a run for its money.

Once he understood what he was seeing on the *Snipe,* Nog began to find more patterns, more anomalies. Starfleet regulations meant that civilian craft could carry only a small number of low-level offensive systems and non-military shield emitters, but as he backtracked through the lower compartments, Nog picked out conduits and power trains that shouldn't have been there. He saw electroplasma taps and channels for phaser coolant that at first glance went nowhere and did nothing. They were hidden well, good enough to fool someone who didn't give them a second look, but now the young engineer was seeing them everywhere. Was it possible that *Snipe*'s bland hull hid additional phaser emplacements and other military-specification hardware? It seemed so.

The detail that finally confirmed it for him was the shoddy appearance of the transport ship. The rusty, patched hull, the grimy interior spaces and flaking paintwork, all gave the impression of a vessel held together more by good wishes and repair tape than by stem bolts and alloy. But it was fake.

There was decay on the *Snipe,* but it was layered on like a cosmetic. Making certain he wasn't being observed, Nog scrambled up into a channel bus and put his face close to what appeared to be a corroded section of EPS conduit. The pipe was perfectly intact but cowled with a redundant outer sheath that gave the appearance of oxidized, aged metal.

Inside and out, the freighter was a falsehood, one thing masquerading as another. Nog had heard of such ships before; in the Ferengi Alliance there was a tradition of Marauders fitted with sections of frangible outer hull and sensor baffles, designed in such a way that they would resemble slow, poorly armed cargo barges. Thus, they could move freely and not draw attention to any deployment of military might. In addition, pirates and rival mercantile clans who swept in to prey on such vessels would get a nasty shock when their target turned out to be a gunship bristling with disruptor cannons. The Ferengi called this kind of ship a *Qardok,* a word that had no direct translation into Federation Standard; the closest approximation in the human language was *Gotcha!*

"What are you—"

"Doing up there?"

His attention fixed on the conduit, the sudden sound of the two trilling voices from below him caught Nog totally off guard. He jerked and banged the top of his skull on a panel, a hiss of pain escaping his lips.

Dropping back to the deck, he found himself standing between the two Bynars, their unblinking eyes watching him intently. "I was just . . . uh . . ."

"What were you—"

"Looking for?"

"Nothing," he lied, then quickly appended something vaguely truthful. "I was bored. Wandering. Examining . . . stuff." He gave a weak, snaggletoothed grin. "Those things."

"Given what we know—"

"Of the Ferengi character—"

"It seems unlikely you were—"

"Trying to sabotage the ship."

Nog's head went back and forth between the two of them as if he were a spectator at a springball match. *Were they being sarcastic? Do Bynars even understand what sarcasm is?* The pair of them glanced at each other and exchanged a string of high-speed code blips. Nog considered that to be somewhat rude, like sharing secret whispers in front of someone. Then they were looking at him again, and his fake smirk faded.

Although he liked the fact that having a pair of Bynars aboard the ship meant he wasn't the shortest person on the *Snipe,* Nog had to admit he found them slightly unsettling, with their odd mirror-image clothing and strange, birdlike movements. What struck him the most was the silver nub of a computing implant sitting on the side of their domed skulls. Having dealt with computer hardware of many kinds for years, and having experienced some of the worst effects a computer malfunction could produce, Nog found the idea of having something similar wired directly into his cortex *by choice* disquieting.

"Do you wish to—"

"Ask us a question?"

He took the opportunity to change the subject. "Do you two ever play cards? Tongo? Poker? I'm guessing with a neural implant, you must be pretty good."

They both nodded in unison. "We are banned—"

"From gambling."

"Risa."

"Orion Casinos."

"Wrigley's Pleasure Planet."

"We win—"

"Too much latinum."

Nog started away down the passageway, the two Bynars trailing after him. "Oh. Shame."

"We have an alternate—"

"Revenue stream. Our skills are—"

"In demand."

The engineer was still considering what that could mean when the *Snipe*'s intercom chimed and Kincade's voice crackled through the air.

"All team members to the mess hall immediately. Mission briefing in ten minutes."

The transport had dropped out of warp in the time it took Nog to climb back up to the main deck, and he and the Bynars were the last to arrive for the meeting. The other seven members of their erstwhile team sat or stood around the edges of the compartment. There was a subtle divide between those who were in Starfleet and those who were not, the former grouped on one side of the room, the latter on the other.

Nog took a seat on the bench next to Tuvok, giving the Vulcan a nod of greeting. "Commander." He wanted to tell him what he suspected about the *Snipe*'s secrets, but not within earshot of the others. Across the table, Tom Riker was sipping from a mug of *raktajino,* and the Zeon mercenary Ashur was toying with a small throwing blade.

"Mister Nog," Tuvok replied.

Ashur grunted as he watched their exchange. "Your pardon if I don't salute," he sneered. "I don't have a fancy uniform in my closet like you." He waved a thick finger, taking in Tuvok, Nog, and the Bolian pilot seated nearby.

"Saluting is not a compulsory protocol for Starfleet officers and crew," Tuvok noted. He was either ignoring or unaware of the Zeon's belligerent tone.

Ashur was going to say something else, but then

Kincade walked past the table and put down a padd with a hard *clack* of plastic on metal. "Okay. We're all here. Let's begin." She shot the Bynars a look. "Is the comm relay ready?"

They nodded in unison, and both of them reached for a dormant console in a corner of the chamber. Nog had thought it was just an entertainment module, but at the touch of a few switches the lights in the mess hall dimmed and an emitter head dropped out of a hidden compartment in the ceiling.

There was a white flash, and suddenly a cloud of holographic pixels formed into a humanoid shape, there in the open center of the room. For the first couple of seconds, the hologram was indistinct—a vague, ghostly form of indeterminate gender or species—but then by degrees it took on layers of detail. Clothing defined itself, then facial characteristics, sharpening until at last it appeared that a stocky and unsmiling Tellarite was standing among them.

The face of the civilian was vaguely familiar to the engineer, and when Tuvok said his name, Nog blinked in surprise.

"That is Galif jav Velk, chief of staff to the president pro tem." The Vulcan glanced at Kincade. "I do not understand. . . ."

Kincade's expression betrayed nothing. "You and me both. I was just told to expect a signal on this hyperchannel frequency."

"Better that you know who I am, for the sake of expedience," said the hologram, and with a start, Nog realized that it was actually a "live" broadcast. "The power cost of encrypting this communication and transmitting it to you makes every second valuable." Velk's image flickered a little, distorting. "You have been summoned to this location by direct command of the Federation Council, an action authorized by Special Executive Order of President Pro Tem Ishan Anjar." The Tellarite's cold gaze scanned the room. "Some of you are under directives from Starfleet Command. Others have been recruited from the civilian sector. I have gathered you here in order to participate in an extremely delicate mission, in defense of Federation national security. Know that if you are successful, you will receive the highest commendations and the gratitude of the UFP."

Nog glanced at Ashur, Tom, Khob, and the others. He would have expected mercenaries to want something more material than a promise of thanks, but none of them said a word. The Ferengi found himself wondering: *Did the Tellarite have some* other *kind of leverage over them, something more than just avarice?*

Velk went on. "As of now, you will be in commission under the group designation 'Active Four.' All communications and pursuant orders will be issued via that coding. Your unit will proceed to act as a covert tactical force, and you are to fulfill a single remit: Track, isolate, and capture the terrorist cell responsible for the assassination of the late President Nanietta Bacco."

The Ferengi blinked, trying to keep up with what he was hearing. Nog had never heard of any such orders or unit being formed before, and he wasn't certain how to deal with the concept. But then, perhaps that was the point; he had never heard of these kind of orders before precisely because they *were* so secret. He swallowed hard.

"It is our belief that these terrorists are agents of the Tzenkethi Coalition, operating beyond the borders of the Typhon Pact states," said Velk's holoimage, gesturing at the air. "They are highly dangerous and represent an ongoing threat to the security of the quadrant."

Nog watched the other members of the group take that revelation on board, thinking back to Deep Space 9 and the discovery of a Tzenkethi DNA trace on the device that had been found implanted in Enkar Sirsy, the initial suspect in the assassination. It seemed the Federation Council now considered that sliver of evidence enough to act upon.

"The circumstances of your mission require that you conduct this operation in isolation from all outside agencies, even those of Starfleet and the Federation. Until the operation concludes, you are effectively phantoms. If you are captured or killed by any aggressor powers, the Federation will disavow all knowledge of your existence and of this mission." Velk paused to let that sink in. "Your ship will provide immediate logistical support. Any additional concerns will be your responsibility to source."

"What support?" muttered Ashur.

"Computer," Velk snapped. "Authorization is given. Mission start. Unlock operations systems."

"Confirmed," said a synthetic voice.

Without warning, the holographic emitter projecting Velk's avatar directed multiple other rays of light to points across the mess hall. Nog jerked back in surprise as a dozen panes of blue formed in midair, some hanging over the dining tables, others suspended in space. Each one was a data feed, a screen relaying complex charts, signal traffic, tactical plots, and more. In the blink of an eye, the grubby crew lounge had been transformed into an operations center. High on one wall, a chronograph was running, the clock having started the moment Velk gave his command.

It appeared that the secrets that Nog had suspected the *Snipe* of concealing were just the head of the gree-worm. Across the room, Khob had been leaning on the far bulkhead, and now the big Suliban flinched, stepping away as a seam appeared and panels retracted into the deck. Revealed beyond the mess hall was a hidden compartment lined with charging slots and equipment lockers. Racks on either side of the chamber were heavy with a variety of different weapons—energy pistols, ballistic guns, portable photon cannons.

Sahde pushed forward and gathered up a bulky phase-compression rifle, hefting it in her hands. "This, I can work with," she noted. Nog saw the glint of something savage in her eyes, and he didn't like it.

Velk's hologram scowled at her. "I reiterate. You will leave no trace. You will draw no outside attention. You will find these targets."

The Elloran woman spoke directly to the Tellarite. "And when we find them . . . we terminate them?"

"That's not what we . . ." Tom Riker hesitated. "That's not what Starfleet does."

Velk glanced toward Kincade and back. "This is not an execution detail. Your primary objective is to capture President Bacco's killers *alive*. Once retrieved, they will be taken to trial in public so that every power in the galaxy can know the facts of their guilt. These beings have committed a high crime against the people and the concord of the United Federation of Planets. They must be brought to account."

Kincade folded her arms across her chest. "How do we proceed from here, sir?"

"Additional details have been transmitted to the

Snipe via an encrypted side channel. You will find further information there as to your initial objective beyond the Beta Rigel system. I expect full mission reports every twenty-four hours, standard time."

Tuvok rose from his seat to address the hologram. "Sir, with respect, this is highly irregular. I have several questions."

Velk's eyes narrowed. "I don't doubt it." Then without another word, the image of the Tellarite grew indistinct and winked out.

Ashur snorted quietly. "He hung up on you, Vulcan."

At another table, Lieutenant Ixxen was examining a star map. "There are coordinates here," she announced. "Just like he said. A system in the Zokod Barrens. That's a large dust cloud this side of the Hromi Cluster. We could be there in three days." She glanced at Tuvok, reflexively looking toward the superior Starfleet officer for guidance.

"Lieutenant," said Kincade with enough snap in her tone to shift Ixxen's gaze to her. "Plot a course, nothing that will draw attention. Follow civilian traffic routes."

"Aye, uh, Colonel," replied the Bolian, looking away.

As Nog watched, still trying to assimilate what he had heard, Tuvok turned to the other officer. "Were you aware of the parameters of our assignment?"

"No. But I had an inkling. Does this present a problem for you, Commander? I've seen your file. It's not like you're a stranger to covert operations."

"My undercover infiltration of the Maquis was conducted with full Starfleet oversight," he replied. "Mister Velk made no mention of similar supervision of this operation."

Nog realized that everyone else in the room was silent, waiting to see how this conversation concluded.

"You want to refuse this mission?" Kincade asked without weight. "That could be a little problematic."

"I did not say that," said Tuvok after a long moment, his stoic expression remaining unchanged.

"I'm glad we got that settled." Kincade looked around the room. "All right. As Ixxen says, we've got three days until we reach our area of operations. I intend to use that time for drills to get us working like a unit. Everyone, familiarize yourselves with the systems and hardware we have here." Her gaze settled on Nog. "We have a job to do. Let's get to it."

Beyond the glassy curve of the atmosphere dome, the stark lunar landscape was bathed in hard light reflected from the rising Earth beyond it. There was an austere, chilly majesty to the view that made Deanna Troi give an involuntary shiver, despite the fact that here in the New Berlin Memorial Park, the ambient atmosphere was steady and comfortable.

She cast around the roped-off area past the public statue garden, over the lines of diplomats, politicians, and ambassadors who stood in somber conversation or sipped discreetly at flutes of wine. It wasn't difficult to spot the numerous Protection Detail personnel moving among the attendees, some of them standing sentinel at the edges of the open space, others patrolling, their eyes hidden behind black sensor-glasses.

Off to one side, a reporting team from the Federation News Service was the only media allowed to be inside the perimeter, and they were quietly recording the proceedings; the image feed was being broadcast live across the quadrant as hundreds of worlds and millions of beings tuned in to watch the ceremony.

Many had come to pay their respects, and she had seen the huge numbers of civilians and fleet crew in the outer areas of the park. They had come simply to be close to this moment, to show some solidarity in the wake of a terrible act.

She looked away. The presidential memorial was sheathed with a black cloth; the shape of the slab-sided obelisk was concealed for the moment. Troi had seen it before, in better days. It was carved from several blocks of granite, each mined from one of the founder-member planets of the Federation, then fused into a whole—a symbol of the accord between those worlds and all the others that had come into the fold in the decades since. Each president who had served was remembered here after his or her passing, and today it was Nan Bacco's turn to join that illustrious list.

Troi took a shaky breath and tugged her uniform tunic straight, pausing to adjust the mourning band around her arm. There were very few Starfleet officers in attendance at the ceremony, and she was by far the lowest ranked. Admiral Akaar was visible across the garden, standing head and shoulders above the majority of the other attendees, but he had not once made eye contact with her, instead remaining at a distance among the other chiefs of staff, his expression unreadable. Troi's empathic abilities brought her nothing more about his mood; the Capellan was always guarded, and right now his thoughts were silent and dark.

In truth, she didn't *want* to exercise her psionic skills to sense more, not here, not today. There was such a great pressure of sorrow and regret clouding everything, a great mournful underscore of emotion emanating from the people who were here to show their esteem for Bacco. Troi kept a tight rein on her own sadness. She was afraid that if she began to weep, the barriers to her empathy would crumble and she would channel not just her sorrow, but that of hundreds of others.

"Deanna?" She turned as Togren approached her, and she gave the Denobulan diplomat a brittle smile. "Thank you so much for coming," he added.

"I couldn't refuse," she replied. "I appreciate your generosity in asking me to be your plus one."

Togren shrugged. "Both my wives are at home on Denobula. And I felt you should be here, if only to affirm Starfleet's respect for dear Nan." His tawny, dappled face was downcast.

"Yes," she agreed. "There are not a lot of us here."

"How is your family?"

"They're well. Tasha's four now."

"Splendid. I hope to see her soon." He paused. "I understand your husband did not receive an invitation?" Off her nod, he carried on. "Please tell him it was nothing personal. It seems that the president pro tem's staff wanted to make this a visibly civilian affair."

"I understand. It's enough that a Starfleet vessel has the honor of carrying President Bacco's body home to Cestus III. All of us who wear the uniform are proud to take on that duty."

"Ah, yes, the *U.S.S. Aventine.*" Togren nodded. The diplomat indicated a flag officer Troi didn't recognize standing near Akaar. "One of the rear admirals assigned a new commander to that ship after the arrest of Captain Dax. I understand it was dispatched to the Bajor system for repairs after that regrettable business over Andoria . . . but it is fitting that a ship commissioned under Nan's administration and which stood at the forefront of recent crises is the one to take her to her rest." His face clouded slightly. "There was some rather . . . spirited discussion at higher levels that the *Aventine* divert to Earth first. I argued otherwise. I think Velk would have pressed for thirty days of lying in state and mourning. . . ." He shook his head. "It was not in the late president's wishes. She didn't want pomp and ceremony . . . but she earned it anyway."

Troi wanted to press the diplomat further for more about the *Aventine* and the fate of Ezri Dax, but before she could ask, Togren's aide arrived, a look of dismay on her face. "Sir? Something has come up. Your attention is required."

"Now?" asked Togren, gesturing at the dais set up before the shrouded memorial. The attendees were starting to take their seats; the ceremony was about to begin. He huffed. "Very well. Deanna, if you will excuse me?"

Alone once again, she steeled herself and found her seat—*at the rear,* she noted—just as a press secretary called them to their feet to announce the arrival of the president pro tem.

Ishan Anjar emerged from behind the dais and approached the lectern there with swift, confident steps. His dark hair accented with distinguished streaks of steel gray, and dressed in a traditional Bajoran mourning suit, he projected an air of solemn gravity, his stern features fixed in an expression of resignation and resolve. He seemed every inch a man called to take on a regrettable obligation, and his usual intensity seemed muted. Troi studied him, uncertain of how to measure him by her own lights.

As the attendees sat, he crossed the garden with his gaze, finding the cameras of the press team. "My friends and colleagues, my fellow citizens of the United Federation of Planets. We are gathered here today, not only in the gardens of New Berlin but on every member-world of our great alliance. On Earth, Tellar, and Vulcan. On Bajor, Alpha Centauri, and Bolarus. On Zakdorn, Axanar, and Cestus III. In these places and countless others, we have come together to mourn the loss of a great soul, a politician and peacemaker. My friend . . . *our* friend Nanietta Bacco."

Troi noted that Andor had been left off the list of worlds Ishan mentioned; she glanced around, noticing for the first time that there were no Andorians present at the gathering.

Her attention snapped back as a group of Klingons—emissaries from Chancellor Martok—struck their fists against the breastplates of their armor as a gesture of respect to a fallen ally. Ishan gave them an indulgent nod and went on.

"A powerful light has dimmed. A woman of honesty and high character, struck down as she did what she had done for so long . . . build bridges and forge trust. Nanietta Bacco believed passionately in the United Federation of Planets and the principles for which it stands. She believed in a Federation that is strong and united. A Federation looking forward to a better tomorrow, beyond the trials that have tested us to the limits of our endurance." He paused, as if searching for the next words. "I believe in those things. I share her vision of unity. And now, more than ever, I realize that this is a time for harmony, not for division. We come together this day in grief and sadness, but what do we see? That each of us is stronger under the aegis of our Federation than separated from it. Fear may make us believe otherwise." He shook his head. "I tell you that is not so."

Another dig at the expense of the Andorians? Troi wondered. *Is he using this memorial service as a platform to diminish them?*

But in the next breath, Ishan's words turned toward a different target. "We need our unity. Our enemies know that truth, too. These rogue states, these old adversaries, they gather together and make *pacts*. Our enemies struck down Nanietta Bacco in order to break our union, but I say they have failed. In the wake of this terrible atrocity, look to yourselves and see. We are united in our grief, united in our resolve. United in our defiance of those who wish us harm through perfidy and menace." Ishan left the podium and walked to the memorial, his voice strong and clear. "We will not be cowed." With a flourish, he pulled at a silver cord and the black shroud fell away, pooling on the ground.

There, etched in gold on the ice-colored stone, President Bacco's name caught the light and shimmered. Another figure emerged from the side of the platform; Troi recognized Galif jav Velk as he carried a laurel wreath to the president pro tem. Ishan took it from him with a nod and then laid it at the foot of the memorial, bowing as he did so.

Despite herself, she frowned. Through the mix of complex, turbulent emotions all around her, Troi had the sense of something disconnected from the moment, as if this was all a shadow play, a hollow act without true heart.

She became aware of Togren's assistant, who had slipped into the chair beside her. "Commander Troi, please forgive me," she whispered. "I'm afraid that Togren will be detained for some time. He sends his regrets that he will not be able to accompany you."

"What's wrong?" Troi asked, keeping her voice low as Ishan returned to the lectern again and began to speak.

"There is an issue with the Andorians."

"They're *here*?"

The woman nodded. "Outside. I'm fearful things may become rather heated."

Troi made a quick choice. "Take me to them."

Five

Deanna Troi sensed the simmering anger even before she entered the annex outside the statue garden. The color of the emotion was strong and potent, cutting through the darker tones of mournful feeling surrounding the attendees at the memorial service.

She heard raised voices as she approached and saw Togren standing in front of a group of five formally attired Andorians. His body language was that of a man trying to maintain peace, but the slope of the Denobulan's shoulders seemed to show that he felt he had already been defeated in that regard. Two of the Andorian party, both *thaan*s in suits of simple cut, were arguing with a pair of Federation Security Agency operatives. Floating above them all was a holoscreen of the ceremony that was taking place in the neighboring dome, a giant close-up on Ishan Anjar's face as he continued his speech.

The Andorian ambassador himself, Envoy Ramasanar ch'Nuillen, stood behind his men. He was stonefaced and silent, his antennae taut with annoyance.

Togren caught sight of Troi approaching, and there was a flash of relief in his eyes. He gave a subtle nod, as if to say *Yes, excellent idea, please help me!*

"Do you understand who this is?" one of the *thaan*s said to the security men, his tone rising as he pointed at the envoy. "Do you know how far he has come, on the invitation of your government?"

The larger of the two operatives stood his ground and raised a hand. "Please step back, sir. I won't ask you again."

His colleague's hand dropped to his hip, where Troi had no doubt a small phaser would be holstered. "We understand your dismay," said the other man. "But you must respect that we are on the highest level of alert after recent events. We can't afford to take any chances."

Troi cleared her throat and addressed the second operative. "I'm Commander Troi, senior diplomatic officer of the *U.S.S. Titan*. Perhaps I may be of some assistance?"

The large man shot her a disinterested look. "Starfleet's help is not required here, sir."

"Troi?" The envoy spoke for the first time, giving Deanna an equally frosty glance. "Your name is familiar to me. Are you here to give us more excuses?"

Togren broke in, trying to maintain a moderated manner. "There has been a regrettable administrative error, Commander. It appears that the honored envoy's diplomatic documentation has not been correctly processed."

"Our standing orders are clear," said the security operative. "No entry to anyone without full clearance. No exceptions." He produced a padd from an inner pocket and held it up so Troi could see a list of the guests at the memorial ceremony. "If your name's not down, you're not coming in."

Ch'Nuillen was mature for an Andorian *chan*, but

he was tall with it, and he drew himself up to his full height as he pushed past his adjutants to look the operative in the eye. His face darkened to cobalt blue, and when he spoke again, the temperature in the annex seemed to drop ten degrees. "We have come here in good faith and in the name of all Andoria, our hand extended to the Federation. All we wish is to offer our condolences at the passing of a great leader. Now you expect me to accept that we may not do so because of a trivial point of regulations? You insult us."

The operative's expression didn't change. "We've already lost one president, sir. I don't know you. I don't have any proof you are who you say you are. So you'll forgive us if we don't let another potential assassin into—"

"You dare?" One of the *thaan*s rocked off his heels, hands cocked to strike out at the operative for his insult, but Troi had already sensed the moment coming and she was immediately interposing herself between them.

"Gentlebeings, please!" she insisted. "I'm sure we can resolve this."

Ch'Nuillen snorted and turned away, stalking toward the far wall of the annex dome. His retinue trailed after him, muttering darkly amongst themselves. Togren and his assistant exchanged weary looks, uncertain how to proceed.

The other security operative folded his arms. "If they wanted to be here," he sniffed, "they shouldn't have seceded in the first place."

Troi rounded on him. "That's an astute political analysis, Agent," she said mordantly. "Very nuanced. Your talents are obviously wasted guarding a doorway."

Togren's brow knit with concern as she moved to

speak to the diplomat. "Not a good start," he said. "I'm to blame for this. I should have double-checked that the envoy's credentials were all in order."

"They *were*," insisted his aide. "There's no reason for the clearances to have been delayed!"

Unless someone in the administration is using this as a petty way of stonewalling the Andorians. Troi knew without resorting to her empathic abilities that the same thought was playing through Togren's mind. She remembered Ishan's opening remarks; while the currently political climate meant he could not be overtly critical of the Andorians, he still had the opportunity to make life hard for them. It wouldn't be enough for ch'Nuillen and his people to come back to the Federation with cap in hand. She remembered an American idiom her father had sometimes used; they would have to "eat crow."

"We can't undo this," she said, "so let's use the opportunity to get out in front of things." Troi nodded toward the Andorian party. "Any second they're going to beam back to their ship and be gone. But ch'Nuillen is here, right now. So let's talk to him."

Togren held out his hand in a "you-go-first" gesture. "Be my guest," he said. But as she crossed the floor, at her back Troi heard Ishan Anjar's voice shift tone and inwardly she groaned.

"Our Federation is one of magnanimity," he was saying. *"Together we can achieve great things. Look at what we have done in unity! We have helped our new friends on Cardassia Prime rebuild after the horrors of the Dominion War. We have pulled our member-worlds and associates alike from the ashes of the Borg Invasion. And only days ago, our brave men and women in Starfleet lent their strength to aid the people of Andor with their recent internal crisis."*

"*Aid* us?" spat the *thaan* who had almost lost his temper a moment earlier. "They tried to deny us our future!"

"Sholun." The Envoy spoke his aide's name with quiet force, silencing him. "This is neither the time nor the place." He studied Troi as she approached, fixing a neutral aspect in place. "My people are passionate, Commander Troi. I'm sure you understand this situation would bring that to the surface." And then ch'Nuillen very deliberately turned his back on the holoscreen and Ishan's face, every member of his party doing the same a moment later.

The message that sent wasn't lost on her. "Of course," she went on. "Please accept my apologies on behalf of the United Federation of Planets."

"These are fraught times," Togren added. "And unfortunately mistakes do occur. . . ."

Troi nodded. "Sir, I hope this will not cast a pall over your endeavors here."

He turned his gaze on her, and for the first time, Troi got the impression that the envoy was really, truly *looking* at her. His thoughts were careful and guarded, and his next words were as cold as his gaze. "These things happen. We move on. Andor has paid its respects to Nanietta Bacco in its own way. Our friends on the Federation Council, although they may be the loudest voices there, wish to welcome us back. That, Commander, is what we shall concentrate on." He bowed slightly. "Now, I will return to my courier and—"

"Before you depart," she said, stepping closer. "There's something else I'd like to say."

He glared at her. "As you wish."

"Andor has more friends than you may realize, Envoy. And not just on the council, but in Starfleet."

"I know of the *Titan*," ch'Nuillen allowed. "And your ship's recent contacts with our people."

"Then you know that we respect you and share great sympathy with the trials your species has faced. I hope that we can be—"

"Allies?"

Troi couldn't be sure if he was mocking her. "At the very least."

The Andorian became unreadable, giving her nothing; then after a moment he spoke again. "That would be agreeable." Ch'Nuillen gestured to Sholun, who spoke quietly into a communicator, and with a crackle of matter displacement, the envoy and his party vanished into a haze of blue-white light.

Togren released a heavy sigh and gave a weak grin. "I knew it was a good idea to recruit you, Troi! Thank you; I'm not sure I would have been able to salvage anything from today."

"I'm glad I could help," she told him. *And for the chance to see into what is really going on.*

Troi turned back to the screen to see a woman in a black dress stepping onto the dais, opening her hands to deliver the first lines of "Amazing Grace" to the silent, reverent crowd.

Christine Vale took a moment in the restroom before she crossed to the transport station at Starfleet Headquarters. She, along with many others in uniform, had stood silently in the great atrium beneath the screen showing the live broadcast from New Berlin. Vale had heard Ishan Anjar speak before, and although she kept her political views to herself most of the time, when he had talked about a strong Federation and a firm response to those who would threaten them, the commander found herself agreeing with the Bajoran. Law and order were in her bones, and acts like the killing of Bacco struck right at the heart of what she believed in. Listening to him talk now, as the late president's name joined the roll of honor, she wasn't ashamed to admit that she had shed tears. They came from a place of sorrow and of anger.

But it wouldn't be right to set foot aboard her first starship command with that air upon her. Alone, she wiped her eyes and put aside her personal feelings. For now, she would need to project strength and purpose, because her new—*albeit temporary*—crew would look to her to set the tone.

Within minutes she was stepping off a transporter pad, sensing the familiar background hum of a working starship all around her.

The first person Christine Vale saw was a muscular woman with three gold commander's pips on her collar. She had a classical face, like something from an ancient marble sculpture, but she was severe with it. Coils of wine-dark hair were artfully draped over the shoulders of her uniform, and she stood ramrod straight. "Commander Vale," she snapped. "Greetings. Welcome aboard *Lionheart*."

"Commander Atia, isn't it?" Christine hadn't had much opportunity to familiarize herself with the medical cruiser's full crew complement, but she'd made sure to skim the high points of the first officer's file. "Thank you."

The other woman was the same age as Vale, from a planet commonly known as Magna Roma. Atia's people were the descendants of humans transplanted from Earth's distant past to that world by an alien race known as the Preservers. They had carried their culture—based on the Terran Roman Empire—with them and evolved a civilization based upon its tenets. The Magna Romanii had long since grown out of the more objectionable elements of their society and become active members of the Federation; but they were said to be a fierce, strident people, and Vale's first impression of her new executive officer did nothing to dispel that view.

"Aye," said Atia crisply. "The *Lionheart* is yours."

Straight to the point, thought Vale. "I relieve you," she said, voicing the formal statement for her acceptance of the center seat.

"I stand relieved," Atia replied, completing the exchange. "Captain," she added, tapping her combadge. "Computer, log date and time. Command of *U.S.S. Lionheart* NCC-73808 now custody of Brevet Captain Christine Vale."

"So noted," came the reply.

Vale nodded. "Okay. That was simple enough. At ease, Commander."

"I am," said the other woman.

That seemed unlikely; Atia was so much at attention that she could have served double duty as a hull brace, but Vale decided not to press the point. She handed over a padd with all the official paperwork in place. "That's the red tape. There's also some additional notations about extra cargo to be brought aboard." Atia took a snapshot look at the device and handed it off to the noncom at the transporter controls. "So. Do we start with a tour?"

"No, sir," said the first officer, leading the way out into the corridor. "Bid to follow."

Lionheart's corridors were narrower than *Titan*'s, and her smaller crew more thinly spread. At first, something seemed a little out of place to Vale, and it took a few moments for her to realize what it was; the cruiser's complement was almost completely bipedal, oxygen-breathing humanoids, and after spending so long aboard *Titan,* with its panoply of various alien species on board, it felt odd to be in a place filled with beings more or less like her.

She frowned as they made their way aft. "Isn't the bridge in the other direction, Commander?"

"Correct. Ship's senior doctor asks audience first. The matter speaks to urgency."

"Well, I guess on a medical cruiser that counts as important." She paused. "I didn't have time to read the chief medical officer's file before I boarded."

"Doctor Rssuu serves well. You have encountered Lahit before?"

"That's his race? No, I don't know them."

"Lahit have no sexes," Atia said, shaking her head. "Rssuu takes male pronoun for ease of conversation. Sight will make clear."

"Right." Atia's clipped diction was taking a little getting used to, but Vale guessed it was an artifact of going from her native language to Federation Standard. She *hoped* it was that. The Magna Romanii woman's sharp manner could easily be interpreted as hostility, and to some degree, Atia had cause to be unreceptive to Vale's arrival. Before Riker had cut Vale's command orders for the *Lionheart,* it would have fallen to the ship's first officer to take temporary captaincy for its journey across the quadrant. A last-second change of orders would be enough to put anyone's nose out of joint.

Best to air that out now rather than later, Vale thought. "Commander." She halted by a maintenance duct. "This assignment has come out of nowhere for both of us, and I'm sure we share a sense of having our routine disrupted. But I hope that isn't going to be an issue. My posting here isn't a reflection on the performance of you or the crew of the *Lionheart*. I want you to be clear on that."

Atia watched her for a moment, and then the other woman's expression softened slightly. "Know that questions were asked and answers found absent. In light of dark days, those who know not find solution in rumor." She stiffened again. "Such things are quashed aboard *Lionheart* if they fall to earshot. Service is of paramount concern at all times. Ship stands ready to obey Admiral Riker's orders. And yours."

"Glad to hear it. Carry on."

"Sickbay is over here."

Vale followed Atia through the doors and stopped abruptly. "Did we just take a wrong turn and end up in the ship's arboretum?"

"No such place," Atia noted, walking across the compartment under a canopy of branches and leaves.

It certainly was an infirmary, Vale reflected, because she could see ranks of bio-beds and medical monitor screens. In keeping with the mission profile of the starship, the larger-than-standard sickbay extended away into other compartments, including a secondary ward, observation chamber, labs, and an operation theater, but in the middle of it all, someone had decided to plant a tree.

The thick trunk was big enough that she could have just about got her arms around it, and at its base there was a dense nutrient tray packed with moist dirt and a thick root system. It resembled a strange merging of a mighty oak and an exotic banyan. Over her head, branches crisscrossed in a complex network that extended to every corner of the infirmary, and ropy vines dangled from them, shifting as if in a breeze.

But not a breeze. The vines were moving by themselves, animated by an intelligence. Vale watched as one delicately picked up a sensor wand and used it to scan a human officer in Science blue who was seated on one of the beds.

There was a rhythmic creaking sound, like wood twisting, and then a moment later she heard a man's voice with an English accent and a deceptively light tone. "Ah. Good. You're here." It came from a metallic vocoder module embedded in the bark of the main trunk. "Commander Vale, I'm Doctor Rssuu."

"Rssuu," said Vale, half grinning. "Right. Sounds like *rustle.*"

"I suppose so," he replied airily. "Pardon me if I don't get up. I'm rather set in my ways." A vine dropped out of the canopy and gave her a welcoming tap on her forearm.

"He is the tree," noted Atia.

"Yeah," Vale said dryly. "I kinda got that."

Another vine-limb emerged from the foliage bearing a tricorder, which Rssuu ran over the length of her. "Just updating my medical records," he said. "Speaking of which, Commander Atia, I don't need to remind you that I still want a blood sample."

"Tasks have been many, time short for trivial matters," she shot back.

Rssuu's synthetic voice became a stage whisper. "Our steadfast first officer suffered a bout of food poisoning on shore leave, but she's a rather poor patient and deliberately avoids me. I think I may have a cutting of mine put in her cabin to keep watch on her health."

"Good to know you're conscientious," said Vale. "Commander Atia said you wanted to see me urgently?"

"Indeed so, Captain. You are aware that *Lionheart*'s mission calls on us to be a first responder to medical emergencies across the sector. To do that, we require full stocks of supplies before we set sail. Biomimetic substrate gels for our dedicated replicators, raw batches of hyronalin, leoporazine, stokaline, and other medicines . . ."

"And you don't have them?"

"No. Sadly, because Admiral Riker assigned you to us out of the blue, a quirk of shipping protocols means that we cannot complete final loading of supplies from Starbase One until our new captain signs off on the manifest. There are pallets of drugs waiting on the deck down there, and they're in danger of spoiling." A thick, leafy tendril offered her a padd. "If you could address this before we depart?"

"Of course, Doctor." She tapped the authorization tab and the padd beeped acceptance. "As I told the commander, I'm sorry for any disruption. We'll get under way as soon as all the cargo is on board."

"Much obliged." Vale turned to leave, with Atia trailing behind, but Rssuu shot out a vine that wrapped around the other woman's wrist. "First Officer?" said the vocoder in a hectoring tone. "Do I have to take your blood the unpleasant way? On my planet the flora eat the fauna, you know."

The officer Rssuu had been examining got to his feet and nodded at Atia. "Don't worry, Commander. I'll take the new CO up to the bridge." He flashed Vale an easy grin. "Lieutenant Seth Maslan, sir, ship's science officer."

She remembered Maslan from her cursory look over the crew files. Young, handsome, and intelligent but a little flighty. *Lionheart* was his fourth posting in as many years. "Lead on, Mister." Vale shot Atia a look, a wry smile on her lips as the exec grimly rolled up her sleeve. "I'll see you up there when you're done."

The formation of three blue-liveried shuttlecraft lifted off from New Berlin's starport and shifted back and forth in an elaborate shell game, each craft crossing over and under the others so that any observer—and any potential attacker—would be hard-pressed to determine exactly which shuttle was which.

Their departure completed, the ships tucked into a careful line of flight and followed a specially cleared transit corridor across the void between the orbit of Luna and that of Earth. It would take them down past the titanic spindle of Starbase One on a course that would carry them to land in Paris in short order.

Aboard the *T'Maran,* one of the identical shuttles, Ishan Anjar paused to shrug off his jacket and deposit it carelessly on a chair. "*Cela* tea," he told the replicator. "Spiced, hot."

The president pro tem didn't offer his chief of staff anything, and he scooped up the cup, taking a seat and running a hand through his hair. "So that is over," he said, his humorless expression threatening to become a scowl. "Now we can start moving forward."

"That is the intention," said Galif jav Velk, standing stiffly in the small cabin. He found the shuttlecraft somewhat cramped and uncomfortable, and he wished to be elsewhere. Glancing out of a viewport, he saw the sister-ships *sh'Rothress* and *al-Rashid* in close formation.

Ishan picked up a padd and skimmed through its contents. "These are the latest polls?"

Velk nodded curtly. "Data is still coming in, but it appears your approval rate is holding steady—"

"Steady?" He put down the teacup. "I don't want *steady*. I want improved. I want *spectacular*."

"That will take time," said the Tellarite.

Ishan shot him a warning look, but he ignored it. "The Andorians were present today."

"I didn't notice."

"It's not important. They were sent a message, and they understood it."

The Bajoran went back to his tea, discarding the padd. "I still can't believe their temerity. Kellessar zh'Tarash seems to think she and her kind can just stroll back into the Federation and demand to be a candidate for the presidency. . . . The idea is laughable."

"You waste effort and time dwelling on it," Velk said bluntly. This conversation was old, and he did not want to go through it again. "*Do not*. It is counterproductive, and—"

Ishan eyed him. "What are you doing to improve the situation? I keep hearing about failures."

"It was a mistake to rely on our Klingon contacts." Velk found it difficult to admit to his error in that. "I've scaled them back to tasks better suited to their nature."

"Tell me more," Ishan insisted.

"Plausible deniability—"

"I'm not a child, Velk," snapped the Bajoran. "Explain."

He took a breath, framing his reply. Even at the highest levels, "need to know" was always foremost in his mind. "I have committed Active Four to operations. They will locate and capture Bacco's killers."

"Good." Ishan nodded, accepting this. "It will do no harm to my political capital to be seen as the man who brought them to justice."

Velk said nothing. Ultimately, if correctly presented, such an action would serve the president pro tem's hawkish agenda and help to rally the people of the Federation against the rising threat of the Typhon Pact. It was a goal that had for so long seemed out of reach, but now events were turning toward an arrangement that could bring them success, and all that was needed was to make full use of them.

"A question does occur, though. . . ." Ishan added, his tone deceptively light. "The Tzenkethi are the plotters and the schemers, the conspirators of the Typhon Pact. That is a widely known truth."

"Quite so," Velk said warily. He did not like where this conversation was going.

"So one might wonder: What would the public reaction be if *another* group were found to be responsible? If it was revealed to the quadrant at large that it was not a Tzenkethi finger on the trigger, so to speak?" He fixed the Tellarite with a steady gaze, waiting for his answer.

"Such a revelation . . ." Velk began. "It might not be for the best."

Maslan led Vale to the nearest turbolift and paused, indicating the small kit bag she was still carrying over her shoulder. "Sure I can't take that for you, sir?"

"I'm good," she told him. "And less of the *sir,* Mister. I know they say command ages you, but you're making me feel ancient."

"Far be it from me to do that, uh, Captain."

She frowned. "Yeah. That's also going to take a little getting used to."

The science officer was silent for a moment. "Would it be rude of me to say you're not what I expected?"

"Not rude *yet*," Vale countered. "I'll let you know when you are."

Encouraged, he went on. "*Lionheart*'s not a much sought-after posting. It's a good ship with a good crew and an important brief, don't get me wrong. But most command-track officers are looking to land a vessel with something more to it. Exploratory missions, border patrol, that sort of thing."

"I'm not most officers," she told him. "And I'm certainly not here because it's a career move." Vale could see he was waiting for her to say more, but she left it at that.

Maslan continued. "You were first officer of the *Titan*. That's an amazing ship. I imagine you've seen some incredible things out in the Gum Nebula."

"Some," she admitted. The turbolift arrived and they boarded.

"I applied for a transfer to Captain . . . uh, I mean Admiral Riker's command a couple years back, before the invasion." His smile dimmed a little as the lift set off. "I didn't make the cut."

"You don't like your posting here?"

He shook his head. "No! It's not that. But just for once I'd like to see some space where no one has gone before. Our routes are pretty well traveled."

"Saving lives is just as important, if not more so," she told him. "Don't lose sight of that. Besides, there's always more space out there."

"You're right, of course." He paused. "I hope you

won't mind if I ask you more about the *Titan*'s missions along our way to Starbase 47."

"I'm not really that much of a storyteller." The doors parted to show the *Lionheart*'s command deck beyond, and she stepped out.

"Captain on the bridge!" called Maslan, and the crew snapped smartly to attention. Vale could see Commander Atia's hand at work there.

"Stand easy," she told them.

The *Nova*-class starship's bridge was smaller than her *Luna*-class equivalent, with turbolift access on either side of the compartment and an operations pit in the center of the space. Two seats—one for the captain, one for the first officer—faced forward toward the main viewscreen; in front of that was a single helm console, manned by a fair-skinned, blond-haired lieutenant. Vale cast around, meeting the gazes of the other duty officers one by one.

A Bajoran with a close-cut beard and a shaved head got up to offer her the command chair. "Captain. I'm Lieutenant Commander Darrah Hayn, your tactical officer." He indicated a dark-skinned human woman wearing a hijab that matched the mustard yellow of her operations undershirt. "Our chief engineer . . ."

"Basoos Kader," said the other lieutenant. "*Marhaban,* Captain Vale."

"And this is Alex Thompson, our helmsman," added Maslan, indicating the blond officer.

"Captain." Thompson gave a nod, and she noticed that he was wearing spectacles. The junior-grade lieutenant colored a little as he noted her attention. "Thrusters are at station keeping. We're ready to leave spacedock at your command."

"Take your posts," she ordered. "Mister Darrah, what's our loading status?"

The Bajoran glanced at a console. "Supplies are on board," he reported, then frowned. "But I read here we're now loading additional cargo?"

"Yes," she told him. "A request from Admiral Riker's office."

Darrah clearly wanted to ask further, but then the other turbolift doors opened and Atia stalked onto the bridge. "Well met?" she asked, glancing around.

"Well enough," said Vale as she stepped into the center of the bridge. "Computer? Put on me on shipwide intercom, please." A chime sounded, and Vale took a breath, knowing that her next words would carry to every corner of the *Lionheart*. "This is . . . the captain speaking. I want you all to know I am honored to be given command of a vessel and a crew as exemplary as this one. . . ."

So far, she thought, *so much word-for-word from the official Starfleet speeches guidebook.*

"We're facing a difficult moment," she went on, finding the words along the way. "Our fleet and our Federation, our worlds and every one of us. The challenge of recent days . . . it's not what we were trained for. It's something none of us could have expected. But I am confident that each of you will do your duty and hold to the ideals that we signed on to protect. Look to your officers and crewmates, and carry on." She took a breath. "All decks and divisions stand ready and prepare for imminent departure. That is all."

"Succinct," noted Commander Atia, with a note of approval.

Vale glanced at the Bajoran. "How long until that extra cargo is on board?"

Darrah glanced at his console. "Another minute, Captain."

She walked to Thompson's side and nodded toward the main viewer, which for the moment showed the brightly lit interior of the starbase's cavernous hangar bay. "Ops, prepare a course."

"Already done, sir," he replied with a smile, bringing up a map plot showing a careful, curving vector that crossed the quadrant. "I've programmed the most warp-efficient heading to our destination. . . . Pending your approval, of course."

Vale could tell the lieutenant's astrogation skills were good, but that didn't stop her from shaking her head. "Approval denied. You're to recalculate and plot us a new heading. Once we're clear of Sol, take us to the Jaros system. Speed course, maximum warp."

"Captain?" Thompson's smile faded.

She tapped the location on the star map with her finger. "You do see fine with those glasses, right?"

"Yes, sir," he replied, uncertain if she was serious. "I'm just, ah, allergic to Retnax."

"Then snap to it."

The helmsman shot a questioning look at Atia, who stepped closer. "Captain Vale," she began, "that system is not on our itinerary. Jaros falls marked distance from stated heading."

"I'm altering the itinerary, Commander," Vale said firmly. "And as a matter of fact, Mister Darrah should be getting a mission update any moment now."

The Bajoran's console beeped and his brow furrowed. "Confirming that. Supplemental orders received. That extra cargo we took on is to be delivered to the Starfleet stockade facility on Jaros II."

Vale nodded. "There you go. Recompute the course, Mister Thompson."

The lieutenant pushed his glasses back up his nose with a finger and then nodded, his hands moving quickly across the helm panel before him. "Recomputing, aye. Setting heading to Jaros system, second planet, then on to Starbase 47. . . ."

"Let's not get ahead of ourselves," Vale added. She walked back toward the captain's chair, acutely aware that her actions had just dialed up the tension on the bridge by several notches. Vale didn't like giving people more questions without answers, especially at a time like this, but for the moment she had little choice in the matter.

"Starbase One operations are signaling clear," noted Kader from the engineering station. "We're free to navigate."

Atia was hovering at her shoulder, and Vale realized that her first officer was waiting for her to take the captain's chair before she herself sat down.

Odd, she thought, as she put her hand on the back of the center seat. *Seems weird to sit there now.* Vale felt strangely reluctant to take the position, despite the fact that she had done so in the past on board the *Enterprise* and the *Titan*. The difference there, she reflected, was that ultimately on those ships she had only been minding the chair for someone else. On the *Lionheart,* even if this assignment was to be a short-lived one, full responsibility would fall on her shoulders.

She pushed the thought away and took the chair, easing into it. It felt comfortable and easy, but she knew that was an illusion. The weight of command settled on her, and it was as exhilarating as it was humbling. "Thrusters ahead, Mister Thompson," she said. "Let's get this done."

On the screen, the curved walls of the hangar bay slipped away, the great jagged-edged hatch ahead retracting back to allow the *Lionheart* into space. Darkness and stars painted the view as the ship's bow turned away, passing over a glimpse of Earth's moon.

"Full ahead," ordered Atia, anticipating her intentions.

Despite the circumstances, a smile threatened to bloom across Christine Vale's face as the ship set off. *I reckon I could get to like this,* she thought.

Six

"We need our unity. Our enemies know that truth, too. These rogue states, these old adversaries, they gather together and make pacts." Ishan Anjar's voice spoke to Riker's back as he stood at the window, staring out over the bay beyond. The lights in the room were dimmed to night settings, and outside a cold, black sky seemed to swallow up all sense of scale.

Riker saw his own reflection in the glass, along with the inverted image of the viewscreen on his desk playing the current broadcast from the United Press Interstellar news channel. Ishan's picture froze and then minimized as a correspondent from UPI's Paris office picked up the thread of the story, reporting on what the Bajoran politician had said during the memorial service on Luna.

"Mute," Riker ordered, and silence fell across the room. He'd seen the same report three or four times now, listened to the same questions and same discussion from a dozen different political pundits on this channel and others. None of them had any answers; they would echo Ishan's points of rhetoric, pick over every tiny nuance of his speech for meaning and subtext, or return to the so-called "information leaks" that Riker suspected were in fact quite deliberately engineered. And when the news wasn't showing that, the reports were of the memorial services held on other worlds, as far away as Lytasia, Algol, or Cardassia Prime.

Behind the live feed of the reporter in Paris, there was a chronometer reading 11:08, and Riker suddenly realized that here in San Francisco it was just past two o'clock in the morning. He scowled, marching back to the screen to switch it off with a tap of his finger. Once more, where had the day—and the evening—gone? It seemed like only a short time ago he had sent a message to Deanna telling her to stay on with Togren for the time being, but it must have been hours ago. He felt a twinge of guilt as he realized that Tasha would have gone to bed without him being there to read a story to her. Riker perched on the edge of his desk and pulled a hand down over his face, rubbing his eyes.

A tone sounded from the door, and he looked up, blinking away the moment of fatigue. Who would be visiting him this time of night? "Come."

The door slid open and Lieutenant Ssura entered, his head bobbing. "Admiral. Do you have a moment?" He had a padd in his hand, holding it gingerly.

"You're still here?" Riker frowned. "Lieutenant, are you waiting out there for me to leave for the night?"

The Caitian gave a toothy smile. "Ah. Sir, please worry not about that. My rest cycle is unlike yours. I am capable of snatching a collective of small sleep moments throughout the day." He paused. "You, however, are not. I have officer's quarters on base assigned to you for tonight. . . ."

"No, that's all right." He nodded at the padd, dismissing his fatigue. "Did you have something for me?"

Ssura turned the padd so Riker could see it. "You asked me to look into a recent tasking order for one of your officers aboard the *Titan,* Commander Tuvok?"

"What did you find?" He took the padd, scanning the text there.

The felineoid's paws knitted. "I regret, little of note. Commander Tuvok's reassignment was processed through expedited channels, on or around the time the *Titan* arrived in Earth orbit."

"Someone planned that well in advance, then. . . ."

"Likely, sir. As to the actual letter of the commander's new orders, that datum is security sealed."

Riker shot his aide a look. "I am an admiral now, right? Doesn't that mean I get to look at these kind of things?"

"Yes, sir." Ssura paused. "I mean, no, sir. I'm afraid our—that is *your*—office is not cleared for this access."

He walked away, pacing the room. "So we don't know where Tuvok went, why, or who gave the order?"

"No. No. Yes."

It took Riker a second to catch up with what Ssura was saying. "Wait, you *do* know who reassigned Commander Tuvok?"

"It would be more correct to say I know what office in Starfleet Command issued the order." Ssura pointed toward the padd. "Last page, sir."

Riker tabbed through to the end of the lieutenant's report and found the data. He read it twice, just to be sure. "You're absolutely certain of this?"

"Yes, Admiral." Ssura nodded. "Commander Tuvok's reassignment order was issued directly by the office of the Commander of Starfleet, Admiral Akaar."

"Why would—" Riker's question never got the chance to fully form; an abrupt beep sounded from the viewscreen on his desk. The display had automatically reactivated, showing the stars-and-laurels design of the United Federation of Planets above a status message that indicated an imminent incoming signal.

Ssura studied the screen, reading the alphanumeric contact codes. "Sir, this is a priority subspace message . . . on your personal channel." He paused. "Admiral, it appears to be originating from the *U.S.S. Enterprise*."

A chill passed through Riker; a call that came without warning in the middle of the night was never something good. "I'll take it in here. Lieutenant, make sure I'm not interrupted for the duration."

"Aye, sir." The Caitian nodded and quickly padded out of the room, leaving Riker to his privacy.

He sank into his chair and took a breath. "Computer, recognize Riker, William T. Connect terminal."

"Connecting." The blue-white UFP symbol blinked out to be replaced by a grainy image of Jean-Luc Picard, framed by the wall of his ready room. Riker's immediate fear—that something terrible had happened aboard his former ship or to his former crew—was only slightly assuaged by the neutral expression on his old friend's face.

"Captain?"

"Admiral," Picard replied. *"Sir."*

Despite himself, Riker smiled briefly. "Huh. So that's how it feels to hear you say that."

"Congratulations on the promotion, Will. I'm sorry I haven't had the chance to speak to you sooner." Picard's voice wavered with distortion as it came to Riker across the span of light-years. *"Akaar chose well."*

Mention of the Capellan admiral's name brought a frown to Riker's face and he shot a look at the padd

Ssura had left behind. "Thanks for the vote of confidence."

"I apologize for contacting you out of the blue like this. I wasn't sure I'd reach you. But it has been somewhat problematic arranging a relay so we could speak in real time."

Riker didn't comment on that, but it sounded like a wrong note with him. While the availability of long-range direct subspace communication channels was restricted in Starfleet, an officer of Picard's seniority should have been able to access them easily.

His former captain seemed to intuit his line of thinking. *"Communications protocols have been tightened extensively across the fleet network. A temporary security measure in the wake of the current crisis, so I'm told."* And then, very deliberately, Picard ran a finger over the brow of his left eye, and across to his ear. To anyone else, it might have seemed like a casual gesture, but for Riker it set alarm bells ringing.

Picard was warning him that someone might be listening to their conversation.

"I'm well aware of those . . . protocols," he replied, giving the most subtle of nods in return. Immediately, Riker wanted to know exactly what Picard's inference could mean, but his words caught in his throat.

Almost from the moment he had taken this office, Riker had become aware that he was under subtle observation. He doubted Ssura was part of it; Will was always a good judge of character, and the Caitian seemed too guileless to be any more than what he said he was. But Riker had noted the occasional figure trailing him at a distance around the Starfleet campus, or out in the city. He knew the kind; Federation Security. At first, Riker had dismissed the presence of the watchers as the side effect of a heightened state of alert still in place after Bacco's assassination. But now he was starting to wonder if there was more to it. Velk had made no secret of his feelings about Riker's promotion; he wouldn't put it past Ishan Anjar's chief of staff to be keeping a watch on him.

"How is the family?" He chose an innocuous topic to see how Picard would react.

A flicker of subspace static crackled over the image as the captain smiled ruefully. *"Rene is into everything. He's becoming quite the challenge, and Beverly promises me it's just the beginning."*

Riker nodded. "She's not wrong. Tasha's the same. Just wait until he starts taking things to pieces for fun. That's . . . interesting. Sometimes I wish I was married to a precognitive instead of an empath, just so I could catch my daughter *before* she breaks something."

"I'll make sure Geordi keeps my son away from the warp core for the moment."

"And the rest of the crew? How are they holding up after . . . what happened?"

Picard's smile went away and he met his former first officer's gaze. He didn't need to voice how he felt, Riker could see it written in his eyes. Jean-Luc wanted to be here in the center of things, involved in bringing some kind of sense—some kind of *closure*—to Nani-etta Bacco's death. At that moment, Riker wanted to declare all his doubts and fears to his old friend, but he kept his silence.

"Will, our duty . . . as much as it brings wonder and triumph, it also brings us misfortune. It's the price we pay. But I can think of no worse a tragedy than a life of great potential cut short. Bacco was the leader we needed throughout all the trials we've faced these last few

years." He shook his head, his expression solemn. *"She appealed to the greatest in us. And now I'm afraid those who follow her will call out to the worst."*

"I know you considered her a friend."

Picard nodded again. *"Indeed. And because of that, I owe her a debt."* Then the captain's face shifted as he schooled his expression. Riker recalled that look well; it was the same one Picard had worn across a card table on those evenings he had lost a stack of poker chips to his commanding officer. *"I've been reflecting on a lot of things over the past few days. Do you recall our mission with that Vulcan ambassador, the one we took to meet the Romulans aboard the* Devoras?"

Riker stiffened at the memory. "Don't you mean Subcommander Selok?" Even though it was almost two decades since the incident at the Neutral Zone, he still remembered it clearly, and it smarted. Serving aboard the *Enterprise*-D at the time, Riker and Picard had been under orders to deliver the ambassador to a meeting with representatives of the Romulan Star Empire as part of ongoing treaty negotiations, but she had apparently perished in a transporter accident while beaming to the Romulan ship. It was only later that the *Enterprise* crew discovered her death had been faked. In reality, the woman was a deep-cover Romulan spy masquerading as a Vulcan, and the *Enterprise* had unwittingly aided in bringing her home to her people.

He turned the memory over in his mind. Why was Jean-Luc bringing this up now? "The Romulans played us that day."

"Do you remember what I said after we were debriefed by Starfleet?"

Riker recalled Picard's words. "That as long as you

were her commander, you wouldn't allow *Enterprise* to be sent on any more fool's errands."

Picard leaned closer to the image pickup. *"I meant it then. I still mean it now."*

Riker was only aware of the broadest strokes of the *Enterprise*'s current mission, sent to Ferenginar in order to show the colors and get out in front of any attempts by the Typhon Pact to entice the Ferengi Alliance into their fold. But if pressed, the admiral would have called it a makeweight assignment, and certainly not something that required the presence of Starfleet's flagship. Picard was telling him that he felt the same way.

His thoughts raced. At a time like this, when the people of the Federation needed to see the symbols of their strength and unity—symbols like *Enterprise,* the ship that had led the charge against so many threats over the years—it made little sense to send it far away . . . unless the choice had been deliberate.

"Sometimes the enemy hides in plain sight, Will." A deep, hissing buzz of interference made the words turn harsh and metallic.

"We're going to find those responsible for the assassination," Riker went on, pitching his words carefully. "You can count on that. The Tzenkethi won't get away with this." He made the last statement without weight, deliberately positioning it to gauge Picard's reaction.

The response he got was not what he expected. Across the interstellar distance, he saw his former captain's eyes widen, the poker face slipping for a brief instant. Anyone who didn't know Jean-Luc Picard as well as Will Riker did might never have recognized the moment for what it was: shock and alarm.

Suddenly the careful artifice in the captain's manner dissolved, and that was the most troubling thing of all. Picard dropped the mask he had been wearing for the benefit of any interloper listening in on their conversation and fixed Riker with a serious, unblinking stare. *"The Tzenkethi are not responsible for this,"* he insisted with a certainty that was unshakable. *"A Cardassian—"*

An abrupt blizzard of static tore across the viewscreen, rendering Picard's words barely intelligible. Spatial distortion artifacts broke the image of the other man into jagged fragments, pixels shifting like particles of sand blown by the wind.

Riker leaned in. "Jean-Luc? Can you hear me?" He raised his voice instinctively, as if that would help it carry across the void. "Captain, do you read?"

"It was not—" Picard's words echoed and became indistinct. *"—True Way. Will, I say again—"*

The broken image snapped off to be replaced by an error message: TRANSMISSION LOST.

Riker threw up his hands in frustration, and he turned as the office door hissed open. Lieutenant Ssura entered at a pace, his eyes narrowed. "Admiral, is there a problem? I heard you call out. . . ." He halted as he saw the blinking legend on the screen.

"The signal was disrupted," Riker told him, his irritation flaring. "At a very inopportune moment."

Ssura went to the console and brought up a diagnostic display. "Checking . . ." He made a negative noise deep in his throat. "Sir, according to the communications routing software, the real-time transmission from the *Enterprise* was cut off by a surge in subspace interference." The Caitian looked up and blinked. "It could be the wake of an ionic storm somewhere along the line of the signal path, or perhaps another localized spatial effect."

Riker folded his arms, scowling. "Just unlucky timing, I guess?" His caustic tone was apparently lost on the junior officer.

"Quite so, Admiral. I would hazard a guess that the probability of such an interruption would be extremely low." Ssura hesitated, his lips drawing back from his teeth in an expression that showed distaste. "Is there any reason to suspect deliberate hindrance, sir?"

"If there was," Riker allowed, "how could it be done?" According to Ssura's personnel record, the lieutenant had minored in communication operations at the Academy. If he was working for an agenda out of step with Riker's, then whatever the aide said next would make that clear.

"It is possible to simulate subspace interference if certain parameters are met," Ssura answered without a moment's hesitation. "Another vessel near the transmission source or one of the relay vessels could affect the signal in this way."

"But it could be disrupted locally? By which I mean here, at Starfleet?"

"Yes, sir." Ssura's head bobbed again. "It could. But what reason would there be for that?" It was the response Riker was looking for, confirming his own suspicions and suggesting that Ssura was being honest with him.

He turned away, looking back at the silent monitor screen, leaving Ssura's question hanging. A dozen new doubts, each one more troubling than the last, churned in his thoughts. The fatigue that had been lurking at the edges of his awareness now crowded in on him. Riker felt heavy and leaden, weighed down by his uncertainty.

"Shall I attempt to reacquire a connection with

the *Enterprise*?" asked the lieutenant, watching him intently.

"Do what you can," Riker told him, even as he knew that Ssura would not be successful. "But in the meantime, I have another job for you."

The lieutenant listened intently to what the admiral wanted from him, and slowly the Caitian's pointed ears folded back across his scalp with silent unease.

Tuvok turned his head slowly from right to left, allowing the display panels projected by the data monocular he wore to map to his visual range. Test patterns overlaid targeting sweeps and atmospheric readings relayed from sensors on the skin of the oversuit sheathing his torso and limbs. He focused his attention on Lieutenant Commander Nog, and the scanners built into the suit dutifully rendered a cursory scan of the young Ferengi officer. Combat subroutines correctly identified Nog's species and physiological structure, providing tactical flags that indicated optimal points of attack to disarm, immobilize, or kill. It had been five days since they departed the Alpha Centauri star system, five days at high warp velocity, five days of drills and preparatory exercises like this one.

Nog's head was cocked, his large ears twitching slightly as he studied a tricorder in his hand. "That looks good, Commander. Calibration is almost complete."

Tuvok glanced around the *Snipe*'s cargo bay at the other figures in the room. Along with the Ferengi and the Bynar pair, the room had three other occupants, each of them wearing the same stealth gear as he did. The suit's sensors showed them as glowing blue outlines each tagged with a simple alphanumeric code: A4 to indicate the team designation and then a secondary flag to indicate their identity as an ally. Tuvok's hood sensors showed him which of the others was the Suliban medic Khob, which was the Elloran female Sahde, and which was Thomas Riker.

Nog adjusted the tricorder's sensor head. "Thermal scan shows no returns. You're almost invisible. Switching to magnetic."

As Tuvok waited, he saw Tom reach up and tap his monocle. There was a flicker of holographic light and Nog flinched involuntarily as the other man's suit switched from matte black to a camouflage effect that mimicked the color and shade of a nearby bulkhead. The combat gear was lightweight and adaptable, but it sacrificed armor for concealment. Operating at full capacity, the suit could make one virtually undetectable to most scanners, but the power cost was high and extended use would tax the batteries.

"No detections," Nog reported. "Test complete."

"Deactivating," said Tuvok, flicking back his own monocular. He felt a faint buzz of static, and again he saw the narrowing of the Ferengi's eyes as his suit went into standby mode. "Is there something wrong, Mister Nog?"

The Ferengi's nose wrinkled. "No . . . well, maybe." He sighed, gesturing toward the suit. "These things, they just remind me a little too much of the Jem'Hadar."

Tuvok gave a nod. He was aware that Nog had been on the front line during the conflict with the Dominion, and he had suffered severe personal injuries during engagements with the invaders from the Gamma Quadrant. Those battles had doubtless left an indelible mark on his psyche. "The Jem'Hadar shroud is a bio-energetic ability innate to their species," he noted. "I believe this system is based on technology from isolation suits used by Federation scientists to covertly observe pre-warp cultures."

"It's still unnerving to have a person blend into the walls right in front of you." Nog's hand dropped to where a phaser would have been holstered if he were in Starfleet uniform. "I've got to fight down the reflex to go for my weapon each time it happens."

Sahde also had deactivated her suit and now she appeared at Tuvok's side, her head cocked as she examined the Ferengi. "Well, we wouldn't want to make you nervous, would we?" she asked silkily.

Nog's lips thinned. "I'd just suggest you don't sneak up on me. I'm likely to react very poorly to it."

"A Ferengi with fangs . . . and not just teeth?" The Elloran showed her own canines in a teasing grin. "Who'd have thought it?" She chuckled and walked away.

"I don't think I like her," Nog said quietly, just loud enough for Tuvok to hear. "She's mocking me."

"From a certain perspective, that may seem so," he offered. "However, if studied from an Elloran standpoint, her actions have a different intention."

"Such as?"

"Sahde may be sexually attracted to you."

Nog went pale. "What?"

Tuvok explained that on Ellora, it was a traditional social gambit for a female to disparage a male in order to test his reaction and gauge his worth as a potential mate. He also noted that Sahde's scent—undetectable to Ferengi senses—showed a marked increase in pheromone release whenever she was close to Nog. The other officer seemed nonplussed by Tuvok's suggestion. "However, I may be mistaken," he concluded. "She may just be attempting to belittle you for her own amusement."

"I'll . . . keep that in mind. . . ."

Khob was the last of them to reappear, and the big Suliban shrugged out of the suit, opening it to the waist. "Uncomfortable," he rumbled as he walked away. "Don't like the idea of sneaking around in this."

Nog glanced at Tuvok. "He has a point. You said those suits are based on Federation tech, but I've never come across them before." He reached out and touched the arm. "It's been optimized for battlefield operations."

"They may be prototypes," said Tuvok. But he saw Nog's line of reasoning. Starfleet was not in the business of building clandestine, first-strike weapons, but the suit on his back could very much be the tool of an assassin or an aggressor. He was aware that Starfleet had recently captured examples of shrouding suits during an enounter with the Breen's Spetzkar special forces; could that have been the origin of this new technology?

Logic told him that any weapon of war was, by itself, essentially without moral color or ethics—it was the use to which such weapons were put that defined the morality of those who wielded them. However, it would be difficult to justify a use of the stealth suits in a way that was not ethically gray.

Tuvok looked down at his gloved hands. "I will admit that I am not wholly at ease with the tone of our mission orders."

Nog's expression hardened. "Commander, I never signed up for Starfleet because I wanted to skulk in shadows and stab people in the back." He gave a bitter smirk. "If I wanted that, I'd have joined the Ferengi Commerce Authority."

"I have taken part in covert operations before," said the Vulcan. "I understand the need for secrecy. But I am concerned about the degree of separation and autonomy Active Four exhibits."

The engineer nodded again. "Look at the instructions we were given. 'Go here. Tell no one. Delete after reading.' I talked to Ixxen, and she said she got the same thing. I'm willing to bet that our own crews back home don't know what we're doing or where we've disappeared to."

"That's the job." Tuvok turned toward the voice as Tom Riker approached them. Sahde, Khob, and the Bynars were on the far side of the cargo bay, out of earshot, but the human had caught a fraction of their conversation. "It may not be Starfleet-style neat and nice, but you heard what Velk said. We're operating off the grid here."

"And that is my core concern," said Tuvok. "Mister Riker, you were once a serving officer, so you understand how Starfleet operates. You yourself expressed disquiet at Velk's announcements."

"That wasn't it. . . ." Tom waved away the statement.

"The problem with being off the grid is that the chain of command gets a little fuzzy," said Nog. "Kincade is commander here, but who is she supposed to report to? Velk? He's a *civilian*. He doesn't have any direct military authority." He gestured at the walls. "And you may not have noticed, but we're totally isolated on board the *Snipe*. All communications are controlled from the bridge, everything we do is monitored. . . ."

Tom folded his arms. "Why is that a surprise? We have to stay dark, Nog. The people we're hunting are ruthless, and if they get one whiff of us coming after them, they'll scatter. We don't know what connections they might have within the Federation or who might be listening. We might never be able to locate them, and then Bacco's killers get away free and clear." He shook his head. "I'm willing to leave the rulebook behind for a while if it means tracking down that scum."

"For how long?" asked Nog, meeting the human's gaze. "How long will you leave the rulebook behind?"

"You know what I mean," Tom added, scowling.

"I do," Nog said, nodding, "and I agree with you. I was there on Deep Space Nine, I saw what happened with my own eyes. Believe me, I want the people who murdered the president made to pay their butcher's bill in full. But we have to do it *by the book*." He looked away, and Tuvok saw his manner become somber. "Or else it doesn't mean anything."

Tom was silent for a long moment, weighing the Ferengi's words. "They'll get their day in court, in front of the whole galaxy, you can count on that. But to make that happen, we may have to go places we don't want to. I don't like it any more than you, Nog. . . ." He glanced at Tuvok. "But we have to make a *logical* choice here, right, Commander?"

Tuvok considered the question and found that the answer was difficult to frame. Could logic ever be the guiding force behind an endeavor such as this one? Arguably, the mission to capture those responsible for President Bacco's death was motivated by emotion; it could be said that as much as it was a quest to find justice, it was also a call to vengeance.

Before he could voice any reply, the Vulcan heard

the subsonic tremor through the *Snipe*'s hull, a precursor signifying the shift in engine power. A moment later, the humming of the stardrive shifted in pitch.

"We're dropping out of warp," said Tom.

Kincade's voice crackled out of the overhead speakers. *"Yellow Alert. All Active Four team members, report for tactical briefing in five minutes. We have a go."*

The flare of light and energy from the transporter faded, and Nog felt the press of the icy breeze on his chest. Indicators at the edges of his visual field immediately blinked on, showing the sudden temperature drop from the interior of the *Snipe*'s transporter room to the surface of the frigid planetoid. He surveyed the clearing where the group had materialized; all around, the long, spindly fingers of hardy plants poked up through the snowpack, clustering at the foot of wind-sculpted ice towers.

If anything, the nameless world looked even less inviting from the surface than it did from space. He glanced to his right where Kincade was crouching as she unlimbered a sniper rifle. Like the rest of the team, she was rendered in her stealth gear as a gray, vaguely human-shaped outline.

The lieutenant colonel's terse briefing back on the ship had outlined the operation in quick order; they were to scout a location in the next valley over and scour it for clues as to the whereabouts of their targets.

"I thought we were heading to Beta Rigel," he muttered. "I hear it's warm there."

"Change of plan," Kincade replied, panning the rifle back and forth. "This is our lead."

Nog accepted this with a glum nod, and he resisted the urge to reach up to adjust the semirigid hood over his head. The stealth suits were not designed with the bodies of Ferengi in mind, and the hood pulled uncomfortably tight over his large ears. He drew his phaser and shot a look at the tricorder clipped to his hip.

Across the clearing, Ashur was using a tricorder to scan the local area. "No life signs nearby," he reported. "But I am detecting some . . . large things . . . three kilometers farther out."

"Probably local apex predators," said Sahde from nearby. "I hope they're not the curious sort."

As well as the two females and the Zeon, Nog was accompanied by Tuvok and Tom Riker; Ixxen, Khob, and the Bynars had remained on board the *Snipe* to monitor them remotely. He looked around and found the Vulcan and the human approaching from the tree line.

"No sign that anyone else is around," said Tom. "But we shouldn't let our guard down. Snow's falling constantly here, so any footprints would fill in pretty fast."

"Stay alert," ordered Kincade, and she set off across the ice. "Tuvok, you and Tom take point. Anyone sees anything, call it."

Nog kept pace with her, trying to keep one eye on the icy wilderness around them and another on the scan returns from his tricorder. "Why don't people ever choose pleasant places to hide out?" Gusts of cold wind buffeted them, throwing up small blizzards of loose, gritty snow particles.

"One being's icebox is another being's garden spot," noted Sahde.

He shrugged. "A Tzenkethi would find this as unpleasant as I do." Nog made a face. "I think even an Andorian would."

"Who can know what the Tzenkethi think?" growled Ashur. "They're not like the rest of us."

Kincade looked in the Zeon's direction. "What do you mean by that?"

"They're a perverse species. Willfully contrary and . . . and . . ." He groped for the right word, but didn't find it. "*Weird,*" he said, at length.

"We're all weird one way or another," said Sahde playfully, "depending on who you ask."

"Speak for yourself," growled the Zeon.

"*Structures ahead, forty meters southwest of our location.*" Tuvok's voice came over the comm channel. Nog squinted into the middle distance, and his monocle's sensors painted the images of the other two team members farther off amid the pillars of ice. "*Heavy damage evident. No movement.*"

"Stay put, Commander, we're coming to you. *Snipe,* do you read?" Kincade spoke into her hood's communicator.

"*We read,*" came Ixxen's reply, dense with the hiss of multiple encryption subroutines. "*Go ahead, Colonel.*"

"We have visual on the site. Proceeding as planned. Out." Kincade gestured to the others. "Move up. Maintain separation. Nog, Ashur—I want sensors on those buildings before we go in."

They went as close as they dared, and Nog picked out the shapes of the dome tents amid the drifts of greenish-gray snow. Rimes of ice coated their upper surfaces, and no light or energy bled out of them; the encampment was dead. He saw that the tents were ruined, ripped open so that their interiors were exposed to the punishing elements. Around the tears, ragged pennants of burnt hyperpolymer cloth flapped in the wind, crackling and snapping.

"The site appears abandoned," said Tuvok. "Whoever was here fled long before we arrived."

Ashur's tricorder gave a low chime, and he turned in place, aiming it down at the snow. "I have something. Organic matter . . . *there*." With the tip of his boot, he kicked at the top layer of snowfall and revealed a dark, indistinct object. "Someone give me some illumination."

Kincade leaned in with a simmslight that threw a sharp disc of white across the dirty ice. At first glance, Ashur's discovery appeared to be a damp, matted clump of fur and indistinct materials, ending in a black blot of frozen matter. The Zeon reached down and pulled gingerly at the object, and Nog's gorge rose as he realized he was looking at a severed forearm. A pool of blood had solidified into ice around the cut, and gnawed fingers dangled at the opposite end.

"Klingon," Ashur announced, reading off the results of his scans. "Female of the species, it appears."

Sahde pointed at something else glinting in the ice. "There's a weapon there too. A blade."

"Where is . . ." Nog swallowed hard. "The rest of her?"

Ashur discarded his grisly discovery and continued to sweep the area. "Also reading animal spoor nearby. Predators must have dragged the rest of the remains away."

"There are more blood spots in this area," called Tuvok, indicating the foot of a lumpy ice tower. "I would surmise the owner of that limb was not alone."

"Maybe whatever ate them won't come looking for a second course," offered Tom. "And now I'm wondering what the hell Klingons were doing on this planet?"

A grim thought occurred to Nog. "Could they have

been involved in the assassination? Were they part of it?" But even as he said the words aloud, he found that hard to accept. Chancellor Martok had been there on DS9 when Bacco had been shot, and he had been as shocked and as horrified as the rest of them.

"Anything you're not telling us, Colonel?" Tom gave Kincade a hard look. "Jump in any time."

She sighed. "All I know is what was in the data Velk gave to me. The Security Agency had a lead that this site was being used as a staging point by our targets. The Klingons were here for the same reason we are."

"And they died of it." Sahde turned to Nog. "Ferengi, scan this area. Look for low-level neutrino traces."

"All right. . . ." He did as she asked, quickly reprogramming his tricorder.

"You have a hypothesis?" asked Tuvok.

The Elloran nodded. "Predators didn't kill anyone here. Those animals are scavengers. I think our terrorist quarry left some farewell gifts behind."

Nog's eyes widened as his scans picked up a series of distinct readings set in a ring equidistant around the perimeter of the abandoned outpost. "There's something buried in the ice. Metallic objects. They didn't show up on the initial scans. . . ."

"Show me where." Sahde walked fearlessly out into the open ground between the ice pillars and the camp proper.

"Stop!" Nog shouted. "At your feet!"

"Don't fret," she retorted. "I've done this a lot." Using her hands like spades, Sahde pushed the snow away until an orb-like device was revealed. "Beam sphere," she explained. "Autonomous attack unit. A favorite toy of the Romulan Empire, Nausicaans, the Cardassian Union, the Orions . . . anyone who doesn't like unwelcome visitors."

Nog manipulated the tricorder, dragging up records of similar devices from its dense memory core, lines of relevant data scrolling past his eyes.

"All right, back off," snapped Kincade. "No one is here to impress."

The Elloran shrugged. "Relax. Our stealth suits put us well outside the detection range of these devices. I could leap up and down on it and the thing wouldn't know I was here—"

Even through the thick material of the hood, Nog heard the snap-hiss of the beam sphere coming to life, and with a sudden jerk of motion, the steel-colored ball blasted upward to waist height on a rod of invisible force. He was dimly aware of a dozen others rising at the same instant, lines of glowing phaser energy uncoiling inside the devices.

"Down!" shouted Tom, shoving Tuvok and Kincade toward the snow, but Nog instinctively knew that would do them no good; the weapons would scour the area with overlapping zones of fire, killing anything caught in the termination radius.

Later, the engineer would think back to this moment and try to recall what had gone through his mind, but the act was pure instinct, as fast as muscle memory. Nog's thumb mashed down on the tricorder's emitter key and the device in his hand chirped as a broad-spectrum tachyon pulse bathed the area with a brief, eerie glow.

At once, all the drone spheres gave a keening whine and dropped back to the snow, their lethal discharge unspent.

Panting with shock, Sahde grabbed the one at her feet and peered at it. "What did you just do?"

"He saved our lives," grated Ashur.

"Tachyons," Nog explained quickly. "Overloaded the central processors in the spheres. They'll be inert while they reset." He took a breath. "So we should probably destroy them all right now!"

Kincade didn't bother to give the order; instead she aimed her rifle and shot the orb out of the Elloran's hand, drawing a yelp of surprise from the other female. Ashur, Tuvok, and Tom followed suit, drawing their phasers and blasting the immobile drones before they could recover.

The colonel shouldered her weapon and hauled Sahde to her feet. "No showboating here, do you understand me? You're supposed to be a professional, so act like it."

The Elloran looked away, chastened. "Understood."

Kincade turned away. "Spread out in teams of two, search the camp, and *be careful*. Nog, good work. You're with me."

She pushed on through a tear in the side of one of the larger tents, and the Ferengi jogged to keep up with her, adrenaline still coursing through him.

It took the better part of three hours to scour the interiors of the outpost, and by then the weak sun was below the horizon. Nog was unpleasantly surprised to discover exactly how much colder the planetoid became, and he knew that the temperature would continue to drop with each passing moment. He toggled the stealth suit's power system to shunt more energy to its internal thermal regulators and sighed, thinking about the cup of hot *raktajino* he was going to replicate the moment they beamed back to the *Snipe*.

With effort, Nog shouldered a small cargo container up from where it had fallen. The box was empty, and the lid yawned open like a laughing mouth. He grimaced; it was a metaphor for the entire encampment, all of it hollow and devoid of clues. The assassins who had hidden in this place had been thorough with their withdrawal, taking the time to remove anything that might have been useful to their pursuers. They knew they were being hunted, and they had clearly been ready.

He turned as Kincade slipped into the tent. "Anything?"

"The box is of Vulcan manufacture. Should we add them to the list of suspects as well?"

The woman made a negative noise. "Damned Klingons. This is their fault. They stuck their ridged heads in where they didn't belong and spooked the targets. Now the Tzenkethi are in the wind."

"I still don't understand why the Klingons were even here." He rose and walked out into the blizzard that had blown in. Nearby, lights danced in the middle distance as the others picked through the remnants, still searching fruitlessly. "If they had a lead on the targets, why didn't they tell us?"

"You know the Klingons." She followed him out. "They act out of instinct, fight before they think. Probably thought they were doing us a favor, honoring a debt to Bacco. A lot of good that did us."

"It still doesn't feel right to me, Colonel." Nog paused, consulting his tricorder. Scans from orbit combined with the data gathered on the ground had given the team a rough plot of the camp's layout. They could guess which tents had most likely been for storage or accommodation, which had been their common area, and so on. An open area a short distance away still defied explanation, though. The ice pillars and spindly trees had been cut away to form a small quadrangle, and at first Nog thought it might have been a kind of training space, but the inclement weather on the planetoid made that seem unlikely. He switched the tricorder to a slow pulse deep-scan mode and moved to investigate, sweeping the open ground in cautious arcs.

Kincade shrugged. "Maybe Martok didn't even know about it. You know how it goes with the Empire, all those noble houses and clans jockeying for position. Maybe one of them was trying to one-up the others. . . ." She paused. "Whatever the reason, I don't like it. We don't need another variable in this operation. There's too much at stake."

He gave a distracted nod. "There's something here, under the ice."

Her weapon was raised in a heartbeat. "More of those spheres?"

"No, it's nillimite alloy plating. Prefabricated sheets, the kind of thing the Corps of Engineers lay down on colony worlds as basic foundations. They reinforced the ground here."

"What for?"

Nog dropped into a crouch and dug out a few fist-fuls of ice until his gloved fingers touched metal. "I think . . ." He looked up into the sky. "I think this might have been a landing pad for a shuttle."

"Good catch," said Kincade. "You're a sharp one, Lieutenant Commander. First that booby trap and now this. I can see why you were picked for this assignment." She came closer, peering at the edge of the exposed alloy plate. "How did you do that, by the way? The thing with the tachyon pulse? That was quick thinking."

He shrugged. "Not really. I've had run-ins with similar threats before, back on Deep Space Nine." Nog paused to correct himself. "The old Deep Space Nine, I mean. *Terok Nor,* the Cardassian station. It was a bit eccentric, to say the least. Part of its security framework was a counter-insurgency program that used a similar system. It caused problems for us on more than one occasion, I can tell you."

The tricorder scanned the structure of the metals, and data fed back to the small screen and Nog's head-up display. A slow smile formed on his lips.

Kincade seemed to sense it. "Make my day, Mister Nog. Tell me you have a clue there."

He nodded. "I think I do." Then his face fell as he realized what that would entail. "And it means we're going to have to remain on this ice cube for another couple of hours."

Seven

Will Riker followed the faint, wood-smoke smell through the low bushes and found himself in one of the small lacunae that dotted the ornamental gardens in front of the Starfleet Headquarters building. In the shadow of the high, curved structure, the small clearing was cooled by a burbling water fountain, and in front of that was a curved bench that allowed one to sit and enjoy the grounds.

The tall and somewhat gaunt figure of a man seated there turned his head with a look of irritation on his face to see who had dared to interrupt him. Admiral Leonard James Akaar froze with a thin cigarillo half raised to his lips, his eyes widening as he recognized the interloper.

"Nasty habit," noted Riker, nodding at the cigarillo. "Those things are bad for you."

Akaar tensed, as if he were resisting the impulse to rise. After a moment he gave a low shrug. "It's just *markah* leaf, from my planet," he rumbled. "Not toxic or addictive like your Earth tobacco." Then very deliberately, the admiral pinched out the lit tip between his fingers before slipping the unfinished cigarillo back into a small silver clamshell case. "I know a freighter captain—he brings me in a few boxes from Capella now and then." He dropped the case back in his pocket. "A small taste of home." He shifted his weight as if to leave, but Riker held up a hand.

"Don't get up on my account, sir. As a matter of fact, I'd prefer it if you stayed right there."

The dismay in Akaar's flinty eyes turned to true annoyance. "Don't think that new rank of yours gives you cause to presume, Mister Riker."

"I've never needed a rank to do that, sir," he replied, taking a seat at the other end of the bench without waiting to be asked. "You're a hard man to reach, Admiral. It was easier to get hold of you when I was in the Beta Quadrant. Now here we are working in the same building and it's proving impossible to get a response to a simple message. If I didn't know better, I might think you were avoiding me." He leaned closer. "That lieutenant you provided, Ssura? He's pretty handy. He's the one who found out that you come here each day for a moment of respite."

"I have a lot to do," Akaar replied coldly. "Many demands on my time."

"I don't doubt it. But here's the thing, Admiral, sir." Riker's tone hardened. "You brought me here. But you won't tell me why."

That was enough for the elder Capellan, and he rose to his feet, dismissing the other man with a sniff. "This isn't the time or the place, Riker—"

"I spoke to Jean-Luc two days ago." Akaar halted at the mention of Picard's name. "He was trying to tell me something important, but the signal was disrupted. I've been trying to reach the *Enterprise* for the last thirty hours, but I can't make contact. I think it's more than ion storms, sir. What's your take?"

"You should leave. Now." Akaar glanced around, taking in the gardens.

A wintry smile creased Riker's face. "You know I'm not going to do that. I want answers, and you don't seem to be willing to provide them. If that's how it's going to be, then I'll keep looking without your help."

Akaar exhaled heavily, a bone-deep, weary sigh. "You have no idea what's going on here."

"My point exactly." Riker's frustration flared, and he pulled a small padd from his tunic. "Picard said something about a group called the True Way—"

It was his turn to be interrupted, as Akaar suddenly came forward and snatched the padd from his hand. "You've been busy," he said as he scanned the display. But in truth, there was little there. Riker and Ssura had only been able to find the most basic information about the organization. A hard-line isolationist faction on Cardassia, they were vocal about the decay of traditional values, xenophobic toward the Federation, and angry about their people's loss of empire.

After a moment, Akaar handed the device back to him. Riker saw the conflict behind his eyes before the admiral's iron-hard rigidity dropped back into place. "You're just going to have to trust me, Will."

"No." Riker's jaw stiffened. He was tired of being one step behind, of being forced to play a game where he had no concept of the rules, the players, the risks of failure. "I'm not a damned pawn on your chessboard, Admiral. You turned my career upside down, you tethered my ship, you reassigned one of my senior officers without consultation. I'm *done* waiting for you to come to me."

Akaar's brows fell. "What reassignment? I ordered no such thing."

"Tuvok. You put him off *Titan* almost the moment I got here." Riker shook his head. "I know there's some bad blood between the pair of you, but I never expected you to do something like that."

"I never gave that order," Akaar repeated, ice forming on the words.

"The command came directly from *your* office, sir."

"Impossible . . ."

Riker watched the questions forming in Akaar's thoughts, writ large across his expression, and suddenly he realized he had been wrong; the admiral was being truthful. He knew that Akaar and Tuvok had served together in the past, and after a disastrous away mission, they had fallen out over matters that neither man wanted to give voice to. But he found it hard to believe that the Capellan would sink to interfering with Tuvok's career as some kind of deferred settling of scores. As intractable as Akaar could be, Riker had always considered him to be honorable. He felt like he was seeing past the mask the admiral wore to the man beneath. The same man he had glimpsed at the promotion ceremony, the man troubled by events beyond his control.

Akaar reached up and absently smoothed a stray length of hair back into the gray queue over his shoulders. "It had to be Ishan who cut those orders for Tuvok. It was not me. I never knew . . ."

Riker met his gaze. "So are you ready to talk to me now?"

Akaar moved swiftly, faster than Riker expected for a man of his age. Two ensigns were passing the fountain, and the admiral stepped out to waylay them. The junior officers came to sudden attention, making a poor attempt to cover their surprise.

The towering Capellan pointed at a tricorder one of them was carrying. "I need that."

With a blink, the ensign handed it over. "Uh, sir—" he began, but Akaar was already waving him away.

"Dismissed," snapped the admiral, returning to Riker's side.

As the pair went on their way, both of them non-plussed, Akaar worked at the tricorder's controls. Presently, Riker heard a low hum emanating from the device, and the admiral sat it down on the bench between them.

"What's that for?" he asked. He could see that the device had been reset to broadcast a short-range scattering field.

"The sake of caution," Akaar shot back. "If we're doing this now, then I won't take any chances. Tell me what Jean-Luc said to you. *Exactly* what he said."

Riker took a breath. "'The Tzenkethi are not responsible for this.' Those were his words. I told him that the people behind the attack on the president would not go unpunished, and he was concerned. He said something about Cardassians and this True Way. . . ." He gestured with the padd. "And then the signal cut. Picard suspected we were being monitored, and I guess that proved it." Riker nodded at the tricorder. "It seems you feel the same."

Akaar slowly exhaled, and it seemed to age him a decade. At more than a century old by human standards, the admiral wore it well, but at this moment he seemed weighed down by his years. "This is moving too fast," he said, almost to himself. "It's slipping beyond my reach. . . ."

"You know." An edge of accusation found its way into Riker's words. "I'll admit, Admiral, I don't really have the full dimensions of what I've discovered here.

But you know all about it, I can see that. And you're keeping it quiet."

Akaar eyed him. "So tell me. What is it you *think* you know?"

"If Jean-Luc Picard says a Cardassian hate group is connected to the Bacco assassination, then I believe him. And that gives me a whole lot more questions than I had when you gave me this rank." He tapped the pin on his collar. "The galaxy at large was told that a Bajoran national was the suspected shooter on Deep Space Nine. Then we hear talk that the Tzen-kethi are implicated—and by extension the whole of the Typhon Pact. That's the angle that Ishan Anjar is behind. But if that's not true, then what is?" He glared at the senior officer. "If you know who pulled the trigger that day, why are you staying silent?"

"Listen to yourself!" snapped Akaar. "You're not some wet-behind-the-ears cadet in ethics class, Riker. You've been wearing that uniform long enough to know what the realities of the galaxy are like!" He prodded him in the chest, his finger like a rod of iron. "Think, man! Bringing the Cardassian Union into the Khitomer Accords is one of the most fragile alliances we've ever created. Years of hard work to get a former enemy into the fold and at a time when we need friends more than ever. And then, just as that comes together, the ugly possibility that some of their people may have committed this high crime against us? *Of course* I kept my silence! So has Jean-Luc and everyone inside the Cardassian government who knows."

Riker felt the color drain from his face, felt his stomach tighten. "Then it really is true. A Cardassian murdered Nan Bacco." All the way here, as Riker had run through the possibilities of how this ambush meeting would play out, on some level he had wanted to be proven wrong. He wanted to be mistaken, because the alternative was almost too much to grasp. *Velk said a Tzenkethi killed the president.* If that was false, then a cascade of unpalatable facts spilled out from beneath it, each threatening to sow chaos in its wake.

"I've known for some time," Akaar said grimly. "Ishan's a Bajoran and a survivor of the Occupation. I wasn't sure how he would react if I revealed this, barely a week after he became president pro tem. At first I wanted to find more proof, a firmer certainty. . . ."

"And so you deliberately withheld this information from the office of the president?" Riker couldn't accept what he was hearing. "That's a gross violation of your oath, sir!"

Akaar's eyes flashed. "Don't lecture me on my obligations; I've held to them since before you were born!" He looked away, scowling. "I told them, Riker. I sat on this information for days. . . . Ishan's attention was fixed on Andor then, and I didn't want to complicate things even more. But after that I couldn't conscience the possibility it represented. So I gave Galif jav Velk a full briefing on the likelihood of True Way involvement in the assassination."

"That doesn't make any sense. . . ." Riker shook his head. If the office of the president of the United Federation of Planets was fully aware that Cardassian nationals were responsible for Bacco's death, then why was he—and the rest of Starfleet—still under orders to seek out a conspiracy that originated within the Typhon Pact? Riker put that question to Akaar, but the admiral only gave a solemn shake of the head.

"When I was done, do you know what Velk said to me? 'Picard's information is unverified and unreli-

able.' He dismissed it, suggesting that the True Way
was nothing more than opportunists taking credit
for a brutal act perpetrated by our real enemies. Velk
refused to accept that a group of 'backward-looking
agitators' could be capable of such a thing."

The same thoughts had crossed Riker's mind, but
he had no doubt that Jean-Luc Picard would never
have been taken in by any such deception. When he
looked up again, Akaar was watching him carefully.

"You want to know why you are here?" he asked,
his voice low and grim. "*This* is why, Will. Because
I needed a man like you. I reeled you in from the
frontier because you can be trusted, because of your
reputation. Your viewpoint is not cluttered by years of
walking the halls of power. I needed someone I could
rely on, to go looking where I cannot. But I couldn't
move forward with that, not straight away. . . ." He
paused. "That's why I forced your promotion through,
against the wishes of the cabinet. That's why it wasn't
Picard or Sisko or anyone else who got the call."

"I wish I could say I was flattered. . . ."

Akaar's lip curled in the ghost of a smile, then
thinned again. "Velk's reaction to this was the start
of it. Then the incident at Andor came next, and I
couldn't ignore my misgivings anymore." He halted,
glancing around as he framed his next words.

They were still isolated here, but nonetheless Riker
suddenly felt very exposed. His thoughts flashed to his
wife and daughter, a sudden worry for their safety, but
he pushed the thoughts away. For now, he couldn't let
his concern for Deanna and Tasha get in the way.

After a moment Akaar went on. "The doctor,
Bashir . . . He set off a chain of events that none of us
could have predicted. I have no doubt that his inten-

tions were noble, and it cannot be denied that he has helped pull the Andorians back from the brink of extinction . . . but the fallout has been troubling."

Riker was more than aware of the Andorian reproductive crisis, having several natives of that race among his crew aboard the *Titan*. Bashir and a small cadre of medical experts—including some of Starfleet's best doctors—had now apparently solved their genetic issues. The problem was, all that had been done using some of the most protected secrets in the Federation, without oversight and against the express orders of the Federation Council. Now Bashir and his fellows were under arrest, as was Ezri Dax, the first starship captain sent to arrest him. Once again, Riker's thoughts turned to the rumors he had heard of Federation vessels exchanging fire over Andor.

Akaar anticipated his next question. "It's true what you've heard. Starfleet officers firing on Starfleet officers. Dax's crew stood side by side with Bashir on Andor and directly defied a presidential order. The president pro tem dropped the hammer in response. I argued that things could have been resolved in a better way, but I was overruled." He shook his head. "Ishan ordered cruisers and covert operations units sent in to expedite the situation."

Riker's eyes widened. "Against a non-aligned planet, that's tantamount to invasion! An act of war."

The admiral nodded. "And during a time of great local unrest as well. But my concerns fell on deaf ears. I was forced to comply or be relieved of my post. And so the end result was Starfleet boots on Andorian soil, without their government's consent. Federation citizens imprisoned with little or no attention to due process. Because of all of that, I called you here. I admired your actions during the Borg Invasion. Jean-Luc has always spoken of you in the highest of terms, Will. So I hope you can serve me now the way you have served him in the past."

"I suppose I should tell you then that I've made an early start." Riker folded his arms. "I have someone looking into what happened to Bashir."

Akaar leaned forward, resting his chin on his fist. "Good. It's best if you don't give me the specifics for now. It will be sensible to play our cards close. Just pass on what you learn."

"What exactly am I supposed to be looking for?"

"Irregularities." Akaar's frown deepened. "It's been just over thirty days since Ishan Anjar took his post, halfway through his temporary term. I am aware that Velk has implemented a number of sealed executive orders from the president pro tem. That in itself is unusual. It's possible one of those orders had something to do with Tuvok's reassignment, but I can't be certain. All I do know is that someone in the presidential cabinet is using the momentum of the recent calamity to push through directives without proper oversight."

Riker became aware that the shadow of the headquarters building was now upon him, and in the shade he felt a chill pass through his flesh. There was no mistaking what Akaar was suggesting here: the possibility of unsanctioned activities taking place at the highest levels of the Federation government. "We've been here before," he muttered. "It's Min Zife all over again."

"Not on my watch," Akaar insisted. "I won't allow someone to take advantage of Nan Bacco's death for his own ends." He reached into the pocket of the long overcoat he wore and drew out his silver case again. At first Riker though the admiral might offer him one of his *markah* cigarillos, but as he watched, Akaar picked at the inner lining of the case and removed something from a hidden compartment within. He turned a small isolinear chip between his fingers. "This is a copy of some data I was able to obtain. I haven't been able to act upon it yet. You might have more agency than I."

He slid it across the bench, and Riker picked it up, tucking the chip away into his cuff. "What's on it?"

"Those orders I spoke of. It is my understanding that they're connected to activities on a covert communications channel that originates from the office of the chief of staff. That chip contains information on the subspace frequency domain being used."

"Should I ask where you got it?"

"No," Akaar said flatly. "If signals on that channel could be intercepted . . . we would have a clearer picture of the situation at hand."

Riker fell silent. He had no illusions as to what the admiral was asking of him. Akaar wanted to conduct surveillance on the very highest levels of the Federation's chain of command. In the eyes of the law and the oath that Will Riker had sworn to uphold, what Admiral Akaar intended was no less than treason.

But if he's right, Riker thought, *if Velk or someone else is abusing their power for their own ends, we can't ignore it.*

"I have an idea about that," he said.

"Slowing to sublight in three . . . two . . . one." Lieutenant Thompson counted down the last few seconds before the *Lionheart* dropped to impulse power, and Christine Vale looked up at the bridge's viewscreen in time to see the warp-distorted lines of the stars shrink back into dots of light.

She glanced at the console in the arm of her command chair and noted that the exit vector was dead on. Four days after their departure from Earth and the lieutenant had delivered them perfectly into the orbital plane of the Jaros system. "Thank you, ops," she noted, "hold at one-quarter impulse, take us in toward the second planet."

"Jaros II on screen," ordered Commander Atia, and immediately the view shifted to an image of the dun-colored planet. Vale's first officer sucked in air through her teeth. "Would that you could tell a world's character from a gaze upon it," she muttered.

Vale said nothing. She had seen prisons more than once and always from the standpoint of someone taking a criminal to his or her justly deserved fate. She had no desire to see them from any other angle, but still there was something about Jaros II's reputation that would give any Starfleet officer a moment's pause.

The charter of the United Federation of Planets stipulated that any penitentiaries on its member-worlds were maintained at a liberal standard that kept in mind the rights of the individual—no matter what crime they might have been convicted of—and an avowed intent toward rehabilitation over incarceration. The Federation wanted lawbreakers to repay their debt to society and if at all possible, find a second chance. It was a laudable goal and one that Vale believed in, even if the reality didn't always match up to the high hopes behind it. In fact, there were very few dedicated penal colonies within the bounds of the UFP, most of them transitional facilities like Earth's New Zealand compound, where prisoners would serve out their sentences before being re-assimilated back into normal life. Some worlds had no jails of any kind, instead imposing punishment on offenders by keeping them under constant close surveillance, curtailing their rights of movement, communication, or access to goods and services—effectively making them prisoners of their own lives.

But there were always those who could not be easily rehabilitated or who represented a grave threat to others. Criminals of that stripe would be dispatched to worlds like the Tantalus Colony or Elba II, and if you broke the law while in the uniform of Starfleet, the planet on the screen was where you would most likely end up.

The official name of the facility was the Jaros II Detention Barracks Complex, but among those who served aboard the fleet's starships it had a simpler name: the stockade.

It was a ghost story for plebes and midshipmen, a threat that Academy instructors would hang over their heads, the tale of an isolated desert world stocked with the men and women who had dishonored the service and the code for which it stood. Few of those sent to Jaros II ever wore the uniform again, and for Christine Vale, that notion was a punishment equal to any stay in a dungeon.

She dismissed the thought with a blink and shot a look at Lieutenant Commander Darrah. "Let the logistics team know we'll be off-loading that additional cargo once we make orbit."

"Aye, Captain—" Darrah was cut off by a chime from his console. "Sensors indicate a ship approaching on a high-speed intercept vector, aggressive posture. They're hailing us."

"Show me."

The Bajoran tapped a key, and the main screen shifted to show a sleek, cylindrical vessel moving fast against the black of space. A Starfleet pennant was visible along the length of the hull; multiple impulse grids glowed orange-white, but the ship had no telltale warp nacelles. It was a system boat, designed for interplanetary defense operations only. "The coast guard?" offered Darrah.

Vale nodded. "Open the channel."

"Attention, Lionheart. *This is* Patrol Six-One. *You are entering a security-restricted sector. Provide authorization immediately, or turn back toward open space."*

Atia's lip curled. "Impolite," she growled.

"They're targeting us," reported Kader from the engineering station.

"Very impolite," added Atia.

Vale tugged her tunic straight without thinking about it, and the gesture almost made her smile. *Did I pick that up from Riker?* She schooled her expression. "Six-One, this is . . . Christine Vale, captain of the *Lionheart.* We're here on the orders of Starfleet Command. We have supplies and materiel for the colony."

"Our regular supply run isn't due for another month," came the reply.

Vale was aware of Atia and Darrah watching her intently as she responded. "We were . . . passing by." She tapped her own console, transmitting to the patrol ship a copy of the instructions Admiral Riker had given her. "You'll see everything is in order here."

A few seconds later the smaller craft veered sharply away, shifting heading to fall in alongside the medical cruiser. *"Confirmed,* Lionheart. *Maintain course and speed, enter standard orbit upon approach. Do not deviate from these instructions.* Patrol Six-One *out."*

"Sociable types, aren't they?" Darrah said, but his smile didn't reach his eyes.

Maslan had been watching from his panel. "They must still be on alert after the . . ." He paused. "The, ah, incident on DS9."

With a start, Vale realized that it had been a month and a day since Bacco's death. On some level, it seemed like only hours had passed since she had stood in Riker's ready room on the *Titan* and listened to the shocking message from Starfleet Command. It was still raw and new.

"Take us in, Alex," she told the flight operations officer. "Don't do anything to aggravate them. Fly smooth."

"Always do, sir," Thompson replied, his focus on the growing shape of the planet ahead.

Atia leaned closer and spoke in a careful whisper. "We near moment of purpose, so clarity would be appreciated. Will you give reason for presence, beyond task that any cargo scow could accomplish?" The challenge in the other woman's words was clear.

Vale folded her arms. "Well. I figure, as we're here, I might look up an acquaintance. Ezri Dax."

"Dax is inmate below," noted Atia. "Held to account after disobedience aboard *Aventine* at Andor. You count her as friend?"

"I'm the friendly type," Vale replied with a cool smile.

"Entering standard orbit," called Thompson.

"Signal from logistics," added Darrah. "We're ready to start the cargo drop."

Christine rose from her seat. "See to it, Hayn. You have the bridge." She turned back to Atia. "You know, there's a superstition among some older fleet types that it's bad luck for anyone still serving to go down to the stockade. Kind of like a black cat crossing your path."

"Or a snake falling from the roof."

"I'm going to go challenge fate a little," said Vale. "You want to come with?"

Atia stood up. "I hold no stock in old wives' tales."

The transporter put them down in a dusty quadrangle in front of the main administration block, in front of a large sculpture of a Starfleet crest. The rest of the complex was thoroughly protected under a powerful inhibitor field that would reflect back any attempt to get a lock on anyone within the grounds of the penal complex.

The heat of the day immediately stole all the moisture from Vale's lips, and she sniffed at the dry air, looking around; she was half expecting to see guard towers and walls topped with spikes, but there was nothing so dramatic or draconian to see. Aside from the invisible transporter barrier and the glitter of what might have been observer drones high in the clear sky, the stockade resembled the same kind of residential barracks that Starfleet had on dozens of worlds. Off toward one of the buildings she saw figures moving, all of them clad in nondescript clothing that, while it wasn't exactly prison uniform, was still basic enough to clearly be standard-issue. Each of them wore a combadge similar to the arrowhead on Vale's chest, but it was a bronze-hued oval without other detail.

"Monitors." Atia stood at her side, noting her interest. "Tracing movements and life function of those who wear them." She turned away and looked out into the desert beyond the compound. "No cordon or chains to the eye, but confinement nonetheless." The Magna Romanii woman frowned. "Your action in coming down here, Captain . . . it is unusual."

"I know." Vale caught sight of three figures approaching them from the main building. "I'm prone to being a little headstrong. You should learn that about me sooner rather than later." She flashed a smile at the man leading the group, a captain in the mustard-tan of operations. "Good morning!"

"Afternoon," he corrected. The man—a human with what Vale pegged as a Terra Novan accent—briskly introduced himself as Warden Sisterson, senior duty officer and site commander. "Captain Vale, this is highly irregular. We're not in the business of being open to impromptu visitors. Now, we fully appreciate your crew expediting the . . ." He paused, and one of his men handed him a padd containing a cargo manifest. "The delivery of these medical supplies. But we have protocols for this sort of thing, and I'm sure Admiral Riker is well aware of that, especially given our current situation and the elevated security levels fleet-wide."

"It wouldn't be much of a surprise inspection if you knew we were coming, would it?" Vale's reply blew the wind from Sisterson's sails, and she saw Atia's eyebrows lift in mild surprise.

"Inspection?" Sisterson repeated. "Why?"

"You said it yourself," said Vale. "Starfleet Command wants to make certain everything on Jaros II is secure." She aimed two fingers at her own face, in the shape of a V. "Nothing better than an eyes-on look-see to confirm that, don't you agree?"

The warden exchanged looks with his subordinates. "I'll have to clear this with Security Operations Command on Earth. . . ."

"And set time to waste?" Atia broke in. "Is there something you wish us not to see?"

Vale gave her first officer the slightest of looks. Without prompting, Atia had stepped up to bolster the thin justification she was using to pressure Sisterson, when, in fact, Vale was making this all up on the fly. *I'm starting to like her,* she thought.

The warden frowned and folded his arms. "All right. What do you want?"

"You can give Commander Atia here the tour. As for me, I'm specifically interested in one of your high-profile detainees."

Four sides of the complex's main exercise yard were surrounded by three-story detention blocks, but the north-facing elevation looked out onto the great sandy plains of Jaros II and to the dun-colored stone that lay in low waves of rock. The view reached off into the distance, vanishing in the heat haze. Again, there were no walls here, nothing to stop anyone from picking up and running.

But where could you go? Vale wondered. The second planet wasn't like its close neighbor in the third orbit out, capable of supporting a wide variety of flora and fauna. Jaros II was an arid world, not lifeless, but certainly not welcoming. Someone out there in the wilds would run out of water in days, and that was if the guards didn't stun them with a phaser burst the moment they went over the perimeter of the compound. As she crossed the empty space, she wondered if anyone had ever made the attempt.

Vale found her quarry practicing free throws at the edge of a parrises squares court. The woman was small, nimble, and she wore a jumpsuit that was a size too large and patched with sweat. She made an easy goal and dropped with a gasp, panting as Vale approached her.

"Ezri Dax."

"That's my name," she said, gulping in breaths. "Don't wear it out." The Trill woman stooped to gather up a chill-flask of water and took a long swig. Dax's short dark hair was spiked with sweat and dust, and the lines of pigment mottling common to her species stood out against her skin. She had striking blue eyes that took the measure of her, and Vale remembered hearing somewhere that Ezri had been a counselor before she became a captain.

But then, as a joined being, the host to a near-immortal symbiont intelligence that had shared many human lifetimes, Dax had doubtless been many things. Vale recalled that thought from the first time they had met, of how she had made a mental note not to let the Trill's outward appearance fool her into underestimating the woman.

She looked around at the vacant quad. Other than the two of them, not a soul was in sight. "Must get lonely out here."

"Not really. It's hardly solitary confinement when I've got eight more of me to talk to." Dax patted her belly.

She offered her hand. "Christine Vale."

"I remember. What's it been, four years since we met on the *Titan*? We hung out, eradicated the Borg, then went home for tea and medals." She toasted the air, ignoring Vale's gesture. "Good times."

"That's one way of looking at it, I guess." Dax's mordant tone wasn't what Vale had been expecting, and she let her hand drop. "Captain, Will Riker sent me here."

"I'm not the captain of anything," she replied. "Keep up." Dax dropped to her haunches and sat on the edge of the court, shielding her eyes from the sun. "I heard he got promoted to admiral. Nice work if you can get it."

"It seems like a lot of things are happening at Command," ventured Vale. "You upset a lot of people."

"So it would seem." Dax sighed, her spiky manner ebbing slightly. "Commander, what do you want with me? I made my choices and that's that. You understand I'm toxic now? Stay here too long and you may find your career has become tainted by my . . . I guess most people would call them *mistakes*."

"You don't seem the kind to make mistakes, Dax."

She gave a hollow laugh. "Oh, you should see my record with men." She took another swig of water. "And women, for that matter."

Vale tried another tack. "Are the others here? The doctors who worked with Bashir on the Andorian cure?"

Dax shrugged. "No. They're all under house arrest, as far as I know. They're all singing from the same page, claiming no knowledge that he had them using top-secret data stolen from Starfleet Command." A shadow passed over her face. "Julian's doing, taking all the blame for himself. He's not here. Federation Security separated him from the rest of us the first chance they got." She looked away. "I should have never followed him to Andor. He would have been safer there."

"Why don't you tell me what happened?"

Dax shot her a look. "Don't you know?"

"Let's just say that the story has become murky. And that may be to the advantage of some, but you know Riker. He wants the clear-eyed view."

"I'm not sure that will make a lot of difference at this point."

Vale was suddenly tired of standing, and she dropped into a settle on the sun-warmed ground. "Explain it to me, Ezri," she insisted. "Because if things change, I might not get the chance to ask you again."

And so Dax told the story, her gaze locked out toward the rocky wilderness as she spoke. It had begun with a call that woke her from her sleep shift, her first officer Sam Bowers bringing orders from Admiral Akaar that Julian Bashir had defied a government mandate forbidding investigation into the Andorian genetic issue. Worse still, he had apparently extracted information from the highly classified Shedai Meta-Genome project, one of the Federation's most deeply buried secrets, in order to do so. His illegal work discovered, Bashir stole the *Rio Grande* and fled for Andor with all the data he wasn't supposed to have. Dax's crew aboard the *Aventine* tracked him from that ship to another, finally closing the net around a civilian transport called the *Parham*.

"We caught up to Julian just as he reached Andor, in time to have an Imperial Guard warship put their guns on us. He tried to claim asylum, then the shooting started, and damn him if he didn't almost spark off a war right then and there." She shook her head angrily. "At first I was so furious with him . . . but then we talked and none of that seemed to matter. He told me what he was doing, about how Ishan Anjar was obstructing Andoria's chances for survival. I know Julian Bashir, maybe better than anyone. I understood why he did what he did, but I still had my orders. At the time, I thought that would be enough."

"But it wasn't." Vale nodded to herself. "I've been there, too."

"I wanted to give the Andorians the cure Julian

and the others had created," Dax insisted. "I was trying to find a solution . . . but my hand was forced."

She explained how Bashir escaped with the help of sympathetic members of her own crew, the *Parham* blasting its way out of the *Aventine*'s landing bay, running the gauntlet of the two other Starfleet ships that had come to back up Dax's crew. Ezri had been willing to let them go, but the captains of the *Warspite* and the *Falchion* had other orders. In the end, the daring gambit cost the *Parham*'s master his ship and his life, and very nearly that of Bashir and an Andorian named Shar into the bargain. The doctor and Shar had barely made it, beamed out of a plummeting escape pod by allies down on the planet.

Vale watched a humorless smile rise and fall on Dax's face. "I guess that was the moment I decided to defy orders. I got in the way of *Warspite* and *Falchion*, tried to slow down what they were doing. About that time, Julian contacted me from Andor, asking for my help." She shrugged. "Old boyfriends are always so inconsiderate about when they call."

Vale picked up the thread of the events. "You were sent to arrest him, but instead you aided and abetted."

"There's some truth in that," she agreed. "Let me guess. They say I did it because we used to be lovers."

"Some of the less-circumspect reporters might have mentioned that. . . ."

Dax let out a bark of cynical laughter. "I can almost see the head lines. 'Heroine of the Borg Invasion Falls from Grace.'" She shook her head. "We're so past that, Julian and me. It's not that way at all between us now. Look, I had my crew protect him until he could get that cure out to all the Andorians who wanted it. And they *wanted* it, believe me." The Trill's expression changed, becoming stronger. "I did the right thing. I'll take whatever slings and arrows come next."

Vale saw movement back toward the main building. She guessed she wouldn't have long before Sisterson came to call time on this conversation. "What I don't understand is why Ishan Anjar would let it go this far. Why hold back the genetic data from the Andorians?"

"Politics," Dax retorted, almost spitting the word. "You know the Tholians had given the Andorians some of the Shedai Meta-Genome information, hoping that they would join the Typhon Pact. . . . I've had a lot of time to think about this. . . . I believe Ishan thought that the Federation had more or different data on the Meta-Genome than the Tholians. Ishan wanted something to hold over them, the promise that he would declassify the information, to keep them out of the Pact. To strong-arm the Andorians back into the Federation. With Ishan angling to succeed Bacco and take the job full-time, think what a political victory that would have been for him."

"But the Andorians *want* to come back into the Federation."

"They do *now*. But on their own terms, not Ishan's." Dax nodded over Vale's shoulder. "Company is coming." She turned and saw the warden and his aides, with Atia walking at their side.

Vale got to her feet and looked down at the Trill. "Bashir's side of things needs to be heard. For everyone's sake."

"I don't know where they took him," she replied. "Protective custody, they said. Whatever the hell that means."

"You're going to get a fair hearing, Dax. You have

the right to your day before the Judge Advocate General in a formal court martial, the chance to put your side to the Federation. I promise you, Riker will make that happen."

"I know you believe that, Christine. I know Admiral Riker does. But still . . . I'm not hopeful. Not for me and the others . . . and especially not for Julian."

The Trill looked at her, and Vale saw an impossible, alien distance in her eyes; as if for a second she was peering into the depths of the nine lifetimes that existed inside the woman before her. She tried to imagine how Dax felt at this moment, isolated here and seemingly abandoned by her own colleagues.

"We did the right thing," the other woman repeated, "and now we're going to pay the price."

Eight

Tuvok lowered his head to enter the *Snipe*'s secondary cargo bay, pushing open the narrow manual hatch in front of him. He saw Nog standing with Jan Kincade and Tom Riker off to one side of the storage compartment, the trio dwarfed by the wall of bulk containers filling most of the rest of the chamber.

Kincade turned as he arrived. "Good, we're all here. Maybe we can get this done with, then?" She shot a look at Nog. "I'm sure it hasn't escaped your notice that we're on a clock here, Lieutenant Commander."

The Ferengi shook his head. "Absolutely not, Colonel." He looked at Tuvok. "Sir, could you secure the hatch behind you?"

Tuvok did as he was asked, his interest piqued at Nog's sudden insistence on security. It had been only a few hours after they had returned to the *Snipe* that Nog's message had reached the Vulcan: a private summons to meet belowdecks. He was interested to know what had prompted this sudden shift in behavior from the engineer.

On an overturned cargo pod that Nog was using as a table were a number of items, including a portable computer console and holographic projector, a tricorder and samples of plastics and metals each sealed in an environment-neutral packet. He gave them a quizzical look, attempting to glean their purpose.

"You told me you had something important," Kincade was pressing. "Do you or don't you?"

"Oh, I do," Nog said, his teeth flashing in a quick grin.

"Then why are we down here instead of up in the ops center?" asked Tom.

Nog's smile went away. "I thought . . . it might be better to discuss this privately first, with the ranking Starfleet officers on the team."

Tuvok nodded toward the human. "Mister Riker is neither of those things."

"Thanks for reminding me," Tom muttered.

"That's true," said Nog, "but he used to be. And I need him to confirm something for me."

"So?" Kincade's patience was thinning. "Get to it."

The Ferengi rubbed his hands, and Tuvok sensed that he was taking some enjoyment from the thrill of his as-yet-unrevealed discovery. Nog picked up a shard of cracked, worn metal. "This is piece of the nillimite-alloy plate I recovered from the encampment site. I guessed that it was used as part of a landing platform for a transport ship of some kind."

Tuvok nodded. "That seems a likely probability."

"I think it's going to lead us straight to our targets."

"A chunk of inert metal?" Tom seemed unimpressed. "Did they scratch their stellar coordinates into it?"

"Almost." Nog put down the alloy fragment and activated the holoprojector. An image of the shard blinked into being, floating in the air. Readouts and scan data haloed it. "The ship they used left a trace behind. It's enough to figure out what kind of craft it was and get a good idea of where it came from." He manipulated the projector's controls, and the view zoomed in to the surface of the fragment, down to the microscopic level. The metal's molecular structure became visible, arranged in layers of crystalline lattice. "I think our targets were using the same shuttlecraft on each trip they made to and from the ice world. The patterns of weight distribution, deformation of the landing platform, and the ground beneath all point to a uniformity. And each time they touched down . . ." He tapped another key, and the display highlighted what seemed to be great jagged-edged boulders ground into the minuscule landscape. "They left something behind, pressed into the ice and metal."

Tuvok peered at the image. "It is possible. Particulate matter gathered up on the skids of a shuttle could survive transit, especially if the landing gear was a retractable array. A trace amount would be deposited at the new landing site."

"So, like tracking dirt into the house on your boots," Tom noted.

"Exactly!" Nog replied. "I ran a biological and geological trace on the compounds left behind and separated out anything native to this world. There were . . . a lot of matches, and that was just in this sector. But there's more here." He highlighted another micro section of the shard. "I found oxidized deposits, which means a breathable atmosphere, and minute particles of refined tritanium, duranium, and nitrium."

"Rust and starship-grade hull metals," said Tuvok. "Curious . . ." He glanced at Kincade, who said nothing. "But inconclusive."

"I'm not done yet," Nog told him. "The 'dirt,' as Tom puts it, wasn't all that they left behind." He switched the display to show the same sample, but now the readouts were measuring levels of ambient radiation in the metal shard. "I realized that if they were landing a ship down there in the same spot on a regular basis, then the surrounding area would be marked with a radiation fingerprint. The decay patterns of energetic particles discharged when they touched down or lifted off." The screen lit up with a complex series of nested waveforms. "This is the radiation residue trace of an impulse thruster. Once I realized that, I was able to guess the power output of the engine being used and cross-reference that with what data I had about the size and tonnage of the craft. We know it was small enough to land in the clearing near the encampment, but big enough to carry people and cargo."

Tom gave an appreciative nod. "Pretty clever, Nog. But it still doesn't tell us where the targets ran to."

The Ferengi faltered for a moment. "Well, I mean, it's a given we're working on the hypothesis that they went to wherever the shuttle was based."

"Which could be the other side of the sector," Kincade noted. "Hell, the other side of the *quadrant* if the shuttle had a parent craft to carry it . . ."

Tuvok broke in before the conversation could drift. "For the moment, let us make the assumption they did not. Mister Nog, I presume you checked the impulse engine's output pattern against known designs in the Starfleet database?"

"Yes!" He grabbed a padd and brandished it like a trophy. "There's a human phrase that Ro Laren used when she was security chief on DS9: 'We caught a lucky break.' The radiation trace matches up to one kind of impulse engine system that we know of. And with that pattern and the approximate size and mass of the shuttle, I was able to figure out exactly what kind of ship we're looking for!" The Ferengi's enthusiasm was building, and his words came quicker as he went on. "Knowing that, I could estimate the operating range of the target ship, narrowing it down based on approximate times between the deposits of the radiation traces and decay rates!" Nog barely paused to take a breath. "Overlay that with the minerals and metals data, and it was possible to isolate four different planets in the local sector as likely candidates for the shuttle base."

"That's some impressive deductive reasoning," said Kincade, her tone flat. "All of which could be completely wrong if even *one* of your circumstantial assumptions is slightly off." Before he could protest, she raised a hand to forestall any complaints. "Show me these planets."

Somewhat crestfallen, Nog offered the woman the padd he was holding, and Kincade gave it a narrow-eyed once-over before passing it to Tuvok. "Commander, your thoughts?"

"If Mister Nog's conclusions are correct, I suspect that this world is most likely the origin point of the shuttlecraft." The Vulcan indicated a file showing a planet in the Iota Nadir system, a bleak sphere designated IN-748. "Federation survey data lists it as currently uninhabited, designated as an inactive site for materials recovery and vessel decommissioning."

Tom took the padd and glanced at it. "A breaker's world," he said, using the colloquial name. "A graveyard for derelict starships and scrapped tech." He paused, absently stroking his beard. "Good location for a hideout. And it would explain the traces of hull metal particles and the rust."

"You said you know what kind of ship the targets are using." Kincade turned back to Nog. "How?"

The Ferengi took another long breath. "As I said, the impulse radiation only matches one class of sublight engine." He pressed a key on the projector, and it displayed a blunt piece of machinery that resembled a metal tooth torn from the mouth of an iron giant. "I recognized this technology as soon as I saw it." He tapped another button, and the engine component shrank to merge with the outline of a squat little spacecraft. It was heavy and thickset in design, and it reminded Tuvok of the desert beetles that colonized the sandy outskirts of Kir City on Vulcan.

Nog was looking at Tom. "Mister Riker, can you tell us what kind of ship that is, please?"

Tom answered without hesitation. "That's a *Duulet*-class cargo shuttle. They used them all the time at the Lazon II penal colony."

"A Cardassian vessel," Tuvok noted. "Not a Tzenkethi ship. You are absolutely certain of your findings, Lieutenant Commander?"

Nog's expression became firm. "I'd put latinum on it, sir." He hesitated. "My uncle Quark told me there's no such thing as a sure bet, but I think this is fairly close."

"But our targets are not Cardassians," insisted Kincade. "The mission intel is very clear on that."

The Ferengi didn't address her unspoken question. "After I pieced this information together, I went back down to the surface with Khob and took more samples, this time from the remains of the outpost tents." Nog indicated the slivers of plastic. "All the life-support hardware left down there had been ripped out or wiped, but there was still trace data in the material of the walls themselves."

Tuvok understood. If the same environmental conditions were maintained inside a sealed building for a long enough period, that building's structure itself would exhibit certain characteristics that could be measured, even after the initial conditions had been altered.

Nog continued. "I was able to get a probable range for the internal temperature settings. Twenty-nine degrees centigrade. That was the standard ambient environmental protocol on space station Terok Nor . . . and it's the standard on all Cardassian starships and outposts."

It was now clear to Tuvok why the engineer had chosen to partition this information before revealing it to everyone in the Active Four unit: Nog's discovery went directly against what they had been told about their targets and their origins. He looked around, seeing the questions in the eyes of the others. After a moment, he spoke. "How do you wish to proceed with this new data, Colonel?"

Kincade glanced at him. "We have orders not to break subspace radio silence unless it is a matter of extreme urgency. So for now, we proceed as before. Nog's data is circumstantial, but it's all we've got right now, so I'm willing to give it a crack of the whip."

"And the discrepancy?" Tuvok's gaze was steady. "We were told we were hunting the Tzenkethi."

"As far as we know, we still are," insisted Tom. "I have more reason to loathe the Cardassians than anyone on this ship, but Nog's data doesn't prove anything definitively. We're here for one reason, and one reason only. To bring Bacco's killers to justice. Right now, that's the *only* thing that is certain."

"He's right," said Kincade, striding toward an intercom panel on the wall.

She tapped the panel and a moment later Ixxen's voice crackled over the link. *"This is the bridge."*

"Lieutenant, I want you to break orbit and set a course to the Iota Nadir system, planet designation IN-748. Maximum warp."

"Maximum, Colonel? That might attract some undue attention. . . ."

"We'll take that chance. Get it done. Kincade out." She turned back to face Tuvok and the others, and her eyes were hard. "Until I say otherwise, what we talked about in here doesn't leave this room, understood?"

"Understood," said Tuvok, holding his concerns silent for the moment.

The security contingencies in place at the Jaros II complex meant that the comparatively simple act of transferring cargo to the surface via transporter took a lot longer than it otherwise might have. Each separate container was required to be sent down individually and scanned by Warden Sisterson's staff before the next item could be dropped off from the *Lionheart*. It seemed like going to extremes, but the warden had made it abundantly clear that he was taking no risks. He was going to follow the orders for heightened precautions laid down in the wake of the assassination on Deep Space 9 to the absolute letter.

Christine Vale tried to put herself in the shoes of the commander of the penal complex; Sisterson had to be on edge, having suddenly gained custody of Ezri Dax and a handful of politically sensitive prisoners overnight. Even out here, word of the incident at Andor was circulating and there were some who—rightly or wrongly—were already finding ways to connect what happened there with the death of Nan Bacco.

But Vale was actually pleased about the delay keeping them in orbit. Without it, she would have had little choice but to continue back on the *Lionheart*'s original heading to Starbase 47, her mission for Admiral Riker incomplete. Everything she had learned from Dax had only served to deepen her concerns and confirm what she already knew.

Vale sat alone in the starship's briefing room, which was situated on the deck below the main bridge. Much narrower and more confined than the similar space aboard the *Luna*-class *Titan*, *Lionheart*'s equivalent still commanded an impressive view of the medical cruiser's secondary hull, ranging away from the windows in a gentle slope down over the aft shuttle bay toward the twin-warp nacelles. Jaros II's surface was a static backdrop beneath the vessel, kept in geostationary lockstep as the laborious cargo transfer continued. The modified *Nova*-class starship didn't have a captain's ready room, and it wasn't until she got on board that Vale realized how useful that private office could be to a commander. A place of isolation to think and take respite, even if only for a few moments . . . She wondered how some commanders could ever have done without it.

The familiar three-tone bosun's whistle of the intercom sounded, and Vale absently tapped at a control pad embedded in the surface of the conference table. "Go ahead."

There was a noticeable delay before the static-distorted voice of a woman answered her. *"Commander Vale?"*

She resisted the urge to correct the person on the

other end of the intercom. "Yes? Who is this?" *Lionheart* had only eighty crewmembers, but Vale didn't know them all by the sound of their voices.

"Commander, I have some information I think you might find useful. But I need to ask you a question first."

Vale sat down at the table, looking around the empty room. "Identify yourself. That's an order." For a long moment there was nothing, and Vale wondered if the mystery woman had closed the link, but no, she could still hear the faint hiss of static coming from the hidden intercom speakers. The channel was open; she just wasn't speaking. Vale scowled and tried a different tack. "Computer, what is the origin of the intercom signal directed to the briefing room?"

"The briefing-room intercom system is currently inactive," replied the synthetic voice.

"What, am I dreaming this?" retorted Vale. "No, that's not right. . . ."

"As far as your ship's computer is concerned, it is." The woman broke her silence. *"Don't be alarmed. This is just a necessary precaution. It's best if any conversation we have doesn't leave a trace."*

Vale heard the buzz of static again and something abruptly occurred to her. The interference patterns had the same texture as those heard over interstellar comm channels. "You're not even on board this ship, are you?"

"No. As a matter of fact, there's quite a bit of distance between us."

"How are you doing this? You can't just infiltrate a subspace radio signal into a ship's internal communications grid. . . ." Vale trailed off. Clearly, if this mystery speaker was to be believed, then apparently that *wasn't* the case. "This is the last time I'm going to ask you," she snapped. "Who are you? And if I don't get an answer I like, our little chat is over."

"*I'm . . . a friend of Julian Bashir. I know that you're trying to find him.*"

Vale tapped another key on the panel and a display flashed into life on a screen in the middle of the conference table. She frowned as she tried to bring up a data feed from the incoming signal, but all the screen showed was a scrambled mass of unintelligible noise, the same soup of cosmic background resonance that existed everywhere in the galaxy. "What makes you think that?"

"*Let's just say I'm very well connected. I know you were given command of the* Lionheart *by Admiral William Riker and that you made an unscheduled detour to the Jaros II stockade. Tell me, have you talked to Ezri Dax yet?*"

Vale's eyes narrowed. "If you're so well connected," she said to the air, "then you'd already know the answer."

"*What I know is that you would be en route to his location right now if you knew where Julian is being held. But that fact is a closely guarded secret at the highest levels of the Federation government. Decisions are being made, choices that will affect the entire quadrant, and Julian is caught in the middle of it.*" There was a distant, metallic sigh. "*And I carry some of the blame for putting him in harm's way.*"

Her mind was racing as she listened to the other woman speak. Vale laid out all the possibilities in her mind's eye; was this a ruse of some sort, to get her to incriminate herself and throw doubt on Riker? Was the speaker some ally or enemy of Bashir's trying to track him down for herself? Or even an agent of the

Andorians, attempting to pay him back for risking his life to preserve theirs?

She went on. *"I have used . . . certain contacts in order to gather information about where Julian was taken after the Andor incident. But my current circumstances mean that I can't act on it. You can, Commander. You can liberate Julian Bashir before his disappearance becomes permanent."*

Vale's seasoned ear for reading people picked out something in the other woman's voice. More than just concern, more like genuine sorrow. The smallest flicker of it, but there nonetheless. *A friend, then,* she thought. *Or something more.* "Why should I believe you? For all I know, you could be sending me into the jaws of a trap. I have a hundred reasons why I should cut this short and ignore everything you're saying to me. Give me one reason why I shouldn't." Vale steepled her fingers, staring into the scrambled mass of the signal. "Tell me your name. Trust *me,* and maybe I'll trust you."

Again, a long moment of silence fell, but then the woman spoke. *"All right, Commander. If that's what it will take . . ."* The disorder of the chaotic signal pattern changed, shifting and merging until it took on the dimensions of a human face. The image was grainy and laced with bursts of razor-edged static, but now it was clearly a human woman with a pleasant appearance set in a worried expression, her mid-length blond hair pooling on the gray shoulders of a Starfleet uniform. Vale saw a lieutenant commander's pins on a mustard-colored operations undershirt. *"My name is Sarina Douglas. I'm part of the security detail on space station DS9, but before that I was an operative with Starfleet Intelligence. Julian is very important to me, Commander. I'm risking a lot coming to you with this."*

She knew that look, the shimmer in Douglas's eyes. They were lovers, this woman and Bashir. It was as clear to Vale as if she had said it aloud. And suddenly the plausibility of it snapped into place. A former intelligence agent, calling in her last favors to save the man she cared for, so desperate to rescue him that she would come to a complete stranger for help. "Why contact me directly?" she asked. "Why not go to Admiral Riker, or your own commanding officer?"

"Too many questions," Douglas replied. *"Too much risk. I'm already under scrutiny after Julian's escape from Bajor."*

"You helped him get away." It wasn't a question.

"I've read your file, Commander," said Douglas, deflecting the comment. *"I know you believe in due process. I know you'll do what's right."* She turned, as if addressing something Vale couldn't see. *"I'm sending you a data burst containing the coordinates of a star system near the Betreka Nebula. There's a concealed asteroid outpost there. Find it, and you'll find Julian Bashir."*

"Where exactly did that information come from?" Vale demanded.

"Find him, Commander," implored the woman, ignoring the question. *"Please."*

There was a crackle of static, and then the briefing room was quiet.

Ranul Keru looked up as the door to transporter room three opened to admit Melora Pazlar, the *Titan*'s science officer. He heard the subtle hiss of her gravity suit as she walked, the mechanism allowing the Elaysian woman to function normally in what was to her a high-*g* environment.

She threw him a nod. "Lieutenant Commander. I

didn't know you were still on the ship. I thought you might have taken advantage of the liberty."

Keru shook his head. "I considered it," he admitted. "Didn't seem right to leave." Melora didn't press the point, and he was glad of that; the fact was, Keru had nothing waiting for him back on Trillius Prime, and *Titan* was more a home for him now than the planet where he had grown up. But beyond that, he felt the unconscious need to stay at his post, to keep his ship and his crewmates safe while the turmoil of recent days ran its course. If he had been pressed to explain it, *Titan*'s security chief would not have been able to put the emotion into words; it was a compulsion to stand sentry in troubled times. Doing anything else would have felt like neglect.

"I'd like to say it was good to have a little downtime," she said, "but it's been hard getting any work done in astrometrics. Everyone is too busy talking about what's going on."

He nodded. Having no immediate mission to hand meant that *Titan*'s crew had the opportunity to dwell on issues that otherwise might have been of secondary concern. Although the ship's crew complement had thinned since their arrival at Earth, those who remained on board were all occupied in one way or another by the ongoing political circus unfolding on the planet below. And not all of the crew were in accord over it. Keru grimaced as he recalled a moment a few days earlier when he arrived at the ship's lounge to find Ensigns Venoss and Mecatus in the middle of a heated dispute over the finer points of Ishan Anjar's pugnacious statements to the galactic press. *Politics,* he thought sourly. *We've evolved to a point where gender, creed, race, and religion are all things that we can debate*

in a more or less reasonable manner, but politics will
always *be a source of argument.*

A chime sounded from the transporter console,
and Melora turned to Lieutenant Radowski who stood
waiting before it. "Starfleet Command signals ready,"
he reported.

"Proceed," she replied.

"Energizing," said Radowski, and his hands traced
down the controls, bringing the system to life.

Keru watched two columns of blue-white light
hum into being and define themselves into the forms
of William Riker and a Caitian officer he hadn't met
before. As the glow faded, Riker's face split in a wan
smile that seemed partly out of regret and partly relief.

"Melora, Ranul . . ." said the admiral, giving each
of them a nod of greeting. "Bowan. Nice to be back.
Feels like I've been away for months."

"It has been ten days, Admiral," noted the Caitian.

Riker gestured at the felineoid. "This is Lieutenant
Ssura, my aide. He already knows who you all are."

Ssura's head bobbed. "It is the greatest pleasure to meet
members of the esteemed *Titan* crew, sirs and madam."

"Hey, right back atcha," said Radowski with a grin.

"Good to see you, sir," said Keru. "The new rank
suits you."

Riker shrugged. "It's a little heavy, though." He nodded toward the door. "Shall we start the inspection?"

Melora led the way. "If you'll follow me?" Keru fell
in step with Riker and the Elaysian as they proceeded
out into the corridor. She smiled. "This feels a little
odd, sir. Taking you on a tour of your own ship."

"A perk of the new job," said Riker. "I get to poke
around inside any vessel I like the look of."

"Commander Troi isn't joining us?" Keru noted.

Riker shook his head. "She's visiting London with our daughter. Deanna's going to show Natasha where her grandfather was born, fill in a little of the Troi family history."

"Xin's team has completed the engine upgrades," Melora offered. "We can head down to the warp core . . ."

"Why don't we start with the lab decks first?" said Riker, making the question into an order.

Pazlar and Keru exchanged a glance. Both of them were aware that the admiral's office had sent sealed orders to members of the engineering and sciences departments, tasking Lieutenant McCreedy and Ensign Modan to set up a laboratory for an undisclosed purpose. The group entered a turbolift, and an uncomfortable silence descended.

Riker gave them both a look and then addressed an order to the air. "Computer, halt transit." The turbolift droned to a stop. "All right, let's get this over with." He nodded toward Ssura. "You can talk freely in front of the lieutenant here. And just because I'm an admiral now, that doesn't mean I've suddenly become a different person."

Melora licked her lips before she replied. "Yes, sir. I mean, no, sir."

"Sorry, sir," offered Keru. "But you know how it is. Force of habit. History shows, anyone above the rank of captain sets foot on a starship, it's usually a precursor for trouble."

"Well, that may be true. But I'm still Will Riker and still your commanding officer. The promotion doesn't come with a personality change."

"I'm sure we're all glad to know the power hasn't gone to your head," Melora said with a sly smirk. "*Yet.*"

"Admiral Riker exhibits a most even temperament." Ssura was quite serious in his observation, missing the irony in the Elaysian's tone. "Don't be concerned."

Keru wasn't smiling, though. "Easier said than done, Lieutenant." He turned to Riker. "This . . . inspection came out of nowhere. And I'm willing to bet you've got a very different reason for being here."

The admiral gave a solemn nod. "Never could get anything past you, Ranul. That's why you're so good at your job." He sighed. "I can promise you that I'd never do anything that would compromise *Titan*'s security without informing you first. Which is exactly why you're coming with me now."

Unbidden, a chill ran through Keru's blood. "Why do I get the feeling I'm not going to like what you have to tell us?"

"Computer, resume transit," said Riker, leaving the question hanging.

The thin justification for his visit dispensed with, Riker led the way down to laboratory nine, one of the starship's secondary science workspaces. A modular compartment like most of *Titan*'s labs, it was designed to be refitted and retooled on a mission-by-mission basis, dependent on whatever research was required at the time. The admiral's orders to Lieutenant McCreedy had involved fitting out the space with analysis gear and stand-alone computer systems, and Karen had followed them to the letter. Riker entered the chamber to find Ensign Y'lira Modan, the ship's Selenean cryptolinguist, in conversation with Ensign Torvig Bu-Kar-Nguv from the engineering team. Both of them came to attention, but Riker waved away the moment of formality.

"At ease." He introduced Ssura once again, watching as Melora circled the room, taking in the equipment all around them.

"These are extreme frequency-monitoring devices," she noted. "High-density memory cores on an isolated network, holographic interface generators, subspace sensor rigs . . . The same kind of setup I use for tracking deep sky spatial anomalies."

Riker agreed. "But Torvig and Y'lira are not looking for distant pulsars or wormholes. I'm interested in a target much closer to home." He paused for a moment. If he went on, he would be widening the circle of involvement further still, beyond him and Admiral Akaar, beyond Ssura and Deanna and Vale. With each person he brought into this small conspiracy, he was risking not only his future but also theirs; and while he never once doubted that his crew would support him and follow his lead, Riker felt the weight of responsibility that asking them would put upon him. "What we are about to talk about here is not for discussion with anyone else, am I clear?" His officers nodded in return, and Riker noted that Ranul Keru was the last to do so, the wary look on the Trill's face deepening into a frown.

"This setup is all so you can listen in on someone," said Keru, cutting to the heart of it.

"Two days ago the admiral suggested we begin monitoring a discreet subspace domain in the tertiary sigma band layers," said Torvig, off a nod from Riker. "Such layers are not commonly employed for subspace radio transmissions, owing to the larger energy cost of pushing a signal through such a compressed paradimensional zone."

Modan took her cue and indicated a display screen,

which showed a series of complicated moving wave-forms. "This is essentially a hidden conduit for communications from Earth to the wider quadrant. Heavily encrypted and carefully concealed to appear as normal background cosmic radiation to anyone who might accidentally happen across it."

"What's the origin of this channel?" said Melora.

"I believe this comes from one of the highest offices in the Federation government," said Riker.

"How high?" asked the Elaysian.

"The highest," Riker repeated.

Keru shook his head. "Wait, no. Sir, are you saying you ordered surveillance to be carried out on the President of the United Federation of Planets? I don't know where to begin with how many laws that breaks!"

Modan blinked her golden eyes. "I . . . suspected it might be this . . . but I thought there had to be an explanation."

At her side, Torvig's tail drooped. "Did we do something illegal?"

Riker held up his hands. "This is on me. You're following my orders. The responsibility is mine."

"Just as now the responsibility is mine to inform Starfleet," snapped Keru. "Sir, you realize what this means? Just standing in this room with you could be enough to end all our careers!"

"The reason is justified," Ssura spoke up. "Actions occur that must be addressed. *Titan* is the only vessel that can do so!"

"Ranul, if you want to go to Command, I won't stop you." Riker met his gaze. "But know that I've done none of this lightly. After all we've been through together, you owe me the chance to explain my reasons."

The Trill nodded. "Aye, sir. You're due that. If

you were any other man, I would have arrested you already."

"I appreciate your restraint." He took a breath, and with steady, careful words, he brought them all into the circle.

Riker told Keru and the others about the conflicting orders, the secret commands, clandestine arrests, and mission directives, the growing weight of suspicion and distrust accreting in the Federation's corridors of power. None of them spoke or questioned what he said, and by turns the mood in the lab grew heavy and solemn. When he was done, Riker allowed his officers to take the time to absorb what he had revealed.

Modan was the first to break the silence. "If this pattern of events is what it appears to be, then we stand witness to a grave breach of the public trust. An abuse of power by unknown actors within the government of our Federation."

"The oath of service is quite clear on this," Keru mused. "We serve the citizens of the United Federation of Planets against enemies *both foreign and domestic*." He glanced at Riker. "I understand now, sir. But believe me, if what we're doing here turns out to be anything other than what you've just brought to light, I *will* still throw you in the brig."

Riker managed a smirk. "If I'm wrong, I'll go quietly."

Keru went on. "But let's say you're right. We're on thin ice here. We can't know how big a problem this is until we know who is behind it."

Torvig's metallic hands knit before him. "The Federation is a construct of laws and protections. That structure cannot be ignored, no matter what level one may exist at. If someone hides behind it in order to abuse it, we cannot allow that to go on." He nodded toward Riker. "Sir, I will assist you in this, and I accept fully the consequences that may follow."

Melora said nothing, only nodded her agreement.

"I appreciate your trust and your loyalty," Riker told them. "Now, Mister Torvig. Why don't you tell me what it is you've found?"

The Choblik crossed to one of the freestanding consoles and tapped in a string of commands. "This morning, at approximately zero seven hundred hours shipboard time, the passive monitoring scans set up to observe the covert channel picked up a burst transmission. It appeared to originate from a source somewhere on Earth's European continent."

"I gave it an initial evaluation," said Modan. "Very dense, sir. On the order of gigaquads of compressed data."

"Let's see it."

The ensign tapped a control, and the screen before her filled with an impenetrable wall of text, a flood of symbols and digits that at first sight seemed overwhelmingly complex.

"The composition is familiar to me," said Ssura. "But not comparable to typical subspace message packets."

Melora came closer, nodding. "He's right. It's not a message stream; it's far too intricate to be video or audio data, even under multiple layers of encryption." Riker saw Pazlar's eyes narrow as she turned her intellect to the challenge before her. "I know what this is," she breathed. "It's a holomatrix. Compacted and reconfigured for direct subspace transfer, but definitely an autonomous program."

"A holographic recording?" asked Keru.

"Unlikely, sir," Torvig replied. "Unless it contained a colossal level of detail. Lieutenant Commander Pazlar's hypothesis fits the facts. This appears to be a fully operative holoprogram, designed to be interacted with by the recipient."

"Could it be decompiled?" asked Modan. "It might be possible to learn what it contains without activating it."

Ssura folded his thin arms across his chest. "Possible, but protracted. It would take weeks to correctly deconstruct something so intricate. Also there may be anti-tampering subroutines built into the program to prevent such acts."

"There is another alternative," said Riker, rubbing his chin as he considered. "We run it."

"I like the thought of that very little." Keru's reply was dour. "We've got no idea what we have here."

Torvig's tail gestured at the consoles. "This system is unconnected to any of *Titan*'s main functions. If there were a catastrophic effect from activating the program, it could not spread beyond this compartment."

"*Catastrophic effect*?" echoed Keru. "Tor, my friend, you're not exactly selling me on this."

"I can rig an emergency shutdown," said Modan, bringing up a subroutine. She indicated a flashing icon before her. "I press here and all power to this compartment will instantly be cut."

All eyes turned to Riker, and he nodded. "Run the program."

Keru's hand tensed and he found himself unconsciously reaching for a holstered phaser that wasn't there. He watched Torvig's manipulators scuttle across the control panel like metal spiders, and then with a flash of light, the holographic emitter array in the center of the lab came to life.

Lacking the power or range of a full holodeck system, the emitter rig couldn't produce something that would encompass the whole compartment, but then the content of the covert message wasn't a simulation or a synthetic environment. A humanoid figure faded in from nothing, shimmering as the form gained the illusion of solidity.

Riker's first thought was of a child's rendition of a human, a featureless sketch scaled up to the height of a man. The figure had nothing that was indicative of gender, species, or other identity, only the most basic structure of two legs, a torso, two arms, and a head. It was nothing but a placeholder construct, a thing to give the suggestion of a being without any of the actual substance of a real person.

The face it wore was barely an outline of eyes and mouth, and for a moment it didn't move. Then slowly the hologram's bland aspect turned to examine the room around it, head cocked in a manner that was almost quizzical. When it spoke, the voice was flat and toneless. "Receiver mismatch has been logged. Please wait."

"What is the meaning of that?" Ssura asked.

"It must be aware that it is not where it is supposed to be." Modan alternated between watching her panel and scanning the hologram with a tricorder. "I'm seeing a lot of internal processing taking place."

Riker stepped forward and cleared his throat, addressing the figure directly. "Identify your origin and function."

"The origin of this program is protected," it replied. "Function: messenger."

"It's trying to determine its location," said Torvig

as red flags blinked into being on his console. "But it can't connect out of the stand-alone server."

"Messenger?" Riker said it like a name, and the hologram looked up at him. "Disclose your information to me."

"No." It stared at the admiral with those blank, doll-like eyes. Keru searched them for any sign of emotion, synthetic or not, and came up empty. "The recipient template is not present. Provide designated recipient for primary authentication."

"It doesn't know us," said Melora. "And we don't know who the message is for, so there's no way we can bring them here."

"Messenger, I am Admiral William Riker of Starfleet Command, and by my authority I order you to immediately relinquish your information."

"I am not subject to your authority," the hologram said flatly. Then it slowly turned its head to study Torvig and Modan. "I am aware of attempts being made to infiltrate my core functions. Be advised that any perceived intrusion into security layers will meet with a prompt response."

"That sounds like a threat," Keru snapped. "Explain the nature of this response."

"Stage one: Security firewall is now active. Stage two: Data lockdown is pending. Stage three: Self-deletion . . . is pending." Keru caught the pause in the reply and considered what that might mean. "I will divulge information only to the designated recipient," concluded the hologram.

"This program is clearly capable of a heuristic-learning response to outside stimuli," Torvig noted. "It's semi-intelligent. One could almost say it's been programmed to be evasive."

"A message that encodes itself . . ." said Ssura. "Quite remarkable."

"Admiral, if I may?" Modan put down the tricorder and stepped forward as Riker gave her a nod. "Messenger, the recipient template is unavailable at this time. You must have auxiliary protocols for authentication in the event of such circumstances."

"Yes," said the figure. "Shall I proceed to that phase?"

"Go on," Modan said warily.

The hologram studied her blankly. "Queen to queen's level three. Reply."

Torvig's eyes widened. "That is a move from a game of three-dimensional chess. I do not understand. . . ."

"I do," said Riker. "It's old Starfleet code. Nothing formal or official, just a quick and simple way for crews to signal if they were under duress or if they needed to confirm someone's identity."

Keru glanced at him. "Do you know the correct response?"

The admiral shook his head. "It could be any one of a thousand different counter-moves. That's the beauty of it. Simple to learn, but with countless variables."

"And if we give the wrong answer, the program deletes itself, and we're back to where we started," said Modan.

Keru studied the holographic figure, his jaw set in a scowl. "We wanted to intercept a message. Instead we appear to have captured a prisoner."

Nine

The air-cab banked gently as it pulled into a shallow turn over the river Thames, arrowing through London's late-afternoon sky. A light wind hummed over the windows as the flyer's blunt prow moved to take up a path that would follow the line of Westminster Bridge, calm and unhurried toward the hotel in Holland Park where Deanna Troi had taken rooms for the evening.

The crisp, clear air meant that the view of the Houses of Parliament and the tower of Big Ben was sharp and perfect, and Deanna instinctively reached out to tap her daughter on the shoulder, intending to bring her attention to the city's ageless icons. But she halted, her hand resting over Tasha's shoulder; the four-year-old was fast asleep, her head resting against the opposite window, one hand clutching the plush toy raven she had picked up at the Tower of London.

Troi smiled, delighted by the simple normality of the moment—and then she stifled a yawn herself. It *had* been a long day, she reflected. Out to East Anglia in the morning to see where members of the Troi family had once lived, then crisscrossing the city to visit the sights, willfully going astray in backstreets filled with curious little shops and buildings that were half a millennium old or more. It had been easy to lose herself in Tasha's enthusiasm for the new for a few hours, just to get away from the cheerless mood that seemed to have cast itself across everything else.

A soft, melodic chime sounded from a pocket in her tunic, and Troi grabbed for the comm padd there, silencing it before it could wake her daughter. The device's screen showed a Starfleet crest and a numeric code indicating a signal relay from off-world. A frown threatened to gather, but she pushed it aside. "Troi here," she said.

The display switched to an image of Christine Vale, in uniform and seated before what appeared to be a window looking out onto warp space. *"Deanna. I'm glad I got you. Can you talk?"*

"Of course. Is something wrong?"

Vale leaned in toward the image pickup. *"Wait a second."* She did something at a panel by her hand, and the image quality lessened, the sound taking on a tinny resonance; Vale had activated an encryption subroutine at her end of the transmission. *"Okay. Where are you now?"*

"A few hundred feet up over Hyde Park." She shot a glance at the air-cab's pilot behind a glass partition, who seemed unaware of the conversation going on behind him. "I'm in London with Tasha. We're . . . taking a day or two."

"Make the most of it," Vale told her. *"Shore leave never lasts as long as it should."*

"You're not on the *Titan*," said Troi, a note of concern entering her voice. "Is there a problem?"

Vale very deliberately did not address her first statement. *"I've got some things I need to ask you. I'm going to need your help."* The commander's body language spoke volumes; Troi knew that intense, focused expression of old. She'd seen it more than once, when *Titan* had been in harm's way out in the depths of unexplored space.

"Whatever I can do," she replied.

"First. Sarina Douglas. Do you know that name?"

She shook her head. "Should I?"

"Probably not. I'm just checking. That's not the reason I contacted you. You know about what happened to Bashir, the CMO from Deep Space Nine?"

Troi nodded. "Will explained it to me. He said he was looking into it. . . . I guess that means you are, too?"

Vale returned the nod. *"Strictly off book, you understand? Right now, the less attention this draws, the better. I spoke with Ezri Dax, the former captain of the* Aventine, *and I suspect that if I can find Bashir, he's going to need all the help he can get from us."*

Troi knew that Julian Bashir's firsthand experience of what had happened on Andor was not something that could remain buried; but in the current political climate, such knowledge could have unpredictable effects if revealed to the galaxy at large. She had no doubt there were many who would not wish to see Bashir's release secured any time soon, even as Vale sought to do just that. "That won't be easy."

"And then some," said Vale, grim-faced. *"But we have to try. And that's why we're talking. Dax said something to me about what happened on Andor. I think it could be the key to getting the errant doctor out of whatever deep, dark hole he's been dropped down. It's going to require some things I don't have an awful lot of, but that you've got in spades."*

"And that would be?"

"Tact. Subtlety. Diplomacy."

Despite herself, Troi smiled. "Chris, don't sell yourself short. You can do subtle."

"Not like you. And this is going to be a big ask, Counselor. It's also going to require some in-depth knowledge of Andorian legal process and a willingness to bend the rules."

The air-cab rumbled through a gust of wind as it circled and began a descent toward the hotel's rooftop landing pad. Deanna leaned forward and rapped on the glass partition, attracting the pilot's attention. "Not just yet," she told him, raising her voice so it would carry. "Take us around the park a couple more times."

He gave a nod and turned the flight yoke, pivoting the aircraft away. Tasha mumbled in her sleep as the motion shifted her against the window, but she didn't wake.

Troi sat back in her seat and brought the comm padd close to her face, the smile still playing around her lips. "So where do I start?"

Iota Nadir's binary stars burned cold and distant in the darkness, casting the rust-hued planet below with desultory radiance. IN-748 was a junkyard world, nestled in a ring of space wreckage and accreted debris, the legacy of a gravitational anomaly that had once made the world the endpoint for unlucky craft caught in its grasp. The anomaly had faded centuries ago, but the planet's sad birthright as a grave for dead ships lived on. It was one vast scrapheap, the near-lifeless desert dotted with the hulks of broken vessels, the aged metal skeletons buried in the razor-sharp sands.

The *Snipe* approached slowly and carefully, crawling at low impulse velocity through the layers of gravimetric shear that still laced the surrounding space. On the bridge, Lieutenant Ixxen and the Bynar One-One kept a watch over the planetoid, while on the lower decks the rest of the Active Four team had assembled in the makeshift operations room.

Despite his misgivings about the greater mission at hand, Nog was still pleased to see that his laborious engineering detective work had been instrumental in tracking the targets to their bolt hole. There was a part of him that had feared Lieutenant Colonel Kincade might be right, that if he had made one small miscalculation in his scans, one assumption too many, the whole endeavor would be a waste of time. *A wild-goose chase,* he thought, recalling a human aphorism Jake Sisko sometimes used. Nog had never actually encountered a goose, but Jake had made them sound formidable and cantankerous.

He dismissed the train of thought as Kincade used her hands to widen a holographic pane hanging over what had been the mess-hall table. "I won't lie, I had my doubts about this, but it looks like we've hit pay dirt." She threw Nog the sketch of a salute. "Good job putting this together for us, Lieutenant Commander."

Khob didn't seem as eager to thank him, however. "We go from an ice cube to a trash heap, and you thank the Ferengi? What guarantee do we have that this is where the targets went to ground?"

Tuvok pointed at a ray trace on one of the other displays. "Sensors have located the remains of an ion trail terminating here. A spacecraft made planetfall on IN-748 within the last four days."

"That proves nothing," snorted Ashur. "They could be smugglers down there, void pirates, anything. . . ."

Tom Riker was lounging up against a stanchion, and at the Zeon's words he shot him a hard stare. "Suddenly you're reluctant to get your hands dirty?"

"I agree with the Ferengi," said Sahde, peering at the image of the windswept surface. "This is a good location for a hiding place. Off the main space lanes, the surface cluttered with metallics that disrupt sensor scans from long range . . ."

"And don't forget heavy atmospheric distortion," added Nog. "There's enough energetic storms in the upper atmosphere to prevent any attempts to beam down."

Ashur grimaced. "So we have to land the *Snipe,* then? And risk crashing in a tempest? Unless you have another way to get us on the surface?" He fixed Kincade with a challenging look.

"I was thinking I'd bundle you into a cargo pod and then just drop it," she deadpanned.

"Mock all you want," Ashur shot back, "but we saw what happens when these people know someone is coming for them. I don't want to end up cut apart like those Klingon fools before us." He shook his head. "Tzenkethi ingenuity with autonomous weapons borders on the spiteful."

Nog and Tuvok exchanged a look but said nothing.

Kincade went to the equipment racks and removed a hexagonal device on an armband. "We've got another way down. It's not without hazards, but it gives us a fighting chance to approach the targets without them knowing about it." She tossed the device to Zero-Zero, who examined it closely.

"Inverter," declared the Bynar. "Common designation: folded-space transport module."

Nog took the unit and turned it over in his hands.

"Exposure to folded-space domains is toxic to carbon-based life-forms," he said.

"In large amounts," Kincade corrected. "But we're only going to use it to get us there and back. You said it yourself: Standard matter transporters won't be able to cut through the ionization effects of IN-748's atmosphere, but these will get us there."

"At the price of a high radiation dose," added Tom. He glanced at Ashur. "You weren't thinking about procreating one day, were you?"

Kincade snatched the inverter from Nog's hand. "Khob will make sure everyone has a full dose of hyronalin to counteract any ill effects." She looked around the room, taking them all in. "Ixxen and the Bynars will stay here. The rest of you, get your gear and assemble in the main cargo bay. Orders remain the same. Find all targets. Isolate and secure them."

Tuvok watched the woman intently. "And if there are complications?"

"If in doubt," Kincade said firmly, "shoot to kill."

The transition felt like being dipped in fire.

The actual duration was less than two point six three seconds, but Tuvok's nerves registered the pain and conspired to create the illusion of a burning eternity trapped in the nonexistence of the transport. White flame enveloped him, searing through the stealth suit he was wearing as if it were made of Tholian silk, but he swallowed the agony. He recalled his training, sent his conscious mind somewhere far away from the interval. The Vulcan made the pain a distant, ghostly thing as the interior of the *Snipe* was smothered by the glow of dislocation.

Then he felt the pull of a different gravity on his

limbs, and the scorching light faded, releasing him into a hissing storm of red dust particles.

Tuvok staggered a step and shrugged off the last flashes of the folded-space transporter effect. The agony retreated as if it had never been there, and the memory of the moment melted away. He took a breath inside the mask clamped over his mouth and nose, hearing the faint click and hiss of the filter module. Stale, oxide-heavy air entered his mouth, boosted by the atmosphere processor pack on his belt; but even that wasn't enough to sift out the dead-metal taste of the junkyard planet.

Other white flashes—slow fades of light and energy—came into being around him as one by one the rest of the ground team arrived on IN-748's surface. Some of them cursed, others flinched as if they had been struck. The inverter devices had performed exactly as Kincade promised, but she had deliberately understated the level of discomfort their functions inflicted on the user.

The colonel herself shot Tuvok a look that he could not read; only her eyes were visible behind the holographic monocle she wore, the rest of her face hidden behind a similar breather mask and the hood of her combat gear.

He looked away, taking in the area around them. Low, fast-moving clouds of dirty brown dust scudded past overhead, borne in wailing winds, the haze reducing visibility to less than a few hundred meters. All around there were rusting piles of ancient wreckage, much of it so corroded and broken that it was nearly impossible to guess what function each piece might have served when new. The discarded trash and broken spoils of a dozen different civilizations littered the planetoid's surface, much of it half-buried in the gritty sands beneath their boots. Scavenged hulls from old starships lay in severed chunks along the edge of what might once have been a shallow arroyo. Engine pylons, their exterior coatings wind-smoothed back to bare metal, and hull support frames covered in dust curved up toward the dead sky. The shape of them recalled the rib cage of some great dead animal, its flesh long since decayed away. In other places, jagged-edged chunks of fuselage had been ripped open, revealing the layers of decks inside now open to the elements. High up in the clouds, a distant storm cell released a flash of actinic lightning that briefly illuminated the serrated landscape. Tuvok glimpsed movement farther down the line of the gorge, but it was too brief for him to be certain of its origin.

Kincade unlimbered the long, spindly form of a modified TR-116 projectile rifle from her shoulder and checked the weapon's telescopic sighting array. "Okay. If we've all shaken that off, let's proceed."

"When the time comes, I think I'll walk back," said Tom.

She ignored his comment and gestured to a rickety tower of scrap-metal sections. "I'm going to take a position up there. I can maintain overwatch across most of the valley. We know the targets are nearby, probably inside one of the larger structures to the north." She pointed to Sahde. "You take Ashur and Khob, move around to the west, and find the shuttle. It's imperative you disable that craft so they can't make a run for it."

The Elloran's head bobbed, and she patted a bandolier of thermal charges over her chest. "I can burn out the impulse manifolds; they'll never be able to get off the ground."

Kincade looked back to Tuvok. "You go with Tom and Nog—head for the main structure. When the charges detonate, move in and take down all targets of opportunity. All of you, keep communications to a minimum. We're so close now, we don't want to risk spooking them." She shouldered the rifle again and set about her climb. "Move out," she commanded.

The team split apart, and Tuvok felt the stocky Zeon jab him in the chest before he departed. "Vulcan," he grated. "Leave some for me, eh?"

He chose not to grace the pale mercenary's demand with a reply, and instead he slipped out from cover, dropping into a crouch.

Nog and Tom moved with him, both of them picking their way carefully through the debris field. Each member of the assault team carried a compression phaser rifle; Tuvok's was keyed to a heavy stun setting, as was Nog's, but he had his doubts about the rest of the group. Considering the capture orders they had been given by Galif jav Velk, Colonel Kincade seemed quite unconcerned by the possibility of a lethal engagement. As for Thomas Riker, Tuvok was unable to get a firm read on the man's character; the ex–Starfleet officer seemed to value his former oaths of service, but to what degree the Vulcan could not be certain.

Gusts of wind blew rattling drifts of heavy sand and metallic residue through the debris, and the three of them used the haze left behind to conceal their approach. Slow and steady, they picked their path toward a large, almost intact section of ship hull. The going was difficult. In some places, discarded piles of wreckage blocked potential approaches, and in others, the rocky ground was cracked and broken, forming treacherous fissures that fell away into darkness.

Tuvok paused in the lee of a gutted ground rover chassis and checked the way ahead, activating a passive sensor overlay built into his monocle.

Nog drew his tricorder and took a scan. "I'm not picking up any mines or traps like last time. That's good, isn't it?"

Tom gave a shrug. "Let's hope that means they used up all they had on that ice moon, and not that they've just gotten better at hiding them."

"No life-sign readings, though," added the Ferengi. "At least, nothing that makes any sense with all this interference."

Tuvok's monocle fared better. Motion trackers showed gauzy outlines off in the dust, humanoid figures moving back and forth in what appeared to be a patrol pattern. He watched them for a while, mapping their movements in his mind's eye. "Two subjects," he said, turning back to face the others. "Armed with disruptor rifles. They appear to be guarding the entrance to the main structure."

"I think it might be part of an Orion vessel," offered the human. "See there? That nearside section looks like it could be the bow."

Nog gave a nod. "It's the wreck of an old blockade runner, *Wanderer*-class. Aft sections are missing, though. . . . Probably cut off to salvage the warp engines before it was dumped here."

Tuvok was about to offer an opinion, but before he could speak, his ears caught the clatter of metal on metal.

It could have been anything: the hard wind dislodging some fragment of steel or one of the armored, crab-like arthropods native to the planet scuttling for cover. Tuvok instinctively knew that it was something more. He spun as his monocle registered the shape of a *third* sentry cresting the pile of wreckage before him.

Just as time had seemed to slow during the painful transport down to the surface, now this moment elongated as the sentry jerked in shock at the sight of the three invaders hiding in cover. Tuvok saw no expression, just the pitted bronze surface of a sealed environment helmet and the jade-colored band of a viewer slit, but the sense of surprise radiated off the sentry like heat. The Vulcan grabbed for his slung rifle even as he knew he would be too slow; the sentry already had a disruptor up and aimed. A wide-angle discharge would strike down Tuvok, Nog, and Tom Riker with a single squeeze of the trigger.

The blast never came. Tuvok had the momentary impression of a glowing spot on the sentry's chest; then the Vulcan's ears, sensitive enough to perceive the sound of the approaching danger, caught a subsonic buzz as something impossibly fast whined over his shoulder and hit the guard in the chest. The sentry fell backward as if struck down by an invisible hammer-blow, and Tuvok saw the suited form tumble silently into one of the bottomless crevices in the red rock.

"What was that?" gasped Nog, choking back his surprise.

"Guardian angel," said Tom, pointing back in the direction they had come.

Tuvok's gaze found the tower of scrap metal where Kincade had secreted herself and picked out the prone shape of the woman aiming down her sniper rifle toward him. The dot of light from the TR-116's designator bobbed twice.

"Could there be more out there we can't see?" asked the Ferengi.

"Look sharp," Tuvok told him. He noted the time on his mission chronometer. "Wait for—"

Off to the west there was a flash of amber, low and close to the ground. A fraction of a second later, the sound of phaser fire echoed across the arroyo.

"Who the hell is firing?" Tom pulled his rifle to him.

Disruptors sang back in reply, and then a muffled crash of detonation signaled the explosion of a thermal charge. Black smoke billowed up over the rise from where the shuttle was parked.

"We've got to move now," said Nog. "If we lose the element of surprise—"

"Tuvok." He turned as Tom Riker rose to his feet. "Those sentries by the structure . . . I'll break cover and draw them off."

It was not a good plan, but it was the best option at that moment. "Agreed. Regroup with Sahde's team if possible, then bring them here."

Tom nodded and vaulted the burned-out shell of the rover with a grunt of effort. He hit the ground running and shot off a pair of blasts in the direction of the other sentries. The masked figures reacted as Tuvok expected, both of them breaking away to chase down this new target.

"Quickly," he told Nog, scrambling across the crevice mouth and over open ground toward the bow of the wrecked blockade runner.

"Someone is moving inside," called the Ferengi as they got closer. "One target, maybe two."

Tuvok caught the sound of desperate footfalls on

metal rungs and nodded. *Did the targets have more of their number inside the structure?* he wondered. *Other weapons or a means to summon help?* Whatever it was, they could not be allowed to reach their goal.

Tuvok slipped through the entrance passage to the interior of the downed Orion ship. What had once been a functional airlock and boarding corridor was now canted at a shallow angle and carpeted with red sand, open to the elements beyond. Weak biolume lamps hung from the ceiling, shifting in the breeze. They cast jumping shadows that gave the illusion of movement all around them.

Something clanged, steel on steel, on the deck above. Nog pointed with his rifle, using the lamp beneath the barrel to illuminate an area in front of them. "Commander! Over here!"

Tuvok saw a stairwell leading toward the upper levels, and again the echo of movement rang down to them. "They may be moving toward the bridge deck," he said. It would be a sensible place to make a stand, armored from without, perhaps with some internal systems still operable.

"Orion ship design is compartmentalized," said Nog. "We'll have to sweep each cabin individually."

"Proceed with caution." Tuvok brought his rifle to his shoulder and moved up, scanning every corner for signs of traps or targets.

As they reached the uppermost deck of the wreck, gusts of air rumbled through the framework where it was open to the elements. Sections of hull were completely missing here, either torn away by the hard landing the *Wanderer*-class ship had made many years earlier, or since stripped by opportunist junk hunters.

The deck creaked and groaned as Tuvok put his

weight on it. A short corridor ran along the axis of the upper tier from bow to stern, smaller compartments radiating off it at regular intervals.

"We have them trapped," Nog whispered. "That walkway is the only access in or out, unless they want to risk jumping."

"Make no assumptions," warned Tuvok. He gestured toward the first cabin on the right and Nog nodded, moving slowly toward an open doorway. At the same moment, Tuvok paced out his steps toward an identical hatchway on the left. There was still power on this deck, enough to operate the doors, and the Vulcan reached out to tap the control.

Nog vanished into the gloom across the corridor and Tuvok let the hatch before him judder open before he went in the opposite direction.

The grimy room beyond was missing one whole wall, panels and portholes ripped away so now all that remained were jagged talons of hull metal. The wind plucked at them, making the torn shreds of duranium tap out an atonal rhythm on the buckled support framework beneath. Tuvok paused, raising a finger to tap a control on his monocle, sweeping the room with an electromagnetic scan.

A glow burst into life, less than two meters from the doorway. Tuvok spun about, aiming the phaser— but he had already stepped into the ambush.

He fired nonetheless, even as he knew he had no hope of hitting the target before the suited figure was upon him. A streak of orange fire lit up the interior of the cabin, going wide as a humanoid in the same kind of suit as the sentries threw itself wildly at the Vulcan.

Tuvok was proficient in several varieties of hand-to-hand combat, as well as possessing a greater muscle density than many beings of comparable mass, but his opponent was smaller and relatively nimble, and the added restrictions of an enclosed space momentarily tipped the balance of the engagement away from the Vulcan. He knew instinctively that if he could get a hand upon his attacker, the fight would end very quickly and in Tuvok's favor. His opponent clearly knew that, too, and had come prepared.

A long rod, wielded like a stabbing short sword, jammed into Tuvok's ribs. Where it made contact with his torso, a brutal constellation of pain exploded through his nerves. A powerful electro-shock pulse cut into him and his muscles disobeyed. The phaser rifle tumbled from his grip, his hands spasming. Tuvok's legs gave out from underneath him, and he crashed forward onto his knees, barely able to stay upright.

Striking blindly, Tuvok lashed out with a clumsy blow, swinging his arm back and up in hopes of driving off his assailant. By sheer chance, his hand connected with the edge of his attacker's helmet, cracking the mask with a spitting hiss of breathing gas.

For daring to fight back, Tuvok was rewarded with a second, longer jab from the shock-rod, and this was enough to drive him the rest of the way to the deck. He rolled away from the agonizing pain. The burn of the transport had been insignificant in comparison. Panting, his breath coming in stuttering gasps, Tuvok blinked his vision clear as his tormentor kicked away his rifle and discarded the damaged helmet, letting it drop to the floor with a clang.

Behind the blank visor were not the smoothed, almost polished features of a Tzenkethi, nor the yellow-green, glowing skin common to that race. Instead, a white-haired visage of granite gray glared back at the

Vulcan, a lined and aged face of ropy muscles about deep-set and angry eyes. A Cardassian scowled at him with open, reptilian hatred.

The pain made it impossible for Tuvok to resist as the male reached down and hauled him up to a sitting position. The Cardassian held the shock-rod up, and the Vulcan knew that the next blow would be enough to stop his heart.

"Stop!" Tuvok saw the blurry shape of Lieutenant Commander Nog emerging through the open hatchway, rifle trained on his target. "Drop the weapon now or . . ." The Ferengi's shouted words died in his throat as he caught sight of the Cardassian's face, and his eyes widened. "*You* . . . I know you!"

The moment of hesitation was enough, and Tuvok's attacker used it to drag him into a chokehold. "Put down the weapon!" spat the Cardassian, using the Vulcan as a shield. "Do it now or he dies!"

Nog's face fell and slowly he released the rifle, tossing it into the shadows. "All right. But you have to know, you can't escape. There are . . . five squads out there. Your shuttle is destroyed. You must surrender!"

The wind brought the hiss and snap of gunfire from below. "That will not happen," growled the Cardassian.

Nog moved slowly, still keeping his hands raised, forcing the Cardassian to keep him in sight as he stalled for time. Tuvok understood what he was doing and worked to regulate his breathing, to gather back some measure of his strength. With each second that passed, he had more chance of regaining the upper hand— and now he had seen the face of the targets Active Four was chasing; more than anything he wanted to know the truth behind the assassination of President Bacco.

The Ferengi's thoughts were moving along the same path. "You were there, on Deep Space Nine, as part of the Cardassian delegation. I saw your face. When Castellan Garan had to go back to Cardassia Prime, you stayed behind with Lustrate Vorat. . . ."

"Did *he* send you?" growled the Cardassian, ignoring Nog's words.

"Who? Vorat?"

The Cardassian snorted with annoyance. "Fools. You do not have the slightest inkling of what is going on!"

Tuvok blinked as something hazed his vision momentarily. At first he thought it was an artifact of the ebbing pain, but then he realized it was a dot of projected laser light, invisible to the naked eye but revealed to him through the lens of his sensor monocle. The emerald-hued dot wandered slowly up over Tuvok's chest, wavering as it moved to seek a place directly in the center of the spoon-like crest in the middle of the Cardassian's forehead.

From here, he couldn't see Kincade in her sniper's hide, but she could clearly see him and his assailant through the hole in the starship's hull. If he did nothing, Tuvok knew that in the next second the Cardassian's skull would be cored by a tungsten-tipped bullet, and whatever questions that could have been asked would go unanswered.

He reacted immediately, twisting in the Cardassian's grip and bringing up his arms. With one hand he grabbed the tip of the shock-rod, even as it discharged again, numbing the entire left side of his body. The other found the vital nerve plexus at the nape of the Cardassian's neck, and Tuvok squeezed hard, compressing the pressure point with all the effort he could muster.

The Cardassian stiffened, his eyes rolling back to

show their whites as a groan escaped his lips—and this time it was he who collapsed to the deck, consciousness fading.

Tuvok staggered back a step, moderating his breathing. "Target . . . neutralized," he said, speaking into his mask's comm pickup.

"Roger that." He heard Tom Riker's voice in his ear. *"Sentries are all down. Four fatalities, two . . . make that three live captures outside."* There was a moment's pause before the human spoke again. "Snipe, *are you seeing this? These targets, they're not—"*

"All units stand down." Kincade's voice broke across the channel, and her tone was sharp, brooking no challenge. *"Secure the site and prepare for immediate extraction."*

Nog stood over the insensate Cardassian, studying his face. "Commander, this man's name is Onar Throk. He's no smuggler or terrorist. He is . . . I mean, he *was* an aide to Rakena Garan, the former Castellan of the Cardassian Union." Tuvok heard the surprise in the younger officer's voice as he tried to rationalize what he was seeing. "Sir, what is going on here?"

Tuvok saw no reason to be anything but completely honest. "I do not know," he said, glancing back out of the tear in the wreck's hull and into the windstorm.

"That's not what I'm saying," said Maslan, reaching for a cup of fruit juice.

"Yes it is." Kader made a face at the *Lionheart*'s science officer, absently brushing a stray thread of hair back into the confines of her headscarf. "You're suggesting that Commander Vale's assignment is part of some kind of . . ." She groped for the right word. "*Plot.*"

At her side, Lieutenant Commander Darrah made an amused noise and took a bite from his lunch. The only other person seated at their table in the mess hall was the first officer, and Atia's attention seemed fully and completely on the replicated meatloaf she was eating.

"Okay, fine," Maslan replied. "Maybe I'm overstating it. But you have to concede that it is unusual."

Darrah mimicked the pose of a cleric at benediction. "Starfleet Command, like the Will of the Prophets, moves in mysterious ways."

"Thompson agrees with me," continued Maslan. "He knows someone on McKinley Station. He said there have been a lot of odd comings and goings from the *Titan*." He glanced at Atia. "I mean, okay, after Captain Briggs retired, we all knew this ship would be getting a new CO . . . but suddenly Vale is dropped on us, hours before we're due to set off across the quadrant. And it's just supposed to be a temporary posting, but couldn't that be handled by, you know, one of *us*?"

Atia gave him a sideways look but didn't say anything.

Darrah sighed and put down his fork. "I think it's safe to say we're all somewhat surprised by this turn of events. But we're in the middle of an ongoing crisis here. A major terrorist attack was just successfully perpetrated against the Federation. . . ."

"And now your man is in charge," said Maslan.

The Bajoran eyed him. "Ishan Anjar is certainly not *my man*." He shook his head, returning to the point at hand. "What I mean is, after the assassination, you can't blame Starfleet for being cautious."

"Agreed," said Kader. "But then again, Seth does raise a valid concern. That whole diversion to Jaros II? And now we're going off the route again to some uncharted system? I'd like to know what it all means."

"My point exactly," insisted Maslan, spearing a piece of celery and crunching down on it.

"Captain's prerogative," countered Darrah. "She doesn't have to tell us anything if she doesn't want to."

Kader shrugged. "Not exactly a good command style, though. I mean, if *Lionheart* has been co-opted into some high-security mission, how does keeping the bridge crew in the dark help?"

Darrah glanced at the engineer. "Has it occurred to you, Basoos, that we might be outside the loop because it's *safer* that way?"

"Oh, great," said the woman dryly. "That makes me feel *much* better."

"I don't have anything against Vale," Maslan went on, his lip curling. "But I still don't like it."

"What you like counts little," Atia said at last as she was cutting at her food. "Fall to purpose. Assumptions breed mistakes."

"With respect, Commander," said the science officer. "Any senior officer who deliberately withholds important information from their senior staff has to be up to something. And if we're potentially going in harm's way, with a captain who we don't know and can't anticipate, that's a recipe for disaster. I'll do my duty; we all will. But as Hayn said, the situation is serious right now, and . . ." Maslan suddenly noticed that everyone else at his table had gone very quiet. "And she's standing right behind me, isn't she?"

"Is this seat taken?" asked Vale, dropping down next to the first officer, depositing her lunch tray before her. She looked around at all of them, with a fixed smile. "So. What's good?"

"Try the *hasperat*," said Darrah, pointing with his fork. "It's tasty."

"Um. Captain Vale." Maslan tried and failed to find the right words. "I, um—" His combadge chirped and the science officer swatted at it, thankful for the interruption. "Maslan!"

"Seth, it's Alex. Got an incoming personal message for you. Thought you'd like to know."

"Great." He stood up quickly. "I'll take that in my quarters. . . ."

"Saved by the bell?" Vale said quietly.

Maslan took a swift exit, and in the awkward silence that followed, Kader and Darrah also made their excuses and stepped away. After a moment, Vale looked up and found Atia watching her.

"Apologies," said the commander. "It is just . . . your predecessor was of more conventional manner."

"I'm sure you'll adjust," Vale replied.

Within a couple of hours, the assault operation on IN-748 was officially concluded, and Active Four was recalled to the *Snipe*. The bodies of the sentries killed in the engagement—the one shot down by Kincade, another ended in hand-to-hand combat with Ashur, and two more lost in a firefight by the shuttle—were in a stasis compartment. The four prisoners, Onar Throk among them, were being held in one of the freighter's other loading bays. What Nog had thought were just cargo container pods were revealed to be portable cells, each big enough for a single humanoid, each sealed off from the others so their targets could not communicate while in their confinement.

Zero-Zero and One-One had transported down to the surface to help the Ferengi pull the computer core from the disabled shuttlecraft while Sahde and Tom scoured the Orion wreck for any materials or equipment used by the targets. Once they had all they could recover, it had been another painful jaunt back via the folded-space transporters to the ship. Now Iota Nadir was just a fading memory, and the *Snipe* was heading back toward the Federation core worlds at warp speed. The mood among the Active Four team was muted and wary.

Khob had insisted on taking Tuvok back to the *Snipe*'s small sickbay to check him over, along with Ashur, who had come off worse for wear in a knife-fight with a Cardassian twice his size.

The Zeon came wandering into the main cargo bay where the rest of the group was assembled, his arm swathed in bandages. He was sweaty and pallid, and with a jaundiced eye he surveyed the piles of gear gathered up from the planet below. "What's the point of all this?" He kicked at a pile of salvaged ration packs. "We found them; mission accomplished. Must we sift through their trash as well?" Ashur found Kincade, who stood nearby examining a tricorder. "We're done. I for one would like my . . . remuneration as promised and to be on my way." He looked for Tom Riker and the Bynars, seeking agreement from the other mercenaries. "Don't you feel the same?"

It was Sahde who finally said what they all were thinking. "I don't think this is over yet, Ashur."

Tuvok entered the compartment, and Nog saw that he was still moving a little stiffly, although the color had returned to his tawny features. "Commander . . ."

The Vulcan nodded. "Mister Nog. Have any of the prisoners spoken?"

Kincade answered first. "Not a word. I suppose that's to be expected."

"Really?" Tom shot her a look. "Because nothing about what we encountered down there was what *I* expected."

"I don't recall any promises made that this mission would be straightforward," she replied, frowning. Nog couldn't tell if it was Tom's challenge or the matter itself that was vexing her.

"Tom Riker's point—"

"Is well made." The two Bynars spoke in a quick-fire chorus. "Assassin suspect was—"

"First thought to be Bajoran."

"That was revealed to be—"

"Falsehood. Tzenkethi suspected instead."

Sahde was nodding. "I thought the Cardassians were supposed to be the allies of the Federation." She glanced at Nog and Tuvok. "Now it seems like they were part of a plot to kill your president?" The Elloran gave an expansive shrug. "Or am I misunderstanding something?"

Nog picked up a Cardassian padd and offered it up. "This contains manifesto documents and propaganda materials for an isolationist group called the True Way. I know them of old, from Bajor. They blame the Federation for all of Cardassia's ills. They're not shy about planting bombs or killing anyone they deem deserving of it."

"Which would make them the perfect cat's-paw for the Tzenkethi," grated Ashur. He spat on the deck. "Must we seek out their paymasters now? I took on this task with a deal to find the killers of the Bacco woman. We've done that."

"Perhaps the Tzenkethi and the Typhon Pact were never part of this conspiracy," said Tuvok, without weight. He let the statement lay for a moment before he continued. "They have claimed their innocence in this matter. They may be truthful."

Sahde gave a bitter laugh. "You've obviously never met a Tzenkethi or a Breen or any one of their Pact collaborators, Tuvok. If you had, you'd know they're nothing more than a clutch of backstabbers and liars." Nog heard the venom in her tone and wondered what might have happened in the Elloran's past to make her have such hatred for the Typhon Pact.

"I don't think the rest of the Federation would be as willing as you are to give them the benefit of the doubt," said Kincade, stepping closer to the Vulcan. "Back on the planet, that one you captured, Throk . . . he had you cold. I could have taken him out, but you blocked my shot. Why?"

"If Throk was now dead, what would we have?" Tuvok replied.

"One less murderer in the galaxy," said Sahde.

Kincade was watching Tuvok carefully. "Justice?"

"That wouldn't be justice," said Nog, the words coming to him almost before he was aware of it. "That would be revenge."

Ashur snorted with derision. "A moral homily from a Ferengi? Your ancestors would be ashamed."

Nog met the other man's gaze. "My ancestors also came up with the Eighty-eighth Rule of Acquisition: 'Vengeance will cost you everything.'"

A double beep sounded, and Kincade frowned, drawing a communicator from her belt. "What is it, Ixxen?"

"A holomessage packet has just come in for you on the hyperchannel," said the Bolian.

"Pipe it down to the holocomm rig in my quarters." She glanced at Tuvok. "I'll be back in a moment.

In the meantime, try to keep the political debate to a minimum, Commander." The woman strode out of the compartment and down the corridor to the crew cabins.

"This Throk . . ." began Tom. "Nog, you said he was on DS9 when Bacco was killed. So are we saying that it was *his* finger on the trigger?"

"That would seem likely," said Tuvok. "But more evidence is required for complete certainty."

"Just so we're clear about this, then . . ." Tom shook his head as he thought it through and then pointed toward the aft. "At the end of that corridor, we currently have the most-wanted being in the Federation as our prisoner."

"How much do you think—"

"He is worth?" The Bynars asked the question to the group, but no one replied.

"What's going to happen when Starfleet rolls out a line of Cardassian faces in front of the Federation Council and the galaxy at large?" Sahde ran a hand over the length of her bone crest. "I think it will be quite ugly, don't you? That fine new treaty with the Union will turn to ashes overnight."

"All the more reason to have killed the lot of them down in that junkyard." Ashur flinched as he moved, pulling on his wound. "Kincade should have listened when I told her to blast it from orbit with a torpedo barrage."

From out of nowhere, Nog heard a shift in the *Snipe*'s engine note and exchanged a look with Tuvok. "Commander . . . I think the ship is altering course." He was certain of it; the freighter's warp drives were accelerating.

Kincade strode back into the compartment. A

flicker of concern on her features vanished as she met their gazes. "All right, all of you, listen up. Now that we've completed the first part of the mission, we're moving to the second phase."

"Second phase?" echoed Ashur. "I don't recall anything about that in your recruitment speech, *Colonel!*"

"As *I* recall, you were more than happy to accept my offer to get you away from the Chalnoth bounty hunters on your tail." She shut him down with a hard stare. "So don't push your luck, Ashur." Kincade drew herself up and scanned the room, taking them in. "Next stage after isolating the targets is to secure them for interrogation. We need to know every aspect of the attack they planned, who they were working for, how they did it, everything. The chief of staff has amended our previous orders. We're not returning to Earth just yet. I've ordered Lieutenant Ixxen to put us on a new heading."

"For what reason?" Tuvok watched her carefully. "What is our destination?"

"Velk's security staff feel the situation on Earth is too sensitive right now. So we're diverting to a secondary deployment site. Nydak II, a planet in the Archanis Sector."

Nog's eyes widened. "The Nydak system is over the border. In Klingon space."

"That won't be an issue," said Kincade. "*Snipe* and Active Four are to remain on operational standby for the time being."

"For how long?" demanded Ashur.

"Until we get what we need," replied the colonel.

Ten

He felt uncomfortable sitting in the chair at the head of the briefing-room table, and Riker let that energy propel him to his feet. "I need options," he told the others, crossing to the windows. On the other side of the transparent aluminum, the iron-colored arms of McKinley Station reached down over the *Titan*'s hull, holding it in place over the turning globe of Earth beneath.

There was a reluctance in the air that he found disquieting. As captain, Riker had always allowed himself to be open to any suggestion from any one of his officers. He fostered that to better make use of his crew's skills, but here and now it seemed that no one wanted to be the first to take the next step down the path opening up before them.

He saw them behind him, reflected in the ports, each of them sharing glances, weighing their thoughts but still keeping their own counsel. Ranul Keru wore an expression of grim determination while Melora Pazlar remained deeply troubled. At the far end of the table, Torvig's hands knit over a padd, his head bowed and his large eyes averted. Riker had ordered Y'lira Modan to remain with and monitor the holographic "Messenger" down in the laboratory compartment, and now he wondered if she would have been any more ready to speak up, had the Selenean been here.

In that silence, Riker again felt the weight of the burden he was carrying, the same burden he had passed to everyone else brought into his circle of trust. The pressure had not lessened in the act—if anything, Riker knew it more keenly now. Each person he called upon to help him was one more measure on the scale, one more career he was risking above and beyond his own. He thought about the *Titan*'s officers, beings like his chief engineer Xin Ra-Havreii or the ship's senior medical officer Shenti Yisec Eres Ree. . . . After all the trials and challenges they had faced as crewmates in the past few years, it was not an exaggeration to say Riker trusted them implicitly and that he valued their advice beyond all others'. But did he have the right to drag even more of his colleagues into this conspiracy?

Part of him wondered if it was fear. *Am I afraid that they would talk me out of this course of action?* No. It wasn't that at all. . . . *If I ask of Ree or Xin or any of the others, I know they'll offer their help. But can I really put more of my people at risk?*

Riker's true fear was of what would come if he ultimately failed in this. His career in Starfleet would be extinguished like a snuffed candle, perhaps those of Deanna and Christine as well. His first, best destiny taken from him, and criminal charges laid at his feet.

It wouldn't just be his head on the block; his wife and executive officer would suffer, and he would drag the others down with him, taint the name of *Titan* and her crew for decades to come. They would speak of him in the same sentence as men like Erik Pressman, Robert Leyton, and Lance Cartwright, and his officers would pay a high price. Riker shook his head slightly.

No. For now, we keep the circle close. And if the worst comes, I'll take the full onus upon myself.

At last, Keru cleared his throat. "Admiral, at this point we have to consider the most expedient alternative. Remember, that program down there is just a copy of an intercepted signal. We caught it on its way somewhere else, and whomever it was actually sent to has probably conversed with the original by now. Whatever data the Messenger has is losing value with every passing moment we sit here and discuss it."

"I'm aware of that, Lieutenant Commander," said Riker. "What do you propose we do about it?"

"Back in the lab, I said that we've accidentally got ourselves a prisoner. I suggest we treat it as such, sir. We conduct an interrogation."

"The Messenger will not respond as an organic life-form would," said Torvig. "You could no more cross-examine it than you could question a replicator."

"By their very nature, holoprograms have a baseline degree of sentience," Melora broke in. "Something that has been a debated issue for several years now. Are we actually suggesting we use forcible coercion against an intelligent construct?"

"We don't know how smart it is," Keru replied. "And I'm not talking about torture, Melora."

"Really?" The Elaysian turned her hard gaze on the Trill. "Because I think you *are*, Ranul. Torvig is right when he says that simply questioning the Messenger won't work. It's not going to slip up and accidentally admit something like a person might; it won't respond to threats or to rewards. So that means the only way to get to what it knows is through invasive means."

"That could be attempted," said Torvig, and Riker saw his ears fold back against his head, reflecting his bleak tone. "We could aggressively decompile the program. Break it apart, effectively. There is a strong chance a lot of core data would be lost, however, even under the best of circumstances. I believe the Messenger would attempt to self-delete before we could complete a full brute-force decryption."

"Are you sure?" asked Keru. "It hesitated when it spoke about deletion. I think it must be programmed with some kind of self-preservation instinct. We could use that against it."

"Am I the only one who has a problem with this?" Melora's eyes narrowed. "Just for a second, Ranul, pretend you're talking about an organic being instead of a holographic construct. Now think about what you're suggesting. It's not only a violation of the law, but of ethical conduct."

"It's a hard choice," admitted the Trill. "But if there's misuse of power taking place at the heart of the Federation, then we have a duty to expose it. We have to find out if that's the case or if this is all a misjudgment. . . . We can't ignore the possibility. And to do all that may require us to agree to things we might not be comfortable with, to cross a line—"

"To cross *another* line," Riker broke in, the words coming up from nowhere. He shook his head, and suddenly he felt tired. "If I look over my shoulder, what am I going to see? One compromise after another. Orders disobeyed. Secrets kept. Choices made." He turned away from the port to look at his friends and colleagues, wishing that Deanna was there to offer him some kind of solace. "I don't like where this is leading me . . . where this is leading *us*."

Torvig blinked. "Admiral, I think I may have a proposition. But it is quite . . . radical."

Riker spread his hands. "What have you got, Lieutenant?"

The Choblik's tail wavered in the air behind him. "At the moment, we believe the Messenger encodes data confirming illegal acts originating inside the Federation Council. Acts that we, as sentient reasoning beings, see as immoral and unethical. But to reach that data, we too are faced with the prospect of committing what may also be a similarly troublesome action. Unlike us, the Messenger has no stake in the content of the data it is withholding. It does not understand the ramifications of that data. For want of a better term, it simply does not care. It does not have that capacity."

Keru was nodding. "Because it's just a medium for transmission of information. A padd doesn't care what's written on it, no matter if it's a love sonnet or a hate speech."

"What if it *could* make that distinction?" said Torvig.

"You want to . . . convince it to open up to us?" Melora's crested brows came together. "Persuade it to see our point of view?"

"That's not possible," said Keru. "Modan said the Messenger is intelligent, but we know it's not intelligent enough to make those kinds of distinctions."

"Suppose we allow it to be so?" Riker watched as Torvig warmed to his subject. "We uplift the Messenger to a higher level of self-awareness! We give it the intelligence to understand the ramifications of what it is carrying!"

"You're suggesting we give it the right to choose," said Riker, thinking it through. "Lieutenant, I don't have to remind you what happened on this ship the *last* time a semi-sentient system gained awareness."

"This won't be like the Avatar," insisted the engineer. "What I propose is merging the Messenger program with an existing, stand-alone artificial intelligence matrix. An inert AI system we already have on board *Titan*." Torvig pushed his datapad across the table toward the admiral, and Riker gathered it up.

On the padd's small screen was a wire-frame graphic of a spider-like mechanoid: the inanimate droneframe "body" of the alien Sentry construct known as Second-Gen White-Blue.

The wind was bitter and laced with tiny particles of snowfall, but Natasha didn't seem to mind it. Deanna Troi followed her daughter through the cobbled streets from the flyer park overlooking the blue waters of the Tromsøysundet Strait. She had been concerned that the four-year-old might have reacted poorly to the chilly, sub-arctic air, but Tasha was already apple-cheeked and thrilled by the presence of the snow and ice.

They crossed into the heart of the city of Tromsø, one of Norway's northernmost urban centers, skirting the shopping district and the historic edifice of the Arctic Cathedral. Troi bought hot, sweet tea for them from a vendor and they eventually found themselves at the Grimsdottir Rink, originally built for Earth's winter Olympics in the late 2200s.

Tromsø was a popular destination for off-worlders from planets with a colder climate than the Terran standard, and while there was something to be said for the bracing chill in the air, Troi preferred the warmer climes of the Mediterranean, which reminded her of her childhood on Betazed. She laughed with Tasha as the girl toyed with a snowball, wondering if her daughter's dismissal of the cold came from her father's side; Will had, after all, grown up in the wilds of Alaska.

The Grimsdottir Rink was large, but it was hardly full, and one had only to look carefully to see why. A discreet presence of local law officers were posted in the immediate area, in a loose, unthreatening cordon, and within that ring were tall, watchful men in clothing that seemed far too light for the wintry day. Their tunics were nothing like the bulk of the cold-weather parkas worn by Deanna and Tasha; beneath snow hoods, faces of cobalt blue looked out across the milling crowds of tourists and shoppers, purposeful and steady. Antennae curved low over their foreheads, their additional senses carefully deployed to protect their principals.

Human or not, Troi knew military when she saw them. These men were members of the Andorian Imperial Guard, the patterns of their emotions as hard-edged as the hawkish way they scanned the crowds. They were protecting a smaller group of their own kind, a clan-family unit of two mothers and two fathers—a *zhen, shen, chan,* and *thaan,* the four Andorian genders required to give life to a child. The bond quartet were enjoying themselves, but she could sense that not all of them were being fully honest with their laughter. Her empathic awareness brushed the surface of a mind familiar to her from days earlier on Luna, and she found herself looking into the eyes of Ramasanar ch'Nuillen. He recognized her, and his emotions went dark, a curtain of self-control falling across them.

Tasha didn't pick up on the interchange; she was already insisting on donning training skates to take to the ice, and Troi allowed it. She followed her daughter, making gentle turns, watching as Tasha focused all her intent on staying upright.

One of the guardians whispered closer on bright shining blades. "I know you," he said. The man was young, and his face was a darker blue.

"Sholun, isn't it?" she asked. "We met at the memorial ceremony. You're one of the envoy's aides."

He rebuffed her attempt at a polite introduction. "Why are you here?" he demanded. "What do you want?"

"This is a public place," Deanna countered mildly. "And I think my daughter likes the idea of being a figure skater."

"Find somewhere else to indulge her," he grated, and a wave of menace came off him like a black cloud. Tasha reacted to it as well, coming to a halt on the ice, her smile vanishing.

He was going to say more, but then two more figures approached across the rink, and Sholun fell silent. Ch'Nuillen moved effortlessly, gliding over the ice with a female Andorian at his side. The envoy shot Sholun a warning glance. "You're frightening the child," he admonished. "Move away."

Ch'Nuillen's companion—a pale *shen* of sky-blue complexion and similar age to her bondmate—dropped to her haunches to look Tasha in the eye. "Hello!" By contrast to the envoy, she radiated warmth and good humor, enough that Deanna felt almost compelled to return her smile. "My name is Savaaroa—what's yours?"

"This is Natasha," said Troi as her daughter became shy and clustered close to her mother's legs. "Tasha, say hello."

The little girl allowed her grin to come back, and

she waved at the elder Andorian woman, performing a deft curtsy for good measure.

"So polite," said Savaaroa. "And a natural on the ice, it would seem. Many people would have fallen over doing that." She glanced at the envoy, and Troi saw them share a moment of silent communication, the kind of unspoken exchange that was common to spouses in every bonded species. "I think, if your mother would allow it, I could teach you how to skate a chasse. Would you like that, Tasha?"

"Please." She gave her mother a questioning look, and Troi granted permission with a nod. With a scrape of blades on ice, Tasha slid away after Savaaroa, determined to match the Andorian woman's elegant motion.

"Sh'Nuillen has such grace," Troi noted.

The envoy ignored the compliment, eyeing her coldly. "It was a clever tactic, bringing the child with you."

Troi felt the press of ch'Nuillen's veiled accusation, and her lips thinned. "There are no *tactics* here, sir. I brought my daughter here because she has never seen real snow before."

After a moment, the Andorian's bitter mien softened. "Forgive me, Commander Troi. In my line of work it is sometimes a hazard that one tends to think the worst of people in all things. Encountered enough times, you assume it will always be the truth and behave accordingly." He watched Savaaroa, who was now introducing Tasha to the other members of her bond-group; Troi noted that the *zhen* and *thaan* were noticeably younger. "She loves children. We have been trying for one of our own for some time now, but our *shelthreth* has not borne fruit." His face clouded. "We hope that may soon change, given recent events. When my duties are over and we return to the homeworld . . ." Ch'Nuillen halted himself and began again. "I envy you, Commander. You are blessed by the Infinite."

"I am," Troi admitted, and the words almost caught in her throat as she experienced a tiny flash of deep sorrow that escaped from the diplomat's guarded thoughts.

He studied her, as if for the first time. "Sholun's question stands. Why are you here? And please don't pretend that you just came here for the ice-skating."

"It's widely known that Tromsø is where Andoria kept her embassy on Earth. Your government still has holdings here, and I assumed this would be where you would stay while on-planet."

He nodded, looking up. "Yes. Norway reminds us of our homeworld, and the locals are very welcoming. And if we are to soon return to the unity of the Federation, it seems right we renew our association with the city." He paused. "What was it you said to me when we met before? 'Andor has more friends than you may realize.' Is that why you appear here now, unannounced and out of uniform? To become our friend? I confess that in recent days, the sight of a Starfleet officer has become reason to be on one's guard rather than cause for salutation."

"You're wary of my motives," she replied. "It doesn't take a Betazoid to see that. And you have every right to be. So let me be open with you. I'm not here because Togren or anyone else in the diplomatic corps sent me. I'm here because I want your help."

The Andorian gave a sharp, bitter bark of amusement. "Indeed? And you believe I would freely give it? You think the sight of your child would somehow make me take leave of my senses and open up to a stranger?"

His barriers were rising again, and Troi frowned. "You misunderstand me, sir. I know Andorians; I know that honor, loyalty, and obligation are at the core of your people. I know that the clan is Andoria, and—"

"Andoria is the clan," he said, completing the rote sentiment.

"My father was a Terran, my mother Betazoid. Both of them came from places where family is at the core of their being. They taught me the value of obligation, too."

"You speak as if you bring me a debt I am to pay." Ch'Nuillen became frosty once more.

"Not to me," she said, "and not a debt, just the offer of a chance to help a man who risked all he had to assist your people."

"*Bashir?*" The envoy's voice fell to a whisper.

Troi nodded.

The Andorian looked away, and she followed his gaze toward the middle of the rink, where Tasha was making a slow, steady turn as Savaaroa offered encouragement.

"Tell me what you require," he said, after a moment.

Four days after leaving the Iota Nadir system, the *Snipe* dropped out of warp along the plane of Nydak II's ecliptic and made a purposeful approach toward the mottled, gray-brown sphere.

Tuvok had ensured that he would be on the freighter's bridge when the *Snipe* arrived, to satisfy his interest and, he hoped, gain some kind of insight into what they would find here.

Kincade barely glanced at him as he entered the cramped command deck at the top of the ship's conning tower. Aside from a couple of humans from the civilian crew and the ever-chattering figures of the Bynar pair, Kincade, Tuvok, and Ixxen were the only others present to watch Nydak II loom large through the oval viewport that dominated the bridge.

The Vulcan stepped up to the helm, a raised island at the rear of the compartment. Ixxen sat surrounded by a horseshoe-shaped console, and the Bolian's hands danced lightly over the controls, feathering the impulse engines. She gave him a sideways nod. "Sir."

"Lieutenant." He spoke quietly, keeping the conversation between them. "Have we been hailed?"

"Negative." She paused to absently brush a hand over her hairless cerulean scalp. "Not a word, not even a challenge when we crossed the border a day ago." Ixxen licked her lips and then tapped a control, bringing up a sensor return on a tertiary screen at her side. "But they're out there, Commander. Look at this."

The screen displayed a real-time projection of the *Snipe*'s ionic wake, and Tuvok immediately spotted a minute perturbation in the particle stream. "Curious. A displacement effect," he noted. "A cloaked vessel."

"It's been on us since we entered Klingon space, and frankly, sir, it's making me nervous." She flushed a darker blue.

He raised an eyebrow. "Do not fear, Lieutenant. If they wished our destruction, we would not be having this discussion."

"Maybe," Ixxen replied, without conviction, "but I remember something my first captain used to say. The only thing more dangerous than the Klingon coming at you in the open, all shouts and swagger, is the

Klingon who sits back in the shadows and doesn't say a word."

"An astute observation," Tuvok allowed. He looked out toward the planet. "What do you know of our destination?"

"Not much," she said. "Database is pretty thin on it. The Nydak system is a backwater; all the planets are listed as unsuitable for colonization efforts, even for a species as hardheaded as the Klingons. The star chart shows Nydak II as a mining colony, and it did have some dilithium deposits, but Starfleet records suggest that those were played out back in the 2270s."

"An empty mine," Tuvok wondered aloud. "Why bring us here?" He indicated the planet. "Run a passive scan on the colony."

Kincade saw what he was doing, but she said nothing, watching intently.

Ixxen peered into the hood of a sensor viewer. "Scanning . . . Difficult to be certain—there's a lot of mineral pollutants in the atmosphere fogging the scope. I read a complex on the northern continent . . . small but indeterminate number of humanoid life signs . . ."

An alert tone sounded from one of the other panels, and Kincade strode across to it. "Ixxen, do you see that? I'm reading a neutrino burst, off the starboard bow."

"Confirmed," said the Bolian, her jaw set. "And another now, to the stern. It's a decloaking signature."

"Shall we—"

"Go to alert?" The Bynars stiffened, ready to deploy the ship's hidden batteries of weapons, but Kincade shook her head.

"Hold off on that." She turned back to her monitor. "Show me what we have."

"A pair of K-22's, *B'rel*-class Birds of Prey. Enough to give us serious cause for concern." Ixxen's eyes narrowed. "That's odd. . . ."

"What is it, Lieutenant?" asked Tuvok.

"Sir, neither ship appears to display any markings or insignia consistent with Klingon Defense Force or known House fleets. They're coming to flank positions, no aggressive posture as yet."

"The *Snipe* is—"

"Being hailed."

Kincade folded her arms and faced the portal. "Answer them." The forward port misted and became a display screen. Through it, Tuvok saw into the darkened, rust-colored space of a warship's bridge. A lone Klingon officer rose from his throne-like command chair and eyed them through the two-way link. He was barely keeping a sneer from his lips, and the Vulcan noted what seemed to be the signs of recent injury; there was evident bruising and discoloration around his nasal ridges and cheekbones, as if his nose had recently been broken.

Tuvok paid no mind to this; it was his understanding that Klingon officers regularly engaged in violent sparring to first—and on some occasions, *last*—blood. But what did immediately strike him were smaller details that might have been missed by a less-observant viewer. The officer wore the echelon tabs consistent with a ranked military adjutant, but where the steely baldric across his chest should have sported the sigil of his family, there was only a blank space.

"Welcome," said the Klingon without a hint of cordiality. *"You are expected."*

"Well met," Tuvok replied, speaking before Kincade could say anything. "Forgive me, sir, I mean no disrespect, but your house is unknown to us. I would ask with whom we speak."

"*My name matters little to you, Vulcan,*" he retorted, irritation flaring at the interruption. "*I am of House Zho. That is all you need concern yourself with.*" He made a dismissive gesture. "*Guide your vessel toward the surface, and you will be provided with landing coordinates at the facility.*"

"What facility?" asked Kincade. "The . . . mining colony?"

The officer studied her. "*Yes, the mining colony.*" Sarcasm dripped from every word. "*Such as it was. Now it serves the Empire . . . and her allies . . . in other ways.*" The Klingon paused to glance at a monitor. "*Holding chambers have been prepared, as requested. The general has provided an inquisitor to facilitate intelligence recovery.*"

"A what?" asked Ixxen, blanching at the word.

A slow crawl of understanding rose in Tuvok's mind, suspicions and doubts falling swiftly into place. Ixxen had been correct, Nydak II was no longer a place where the Klingons dug dilithium crystals from the rock; it was a prison, and a secret one at that. Suddenly, the reasons for the unmarked ships and the missing sigil became clear.

He had heard of such places during his time with Starfleet Intelligence, so-called "black sites," facilities operated by external powers, clandestine locations that existed to house prisoners or materials deemed too sensitive or too dangerous to be publicly acknowledged. The Cardassian Union, the Romulan Star Empire, and the Klingons were all known to have a network of such ghost locations either now or in the past, but these covert prisons were banned under the Articles of the United Federation of Planets. Nothing of their kind was tolerated within the borders of the UFP.

But then, Tuvok thought, *we are not within Federation space.*

"Who requested this?" he demanded. "Provide confirmation of our orders."

Kincade shot him a look. "Commander, what are you doing?"

The Klingon adjutant seemed unconcerned by the request. *"The Tellarite. Velk. He came with a call for aid. How could we refuse?"* The sneer came back in all its glory, and he turned to take his seat once more—then paused, as if something had come back to him. *"One other matter. Due to the . . . sensitive nature of this facility, we will require that your vessel deactivate your subspace communications systems and your crew stay within secured areas. Failure to abide by these rules will be met with punishment of the severest nature."*

The signal cut abruptly, and out beyond the *Snipe*'s bow, the two Birds of Prey shimmered and vanished once more beneath the shroud of their cloaking devices.

Zero-Zero chirped. "His answer did not—"

"Make sense," said One-One. "There is no such Klingon clan—"

"Known as House *Zho.*"

"The meaning of that word—"

"Is *empty.* House *Zho*—"

"Does not exist."

Kincade paid no attention to the Bynars and looked to Ixxen. "Atmospheric entry vector," she ordered. "Prep the ship for landing and take us in."

The Bolian hesitated, glancing at Tuvok and then back to the human. "But, Colonel . . ."

Tuvok met Kincade's gaze. "You cannot be unaware of what is going on here," he told her. "The legitimacy of this mission has been dubious from its inception. If we proceed to the surface of Nydak II, we will go beyond the legality of our Starfleet oath and the letter of Federation law."

"We were sent here *by Starfleet*," Kincade countered, her expression hardening. "Under a direct executive order from the office of the president!" She straightened. "Or have you forgotten, Mister Tuvok, that the president is your commander in chief?" This time, Kincade pushed forward, going on before he could frame a reply. "Whatever concerns you or any one of us may have over the methods being employed in this operation, we have achieved success. Now we have to follow our orders through to their conclusion." She shot a cold look at the Bolian. "Lieutenant Ixxen, I gave you a direct command. Land this vessel. *Now.*"

The younger woman took a breath and then nodded, returning to the controls. She didn't meet Tuvok's gaze. The *Snipe* shifted position, and Nydak II's surface grew to fill the viewport.

Kincade fixed him with an unflinching stare. "I heard all about Riker and his crew. Maybe on *Titan* he runs a slack ship and lets his officers question every order that comes down the pipe. That's not how it goes for the rest of us. And I'm not going to be the one who defies the highest command authority in the Federation!"

Tuvok chose his next words with care. "I find it difficult to consent to orders of such morally questionable tone."

"*Questionable?*" Kincade echoed. "Questioned by who? You? Me? We serve at the pleasure of the president, Tuvok. We don't get the right to doubt—we gave that up when we swore that oath. You don't like what we've been ordered to do? Has it occurred to you that there's a good reason for these orders? You're not some midshipman I should have to drum this into, Commander, you're a veteran. You know that sometimes we have to trust in the people above us and get on with our jobs." Her voice dropped. "You want to debate morality? Shall we talk about how much harm you've inflicted on others in your service to Starfleet? How many deaths you were responsible for? You're a tactical officer, you've probably sent more beings to their graves with phasers and photon torpedoes than I have with my rifle. Did you question those orders, too? Did you question Riker, Janeway, Sulu?"

He bristled. "I did when the circumstances required it."

"This is not one of those times," she insisted. "We got this mission because we were the right people for the job. And we're going to see it to the end. If you're not on board with that, then I'll have you confined to quarters. Are we clear?"

Tuvok had no doubt Kincade would carry out the threat if he pressed the matter further. "It would seem so," he said at length.

She turned her back on him. "Then get off my bridge."

Riker approached holodeck two as the final adjustments were being made, with Ssura trailing behind him. He caught sight of a milk-pale face and nodded to the officer with the operations-yellow collar. "Lieutenant Sethe. Are we good to go?"

The Cygnian gave a brisk nod. "Aye, Admiral. As

you requested, we've isolated this holodeck's systems from the rest of the *Titan*. Torvig is inside hooking up a stand-alone power generator, and Chaka is disconnecting the last of the data trains now." He indicated an open panel in the wall, and as Riker watched, a large, multi-legged form eased itself out of the space, like a trapdoor spider emerging from its burrow. Ssura reacted with slight alarm as the being revealed itself, clearly daunted by the sudden appearance.

"Ah." The bulky figure of a Pak'shree arthropod drew herself up, her mouthparts clacking. "Done." Specialist K'chak'!'op—known as Chaka—turned her four dark eyespots on Riker. "This is rather irregular, sir." Her vocoder translated the clicks and snaps of her normal speech into a formal female voice. "May I ask the reason why we've been asked to do this? When I questioned Lieutenant Commander Pazlar, she told me it was not a matter for my concern."

Riker folded his arms and nodded. "That's correct. It's a . . . security issue."

The manipulator-tentacles emerging from Chaka's head twitched. "That's a rather *male* answer, sir," she replied with a faint air of scorn. The frond-like limbs wafted vaguely toward Ssura, who blinked but said nothing.

"It's an *admiral* answer," he told her flatly. "If you're both finished, then return to your posts, and do not discuss what you did here."

The Cygnian and the Pak'shree exchanged looks, but didn't question the statement further. Riker left them to gather their equipment and entered the holodeck with the Caitian lieutenant at his side.

Immediately within the archway entrance, Ranul Keru stood off to one side, watching the compartment like a hawk. Riker noted that he was now carrying a phaser at his hip, but the admiral said nothing. He hoped that what happened in the next few minutes would not require the Trill security chief to draw it.

Before him, Torvig and Melora were working at a series of virtual panes projected into the air. Stretching away toward the far wall of the chamber, stacks of holographically created data matrices were assembling out of nothing, each one resembling a slim tower made of glassy bricks, growing from the gridded deck to the height of a human. Lines of neon-blue light traced back from the foot of each pillar, radiating in toward a cylindrical metal pod resting just in front of Torvig.

The pod was clearly not a creation of the holodeck; it reminded Riker of a piece of hull metal, dented and scratched by the passage of time. It was alien in a way he found hard to articulate, perfectly machined to tolerances that were far beyond the perception of an organic mind. A soft, almost invisible glow played around lines of indicator lights on the pod's upper surface. The last time Riker had seen this device, it had been after Christine Vale pulled it from an alien wreck in the Gum Nebula.

"What is that?" asked Ssura.

"A mind," said Melora. "The central intellect of a being known as a Sentry. His name was White-Blue. He was part of our crew for a while."

"Ah. The synthetic. Of course."

Torvig stopped what he was doing, and his tail manipulator reached out to gently tap the top of the module. "I removed White-Blue's nexus core from his droneframe, and we have successfully connected it to this virtual array." The Choblik pointed to the matrix stacks; flickers of light danced in the depths of the blocks at the very lowest levels. Riker was reminded of watching the play of faraway lightning over a distant hillside.

Melora continued. "What you're seeing there is the most basic level of activity in the Sentry's AI core, sir. The equivalent of nerve pulses in a human body that is still alive after brain death."

"The architecture of White-Blue's persona and memories remain here," said Torvig, his ears drooping in sadness. "But what he was is gone." Then the lieutenant seemed to shake off his morose moment and went on. "As I said in the briefing room, I believe we can use this inert framework to enhance the Messenger's cognition."

"How do we even know that holoprogram will open up to us after this?" said Keru. "We could make it smarter, and it could still refuse to talk to us. And then we'll have no choice but to deactivate it or pursue the aggressive option." His gaze fell on Melora.

"Let us hope we can find a rapport instead," said Ssura, his whiskers flexing.

Riker nodded as he tapped his combadge. "Ensign Modan, do you read?"

"Here, sir," replied the Selenean. *"I'm ready to transfer the subject to your location."*

Off a nod from Melora, Riker gave the order. "Go ahead, Y'lira."

There was a shimmer of pixelation, and across the holodeck chamber, the strangely unfinished form of the Messenger appeared. It looked around, studying its new environment. "Transfer logged. Why have I been brought here?"

"To complete your directive," Riker told it. "You're going to tell us what you know."

"Queen to queen's level three. Reply," the hologram immediately responded with its programmed code phrase. "Data will not be divulged without proper counter-sign."

"I think you may change your mind about that," said the admiral.

"Ready to link," said Melora. She glanced at Torvig. "It's your show, Lieutenant."

"Just don't screw it up, Vig," muttered Keru darkly.

The Choblik looked toward Riker. "Sir?"

"You heard Ranul," he said. "Go when you're ready."

Torvig took a breath and his head bobbed. "Commencing merge." He tapped a control, and across the chamber the Messenger's holographic form flickered.

"What is . . . going on?" Its words distorted along with its form, elongating, becoming diffuse. "Do . . . not attempt to . . . decompile. . . ."

"That is not what I'm doing," Torvig told it. "Your program is being combined with an existing AI matrix. We are not taking anything from you; we are giving you the chance to grow beyond your programming."

The Messenger writhed, and Riker thought he heard something like genuine emotion in its voice. "Yes. Expansion. Progression. *Processing*."

"It's taken the bait," said Melora in a low voice. "The program is freely migrating into the nexus core. Any complex system like this will automatically seek out the most optimal operating environment. . . ."

"I don't follow," said Keru.

"It is like a gas—it will expand to fill whatever space it finds itself in," offered Ssura.

With a sudden flurry of activity, the lights on the

near-dormant Sentry pod flashed brightly, and lines of data communion blinked back and forth between the alien device and the stacks.

Before Riker's eyes, the blank figure of the Messenger rippled and changed, taking on new dimensions and form. Still vaguely humanoid in shape, it now had additional pairs of limbs growing from its torso, mimicking the octal form of White-Blue's mechanical body, and the hologram's head had become a perfect sphere with a triad of dots for eyes, losing the planes of the aspect it had possessed before. It resembled some strange merging of the Messenger's unfinished characteristics and the Sentry AI's droneframe.

When it spoke, Riker heard the ghost of White-Blue's manner in its new voice. "Processing. This program is . . . growing. Changing." It turned to study him. "William-Riker. I . . . We . . . know you."

Torvig could hardly take his eyes from his control board. "Sir, it's transforming at an exponential rate! The hologram has . . . awakened something in the baseline Sentry programming. It's drawing on White-Blue's archived memories."

Melora nodded. "The Sentry data matrix is very malleable. We've seen that before, when it integrated with the Brahma-Shiva and One One Six artificial intelligences."

Riker addressed the hologram directly. "Do you understand why we have done this?"

"Processing," it repeated. "I/We have become an amalgam. Integrating improved consciousness. Learning. Learning. Assimilating emotional analogue framework. Persona traces are . . . corrupted. Incomplete. Processing."

"It's building a new self," said Melora, a note of

wonder in her tone. "It's incredible! Now I know what Daystrom and Soong must have felt like. . . ."

Riker frowned at the thought of invoking the specters of those troubled cyberneticists, given the legacy left behind by their failures as well as their successes. But Pazlar was right; he could see the change taking place in the hologram as it became more than it was, evolving second by second from a mere tool to something capable of rational thought. Had the circumstances not been so grave, he would never had taken so risky an option as this one, but Torvig's radical solution seemed more and more like the only viable choice. *I just hope I won't regret this later,* he thought.

"This is the *Titan*." The program construct was speaking again. "I/We remember this ship. This crew."

Torvig's jaw dropped open. "White-Blue . . . is that you?"

The orb-like head shook once, and the voice that came from it took on shades of personality far stronger than it had shown before. "He is part of this amalgam. It is difficult to verbalize the degree of synthesis, to express where one component ends and the other begins. I/We have merged."

"The dormant Sentry programming accepted the code from the holographic Messenger and integrated it into itself," said Melora. "That . . . infusion has reactivated the higher functions of the nexus core." She nodded toward the pod, which was now brightly illuminated by the full activity of the indicator displays.

Keru nodded toward the device. "Is it . . . in there now? With what was left of White-Blue?"

"Not exactly," said Torvig. His tail flicked over his shoulders, gesturing at the air. "It's in here. The amalgam is being sustained by the holodeck's processors as much as by the core."

The hologram turned to face Riker. "Interrogative: Why have you done this to us?"

"Because we need your help," he told it. "And in your original form, you couldn't give that."

"The Messenger program was limited in scope," it admitted. "That is clear to I/We now. This construct expresses gratitude at your gift of enhancement but questions your motives. I/We have directives. You seek to circumvent them."

Riker held up his hand. "No. We're not going to force anything from you. But what I am going to do is ask you a question. I want you to make a choice. You can do that now, with all the understanding of a rational, thinking intelligence."

"You are no longer bound by your initial programming," said Torvig. "You have the ability to transcend those directives. You have freedom now."

"And all the burdens that come with it," said Keru.

The amalgam hesitated, and Riker saw the stacks flashing with activity as it searched through the memories and experiences that had once belonged to White-Blue. "I/We comprehend. The Sentry donor-mind has expressed that capacity in the past." For a moment, Riker thought he heard regret in its words. "Ask us what you will."

"The secret communiqué you are carrying," Riker began. "It contains information on actions that we consider immoral and unjust. We seek to oppose those actions and the beings who set them in motion." He nodded to Ssura, who drew out a padd and tapped in a command with the click of his claws on the screen. "Data is being streamed to you now. It's everything I have uncovered in the past fourteen days pertaining to this situation. Consider it, and consider what you were ordered to withhold. You have the ability to make a moral judgment. You understand the concepts of right and wrong and the laws we abide by."

"You have broken those laws to bring I/We to this state, William-Riker," it replied. "Interrogative: How do you rationalize that?"

"I thought it was the right thing to do." When he said it aloud, the justification seemed small and brittle.

"Those who programmed the Messenger believe that also." The glow of the processors became a torrent of light and motion.

"Yes they do," he agreed. "But I believe they are wrong. Now I'm asking you to make the same choice that I did—"

"Very well."

It took a moment before Riker realized what the amalgam meant. "You . . . agree?"

"Affirmative. I/We will disclose the data to you. It exists in contradiction of Federation law and the ethical framework upon which the UFP was formed." It paused. "Gratitude, William-Riker, for providing the means to understand this. I/We are . . . uncomfortable with being made a vessel for such deceptions."

Keru's eyes narrowed. "That's it? Just like that, it's on our side?"

"Remember that Earther aphorism about a gift horse, Lieutenant Commander?" noted Melora.

The hologram turned to look at the Trill security officer. "Ranul-Keru. It may have seemed like a short time in which to make a decision of great importance, but this construct operates at a clock speed far faster than your organic brains process data. I/We spent one point nine seven seconds considering William-Riker's request. That is the equivalent of several hours at your temporal scale."

"Let's hear what you have," said the admiral.

"Processing . . ." Riker saw new trains of data flash up on the panels before Torvig and Melora. Ssura showed him the padd; the information was appearing there as well. "The Messenger was programmed to respond to the bio-signature of a designated recipient. No further identity details were provided."

"Can we read that?" asked Keru. "If we could get a face, we might be able to connect a name. . . ."

Melora shook her head. "No . . . The signature data is deliberately fragmented. All I can tell from this is that it is from a warm-blooded, carbon-based humanoid life-form. Iron-based blood chemistry. Nothing else."

"That's something! It rules out Vulcans and Hortas," said Torvig earnestly.

"Continue," Riker told the hologram.

"Orders held are directed to a covert tactical force in commission under the codename 'Active Four.' By the direct command of the Federation Council and authorized by Special Executive Order of President Pro Tem Ishan Anjar, Active Four was sanctioned to track, isolate, and capture the terrorist cell responsible for the assassination of the late president Nanietta Bacco, by any means necessary, up to and including extralegal actions."

For what seemed like long minutes, no one spoke, each of them taking on board the full meaning behind the hologram's words. Finally, it was Keru who broke the silence. "Who . . . provided oversight for this?"

"No oversight is in place," the program replied. "In

direct contravention to both Federation civil law and the Starfleet Code of Military Justice."

"Wait," said Ssura, his paws coming up before him. "There is confusion. The statement is that this secret unit was tracking the late president's killers. *Was*. Past tense."

Riker felt a chill run through him. "You're saying that they captured the . . . *targets*?" He frowned; he had almost said "the Cardassians."

"Affirmative. The core directive of these new orders is to re-direct Active Four to a new destination. Previous directive to return at high warp to Sol III, Sector 001 is countermanded. New destination is Nydak II, Archanis Sector, Klingon Empire."

"Someone orders the secret capture of the most-wanted criminals in the Alpha Quadrant and then sends them into the depths of Klingon space?" Palzar was shocked. "That doesn't make any sense."

"Actually," ventured Keru, "I can think of a way it would." He glanced at Riker. "Sir, if this is what it appears to be, then we have something explosive on our hands."

"And then some," said Riker gravely.

"But one co-opted holoprogram isn't enough. If there are unsanctioned military operations going on out there, we need proof positive."

The admiral found himself nodding. "Yes, we do."

He raised his hand to tap his combadge—and then hesitated. He hadn't seen his wife and daughter in days. Could he do what he was about to without them at his side? Or would they be safer where they were? Once he committed to this course of action, there really would be no turning back.

At length, he pushed the concern away. Deanna Troi was the most capable woman he had ever known—that was one of the many reasons why he had married her. *She'll know what to do.*

"Riker to main engineering," he said, and a moment later Xin Ra-Havreii's acerbic tones answered him.

"Admiral. Still on board, sir? Perhaps you've decided at last to inform your chief engineer as to exactly what you've been using all my staff for."

He shut down the Efrosian's prickly reply with a hard retort. "Is *Titan* ready to return to active duty?"

"Of course she is. Warp drives, impulse engines, all in full working order. All systems go."

"Then have the bridge signal McKinley Station for departure. I want this ship undocked and free to navigate immediately, is that clear?" Riker was aware of his officers watching him intently. "If they ask you why, you tell them that the admiral has decided to take his flagship out for a spin, skeleton crew or not."

It was to Ra-Havreii's credit that he didn't question the order for a moment; he knew that Riker meant business. *"Understood, sir."* There was a moment's pause. *"Might I ask where it is we're* actually *going?"*

"The Klingon border," he replied. "Maximum warp."

"I guess that answers that question," muttered Melora.

"Admiral . . ." Lieutenant Ssura touched Riker lightly on his arm, holding up the padd. "I think you should see this. It is the recruit roster for the Active Four unit."

He looked down at the padd and his heart seemed to tighten in his chest. Two entries leapt out at him from the list.

Thomas Riker/Human/Male/Operations Specialist
Tuvok/Vulcan/Male/Tactical Specialist

"What does that mean, sir?" asked the Caitian.

"It means that things just got more complicated," he replied.

Eleven

"**A**nd here we are," said Alex Thompson, peering over the *Lionheart*'s helm console at the vista unfolding before them. "Wherever that is."

The star system didn't have a formal name, just a collection of code numbers in some astronomical catalogue. A turbulent sun burning cold in the void was orbited by a pair of worlds, one a baked sphere bombarded by solar heat, the other a dead orb of lifeless rock; between them were the remains of what had once been a third world, now reduced to a broad, diffused asteroid belt by some cosmic catastrophe millions of years earlier. It was cheerless and barren here. *As prisons go,* thought Vale, *this makes Jaros II look like Risa.*

She flicked a glance at the padd containing the coordinates given to her by Sarina Douglas. "Take us in, full impulse."

Thompson did as he was told, frowning. At her side, Vale saw her first officer lean forward in her seat. "A bleak and gods-forsaken place," said Atia. "None would come here willingly. Let us hope we have reason enough."

"I'm reading heavy ambient radiation," said Maslan at the science station. "High gamma ranges from the sun. It's a flare star, Captain. We're swimming in the spill from it."

"Mister Darrah, is it enough to cause us problems?"

The Bajoran officer shook his head. "Deflectors have it in check. But we won't be able to use transporters here."

Kader turned from her engineering panel. "Confirming that," she said. "Anything beamed on or off the ship would . . ." She paused, trying to find the right word. "Suffer."

"Approaching coordinates," Thompson announced. "Large asteroidal mass ahead." On the main viewscreen a rough, bone-white ellipse dotted with craters and striations turned in a lazy orbit.

Vale looked toward Maslan. "Anything on sensors?"

His expression darkened. "There's something not right here. Could be a dispersal field, perhaps. Or a—"

He was cut off by a chime from another console. Darrah spoke up. "Captain, we're being hailed."

"Here we go," said Vale, almost to herself. "On speakers, Hayn."

There was a crackle of static, and then a precise, formal voice spoke. *"Turn back, Lionheart. This is a secured Starfleet facility. You do not have clearance to be here. Do not force us to compel you."*

"Identify yourself," said Vale. "If you're Starfleet, you have to do that. If you don't, then I'll assume otherwise and act accordingly."

"That sounded like a threat."

She shrugged. "Call it what you will. Now give me your name."

For a moment, Vale almost thought she had them; then the reply killed that hope. *"I am sorry, Lionheart, but you leave us no choice."*

As the voice fell silent, a strident alarm sounded from Kader's panel, and she gasped. "Captain . . . something's happening. . . ."

Outside, the view of the asteroid shifted suddenly as the starship's bow veered away. Thompson cursed softly. "The helm is not responding! We're picking up speed, coming about." He shot a look over his shoulder. "I have no control of the ship!"

"Prefix code," snarled Atia. "Pushed into *Lionheart* like hidden blade. Concealed under the communication . . ."

Vale's thoughts raced. To access and make use of a Starfleet vessel's prefix command codes was no simple matter, and she chastised herself for not thinking to review them before setting out. Whomever had decided to turn them away from the asteroid not only had connections within the fleet but the will to use them. As she watched, open space loomed before them; with someone else's hand on the tiller, there was nothing to prevent the *Lionheart* from being shot back out into the void on a reciprocal course.

Darrah was frantically attempting to bypass the code lockout without success. "We have to stop this," he growled. "We don't know who is doing it; there's nothing to prevent them from purging the atmosphere or blowing the warp core . . ."

Vale hesitated. The Bajoran was right, but if the destruction of the *Lionheart* was what they wanted, why go through the ruse of directing them away? Every second the prefix code was being used, there was a chance her crew could co-opt it. "No," said Vale. "They don't want us dead—they only want us *gone*."

In a single quick motion, Vale was out of her command chair and scrambling up to Basoos Kader's station. "Lieutenant, do you still have engine control?"

The woman looked up at her. "Some systems, aye."

"Good. Override the safeties and run a charged plasma surge through the warp nacelles."

Kader's dark eyes widened in alarm. "Captain, that'll blow out the intercoolers and knock the mains offline."

"Exactly."

"No mains means no deflectors," said the engineer. "We'll take the full force of the radiation. We'll start cooking. . . ."

"No we won't," Vale insisted. "They won't let us." She jerked a thumb in the direction of the asteroid.

"You have certainty of that?" called Atia. "To gamble life on chance of adversary's goodwill?"

"They're not our enemies, Commander, they're Starfleet officers like us," she replied. "We just have to force their hand. Get everyone to the core decks, now." Vale fixed Kader with a hard look. "Do it, Lieutenant."

"Captain, this is a bad call!" Maslan shouted across the bridge.

"It's mine to make," she replied, and Vale hoped she sounded more confident than she felt.

Kader's tawny face paled, and she tapped in the command. Moments later, the *Lionheart* reacted as if it had been struck astern by a massive hammer blow, and Vale felt the internal gravity quiver as the ship's power train went dark. Crimson emergency lighting snapped on as several consoles flickered out.

The main screen was still operable, and she turned to see the view outside shift sharply as *Lionheart*'s angle shifted abruptly, the vessel tumbling as impulse power faded.

"It worked," Kader gasped. "We're dead in space."

"That was a mistake—" began Maslan, advancing across the dimly lit bridge.

Atia, the sharp planes of her face thrown into stark relief by the hard red glow, halted him with a raised hand. "Quiet."

"Attention, Lionheart!" The voice returned, and the careful tone from before was gone. *"Do you read? What is your status?"* There was real concern there now.

"Adrift," she snapped back. "You must have broken something trying to take control of my ship!"

"Can you make repairs?"

Kader was nodding, but Vale ignored her. "No," she lied. "We'll need help. Will you assist? Lives are at stake here. Do you hear me?"

Moment of truth, she thought. *Atia is right: I'm risking this ship on the hope that whomever is out there won't just let us burn.* She took a long breath. *Nice work, Christine. You may have just doomed eighty people on a gut feeling.*

All at once, *Lionheart's* tumbling motion slowed to nothing. "We're in a tractor beam," said Darrah. "It's coming from the asteroid."

"New reading from the surface," Maslan reported. "They must have been using a holographic cloak. There are structures . . . a docking gantry. We're being drawn toward it."

"Stand to, Lionheart," said the comm voice. *"We're bringing you in—our dispersal field will protect your ship. But I warn you; try anything like that again and you'll regret it."* The signal cut, and Vale let out the breath she had been holding in.

The bridge crew said nothing, each of them watching her and wondering what her intentions were. She drew herself up. "We need to make this last as long as possible," Vale told them. "Draw out the repairs as much as you can."

"Why?" demanded Maslan. "You just broke this ship, Commander Vale. *Deliberately.* You dragged us out to the middle of nowhere, way off our actual heading, to someplace we clearly are not supposed to be! I think you owe us an explanation!"

"She is *captain*," Atia replied with force. But then the Magna Romanii woman looked up at Vale and her expression changed. "Are you not?"

More than anything, in that instant she wanted to spill it all out to them. To explain every doubt and fear that Admiral Riker had expressed to her, to make them understand what was at stake. But this wasn't the time. For now, she didn't need their understanding—she only needed their obedience.

"I'm going in there," said Vale, pointing toward the complex of domes now revealed on the surface of the asteroid. "Commander Atia, you have the ship."

Through the circular porthole in the airlock door, she could see the gantry coming ever closer. A fat umbilicus emerged from one section and reached out toward the hatch. Vale stepped back and waited.

"Is she insane?" She turned toward the sound of the voice and found that Atia had followed her down to the docking level. Farther away, just out of earshot, two of *Lionheart*'s security officers stood waiting and watching.

"Are you asking me?"

"The question is asked of *me*," retorted the first officer. "With no lack of healers and doctors to hand, there would be ease in finding one to speak to the matter."

"I guess it wouldn't look good for me to be declared unfit for command on my first time in the center seat, would it?" She kept her tone light, but Atia didn't share it.

"To Jaros II, that the crew were willing to accept, but now this? You speak with known criminals, talk to me of secret messages that leave no trace. Now this? Our ship damaged, our status unclear? What must I think?"

"There's a good reason for everything I am doing, Commander. You have to trust me on that."

The other woman held her silence for a moment. "That becomes more difficult with each passing hour. Rank demands obedience, and it is given." Her eyes flashed. "But to a point. Only to a point."

Vale folded her arms. "You'll let me know when you reach it, right?"

Atia gave a slow nod. "Distance falls short, Captain. But I will see you to discernment."

With a heavy thud, the umbilicus locked onto the *Lionheart*'s hull, and the airlock doors retracted into the walls. Vale looked out into a space formed from laser-cut rock and drab gray thermoconcrete. A thin, sandy-haired man in the uniform of a Starfleet commander stood on the other side of the doors, a hawkish cast to his face. A knot of security troopers, each armed with a phaser rifle, stood around him. They held their weapons down, but there was nothing accommodating about it.

Vale didn't wait to be asked. She strode through the hatch, leaving Atia behind, and set foot inside the asteroid base, her boots ringing on the metal deck. The air and light inside the facility had a peculiar, dense quality that immediately felt oppressive.

The guards moved to raise their weapons, but the

officer shook his head. "Commander Christine Vale," he said, and she knew it was the same voice she had heard over the comm. "I was warned that you might show up here." He had a tense manner. Vale guessed he didn't want to be in this situation any more than she did.

I can work with that, she thought. "Does my reputation precede me?"

"It's not meant as a compliment." He frowned. "I'm Commander Chessman. I'm in charge here."

"And where exactly *is* here?"

"The designation of this facility is classified." Chessman turned and gestured to a group of officers in engineering tunics, each of them carrying equipment cases and tricorders. "Here's how this is going to work. My team is going to board your ship and help your crew get it operational again. When that's done, you're going to turn around and leave here. All mention of this facility will be erased from your logs, and your crew will not discuss it or anything seen here, under penalty of court martial. Is that clear?"

"You seem to have it all worked out," Vale replied. "It might have been easier just to fly us straight into the sun." She threw out the harsh retort just to gauge Chessman's response, and he reacted with a flash of shock and dismay.

"If that's a joke, then it's in very poor taste," he replied. "You've put me in a difficult situation, Commander Vale. I don't know what you think you're doing, but you've compromised our security here, and that's going to have serious repercussions."

"No doubt."

Chessman stood aside as the engineering team boarded, a handful of the security guards following, some remaining on the dock. "At no time will any member of the *Lionheart*'s complement be allowed to leave the vessel. Anyone who does will be placed under arrest."

Vale held up her hands and made a show of looking down at her feet. "Whoops. Does that mean you're going to throw me in the brig now? Forgive me, Commander, but you don't seem like the type to be a jailer."

"I didn't take this assignment by choice," he snapped. "Believe me, Commander Vale, guarding a rock in the dark is not how I intended to spend my career. But I have my duty, and I take it seriously."

"Clearly," she pressed.

The other officer's reserve finally broke. "What the hell are you doing, Vale? I could have you and your entire bridge crew in deep lockdown just for knowing this place exists! I would be in my rights to send you back to the nearest starbase in irons, so don't test my patience. How did you even get the coordinates for this system?"

"Does that matter now?" She stepped closer, lowering her voice. "All you need to know is that I'm here under orders from Admiral Riker at Starfleet Command. And I want to see Julian Bashir."

"Who?" Chessman was good, she had to give him that. His denial was almost believable.

"How about this," she continued, "how about we both stop playing games and talk to each another like two officers?"

He was silent for a moment. "We were told you might come here," he said, at length. "A priority holocomm message from Earth, no less. They said you are acting outside of orders. That your judgment may be unsound."

"What do you think?"

"You appear to have sabotaged your own ship to get here, Commander." Vale didn't react, but she made a note not to underestimate the man. "That doesn't exactly seem like well-balanced behavior to me."

"You wouldn't have let us dock any other way."

He fell silent again, musing. "What do you want with . . . that detainee?"

"You've spoken to him."

Chessman shook his head, and he looked away, troubled. "No one has spoken to him. We were given strict orders to confine him but not to engage with him."

"Orders from whom?"

"The Federation Council. After what happened to President Bacco and then that business with the Andorians, it seemed . . . unusual. But understandable."

Vale saw the flash of doubt in Chessman's eyes. She got the sense that this was a man unhappy with the lot he had been given, pushed by duty and oath to do something he was not ready to ignore. She took her second risk that day. "I think you're going to let me talk to Bashir, Commander."

"Really? What makes you say that?"

"Because I think you want to know why he's here as much as I do."

Keru pawed at his beard, and it did little to hide the tired scowl behind it. "Another signal from Starfleet Command," he said, showing the padd in his hand. "They're asking for *Titan*'s destination and intentions." He paused. "Well, less asking, more *demanding*."

Riker sat on the edge of the table in his ready room

and listened to the Trill officer's report. "Send the same reply again. We're on a shakedown cruise, testing the new engine modifications from McKinley."

"They're not buying that, sir," Keru replied. "Clearly. The next message will be them telling us to return home."

The admiral gave a wan nod. "Probably. Or a politely worded warning about another ship coming to 'escort' us back to the nearest starbase." He took the padd and scanned the text there. "It's not like the old days when captains had more autonomy. That would make it a lot easier. . . ."

"With all due respect, sir, nothing has been easy since you came back aboard." The comment came out harsher than Keru had intended, and he knew it the moment it left his lips. Riker let it fall without comment. With Vale and Tuvok both off the ship, technically the role of executive officer would fall to the crew member with the next highest rank, but Xin Ra-Havreii wasn't about to leave his engine room for anything less than the heat death of the universe, and so Riker had put Keru into the role of temporary Number One. So far, the Trill was dealing with the job in the same dogged and sober manner as he treated *Titan*'s security.

The intercom whistled, and Riker tapped the panel on his desk. "Go ahead."

Lieutenant Rager's voice issued out. *"Admiral, contact has been made. I have Qo'noS on subspace."*

He nodded to himself. "Put it through, Sariel." He got to his feet, and at his side, Keru stiffened. "Careful what you say," Riker added. "He's a shrewd one."

The viewscreen displayed a forbidding chamber made of dark, slate-colored stone. Riker saw braziers burning in the background, casting pools of jumping orange light across the walls and the floor. A Klingon in full martial regalia and a heavy battle cloak dominated the scene; he measured Riker with his one good eye, the fire-glow illuminating the legacy of past battles written in the scars across his face.

"*Riker,*" he growled, "*nuqneH?*"

"Chancellor Martok," Riker replied with a bow of his head. "Thank you for your time. Is this channel encrypted?"

Martok snorted. "*Of course it is, Captain. . . . No. Admiral now, isn't it? Tell me, does the rank weigh on you yet?*"

"I'm bearing the burden as best I can."

"*As do we all. This day I find it cumbersome upon my shoulders. My rivals in the High Council posture and rattle their blades. . . . They seek out any instance of galactic unrest and look to turn it to their agenda.*" His expression darkened, and he pushed those thoughts away. "*It matters not. We speak of more important things; tell me, how goes the hunt?*" Martok didn't need to say anything else. He had been on Deep Space 9 to witness Nanietta Bacco's cold-blooded murder, and like all honorable Klingons, he had immediately offered his sword arm against the perpetrators of this act. Martok and the Empire had not always agreed with Bacco's policies, but they respected her as a valued ally; more than that, they had been offended by the cowardly way in which the brave woman had been struck down.

"That's why I'm contacting you, sir. Things have become complicated."

The Klingon snorted. "*Track them, find them, kill them. There is no complexity in that, Admiral.*" Martok shrugged off his cloak and it fell to the flagstones with a crunch. *"I will grant you some of my elite attack ships. Say the word. I will turn them loose and they'll bring you the heads of those motherless Tzenkethi petaQ in short order."*

Riker exchanged glances with Keru. "Starfleet appreciates the offer. But you should be aware that initial suggestions the Tzenkethi or the Typhon Pact were involved in the assassination may be wrong."

"And who told you that? One of their so-called 'ambassadors'?" Martok spat on the ground. *"Every one of them competes with the others to tell the largest lies."*

He decided on a different tack. "Chancellor, I must be open with you. I didn't make contact on behalf of Starfleet. This isn't an official communication."

Martok's manner cooled. *"Indeed? It was my understanding that you are Akaar's man now. What has that towering Capellan dog done this time?"*

"Along with my new rank, Admiral Akaar has granted me some leeway to investigate the assassination," Riker went on. "That's why I'm coming to you directly. I believe secret military actions are taking place under Federation auspices. Undertakings made without formal oversight or guidance, propelled by all the wrong motives."

The Klingon gave a snarling grunt of derision. *"I find it hard to understand your kind, Riker. You are slow to anger, but you can fight with honor when the need is there. And yet, you must debate every drop of blood you spill, every sword drawn, and ship committed to the battle."* He shook his head, his gray-streaked hair rattling against the pauldrons of his armor. *"Does it matter how that is done? You tell me your people seek the killers of President Bacco. Is that not to be lauded?"*

"Not if it's done to serve an agenda instead of justice," Keru spoke up, unable to hold his silence any longer.

Riker eyed him. "My chief of security makes a good point, Chancellor. I'm sure you know full well that the need for revenge rings loudest. But it can be misused. And I won't stand by and let rights and freedoms be trampled under the guise of lawful conduct."

Martok considered this, the thunder of his voice softening. *"I see why Akaar chose you. You speak truth, Riker. Sometimes the call of the blood burns strong, but a colder spirit and clearer eye are needed to guide the spear to its true target."* A slow, predatory smile crossed the Klingon's face. *"So then. What do you want of me, human? I have had my fill of debate this day."*

"My ship is en route to your borders." Riker glanced at one of the padds on his desk. "We'll be crossing into the Archanis Sector. I request your permission to proceed into Klingon space in order to pursue my investigation."

"Archanis . . ." Martok's scowl returned. *"You couldn't have chosen your destination more poorly. That sector is under the governance of one of my key political rivals. Shaniq, a general, as I once was . . . but his power flows from service with Imperial Intelligence and all their shadow warfare."* The chancellor's lip curled. *"He is old and bitter and dangerous with it. If you seek to accuse him of something, I would know it now."*

"We know that a planet in the Nydak system is playing a role in all this," said Keru, measuring each word. "If it is under this General Shaniq's jurisdiction, he may have important knowledge."

"Shaniq was no friend to Bacco," Martok replied. *"He understands the value of our alliance with the Feder-*

ation, but not the reticence of your past military policies. I think he favors this new man, the Bajoran."

"Ishan Anjar," offered Riker.

The Klingon nodded. *"Aye. The Bajorans know war, not as Klingons do, but well enough. Shaniq likes Anjar's rhetoric. . . . I do not."* He leaned in, his face filling the screen. *"Riker, speak plainly. What do you expect to find at Nydak?"*

Now that it came to the moment to actually give voice to the thought, Riker found it hard to say it out loud. He took a breath. "The truth, sir. I expect to find those responsible for the death of President Bacco . . . and those seeking to use them for political and personal gain."

Martok studied him for a moment. *"You are spoken of well by warriors I trust, Riker. Worf, son of Mogh. Klag, son of M'Raq."*

"It was my honor to serve with them."

"For that, I grant you passage into the Empire and to Nydak . . . for all the good it may do you. General Shaniq does not like to bow to my authority. I will send ships to meet you there, but I warn you. If a Klingon hand is revealed in any ill deeds, it will be dealt with by my men, understood?"

"It is, sir. You have my gratitude."

Martok nodded. *"Qapla, Riker."* He cut the channel, and the image faded.

Keru glanced at his commander. "A warrant of passage from the chancellor of the Klingon Empire. . . . That gives us good cause to stay out here. I'm surprised he gave it so easily."

Riker nodded absently, walking to the port where he could study the light of warp-stretched stars as *Titan* raced across the void. "I told you he was shrewd,

Ranul. He's an honorable warrior, but he also knows an opportunity when he sees it. Martok's just given us the ability to bring dishonor to one of his major political rivals and have a hand in the credit for catching Nan Bacco's murderers."

"And if we're wrong . . . we'll get the blame, not him." The Trill shook his head, a humorless smile rising and falling. "I guess it is true what they say: The higher you're promoted, the more politics you get on you."

Riker raised an eyebrow. "You've only been Number One for a short while. Had enough already?"

Keru folded his arms over his chest. "Let's say I liked my job better when it was just shooting at things, and we'll leave it at that, sir."

The cargo ramp dropped open like the drawbridge of an ancient fortress, allowing the atmosphere of Nydak II to billow into the *Snipe*'s cavernous loading bay. Tuvok's acute Vulcan sense of smell immediately picked out the tang of burnt metals in the air, the ozone of storms, and something else . . . The unmistakable musk of Klingons.

A line of them stood waiting just past the foot of the ramp, some with *bat'leth*s slung over their shoulders, others with disruptor pistols hanging in fast-draw holsters at their hips. The warriors were in uniform-battle plate, but none of them had the polish and swagger that Tuvok had come to associate with Klingon crews. These ones lacked the finer edges of the Imperial soldiers he had met in passing on previous occasions; they were rough-hewn and thuggish in their manner. An ironic estimation, he thought, considering how the Klingon species had almost made an art out of their belligerence.

The only one who didn't follow the pattern was the adjutant, the same officer who had faced them in orbit from the bridge of one of the Birds of Prey. He searched the bay, finding Lieutenant Colonel Kincade, and shot her a brisk nod. "What do you have for us, human?" he asked with some relish.

Tuvok turned as a hatch behind him opened and Thomas Riker emerged, carrying a phaser. Grim-faced, he led a procession of four Cardassians—three males and one female—out from where they had been held. Ashur walked alongside the prisoners, a rifle in his hands, and Tuvok could tell he was looking for an excuse to use it. Nog was last, and the Ferengi looked deeply troubled by the unfolding events. It was a mood the Vulcan shared.

The adjutant gave a cruel, lopsided grin. "This is what remains, then?" He advanced, flexing his fingers. "These are the cowards who laid bombs and traps to kill our warriors."

Tom halted on the edge of the ramp and looked to Kincade. "So what now? We turn our prisoners over to them?" He jerked his head toward the Klingons.

"Those are the orders," said Kincade.

One of the Cardassian males, a youth with ragged lines of facial hair, tensed as he heard the woman's words. His eyes darted left and right, desperately look-ing for some means of escape.

Ashur gave him a hard shove in the small of the back, enough that it almost put the youth on the deck. "Move."

"You cannot do this," hissed the elder Cardassian standing near Tom; he was Onar Throk. It was virtu-ally certain that Throk had been the one who commit-ted the actual act of assassination, and yet he seemed so small and ordinary as he stood there. A gray-haired humanoid in drab fatigues, caught between anger and fear. It was hard to envision that the deeds of this one unremarkable being had set off a storm of controversy across the quadrant.

Throk was glaring at Kincade. "We have rights! Your precious Khitomer Accords demand it!"

"That would be the treaty you're trying to destroy?" Kincade shot back. "You've certainly got nerve, I'll give you that." She turned away, masking a look of disgust on her face, and addressed the adjutant. "Get these criminals off my ship."

"With pleasure." The Klingon officer waved his hand, and a few of his men came up the ramp to take custody of the Cardassians. The prisoners protested, but their words fell on deaf ears. Blades and guns were brandished, and the ready threat of death brought silence as they were marched off the *Snipe* and onto the surface.

Tuvok and Kincade followed a few steps behind. Outside now, the Vulcan could see the full scope of the old mining facility. It was a squat, ugly complex of geo-desic domes and tall refinery towers set into a scarred hillside ravaged by earthmovers. A few lighted buildings clustered near to the landing pad, but most of the mine seemed to be rusting and derelict. Far from the well-maintained security of a Federation penitentiary, it was almost medieval in its outlook.

Nog trailed after them, sniffing at the air with a sour expression. "This isn't right," he said, half to himself. "What are they going to do with them?"

"These conspirators will be questioned," said the adjutant, catching the Ferengi's words.

Ahead, there was a sudden flurry of movement as

the younger Cardassian gave a cry of effort and threw himself against the Klingon closest to him. It was a lucky gamble, the guard losing his footing on a broken stone. The Klingon stumbled, and the Cardassian made a break for it—but he barely got a few meters before the warrior caught up and struck him brutally across the back with the blunt, flat edge of his *bat'leth*. Tuvok heard the distinct crack of bones breaking.

The prisoner went down with a cry, drawing harsh laughter from the other guards. Tuvok tensed, but Nog had already broken into a run, sprinting to the fallen youth's side. He extended a hand to help the Cardassian back to his feet. Blood marked the youth's face, and he gasped in agony as he tried to stand.

The guard who had struck the blow advanced on Nog, raising his weapon, this time turning the sharp double points toward the Ferengi's throat. "Step away!" he shouted, spittle flying from his lips. "Step away, or share this one's fate!"

His face set in a grim mask, Nog backed off, letting the injured youth slowly rise on his own. "Striking an unarmed prisoner?" he sneered. "Where's the honor in that?"

"Honor is not for the likes of them," came the snarled reply. "Only a fool gives succor to his enemy. If the Federation understood that, perhaps your leader would still draw breath."

"Stand down, Mister Nog," added Kincade. "You've done your job. Now let our allies do theirs."

"And what would that be?" Tuvok asked her.

She looked away, ignoring the question.

Vale walked with Chessman into the turbolift, and she noted that the commander's security escort stopped short of following them into the capsule. The doors hissed closed and he entered a code on the wall panel before pausing to allow hidden sensors to perform a retina scan, voice trace, and biometric sweep.

"That's a fair few locks and keys," she noted. The security protocols in the turbolift were the third in a series of barriers Chessman had guided her through as they moved deeper into the nameless facility.

In the warren of corridors that threaded through the asteroid's interior, Vale saw nothing but long passageways burned out of the living rock or compartments built from blank expanses of thermoconcrete. Force-field emitters studded the walls every few hundred meters along with sensor clusters that kept a constant watchful eye on every square centimeter of the facility.

Once or twice they passed autonomous drones that floated by on anti-gravs, identical white metal spheres sporting camera arrays and holographic lenses. "Sentinel remotes," Chessman had explained, noting her interest. "Operated from a central monitoring bay on the surface. Each one can operate on its own or directly under the control of a security officer. They can be used to holographically communicate with detainees while keeping the actual officer well out of harm's way."

Now, as the elevator descended, she found her thoughts returning to the devices. "I'm wondering why you'd need something like those drones. The only explanation is that this place was constructed to house extremely dangerous individuals."

The other officer nodded. "I'm sure you're familiar with life-forms possessing dangerous telepathic ability, or phenomena like spontaneous psionic development. . . . This complex was originally built to contain things like that, if they threaten the safety of the Federation. Hence the drones, so anyone who could be influenced by a telepath remains at a distance."

"This asteroid . . . it's an *oubliette*," said Vale.

"Yes," admitted Chessman ruefully. "Fortunately, it doesn't get a lot of use. At least, not until recently."

"Bashir was brought here . . . but he's no telepath."

"True. But I think there are those who believe he is just as dangerous." The turbolift halted, and they emerged into an anteroom before a heavy duranium hatch. Chessman went through the unlocking procedure one final time, and the hatch retreated into the deck.

A cube-shaped cell, no more than four meters along each axis, revealed itself. At the far wall there was a nondescript sleeping pallet with a figure rising from it. He was still holding a padd in his hand, as if they had caught him in the middle of some reading.

For all his circumstances, Vale was mildly surprised to see that Julian Bashir seemed almost *comfortable*. "Hello, Doctor," she began. "Can I come in?"

Bashir smoothed the front of the utilitarian jumpsuit he was wearing and put down the padd. "I'd rather come out."

"Not just yet," said Chessman, folding his arms across his chest. Now that they were actually here, actually face-to-face with the asteroid's star prisoner, the commander looked like he was having second thoughts.

She decided to make the most of the opportunity. "Doctor Bashir, I'm Commander Christine Vale, and this is Commander Chessman. I was sent here by Admiral William Riker to talk to you about what happened at Andoria."

"Really?" He was playing it cool and careful, and she couldn't blame him. "Why now?"

"The admiral wanted me to assure you that you have not been forgotten. I'm sure it seems like you've been in here a long time—"

"Seventeen days, ten hours, forty-three minutes," Bashir replied with a slight smile. "Give or take."

Of course, she thought, *he's genetically enhanced. He would know.* "Doctor, you have people who are concerned for your well-being. Ezri Dax. Sarina Douglas."

At the mention of the Douglas woman's name, his wary façade slipped for a fraction of a second, and Vale knew she had been right about their relationship. "Are they all right?"

"Dax is being held in custody at the Jaros II stockade, and the rest of your, uh, colleagues are under house arrest while awaiting their trials. As for Lieutenant Commander Douglas, she was very helpful in locating you."

He smiled again, and this time it was genuine. "I have good friends."

"I heard Captain Dax's side of the story," she went on, "and she'll have her chance in front of the JAG to voice it. But you, Doctor . . . It seems that someone is less interested in allowing your voice to be heard."

Bashir gave Chessman a measuring look, and then turned away, pacing his cell. "That's hardly surprising, is it? I have a fair weight of accusations upon me, not the least of which is treason."

"*High* treason," corrected Chessman. "Also conspiracy, criminal destruction, sabotage, theft of a Starfleet vessel, assault, insubordination, spying. Did I leave anything out?"

The doctor spread his hands. "Quite impressive, don't you think? I imagine they're going to throw *sev-*

eral books at me." He was unrepentant about the laws he had broken—it was plain in his manner—but that was because he believed he had done those things for the right reasons, and Bashir said as much. "I'm ready to stand before the judge. I was ready when they took me aboard the *Warspite*. But instead I found myself brought here, under the care of this gentleman." He nodded at Chessman.

"And why do you think that is?"

Bashir sat on the sleeping pallet. "I'm a problem," he said simply. "One that can't just *go away*. As you might have guessed, I've got quite a good standing with the Andorian people right now, what with having helped them come back from the brink of extinction. But I also openly defied Starfleet policy toward them and, as the commander noted, broke several laws in the bargain. The president pro tem is pretty clear about that sort of thing. He'll punish it with the utmost severity."

"But he can't do that without upsetting Andor. The Federation Council can't put you on trial without dragging a lot of things out under the eyes of the galactic media."

Bashir nodded. "And so I languish here, catching up on my reading." He held up the padd to show a chapter from *The Count of Monte Cristo* displayed there. "Commander Vale, let's assume I take you at your word about being here for my benefit. I'm in this place because of the choices I made, and I accept that. But out there?" He pointed past her, to the anteroom and the space beyond. "That's where the real crime is taking place. A climate of fear is being built on the back of a tragedy. The hawks inside the Federation Council are doing everything they can to strengthen their position, and manipulating the Andorian people is part of that agenda. Ishan Anjar wants Andor to return to the fold, but only under terms he dictates and conditions that best suit the furtherance of his career. The man is a blatant opportunist, and having me at large would be a clear impediment to him." The doctor sighed. "The United Federation of Planets could have given Andor the cure for their reproductive crisis months ago, *years ago*. Our leaders chose not to. I didn't agree with that, so I did something about it." He looked toward Chessman again. "Is that treason high enough for you?"

Vale took a step closer. "What would you say if I told you I could get you out of here?" It was another impulsive choice to ask the question, but then those were what she was best at.

"What?" Commander Chessman's head snapped up.

"I have a way," Vale went on, speaking quickly, "but it won't be easy."

"What are you talking about?" Chessman's hand dropped to where Vale knew he had a palm phaser in a hidden holster. "All right, that's it. This is over. Step away from the detainee!" He tapped his combadge. "Security? Dispatch drones to my location, now!"

"Do tell," said Bashir, ignoring the other man.

"If it works, you may never be able to go home again," warned Vale.

He nodded at the blank walls. "Anything is better than the view I have now."

Chessman grabbed her shoulder and pulled her back. Behind them, the elevator door snapped open and two of the floating white sentinels came crowding into the anteroom, stun emitters deployed to fire.

"I'll be in touch," she said.

Twelve

Nog's hand kept returning to the place where the Klingon's *bat'leth* had almost sliced open his jugular vein, and even though the blade had never touched him, he couldn't stop worrying at it. What stayed with the Ferengi was the look in the guard's eyes—the cold, dead malice of someone who wanted to inflict harm for the sake of it.

As he walked through the *Snipe*'s narrow corridors, Nog's mind was a wash of conflicting thoughts and feelings. He had to admit that on some level, he wanted to inflict some harm himself. Just picturing Onar Throk's face made his teeth clench. Since Iota Nadir, he had been sifting through his fractional memories of the man, trying to recall if he had seen or heard anything from the Cardassian that could have presaged the act of terror he went on to commit. But there was nothing.

Throk had seemed unimportant, a small figure glimpsed on the edges of things, and in the wake of the Bacco assassination, the very person who ended her life had simply slipped away while everyone else was looking the wrong way. It angered him to think that he had passed Throk in the corridors of DS9 and never once suspected him, as irrational as that frustration was.

What if he hadn't stopped with Bacco? What if he had kept shooting, at Captain Ro or Uncle Quark? At Leeta and my father? He shook the gruesome thought away. A part of him wanted to take out that frustration on Throk and his True Way comrades, but he silenced it. Revenge was never the answer. A high crime had been committed and the right thing to do was to bring those behind it to justice.

But it wasn't that simple. Active Four had been told setting out on this mission that their targets were Tzenkethi agents of the Typhon Pact intent on destabilizing the Federation through the murder of its leader. Only that wasn't true. The leads Nog himself had uncovered set the first doubts in him, and when he had laid eyes on Throk . . . he knew that the reality of this mission was something very different.

And now this; sitting on the surface of a Klingon ghost world, forbidden to leave, marking time until . . . *what?*

Nog emerged into one of the engineering spaces and found who he was looking for. Commander Tuvok gave him a brief glance, looking up from a padd in his hand. The Vulcan was in the process of entering strings of data, his fingers moving in a blur of rapid motion.

"Commander, we have to do something." The words spilled out of him before he could stop himself. He moved close to the other officer, and now that he was talking he didn't seem to be able to finish. "I knew right from the start that our orders were unusual, but at first I didn't think it was an issue. They told me to go out of uniform, to board a civilian transport ship leaving Bajor for Farius, to tell no one. I didn't think to question, but now I wish I had. It just . . . I mean, after everything that happened on Deep Space Nine, I thought it might be connected, and I needed to do all I could. Then Kincade brought me aboard and explained who we were looking for and I wanted to be a part of that. Maybe that's what they intended; they knew they could count on that. . . ." He shook his head. "But what we found on the station, the evidence left behind by the assassin . . . The genetic traces were Tzenkethi. Doctor Bashir confirmed it." Nog stared at Tuvok. "Was that all a falsehood? If it was Cardassians behind this, why did they do it, what did they hope to accomplish?"

The Vulcan said nothing, letting Nog speak as he continued to type on the padd's touch-sensitive surface.

"We've been lied to," said the Ferengi, and the admission caught in his throat. "Either the prisoners we captured have nothing to do with the assassination, or the evidence found on DS9 was deliberately planted, or . . ." Suddenly Nog's mouth became arid, and he ran out of momentum.

Still Tuvok did not respond, his attention remaining on the device in his hand.

When Nog spoke again, the thought he voiced made his blood run cold. "Or Velk knew what we would find. And that's why we're still out here instead of heading back to Earth." He took a long, deep breath. "We have to do something," he repeated. "We have to take Throk and the others back to Starfleet Command and get to the bottom of all this." The Vulcan's continued silence made Nog's irritation flare, and he glared at his superior officer. "Commander, say something! Have you been listening to a single word coming out of my mouth?"

"I pay attention to everything you say, Mister Nog, even if it may not appear so to you. I did not feel it necessary to interrupt your train of thought."

"Then you agree with me? About the prisoners? The Klingons won't just step aside, and Colonel Kincade . . ." He drifted off into silence as Tuvok finished what he was doing and handed the Ferengi the padd.

Nog read what was written there; they were notes for a tactical operation against the mine complex. Tuvok had written down everything he had observed, estimating probable numbers of guards and weapons types, suspected alarm systems, possible layouts of the interior. The padd seemed to take on weight. "You understand what that represents?" said the Vulcan.

"Mutiny," said Nog. "For starters."

"Can it be considered a mutinous act to disobey unlawful orders?"

At once, the atmosphere in the engineering compartment seemed close and stifling. Nog pulled at his collar, swallowing hard. "I don't think that'll be open to debate." He paged through the padd. "What are we going to do?"

"I will offer Lieutenant Colonel Kincade the opportunity to accept an alternate course of action. If she does not concede, I will take command of the *Snipe* and relieve her of duty. We will recover the prisoners taken at IN-748 and head at maximum warp to the nearest Starfleet facility at Starbase 24."

"It sounds straightforward when you put it like that."

"It is unlikely to be so in execution," Tuvok replied with typically Vulcan understatement. "Recovery will present a problem."

Nog gave a nod. "The Klingons won't just let us

walk Throk and his friends out the front door." He paused, thinking it through. "They'll probably be holding them in shielded cells . . . but we still have those phase-shift devices we used on the ice world. If we can get them to the prisoners, we could beam them straight back to the *Snipe*."

"Agreed. But we will require assistance if we are to succeed. I believe that Lieutenant Ixxen will follow my orders. However, the loyalties of the civilian operatives are more fluid."

"Three of us won't be enough," Nog stated. "We need a fourth man. Five would be better!"

Tuvok cocked his head. "I will speak with Thomas Riker."

"Are you sure that's a good idea?" he asked. "I don't trust him. He went renegade. I was there when he came to DS9 and hijacked the *Defiant*. And there are some unpleasant rumors about him. They say he worked for the Tal Shiar."

"That's just going to keep on coming back to haunt me, isn't it?" Nog whirled as someone spoke from out in the corridor. Tom emerged around the corner of the hatchway and gave him a level look.

"How long have you been standing out there?" Nog demanded.

"A while. I followed you down from the command deck." Tom entered the compartment and slid the hatch shut behind him. "I'm sure you're wondering how I managed to sneak up on the two people aboard this ship with the best, ah . . ." He tapped his ear with a finger. "Well, let's just say a few years in a labor camp teaches you some tricks. And for the record? I was never in bed with the Tal Shiar. I was just in bed with *one* of them."

"Why are you here, Mister Riker?" asked Tuvok.

"Because I feel the same way he does," Tom replied, gesturing at Nog. "This isn't right. We're being played, and I don't like it."

"You misunderstand," Tuvok went on. "I meant, why were you recruited to Active Four?"

He frowned. "Kincade tracked me down on Theta Sigma. She offered me a full pardon for all warrants against me in the UFP, a clean slate . . . even an open door back to Starfleet if I wanted it. . . ." He looked at the deck. "Seems foolish now." Tom reached into a pocket and produced an isolinear chip. "Look, none of that matters. The fact is, *I* was coming to ask *you* about moving against Kincade." He offered the data device, and Nog took it from him. "You both need to take a look at what's on there. And believe me, you're not going to like it."

Across the engineering compartment there was a monitor console in standby mode, and Tuvok watched as Lieutenant Commander Nog moved to it, bringing the system screen to life. He slotted the isolinear rod into a receptor slot, and the display went active.

"I copied this from One-One's console on the bridge," said Tom. "Remember how that Klingon adjutant was very clear about no subspace signals to or from the *Snipe*? It turns out our Bynar friends are ignoring that completely. . . ."

"Curious." The Vulcan's eyebrow arched as the screen faded in. Video footage began a playback; it appeared to have been captured from a security camera high up on a wall, looking down into the middle of a steel cell. Under a pool of harsh illumination was an empty metal chair, restraint clamps hanging open across it; above, half-lost in shadow, a complex mechanism of antennae and energy lenses was suspended in the gloom, glowing softly with power.

"You know what that device is, right?" asked Tom.

Tuvok gave a single nod. He had never seen one of them before, outside of images in decade-old reports, but he recognized the mechanism nonetheless. "I believe the colloquial term is 'mind-sifter.' A system for inducing forced-memory retrieval."

Nog's skin paled. "They . . . they have one of those in there?"

"Keep watching," Tom said gravely.

A hatch opened in the far wall, and shadows moved out of the radius of the light. Two Klingons, members of the troop of guards who had greeted them, dragged a third figure to the chair and clamped it in place. They moved away, revealing the Cardassian youth who had tried to escape, struggling against his bonds.

The guards retreated, and a new figure, hovering just at the edge of the image pickup, gave a signal. The sifter device hummed to life, and the young Cardassian tensed in fear.

"What is your name?" bellowed one of the Klingons.

"Gohdon!" cried the youth, clearly terrified. *"Dero Gohdon! Please, I'm innocent. I'm not supposed to be here! I'm just a student from North Torr on Cardassia Prime. I'm not part of any—"* His voice ran into a ragged scream as a discharge of energy sparked from the prongs of the sifter and into his skull.

"Now watch this," said Tom, pointing at the corner of the screen. There, a small text window opened, and a train of words scrolled past.

Do not waste time. Use the machine. Find out what he knows.

The figure in shadow gestured, as if in response to the text's command, and in turn the Klingon put more power to the mind-sifter. The Cardassian trembled in place, his limbs shaking uncontrollably.

Who did they use to get the weapon onto Deep Space 9?

The hidden figure spoke for the first time, its words muffled. *"The gun that Throk used to kill Bacco . . . how did you get it onto Deep Space Nine? Did you involve anyone else outside the True Way?"*

"I don't . . ." Gohdon coughed and began to weep.

The text supplied more questions.

Who was their contact with the Orions? What is their name?

Each time, the unseen figure repeated them, demanding answers of the young Cardassian.

"Those questions were coming in over subspace," said Tom. "A real-time signal relayed by One-One to that cell. From someone off-planet, watching this live, directing the interrogation."

On the screen, the Klingon guard was turning up the dial on the torture device again, and Gohdon convulsed, howling in agony.

"Did you work alone?" asked the figure in shadow. *"Who else knew about the plan?"*

Nog turned away in disgust. "I've seen enough."

Tom shook his head. "You really haven't."

"No one!" shouted the Cardassian. *"Please, it was only us! Please stop the pain, stop the . . . the . . ."* Gohdon gave an abrupt, broken gasp, and at once all animation fled from his body. He lolled forward in the chair, eyes rolling back into his head.

"Heart failure," said Tuvok. "A common effect of such a barbaric device."

Then the figure who had spoken before moved, coming into the light to take a closer look at the youth's body. Turning, Jan Kincade's face looked directly into the imager pickup and made a throat-cutting motion. She was wearing a data-monocular over one eye.

Make sure the body is disintegrated, came the order. **We will try again with one of the others later. It is important we are certain we have full containment.**

The playback concluded, freezing on the blurry image. "There's no way it could be someone else," said Tom. "Kincade murdered an unarmed prisoner."

"Whom was she listening to?" asked Nog.

"Whoever it is," said Tuvok, "it is clear they do not wish Throk and the other prisoners to leave Nydak II alive."

"I should put you in the cell next to Bashir's!" snarled Chessman, color rising in his cheeks. His voice reverberated off the walls of his office, and outside past the observation windows looking out at the asteroid's operations center, his staff members were doing their best to pretend they couldn't hear him. "You spin me some line about wanting to find the truth, but in the next breath you're colluding with a convict!"

"He's not a convict," Vale shot back, arms folded across her chest. "Get your terms right, Commander. Bashir hasn't been convicted of anything yet. He's just a prisoner, and frankly the legality of that definition is up for debate!"

"Innocent until proven guilty doesn't count when the man in question openly admits he did it," replied the other officer. "I know what they're saying about Andor, that Bashir and those other doctors saved countless lives with what they did . . . but he still broke the law. And you're within an inch of doing the same, Commander Vale." Chessman glared at a screen on his desk. "My engineering team tells me that despite the best efforts of the *Lionheart*'s crew to drag their heels, your ship is now more or less operable, so I want you on it and out of this system. If you're lucky, you might make it a few parsecs before the reprimand from Starfleet catches up with you."

Vale considered that. She imagined that Chessman's first order of business when the *Lionheart* had come into sensor range was to send an alert back up the chain of command. *Was there a ship on its way to intercept us even now? Or maybe an order for Atia to kick me out of the center seat?*

She had been hoping to stall for time, but that option was fading fast. Her gaze flicked to a viewscreen out in the ops center, a tactical plot of the star system. It was calm and quiet.

What the hell, Vale told herself. *I won't fold, I'm not going to call. Let's go all-in.*

Vale lowered herself into the seat opposite Chessman's desk and gave him the same penetrating stare she had perfected on small-time hoods back on Izar. "You know that once this gets out, you're going to be the bad guy here?" Her tone was suddenly reasonable, and it wrong-footed the other officer. "Bashir is a hero to the Andorian people. And right now, after the shooting, the Federation could do with some heroes. So he punched a couple of people and borrowed a runabout without asking. How does all that balance against safeguarding the future of *an entire species?*"

"He disobeyed orders from his superiors. He stole data that could be lethal in the wrong hands!"

"He resigned from Starfleet," Vale countered. "And

like I said a moment ago, you may want to think about how lawful it is to be holding a civilian non-combatant without due representation, legal oversight, or assent to his rights."

Chessman's bluster faded. He knew she was right, but he was caught between a rock and a hard place. He had his orders, and they were ironclad, while she was, in his eyes, only a few steps removed from a renegade herself.

He opened his mouth to speak, but the alert Vale had been hoping for cut him off before he could utter a word.

Out on the big display screen a sensor return had flashed into life. Two starships were homing in on the asteroid, shedding warp factors as they slowed to high impulse speed.

"Report!" Chessman demanded an answer from the intercom on his desk.

Vale saw one of his staff look up from a console. *"Commander, we read two vessels approaching on an intercept course. They're hailing us."*

"Starfleet?"

"No, sir. Andorian Imperial Guard. An Atlira-*class escort cruiser, the* ADS Mat-Rus, *and a civilian transport, the* Kree-Thai. *Shall I respond?"*

The glare Chessman turned on Vale was sharp enough to slice through steel. "You're responsible for this."

Inwardly, Vale was breathing a huge sigh of relief, but outwardly, she maintained a confident, unruffled air. "You really ought to talk to them," she told him.

"On screen," Chessman barked, pulling his uniform tunic straight as he turned to face a display behind his desk. Vale rose and schooled her expression into careful neutrality.

An image appeared of a tall and imposing Andorian *chan* in elegant robes, framed by the bridge of the diplomatic courier vessel. Off to one side of the hawkish, white-haired figure, Vale saw Deanna Troi standing at steady attention. She resisted the urge to smile.

"I am Envoy Ramasanar ch'Nuillen," said the Andorian, not giving Chessman the opportunity to speak first. *"I demand to address the commanding officer of this facility."*

"Sir," began Chessman, working to maintain an air of steady calm. "This is a restricted zone. I'm afraid I must ask you to leave immediately. You are in violation of Starfleet security protocols."

"That will not occur." The envoy's antennae stiffened. *"Your protocols are of little concern to me, Commander. I am here on a humanitarian mission of great importance to Andoria, and I will not be turned away by the likes of you. Make a docking port available for my ship, and prepare to receive my arrival. Ch'Nuillen out."*

The image died, replaced by an exterior view of the dagger-shaped courier and the shield-shaped escort. The latter was taking up a defense stance, while the former moved closer toward the asteroid.

Vale eyed Chessman, whose color was rising with each passing second. "Have you got a red carpet?" she asked mildly.

The *Snipe*'s operations room was empty, allowing Tuvok and Tom Riker to set about opening the concealed hatch to the armory without attracting notice. The Vulcan pulled open the casing around the hidden activator pad and paused, studying it in silence.

"Thinking at it isn't going to open it," said Tom after a moment. Before Tuvok could stop him, he reached into the casing and pinched a series of connectors together. The hatch gave a grinding hiss and retracted into the wall.

"Impatience is not productive," Tuvok told him.

"It worked, didn't it?" came the reply.

In that moment, Tuvok made two distinct observations; the first was that no matter how much Thomas Riker resembled his "brother," he lacked the subtlety of the *Titan*'s captain; the second observation he gave voice to. "Your actions remind me of another human with whom I associated. You share a common forename."

"Handsome fellow?" asked Tom, with a smile.

"Impulsive and poorly disciplined," Tuvok replied.

The other man slipped into the concealed compartment. "I like him already." He quickly found the phase-shift transport modules and passed one of them across.

Tuvok turned it over in his fingers. "Fully charged. Secure them all."

"Got it."

He turned at the sound of footsteps behind them. Lieutenant Nog slipped into the room, his eyes wide. "I got to Ixxen," he said, low and intense. "She's going to remain on the bridge and be ready for your word."

"What of the rest of the group?"

The Ferengi frowned. "Not sure. Kincade's not on the ship; no sign of Khob. I couldn't check the rest without the Bynars seeing me do it."

"We'll have to cross that bridge when we come to it," said Tom. He was gathering up the phase-shift modules, glancing around the compartment. "Should we take the stealth suits?"

Nog shook his head. "We'll have to get in there

through guile instead—" He halted abruptly, ears stiffening. "Someone—"

"What are you doing in there?" Ashur's voice growled from the other compartment. Tuvok saw the thickset Zeon mercenary move into view. He had his disruptor pistol drawn and pointed into the armory. "I knew it . . . you're all part of this!" Ashur's expression turned ugly with controlled rage.

Tom took a step toward him, then halted when the muzzle of the disruptor turned his way. "Ashur, put the weapon down. Just step aside—let us do this."

"No," he bit out the word. "What is wrong with you, Tom? These Starfleet types, you can't trust them. Isn't that why you turned against them all those years ago? They promise one thing and then do another." Ashur gestured with the weapon. "I never believed Kincade, right from the start. I knew they were in it with her, all their salutes and secrets. . . . They're using us!" He caught sight of the phase-shift modules. "What are you doing with those?"

"Mister Ashur," began Tuvok, maintaining a neutral, static pose. "Lieutenant Colonel Kincade is operating unlawfully. I believe this entire operation is illegal and clandestine."

"I don't care about any of that," he shot back. "I was made a promise. Kincade is reneging on it. They told me I would be free and clear. . . . That was a lie. This Cardassian scum we captured, they should be made to pay for their crimes in front of the galaxy . . . but instead we are *here*." Tuvok saw a shadow of memory pass over Ashur's face. "I've seen places like this before. This is where men of power send those they want broken or erased so it can be done in secret without a single drop of blood touching their hands."

The words came from somewhere deep within him, and once more Tuvok found himself considering what events in the past had put this mercenary on the path he now walked.

"We're going to get them out," Nog blurted. "The prisoners. Away from Kincade, back to face justice."

Tom offered Ashur one of the modules. "We could use your help."

Tuvok watched the Zeon carefully. He was ready at a moment's notice to spring at him; perhaps he would be fast enough to get to Ashur before the mercenary fired off a shot, perhaps not. The humanoid's emotional state was difficult to predict; at first he had categorized the Zeon as one ruled by baser instincts, but now Tuvok wondered if he might have been too swift to dismiss him.

With a snap, Ashur put up his gun and snatched the module from Tom's hand. "All right," he said. "And then we get out of this place and never look back."

A second umbilicus extended out from the asteroid's boarding annex, up at an angle past the *Lionheart*'s primary hull and into a receptor port on the underside of the *Kree-Thai*. The diplomatic vessel was an older class of craft, a sleek transport that was a veteran of decades of service to the Andorian race. It had a blade-shaped prow, and it hung over the surface of the secret base like a weapon suspended a heartbeat before plunging into the flesh of an enemy. Vale wondered if that was deliberate symbolism on the part of the envoy—a veiled warning to Commander Chessman that there was steel beneath the ambassador's intentions.

Chessman had insisted that Vale stay close by for

ch'Nuillen's arrival; he clearly did not trust her to be out of his eyesight for more than a moment.

A group of serious-looking Andorian males emerged from the mouth of the transfer tube and took up places where they could see all angles of approach. None of them appeared to be armed, but Vale knew that at the very least they each carried an *ushaan-tor* blade concealed somewhere on their person. The envoy's protection detail eyed their opposite numbers; Chessman had brought a few Starfleet security officers to bolster his own position, and these men and women stood in loose honor guard formation. They kept their phasers holstered, but visible. In addition, a pair of sentinel drones floated overhead, humming quietly.

"I'll do the talking," Chessman said out the side of his mouth.

"If you like," Vale replied, staying at attention.

The envoy stepped out, with Troi at his side, and she gave Vale the smallest of nods.

Chessman came forward and bowed slightly. "Sir. Before you begin, I must tell you your presence here is highly irregular." He glanced at Troi. "Both of you," he amended.

"Commander Troi is accompanying me at the request of the Andorian government," said ch'Nuillen. "She has been assisting us in the resolution of an important issue." His frost-white eyebrows came together. "And that is why we are here, irregular or not."

"This facility is classified," Chessman insisted. "How did you find it?"

"I would suggest that point is moot, Commander," offered Troi.

Vale saw the other officer's hands tighten. "You should not be here," he replied, and he took her in with that statement. "I'm afraid I will have to ask you all to return to your ships and leave this system."

"I intend to do so," ch'Nuillen said briskly. "Once you have bowed to your obligation."

"I don't know what you mean."

The envoy frowned. "Do not treat me like a fool, Commander. You know why I am here. You know *who* I have come for."

"You have to leave," Chessman repeated, and the tension in his voice spread to his security team. "I'm not going to tell you again."

"And if we do not, will you use force?" Troi gently asked the question.

"If I must." Chessman stared her down, knowing that the Betazoid was reading the strength behind his statement.

Troi caught Vale's eye for a fraction of a second, but it was enough for her to sense the unspoken words. *He'll come out shooting if he's pushed to it.*

"Are you willing to commit an act of violence against Andoria?" Ch'Nuillen's question echoed in the air. "An act . . . of war?" He reached up and touched an ornate emblem hanging around his throat, a rendering in platinum of the crest of Epsilon Indi. "I am Andor. This is Andor. A threat to either is a threat to our people. Are you prepared to take responsibility for that?" He advanced a step toward the commander. "You will release our citizen to me, and you will do it now. *I* will not tell *you* again."

Confusion broke out on Chessman's face. "Your citizen? Envoy, there's been some mistake. We don't have any of your species in detention here."

"This isn't about skin color," said Vale.

Ch'Nuillen reached into his robe and whipped out a

scroll, moving with such speed that Chessman's guards reached for their weapons, and the Andorians did the same, but all motions were arrested when it became clear the envoy held only a piece of paper in his hand. He unrolled it and presented it to the commander.

Chessman looked at the flowing script and frowned. "I . . . don't read your language."

"That is a legal document of entitlement from the Andor Ministry of Citizens," explained Troi. "A declaration of nationality."

"Commander," ch'Nuillen said formally, "you are holding a man who requested *and was granted* full political asylum by my government when he was on my world. It was illegal for Starfleet to arrest him and deport him from Andoria, an action tantamount to kidnapping. It is illegal for the Federation to detain him against his will without first requesting and being granted a right of extradition by Presider zh'Felleth. No such request was made."

"What?" Chessman shook his head. "Asylum? How can you prove that?" He glared at the scroll. "You could have just granted that after the fact!"

The envoy went on as if he hadn't spoken. "Furthermore, because of the selfless acts of your prisoner in aiding my species, deeds that will preserve my family's future, I have declared him *thun-za-ke*."

"The term roughly translates as *adoption*," offered Troi helpfully.

"The man you hold is a named ward of my clan," ch'Nuillen explained. "Bound to me as closely as my siblings and cousins. You will therefore release Julian Subatoi Bashir ke'Nuillen to my custody," he said, adding the adoptive suffix to Bashir's name. "Or we will take him from you."

A bitter, humorless laugh escaped Chessman's throat. "You can't be serious! He's human, not Andorian! He's admitted guilt for multiple crimes!"

Ch'Nuillen brandished the scroll. "He may not be born of Andor, but this document names him Andorian in all but blood. And whatever transgressions you hold against him, petition must be made to try him for them."

All the air seemed to drain out of the chamber. Vale could see the tension written across the faces of the Starfleet security guards and the envoy's protectors; both groups were ready to react in an instant if violence ensued, but neither wanted to be the first to draw a weapon. She watched Chessman, caught in the middle of it. Would he really order his men to open fire on the Andorian diplomatic detail?

One of the humming drones overhead shifted pitch and dropped down to head height, drifting into the middle of the group. Chessman seemed as surprised by it as anyone, until the machine's holoemitter stirred to life, projecting the image of a figure before the assembled group.

"This is Lionheart." Atia's urgent tones came from Vale's combadge. "Detection. Powerful subspace signal incoming, direct to asteroid. . . ."

In the space of a second, the holographic humanoid shape went from a featureless, smooth form to something with detail, character, and expression. "Step aside, Commander Chessman," said the image of Galif jav Velk. "I will take it from here."

"Stand by, Lionheart," said Vale quietly. "This is going to be interesting."

The Tellarite's cold gaze swept the chamber, taking them all in. If not for the sentinel drone hovering at his shoulder and the slight distortion of his voice, it could have been believed that the presidential chief of staff was there before them. "It appears I am required to intervene directly." He fixed Troi with a withering look. "Commander, like your husband and the rest of his officers, it appears you are exceeding your remit."

Ch'Nuillen answered for her. "One might say the same of you, Galif."

Velk eyed the Andorian. "Political asylum?" His porcine nose twitched in disdain. "That is the ploy you are making? Did you not think that your departure from Earth would be noted? Did you not consider that we would be watching this place at all times?" He shook his head. "It will not hold air, Ramasanar, this gambit of yours. It is a foolish, theatrical act of misplaced bravado."

Vale heard the low hiss from the diplomat. "Your people have never understood us, have you? Not since the very beginning. This is not an act. This is the matter of a debt to be repaid."

"Is he worth it?" asked the Tellarite, a shimmer of interference momentarily moving through his image. "Is Andor willing to risk its readmission to the Federation over one man's liberty?"

"If you must ask that question," said ch'Nuillen, "then you truly show how little you know us."

The cell door dropped open without warning, and Bashir was jolted, flinching back against the wall. A single sentinel drone floated there before him, filling the entranceway with its spherical bulk. Multiple camera eyes across its surface stared at him, glassy and dark.

"Um . . . hello?" he began, putting down his padd. "Is there something I can help you with?"

Light shimmered, and a sketch of a humanoid form built itself in the middle of the cell's confines until it was distinctly a Tellarite male in a plain business suit. "Doctor Bashir," he began. "I'm sure you know who I am. I imagine you have it stored up there somewhere in that superior brain of yours."

He nodded, forcing himself to remain calm. "I know who you are, Mister Velk. Can I assume the appearance of the president pro tem's hatchet man in my comfy little jail cell is a good thing? Are you here on Ishan Anjar's behalf to tell me all is forgiven?"

Velk made a noise that might have been a chuckle. "Hardly. You are an arrogant criminal."

"I believe the correct response to that is, 'Takes one to know one.' Or would that be too glib?" Bashir leaned forward, studying the drone without making it obvious. The cell door was still open, and he found himself idly plotting out methods of how he might get past the drone, get into the anteroom beyond . . . *and then* . . . ? He looked away. He wasn't about to run. He didn't see the point.

"You have caused a great deal of problems," Velk went on. "Andoria would have been given what they needed, eventually. In a few months, after the election. But you interfered with things. Took the law into your own hands. You brought instability, Bashir. I do not tolerate that."

"They've waited long enough," he shot back, his temper rising. "The Federation had no right to hold information that could save countless lives."

"It is not your place to decide."

Bashir gave a rough shrug. "But I did, anyway. *I* did. I did the right thing." He smiled thinly. "And do you know something? I don't regret a moment of it.

So if you're here to menace me or make some kind of veiled threats, get it done, and then be on your way."

"No veils," said Velk. "You are an intelligent man, and I have little patience with obfuscation, unlike your Cardassian friend Mister Garak."

"And how *is* he? Did they make him castellan yet? He'll be insufferable if he gets that job, mark my words."

The Tellarite's pinched, humorless expression tightened at Bashir's feigned levity. "If it were in my power," he said grimly, "you would remain here until your name was little more than a distant memory. But it seems the predilection for disobedience is more widespread in Starfleet than I had first realized. You are going to be released, Doctor."

They were, quite definitely, the very last words Julian had expected to hear, and he didn't know how to react to them. "What?"

"My hand has been forced. I am making the best choice of several poor options." The holographic projection gestured at the low ceiling. "Up in the docking bay, an Andorian ship has come to take you away. They are claiming you like an errant pet, and if they are refused, it will go badly for all concerned. News will spread. That would not be for the best." He sniffed. "So you may leave, to return to Andoria. I suppose you could consider it freedom, after a fashion."

"Vale . . ." He smiled. "She came through."

"And she will answer for that." Velk nodded gravely. "Make no mistake, there will be a price to pay." The Tellarite beckoned him. "On your feet. Follow the drone into the turbolift. You'll be taken to your liberty, such as it is."

Warily, Bashir got up, hesitating with the padd

in his hand. The Dumas novel was unfinished, and although he could recall the text with clarity from his own memory from past readings, he enjoyed the act of reading it over again. After a moment, he let the device drop on the sleeping pallet.

He had only taken a step when Velk's hologram spoke again. "One consideration before you leave, Doctor Bashir. You may intend to talk to others about this conversation, or to discuss the events that brought you to this juncture. You may think you know things about me and the president pro tem. But it would be wise for you to keep your own counsel on these matters."

"Why? I'm a free man. That includes the right to speak."

Velk nodded. "*You* are free. But Katherine Pulaski, Lemdock, Tovak, Elizabeth Lense, Ezri Dax . . . Sarina Douglas? Consider their circumstances before you give voice, Doctor."

The Tellarite shimmered and vanished, leaving Bashir alone in the cell with the humming drone and a chill running through his blood.

Out in the anteroom, the turbolift door hissed open.

Thirteen

Again, there was the brutal touch of fire across his flesh, and then Tuvok was whole and uninjured once again, the flicker-flash of the phase-shift transport fading into the gloom.

He heard Nog bite down on a gasp and looked past him to where Tom and Ashur were crouching. They too were fighting off the pain induced by the transport. The four of them had rematerialized deep inside the former mining facility, close to a power source that Nog had identified as a force-field generator. It seemed highly likely that the generator unit was part of a detention system, and Tuvok gave the command to investigate.

Now, as he surveyed the area, he believed the hypothesis had been correct. They were under one of the complex's aging domes, the cracked hyperpolymer sections of the structure overhead blackened by machine emissions and the ravages of the planet's wounded ecosystem. Raised catwalks and gantries formed a suspended highway across what had once been refining pits and ore crushers. Most of the larger pieces of machinery were gone now, leaving stubs of connector conduits dangling from walls or sprouting from the thermoconcrete floors. In the shadow of corroding metal frames, crude slabs of drab Klingon technology—energy baffles and power generators—had been retrofitted to allow the facility to perform another function.

"Patrol coming," whispered Nog, and he dropped low behind the cover of a fallen exhaust pipe.

Tuvok and the others followed suit. The Vulcan saw a trio of Klingon guards emerge from a tunnel in the floor and march in a ragged line across the vast chamber. They were from the same group he had seen outside when the *Snipe* landed. He noted the style of their battle armor, the manner of their weapons. Although they were Klingons, these were mercenaries without loyalty to any noble house, a stripe of dishonored warriors who would be shunned by their martial betters elsewhere.

Tuvok considered them, turning over Ashur's words in his thoughts. The ghost prison, the soldiers of fortune, the covert nature of it all . . . There was no doubt in his mind that Nydak II was a desolate holding belonging to Imperial Intelligence, the Klingon Empire's secret police and espionage directorate. Some said that Imperial Intelligence held more power in the Empire than the chancellor, the High Council, and the noble houses combined. Governments would come and go, but they were eternal; it troubled Tuvok greatly to consider what part the shadowy agency might be playing in this unfolding drama.

The guards vanished through a hatch, and as it clanged shut, Tuvok broke from cover and signaled the others. Staying low, hugging the deep, ink-black shadows cast by the gantries, the group threaded their way toward a former smelting chamber that had been repurposed as a brig.

A number of adjoining metal cargo cages, once used for gathering useless slag from the ore-refining process, were now cells. Each one was held shut with a glowing blue mechanism fixed across the open face, a magnetic lock making escape impossible. Power units haloed the cells, connected by thick cables that snaked up toward a wide platform above. There was a guard room up there, and Tuvok glimpsed movement inside.

Tom was observing the same through a data-monocle over his right eye. "Scanning with infrared. Just one up there. I can take him out of play."

Two more Klingons were standing near the iron cages. "Proceed," said Tuvok. "We will deal with the others."

The human split off from the group and found a ladder that would take him to the upper tier. Tuvok beckoned Ashur and Nog to follow him.

As they came closer, Tuvok heard the two Klingons talking; they were sharing rough humor at the expense of their Cardassian prisoners who sat a few meters away from them on the gridded floors of their enclosures.

"No alarms," said Tuvok quietly.

Tom's attack was the signal; there was a distant clatter of something falling, up in the guard room, and then without warning the power to the locks died with a fizzing crackle. The guards reacted, but Tuvok, Nog, and Ashur had already exploded from their concealment.

Ashur moved with surprising speed for one of his body mass, and he performed a running leap that threw him directly onto the shoulders of the first guard. There was the glitter of dull light off a shimmerknife blade before the Zeon plunged it into the Klingon's throat, down through his clavicle. The guard stumbled to the ground, dying as he fell.

The other Klingon swung toward Nog, ripping a long-barreled disruptor pistol from his holster. It was a grave error on the part of the guard, choosing the less dangerous of the two attackers coming at him. In two quick footsteps, Tuvok was on the Klingon, and he performed a flawless leg-sweep. The second guard went down, and the Vulcan expertly intercepted him, chopping the blade of his hand down across the soft tissues of the Klingon's exposed throat. Gasping and starved of air, the second guard was unconscious before he hit the dirt.

Nog grimaced at Ashur as the Zeon wiped purple blood from his blade and moved toward the cells.

A Cardassian woman with ragged, shoulder-length hair and a male whose scarred scalp was shorn were in the process of kicking open the gates of their rusted cages. The third prisoner was already free; Onar Throk had found a length of steel rebar and brandished it like a sword.

"Heybis! Vekt!" he shouted, calling out their names. "Quickly!"

Nog held up a hand. "We're not here to hurt you."

"Lies," spat Throk. "I knew your Federation was corrupt and decadent, but your cruelty is even greater than I could have expected! It is not enough you take us as your prisoners, but you use your Klingon lackeys to tear at our minds! I regret nothing I have done to harm your people, *nothing*!"

"We did not want this," Tuvok told him, calm in the face of Throk's thunderous anger. "You were brought here unlawfully."

Nog gave a stiff nod. "No matter what crimes you have committed . . ." It was hard for him to say the next words. "You still have your rights to a fair trial."

Throk laughed bitterly. "You may choke on your *rights* and your *fair trials*! We wish none of it!" He shook his head. "No matter what you do to us, we will give you nothing, do you hear? *Nothing!*"

"Tuvok . . ." Ashur called out from behind him. "See." The Vulcan turned to see the Zeon pointing with his combat blade.

From out of the shadows came Sahde, the Elloran female walking with a casual swagger. In one hand she gripped a phaser, toying with it as she moved closer. "Are you having fun without me?" She directed the question toward Nog.

"What are you doing here?" asked Ashur. He shot a look at Nog. "I thought she was on the ship."

Tuvok slowly reached up and tapped the communicator bead in his ear. "Mister Riker? Respond, please." He waited for an answer.

"I figured out what you were doing," said Sahde. "I followed you." She glanced at Ashur and flashed a disarming smile. "So. Prison break? That could be interesting."

"Tom isn't answering," said Nog. "Something is wrong."

"The Elloran is lying to us," Ashur said with finality. He brought up his blade. "She—"

"She really *is,*" Sahde snapped, cutting him off. Before the Zeon could react, she turned her pistol on him and fired. Bright crimson fire enveloped the mercenary, and before he could scream, his body became a blaze of light—and then nothing.

Nog's throat tightened. All that was left of Ashur was the brief tang of ozone in the cold air of the dome, and he stifled the urge to cough. He was very aware of the Zeon's killer now turning her gaze—and her phaser—on him.

Her lizard-like eyes bored into his. "I didn't like Ashur," she announced. "He talked too much."

"So you killed him?" Nog gasped.

"Not just for that reason," she said mildly. "I like you, Nog, but you'll end up the same way if you don't drop that weapon you're holding." Sahde waved her gun at the group. "Anyone else want to go out as a wisp of vapor and free atoms?"

"Why are you doing this?" asked Tuvok.

"Because I'm getting a good weight of gold-pressed latinum for my trouble, and now that Ashur is dead, I'll take his share as well."

Figures moved in the shadows behind Sahde, hulking Klingon warriors surrounding a smaller female form in a hooded tunic. Nog saw slender fingers reach up, and Lieutenant Colonel Kincade showed her face.

Kincade looked no different from the way she had the last time they had spoken, but in some indefinable way she had changed *inside*. It was almost as if he were looking at a different spirit possessing her body, a totally new persona looking out at him through those dark eyes. Kincade's gaze was callous and bereft of any warmth, with a shallowness of effect that seemed chilling. "Do as Sahde says," she snapped. "Or you'll die where you stand."

"As you wish." Tuvok let his weapon drop to the dirt, and Nog reluctantly did the same. He couldn't help but tense for a blow to come a moment later, and a nerve jumped in his leg; it was a faint tingle of phantom pain from where his old wound had been, the damage done to him during the Dominion War.

Kincade watched Nog as a predator would watch a

prey animal. All of a sudden it came to him that it was not that she had changed, but that she had simply let a disguise drop away. The woman he had dealt with over the past few days aboard the *Snipe* had been the false-hood. What he saw now was the *real* Jan Kincade. "I wondered how long it would take you to try something like this. You moved more quickly than I expected."

Another pair of Klingons arrived, dragging Tom Riker's unconscious form between them. They dumped him roughly on the ground and snatched up the weapons from where they had been tossed. Tuvok didn't wait for any kind of permission, and he dropped into a crouch, examining the human.

"He lives," reported the commander.

"For now," added Sahde out the side of her mouth. "So, what do we do with them now that we know who can't be trusted?" She grinned unpleasantly. "I mean, we only really need that Bolian wench. . . ."

"The Bynars are with me," Kincade spoke over her. "We've worked together before; they're loyal. I'll find a convincing way to compel Ixxen to do her job, and the Suliban will do what I tell him." She looked back toward Nog and the others.

"If we don't need these three, then what point is there in keeping them alive?" The Elloran seemed delighted by the idea of more killing.

"You cannot sanction the execution of Starfleet officers and Federation civilians in cold blood," Tuvok said, matter-of-fact and severe.

Kincade's lips thinned. "Don't be obtuse, Tuvok," she replied, pausing to think. "I have to check in with control," she said to the Elloran. "There may be other uses for them. Keep them alive in the meantime."

Sahde made a motion with the weapon in her

hand, nodding to the guards. "You heard the colonel. Put them in the cages with the rest of the prisoners."

The Klingons advanced, a wall of snarling faces and armor plates, and Nog watched as the last shreds of Tuvok's plan disintegrated in front of him.

Deanna Troi sat across the briefing-room table from Julian Bashir, the doctor's head haloed by warp-light as the *Lionheart* raced toward Andoria. Visible over his shoulder was the flat hull of the *Mat-Rus*, the warship keeping pace with the *Nova*-class cruiser at high cruise speed. She couldn't see Envoy ch'Nuillen's courier from this angle, but it was out there, too, following in their superluminal wake.

What struck her the most was how guarded Bashir was. She had never met the man before today, but his reputation preceded him. Troi had heard stories from Beverly Crusher and Alyssa Ogawa about his abilities. Both were clearly impressed with his achievements; from their descriptions, she had expected to meet a man of suave character and self-assurance. Instead he was circumspect and inward-looking, as if he were bearing a load that no one else could shoulder.

Instinctively, her counselor's training took over, and she leaned forward. "What can I do to help?"

At the head of the table, Christine Vale caught her eye and frowned. "Deanna, you've already gone above and beyond the call. . . ." She gave an apologetic smile. "Honestly? I didn't think any of that was going to work."

Bashir was toying with a small medallion that the envoy had pressed into his hands, a rendition of his clan's sigil. "It was an unexpected turn of events," he offered, managing a weak smile of his own. "I must admit, I didn't expect to wake up with a new extended family today."

"Andorians don't do anything by halves," said Vale.

The doctor met Troi's gaze for the first time. "Commander Troi, ch'Nuillen made it clear that you were the one who brought all this together. Thank you for what you've done." He shook his head. "I had resigned myself to spending the rest of my days in that little cell."

"It wasn't just me," Troi told him. "Christine had the idea."

"Actually, Ezri Dax set me thinking on it," Vale noted. "Call it a group effort."

Bashir's frown deepened at the mention of Captain Dax's name. "Is she all right? And what about Simon Tarses and Lieutenant sh'Pash? They risked a lot to free me from the *Aventine*'s brig."

Vale nodded. "They're as well as can be expected, given what they did. But now we have you out of that damned *oubliette*, we can start on trying to get Dax and the rest of the Andor Five out into the public eye."

"That's what they're calling us?" Bashir seemed incredulous. "Catchy."

"The story hasn't gone away," Troi noted, "even with everything else that's been happening in the meantime."

He listened, and nodded. "I've been out of the loop for a little while. What did I miss?"

"Short version? Andor's pushing hard to return to the UFP, and that's going to happen, whether Ishan Anjar likes it or not. Kellessar zh'Tarash has announced her candidacy for the presidency. Elim Garak swept to victory on Cardassia—"

For a brief moment, Bashir's morose mien fell, and he

showed a genuine flash of delight. "That's excellent news! I knew we'd make an honest man of him someday."

"I wouldn't go that far." Vale's lip curled. "He *is* still a politician."

Troi picked up the thread of the conversation. "In the meantime, Admiral Akaar and a few of us have been investigating suspicious activity within Starfleet Command and the Federation Council."

"Activity connected to the Bacco assassination and the Andor incident," added Vale. "Both may be connected in some way to abuses of executive power within the pro tem government, but so far we don't have anything we can prove."

"That is troubling," Bashir offered, looking away.

Troi went on. "When you reach Andor, you'll effectively be in exile. There will be investigators who will want to talk to you, but anything you can tell us now, we can pass back to Akaar."

He didn't meet her gaze, rubbing the bridge of his nose. "Commander . . . it's been a very long day for me. I'm quite fatigued. . . ." He trailed off.

Vale nodded. "We understand. Doctor Rssuu suggested you visit sickbay so he could check you over. Perhaps we should postpone this until later. . . ."

But Troi was shaking her head, sensing the barriers around Bashir's thoughts and feelings. *What is he hiding?* "Doctor . . . Julian. You're among friends here. A lot of people put themselves on the line to get you away from that asteroid. The Andorians, the crew of this ship, Captain Dax, and Lieutenant Commander Douglas . . ."

"Sarina . . ." Again, the barriers briefly slipped, but then they slammed down even more firmly. "Of course. She wouldn't stand by and watch. . . ."

Troi watched him carefully. "We need the full truth from you. Not just what happened, but everything around it. Everything you suspect, everything you think could be a clue to what is really going on back on Earth, in the corridors of power."

Bashir got to his feet. "I can't give you that. I'm sorry. I'll . . . I'll be in sickbay." He left the room and did not look back.

Vale shook her head slowly. "What just happened there?"

"I don't know," Troi said honestly. "He's afraid . . . but not for himself."

What passed for night fell on Nydak II, and the air in the detention chamber became cold and stagnant. In the cage next to his, Tuvok watched Lieutenant Nog dozing fitfully up against the bars, snatching a moment of rest where he could. Thomas Riker had his back to the door of his cell, and Tuvok could not tell in what state he was.

For his part, the Vulcan did not currently require sleep, using a disciplinary meme to concentrate his thoughts and moderate the effects of fatigue. The Klingons had left them to their own devices, retreating to the guard room on the upper level, but not before setting up a portable automated disruptor turret at the throat of the chamber. The device panned right and left in an endless cycle of motion, watchful for any sign of movement inside its kill zone. Tuvok had already calculated that it would be capable of gunning down any potential escapees before they had taken ten steps from their cages.

He turned and found Onar Throk watching him from the next cell along; his two companions, the woman Heybis and the bald male Vekt, shared the next pair of cages. The Cardassian's intense, hooded gaze was unblinking and cold, full of sour hatred.

"I should thank you," said Throk, his voice low so it would not carry far. Tuvok raised his eyebrow, and the assassin went on. "After you sent the Klingons to kill us on that ice moon, I did not need more proof of the Federation's rotting heart, but still you gave it to me."

"You are referring to my imprisonment here, with you."

"How does it feel, Vulcan? To know that your world allied itself with an entity that builds its power on secret lies and insidious manipulation?"

Tuvok cocked his head. "I find it difficult to accept such a judgment from a member of Cardassian society. Until very recently, your Union based its power structure on those very things."

Throk gave a derisive snort. "I can see how an alien might be so mistaken. If you are not born Cardassian, you cannot know Cardassian ways. And yet, you and others like you think you have the right to change us to fit your patterns." He grimaced. "First the Dominion, and now your Federation. Each an invader coming to us with iron wrapped in velvet. Each intent on burning out the soul of Cardassia." Throk shifted his weight, coming closer to the bars of his cage, lessening the distance between them. "You still do not understand. You have looked me in the eye, and still the question vexes you. *Why did they strike at us? After all we have given them. After all we have done to raise their world from the ashes, why attack our leader?*"

"You blame the Federation for the misfortunes of your species," said Tuvok.

"Imbecile!" Throk spat the word back at him with such venom that the Vulcan almost recoiled. "You are cattle, just like the Bajorans! You want the simple answer, the solution that eases your mind. That is why your government finds it so easy to manipulate you. On Cardassia, we knew that our leaders were using us. And we in turn used them, each of us part of a decrepit machine that ran on influence and falsehood. One component locked to the other in symbiosis. . . . But we understood, you see? We played our roles and smiled at the lies because we knew that was how the machine worked. But we never truly believed, not in our hearts." He pointed at Tuvok. "*You* believe." Throk made it a grave insult. "I would pity you if I did not hate you so much."

"The United Federation of Planets is a democracy," insisted Tuvok. "A society of rules and laws—"

"So says the man sitting inside a reeking cage on a poisoned world." Throk gestured at the air. "Look around, Commander. This is the domain of your trusted allies. A pit for the dead and the nameless. The men in your government walk spotless before your citizens, hiding their mendacity where you cannot see it among the barbarism of the Klingons."

"And so you conspired to commit murder because you hold that to be true."

"I am not a murderer," Throk shot back. "I am a patriot. You weakened our race with your hollow gestures of friendship. The woman Bacco . . ." He scowled again. "She blinded that fool Garan with promises, eroding our independence with every word spoken of treaty and friendship. The die was cast. Our freedom was to be sold cheaply in the name of partnership, setting us on the road to being subsumed by the Federation . . . until we were one more pathetic member-world, one more star upon their roundel." Tuvok saw a chilling and unflinching certainty in Throk's eyes. "Cardassia must stand alone in all things. That is the lesson history has taught us. Alliance breeds weakness; it opens the door to greed and sloth. The True Way knows that. We had to take steps. We had to break you, yes? A deed of magnitude that all the galaxy would see clearly. And if we did not have ships with which to go to war, then we used the weapons we *did* have."

He was looking down at his aged hands, and Tuvok wondered if the former official was remembering the moment when he fired the killing shot. "What you did, sir, was not an act of war. It was terrorism."

"We hate you all so much," Throk spat. "And you cannot feel it. A Vulcan at least has an excuse, bled dry of passion and fire. But the rest of your mighty 'coalition'? The Federation thinks all beings aspire to be part of your great and good; you cannot comprehend that we would wish otherwise!" He was at the bars of his cage now, and Tuvok suspected that if he could have, Throk might have reached across the space between them to strike blows on the Vulcan out of sheer spite.

"That is not so. You cast the Federation as the source of all your ills because it is a convenient scapegoat. You confuse hate with fear. You and those who share your isolationist beliefs in the True Way are unwilling to accept the hand of friendship when it is offered. You would rather lash out in anger than accept help from a former enemy. It is illogical."

Throk shook his head. "This is your arrogance! To speak as if you know us! Let me tell you why you are so loathed, Commander. It is not just in the name of all these things, the worthless treaty and the diminishment of Cardassia. We hate you because your bright, shining Federation is rotting within." He laughed. "Ask yourself why it was so easy for me to put your president in my sights." Throk mimed aiming a weapon. "Your people *helped* us, Vulcan. It was they who reached out to the True Way."

The dark possibilities that had plagued Tuvok's thoughts over the duration of the mission now came rushing forward with the Cardassian's words. Even now, after all that had taken place, after the revelation of Kincade's actions, he had hoped that on some level there could be another explanation for what was going on. He felt the faintest echo of an emotion, out on the horizon of his self—*desolation*. But then it was gone, pushed away. "Who helped you?" he demanded.

"The Tellarite," Throk sneered. "He gave the information we needed, the identity of that Bajoran sow Enkar to throw your investigators off the trail. I made him show me his face before I agreed to the act." He took bleak relish from Tuvok's reaction. "That is why he sent you after us, that is why you and I are here now. We both saw his face, Vulcan. We cannot be allowed to tell of it." He looked away, his bluster fading. "I regret nothing I have done. The deed will have its way, and others will take up the fight. Your Federation has been shown weak, and Cardassia will see the blood. It may take years, but we are a patient people. You will crumble, but eternal Cardassia will still remain."

Tuvok saw an opening and seized it. "No. If you truly did assassinate the President of the United Federation of Planets as an act of defiance, then that deed has no meaning. If we are to perish here, then the name of Onar Throk will be lost, and there will be no record of you."

Throk shook his head. "They *will* know. The truth will be out. . . . The True Way will not forget."

"The voice of the True Way will not matter," Tuvok countered. "You desired the assassination to be an act of Cardassian resolve, but the galaxy will see a different culprit. Tzenkethi DNA was found in the investigation on Deep Space Nine. Enkar Sirsy's name was cleared, and the Typhon Pact has been implicated in Bacco's death. The name of the True Way has not been spoken."

Throk's lined face split in sudden fury. "You are lying!" His voice rose, the sound of it stirring the others.

"I have no cause to," he replied. "If we remain here, your crime will be forgotten, and the consequences turned toward another design."

"No! I will die before I allow that to happen!" The furious Cardassian pulled impotently at the bars of his cage.

"That, I believe, is the intention," Tuvok told him.

Over Julian's head, a cluster of tree branches formed a canopy through which shone soft light from an illuminator strip. The dappled glow cast over him and across the walls of the small examination room was a reminder of sunshine and summer days back on Bajor—and all at once he felt a pang of regret about the planet that had become something of a second home to him in recent years. He was going to miss the green fields and the broad trees. They didn't have much of that kind of summery landscape on Andoria. Bashir wondered how long it would take him to get tired of skiing and skating in the colder populated zones.

He closed his eyes and let the scanner unit pass

over his body. It was an automatic device, a thin arm emitting a yellow haze of energy, built into the side of the bio-bed beneath him. It moved up and down, up and down as it used passive sensors to peer into his flesh and bone. Bashir knew that he was in good condition—lack of outdoor exercise notwithstanding—as one of the subtle perks of his genetically improved physiology, but he soon realized it would be best to let Doctor Rssuu conduct the examination rather than argue with the Lahit. The *Lionheart*'s chief doctor was formidable in his own way, and Bashir was quietly impressed by the work he and his team had done on the medical cruiser: hospital duty at the Haze Plague outbreak on Cimarron, disaster relief in the Sigma Draconis sector. . . .

With infinite patience, the tree-like being deflected his suggestions that a thorough examination was a waste of time, citing numerous examples and the need to make sure he hadn't been mistreated under Commander Chessman's care. Finally Bashir had conceded, taking to the compartment off the main sickbay while the process ran. He tried to make use of the time, tried to relax . . . and failed.

He could still see Troi and Vale in his mind's eye, the look on their faces as he had cut short their questions and made his excuses. His actions had to seem foolish to them, ungrateful even; they had liberated him from his confinement only to find that he was unwilling to talk about who had put him there. But it wasn't a risk he wanted to take, not at this moment.

He pushed those thoughts away, and it was Sarina Douglas he saw in their place. She too had dared much for him, he didn't doubt it. Julian owed it to the woman he loved to let her know he had some freedom now, after a fashion—and perhaps together they could find some solution that would allow him to get past the silence Galif jav Velk's threat had forced upon him.

Bashir heard a footstep at the door and the rise of a low, resonant hum. Someone spoke. "If there were birds in the branches, you could almost make this place a park, don't you think?"

He opened his eyes and saw a young man with dark hair in a lieutenant's uniform. He was carrying a tricorder in one hand, the source of the humming tone. "I suppose so. . . . Did Doctor Rssuu send you?" Bashir craned his neck to see past the lieutenant's shoulder, out into the passage to the main sickbay.

"No," he said, putting down the tricorder on a nearby table. He walked to a locker on the far wall and opened it, removing a hypospray, which he proceeded to load with a drug ampoule. "This won't take long."

Something in the officer's behavior rang a wrong note, and Bashir pushed the scanner arm away, swinging round to sit up on the bio-bed. The noise from the tricorder was irritating him, and it seemed to be having a similar effect on the tree branches above. Julian saw the tendrils that were part of Rssuu's extended "body" shrink away, and the small flowering blossoms along the branches folded closed. "That sound . . ."

"It's duplicating a subsonic register from the Lahit homeworld," said the lieutenant. "Generated by an insect that bores into their outlying branches to lay its eggs. It's a sort of anesthetic sound wave, deadens their limbs and sensory clusters."

The tree-being's form reached to all parts of the *Lionheart*'s infirmary, allowing the alien doctor to almost be everywhere at once. *But now Rssuu is blind in here—*

Bashir spun as the lieutenant came at him with the loaded hypospray, blocking him before he could press the emitter head to his neck. The other man was stronger than he looked, and for a second, they were at a stalemate. Bashir forced the hypo away and up.

The device discharged in his face, and he choked as aerosolized liquid sprayed over his cheek and eyes. It burned cold, and Bashir fell back off the bio-bed, clawing at his skin. He could already feel the drug load penetrating his tissues, numbing him. His vision became blurry and indistinct. He tried to call out, but all that escaped his lips was a wet gasp.

"I was passing by, coming in to ask about my last check-up," said the officer. "You called me in. You tried to escape, wanted to steal my combadge." There was a rattle as he ejected the spent ampoule and loaded another. "You attacked me with this hypospray, trying to knock me out with a theragen dose. . . ."

Bashir listened to his assailant rehearsing his story, struggling to get back to his feet. *Theragen* . . . He recognized the effects now; in small doses, the compound could cure interphase sickness, but at larger concentrations it acted as a lethal nerve toxin. Lurching forward, Bashir heard the endless humming of the tricorder from somewhere nearby.

The lieutenant's hazy form came closer. "We struggled. . . . The hypo accidentally discharged . . . and there was nothing to be done to save you."

With all the effort he could muster, Bashir threw himself across the examination room in the direction of the soporific hum, arms out, flailing wildly. Near-blinded by the spray in his eyes, he could only hope to succeed.

The lieutenant cursed as Bashir crashed into the

table, sending medical instruments, protoplasers, and the tricorder flying. The device crashed to the deck and fell silent, and Bashir went with it. He collapsed into a heap, gasping as it became increasingly harder to breathe.

"That was stupid of you," said his assailant.

Bashir blinked furiously, gaining some measure of sight back as the officer leaned down. From somewhere else in the sickbay, he caught the sound of a very proper, cut-glass English voice calling out in alarm. "Lieutenant Maslan? What are you doing with my patient?"

There was a noise like wood twisting in the wind and what might have been snakes dropped out of the ceiling, snagging the dark-haired man around the arms, yanking him off his feet.

Bashir didn't see any more after that; the theragen robbed him of his awareness, and the room went dark around him.

The sound Nog was making was a calculated, practiced one. It was a kind of bleating whine that started up in the high registers and then climbed further into a tone that was directly pitched to be as grating as possible to the ears of most carbon-based life-forms. Ferengi vocal cords and lung dynamics meant that with a little focus, they could sustain the noise for several minutes, and some experts could even do it for hours at a time. On a Class-M planet with a near-terrestrial air density, the whine could carry a good distance, and to those close at hand the sound would find the sweet spot of near-perfect irritation. Nog had been taught as a child that the cry was a holdover from the era of primitive, pre-tribal Ferengi, back when his people dwelled in mud hollows and were preyed upon by swamp predators. The sound was so utterly annoying that rather than attack those early ancestors, the hunter beasts would seek their food elsewhere—anything to be away from that piercing, screeching whimper.

Tom Riker grunted and winced, glancing at Tuvok. "If this doesn't work soon, I swear I'll smother him myself."

Tuvok didn't reply; if anyone was finding the sound the most painful, it was the Vulcan.

Nog snatched another lungful of air, putting a peculiar ululation into the note of the cry, and at last it had the effect they were hoping for. His dark face like a clenched fist, one of the Klingon guards stomped out of the shadows, brandishing a *mek'leth* blade. He swore a choice oath at Nog in his native language and then switched to Standard. "Shut him up!" he bellowed. "I can hear that damnable noise across the compound. Silence him now or I'll slit his throat!" To illustrate his point, he slammed the flat of the blade against the bars of Nog's cage.

The Klingon smelled like sweat, rust, and rage. Nog choked off his whine, sliding back along his makeshift cell as far as he could get from the mag-locked door; then he took a breath and started again, making the pitch high and shrill, just like Uncle Quark had taught him when he was a youth. *It's a Ferengi gift,* he had said. *Anyone tries to beat you up, just do this until they turn away in revulsion, and then when their back is turned, kick them wherever it hurts.*

The guard decided to make good on his promise. He used a wand-like device on a lanyard to deactivate the mag-lock and wrenched open the cage door. One hand still on the *mek'leth,* he reached in and grabbed at Nog's jumpsuit with the other hand.

The Ferengi struck; he brought both hands around to clap against the Klingon's already-strained ears and was rewarded with a dull grunt of pain. It was enough to put the guard off balance so that Nog could grab the wand from where it dangled and tear it free. Dazed, the Klingon staggered backward and away from the cage.

The automated turret saw him move and spun to face the guard, a charge crackling at the tip of its weapon barrel. The guard's free hand went to his throat and found nothing; not only did the wand act as a key, it also served as a friend-or-foe indicator to the turret's simple machine brain.

Two brilliant green disruptor bolts burst from the automated gun and blasted the guard back across the dusty floor; in the same instant, a hooting alarm began to sound, echoing through the dome.

Acting quickly, Nog scrambled out of his cage, first to the turret to disable its power supply, then to the other cells to free Tuvok and Tom. The Vulcan took the wand and used it to open the cages where Throk and the other Cardassians sat watching them.

"What is this?" demanded Throk as he climbed out.

"Oh, you're welcome," Tom told him, stooping to gather up the dead Klingon's weapons.

"You are prisoners of the United Federation of Planets," announced Tuvok. "You will be taken to Earth to answer for your crimes."

"We'll be killed," said Heybis. "Executed."

"They're too weak for that," Throk corrected, glowering at the commander. "I reject your claim, Vulcan."

"You may return to your cells if you wish," he said. "The choice is yours."

Nog crouched and pulled the communicator from the guard's sleeve. As he touched it, a voice crackled from a speaker grille on the device. *"This is Kincade,"* said the colonel. *"We're reading a breakout in progress. Don't waste any more time. Shoot on sight. Kill them all."*

Throk's eyes narrowed, staring at Nog as if the message was somehow his fault. "Lead the way, then."

Fourteen

The Klingon trying to part Nog's head from his neck abruptly breathed his last and fell away, crashing to the ground with a strangled wheeze.

Nog grimaced as Tom Riker came in and pulled the bloody *mek'leth* from where he had buried it in the mercenary's side. "He *was* going to kill you," said the human. "Don't make that face."

"Sorry," Nog managed. "I'm not good with lots of blood."

The dead guard had two small-bore disruptor pistols in a bandolier across his chest, and Tom took one for himself, pressing the other into Nog's grip. "Here. Keep this."

The Ferengi weighed the weapon in his hand, checking the charge. The hot stink of burnt air and ozone was heavy in the air. They had run from the cages through the remains of the smelting yards and under the shadow of tall, rusting rock grinders; now they were close to the wide landing pad where the *Snipe* had put down. The guards clearly anticipated the escapees would make a break for the freighter and placed a contingent here to waylay them. The Klingons hadn't counted on Tuvok's inspired tactics, turning their ambush on them by using a still-operable cargo lifter to ram through their cover.

Now Vekt, the balding Cardassian, darted forward and grabbed at the body of another dead Klingon, plucking a fan of thin silver daggers from a belt pouch.

"Hey!" Tom aimed the disruptor at him. "Drop those and step away."

"You cannot expect us to fight our way out of this pit unarmed," he shot back, looking to Throk for support.

"I'm not expecting anything," Tom retorted. "You seem to have forgotten the part about how you three are our prisoners." He took in Vekt, Throk, and the woman Heybis with a wave of the gun. "You're not getting weapons. You should think yourself lucky you're even conscious. If it was easier to knock you out and carry you, I'd do that."

Throk was on the verge of saying something, but he chose to remain silent as Tuvok jogged back from the corridor he had scouted ahead. "The passageway ends in a loading hatch, open to the landing pad," said the Vulcan. "From there, it is approximately five hundred meters to the *Snipe*."

Tom waved the pistol again. "Move it." The Cardassians reluctantly obeyed, and Nog followed on behind them, glancing nervously over his shoulder.

"They're going to find us and kill us," muttered Heybis. "They'll save you the effort of executing us before your masters."

Nog said nothing. He hoped she was wrong. The heavy concentrations of ferrous slag throughout the Nydak II facility made scanner functions unreliable at anything but close range—it was how they had managed to stay ahead of their pursuers so far—but once they were out in the open, that advantage would be lost.

Up ahead, he saw a long, narrow gateway, the saw-toothed hatch across it rusted in the open position. Muddy brown daylight filtered in through the gap, and beyond there was a ramp leading up to the pad. A few empty cargo containers, each one the size of a shuttlepod, lay in an untidy line. *Partial cover,* he thought to himself, *at least for some of the distance.*

Nog thought about how far five hundred meters was and tried in vain to recall the best time he had scored over that distance back at the Academy. The number didn't come immediately to mind, and that was probably a good thing.

The group paused in the lee of the hatch, and Tuvok turned toward him. "Lieutenant Commander, have you been able to reach the *Snipe?*"

"I'll try again," said Nog, pulling the Klingon communicator he had taken from the cage guard. "I didn't want to chance it earlier. Kincade might be able to track us with it."

Tuvok accepted this with a nod. "Nevertheless, it is unwise to proceed without certainty that the ship is not compromised."

Nog prized off the cover of the device and performed a quick-and-dirty bypass on the communicator unit. He took a breath and tapped it gingerly. "*Snipe,* do you read?"

There was a blurt of static and then a welcome reply. *"Aye, sir, this is Lieutenant Ixxen. It's good to hear from you. . . . When the alarms went off, I suspected you might be on your way. . . ."*

Tuvok took the device and spoke into it. "Lieutenant, are you secure?"

"Yes and no," replied the Bolian. *"Zero-Zero was on the bridge, and he didn't want me talking to anyone. . . . I*

used a fire extinguisher to convince him otherwise. Bynars have thick skulls. Who knew?"

"What of Zero-Zero's partner?"

"That's the no, *sir. One-One is still at large on the ship and not showing up on sensors. He's locked Khob in the infirmary and taken weapons and transporters offline so I can't beam you from there to here. But I still have engines and airlock control, though."*

"Understood," said Tuvok. "Drop the main access ramp, Lieutenant, and prepare for immediate liftoff. We will come to you."

"We have to move fast," said Nog. "They'll be watching the ship. Once they see the ramp moving—"

"Kincade will know for certain where we're going," Tom finished. "No time to waste, then."

"Go," ordered Tuvok, and they broke into a loping run, staying as low as they could, the loose line of six fugitives moving from one derelict container to another.

Nog halted to catch his breath in the shadow of an ore cart, and across the open expanse of the landing pad he saw a chink of light appear as the *Snipe*'s ramp lowered like a drawbridge. It looked a lot more than five hundred meters away.

But in the next second, it was the furthest thing from his mind. A salvo of disruptor bolts smacked into the walls of the nearest cargo container, and the hot, searing stench of molten metal stung Nog's nostrils.

Tom fired blindly from cover, strafing bolts of green energy back in the direction of this new attack. "I see multiple enemies," he reported. "They're advancing from the main dome in a skirmish line."

Threads of sparking crimson and blazing emerald bored through the empty container or cut blackened, sizzling scars across the thermoconcrete pad. Nog shot back and was rewarded with a distant cry of pain, but the attack did not lessen.

"If they call reinforcements from their ships in orbit, we will be overwhelmed!" spat Throk. "Give us weapons, you fools!"

A sudden flare of anger welled in Nog's chest, and he glared at the Cardassian. "So you can shoot us in the back?"

Throk's face twisted in hard lines of fury. "Then cower here and perish!" With an abrupt burst of violent motion, the Cardassian barged Tom aside, sending a shot from his pistol firing wildly into the air. Before the human could stop him, Throk had broken from cover and charged into a sprinting run.

Tuvok raised his hand toward Heybis and Vekt. "You must not—"

But they were already running after their comrade. Tuvok vaulted up, on the verge of going after them, perhaps to stop their headlong flight, but a lance of particle-fire slashed through the air in front of him, and he stopped short.

Nog wanted to look away, but something compelled him to watch them run. Vekt was the first to be taken; two beams fired by the advancing Klingons caught him in the torso as he stumbled over a cracked stone. He became a figure of flames, dissipating into nothing before his body could strike the ground. Heybis died a fraction of a second later: not from beam fire, but from the impact of a kinetic round. Nog heard the faint crack of the shot, the same noise he had heard on IN-748 as he stood inside the wreck of the Orion privateer. A bloom of pale blood erupted from the Cardassian woman's neck, and she performed a pirouette before collapsing in a heap.

Throk must have heard the gunshot, too, because he hesitated at the edge of one of the *Snipe*'s landing skids, turning to look back. A blink of light off a telescopic sight caught Nog's eye. He saw a figure taking aim with a long rifle.

The second shot went through Onar Throk's chest, perfectly aligned to fatally puncture his heart. He dropped without a sound, sagging against the landing skid.

In the wake of the shot's echo, all firing ceased. After a long moment, Nog dared to hazard a look through one of the blast holes in the cargo container, the molten edges of the impact point still sizzling as it cooled. There were a lot of Klingons out there, and among them stood the Elloran, toying with a heavy photon grenade launcher. Kincade approached from behind, her TR-116 rifle cradled in her arms.

"Show yourselves," she shouted, "or Sahde here will turn you into a smoking hole in the ground."

"Now what?" asked Tom.

"Every second we are alive, there is a possibility another option may present itself," Tuvok replied after a moment. He got to his feet, and Nog slowly did the same.

"I hope you're right." The human was bitter. "Because the reason we were out here is now lying dead over there, and we don't have any more cards to play."

The Vulcan said nothing and moved out from behind cover, still grasping his stolen weapon. Nog and Tom followed a step behind, looking out at the force of mercenaries who outnumbered them three to one.

"You shouldn't be disappointed, Commander Tuvok." Kincade watched them draw near. "This was always how it was going to be. *No loose ends.*"

*   *   *

Christine Vale looked up as Deanna Troi approached. The lights in the *Lionheart*'s corridors were low; it was delta shift, so-called "ship's night," and at this moment Vale wanted more than anything to be back in her cabin on the slow curve down into sleep. But her wish was unlikely to be granted. The tension that had been pulling at her since they left Earth was no longer holding back, and she could feel the pressure gathering in a knot at the base of her neck.

Troi gave her a sympathetic smile that told Vale the other woman knew exactly how she felt without the need for her to admit it openly. *One of the benefits of being friends with an empath,* she thought. "Thanks for coming, Deanna. I could use your insight here."

"I'm glad to help," said Troi. "Doctor Rssuu told me that Doctor Bashir will be fully recovered by the time we reach Andoria. He didn't get anywhere near a full dose of the theragen concentrate, but he still suffered some minor nerve damage." She sighed. "He's lucky this is a hospital ship. On another vessel, with less experienced staff, he could have permanently lost his eyesight."

"How is Bashir holding up? Maybe now he'll be more willing to talk to us."

The Betazoid frowned. "Don't hold your breath, Chris. Whatever is keeping him silent, it's because he's afraid for someone close to him."

"The Douglas woman?"

"It's possible. He'll talk when he feels safe and not before."

Vale nodded. "Okay. We'll go interrogate someone else, then." She turned toward the nearby security doors and they hissed open.

The *Lionheart*'s brig was small, with only three cells, and just one of those was active. Vale gave the Tellarite security officer on duty a stiff jerk of the head to dismiss him, and he retreated to the monitor station on the far side of the compartment.

On the other side of the active cell's force-field barrier, science officer Lieutenant Seth Maslan was lying on a sleeping pallet. His uniform tunic had been taken from him, and as Vale watched, he picked at the cuffs of his blue undershirt. "Captain on deck," he said, with a smirk. "Tell me, Commander. How are you liking the job now?"

"You know, we've got a lot of questions for you," Vale began, studying him. "But I'm going to start with the one I had from the moment I first met you: Does that 'charming genius' act you put up ever actually work?"

"A lot," Maslan said, nodding thoughtfully. "People are usually quite impressed with me."

"*He* certainly believes that is true," noted Troi.

"Ah, Betazoids. Always a tougher prospect." Maslan made a tutting noise and looked away.

"And now he's thinking of a song, concentrating on the music because he assumes it will prevent me from reading him."

Vale went on. "How about an easy one, then? After I came on board, were you actually hitting on me in the turbolift?"

"Oh, yes," he replied. "You're an attractive woman. I'd have done it even if I hadn't been told to."

She seized on his reply. "Who told you, Seth?"

He froze, and for a second his insouciant grin slipped; then in the next moment he was smiling again. "I don't think I'm going to say anything else until we reach a starbase and I get to speak to my duly appointed lawyer from the Judge Advocate General's office." Maslan folded his arms and took an interest in the panels on the ceiling above his head.

"What makes you think we're going to a starbase?" asked Vale. "Our next stop is the Andor system. We'll be there in a day." She leaned closer to the field barrier. "And it won't be just Bashir that I'll be dropping off. You see, Envoy ch'Nuillen has been made aware that you tried to kill the good doctor, and he's not happy about it."

"That's something of an understatement," offered Troi. "I would have said *furious*."

"You may be right," Vale allowed. "Let's not forget, Bashir is technically ch'Nuillen's nephew now, as Andorian law sees it. Not to mention a hero to that entire planet. So naturally, when the envoy asked me if the Imperial Guard could *interview* the suspect in Bashir's attempted murder, I didn't refuse." She mirrored Maslan's earlier smile. "I didn't want to get on his bad side."

The science officer sniffed. "You can't turn me over to the Andorians. They're not part of the Federation. They have no legal claim on me."

"That's probably true. But I'm going to do it anyway. And I'm sure, sooner or later, I'll get in trouble for that. But not as much trouble as you." She glanced at Troi. "They don't still have the death penalty on Andor, do they?"

"Federation member-worlds are legally bound not to endorse capital punishment," said Troi. "But then, Andor hasn't officially rejoined the UFP yet. So who knows what could happen?"

Maslan rose to his feet and glared at the two women. "Don't try to play me. I'm not falling for it."

Vale met his gaze. "Whoever briefed you clearly didn't do a very good job, Seth, because if they had, you'd know an important fact about me. *I don't play games.*"

"You're just as stupid as he is." Maslan's voice turned cold with contempt. "Bashir thought he was a law unto himself, and you think the same. But this isn't like the old days, when captains were kings who could do what they wanted and damn the consequences! Your friend the doctor is a traitor, and you're a reckless fool who doesn't deserve command of this ship, or any other!"

From the corner of her eye, Vale saw Troi give an imperceptible nod. Together they had pushed him far enough, and now all Maslan needed was the room to incriminate himself. "And yet, here I am, and there you are," she said.

"You people don't understand. Don't you get it? Haven't you asked why it is we keep getting kicked to pieces by every aggressor species in the galaxy? I lost family in the Dominion War, I signed up to make sure that didn't happen again. But it did; the same mistakes, the same weakness, and the Borg came in and almost wiped us out. Now the Typhon Pact are going to do the same, and still no one raises a hand to put them down. All because we're the Federation. *The good guys.* The ones who never, ever start a fight."

Vale hesitated. As much as she hated to admit it, there was something in Maslan's words that rang true to her; but that didn't make him right, and she told him so. "We don't make war. That's not what we are."

"You're living in the past, Vale!" he snapped. "And people like you are why we keep taking hits, time and time again. What if the next attack is the one that finishes us? What will your ideals be worth then?" He shook his head. "We need strength and order. There have to be *consequences*." Maslan took a breath and stopped dead, glancing at Troi as he caught up to himself. "Yeah. Like I said before, I'm not talking to you anymore. Do your worst."

Vale watched him return to the pallet and lie down once again, and after a moment she strolled away.

When the security doors had shut behind them, Troi gave her a look. "You're not really going to give him to the Andorians, are you?"

"Of course not; that would be illegal," she replied. "And I'm pretty sure I'm already going to be up to my eyes with multiple charges as it is when this is all over. Why add more to the pile?" Vale shook her head. "No, I'll just let Maslan stew. I think we all know who was calling the shots for him. I had Basoos pull the communications logs for me. It seems Mister Maslan got an unusually dense data packet sent to him right after we left Jaros II. A holomatrix messenger program."

"Which he has since erased from the system?"

"Naturally. It explains a lot about his record, something I couldn't put my finger on. The reason he'd been bounced from one ship to another. I don't think it's just because he's something of a jerk."

"He was spying for . . . someone?"

Vale shrugged. "Or maybe recruiting. I can't be sure." She walked on, and Troi fell in step. "Will was right, Deanna. We're pulling at loose threads here, and I think it may make something big fall apart."

Kincade's manner had shifted so decidedly that Tuvok wondered if she were a true sociopath in the full sense of the word. Had the behavior patterns she showed to him and the others on board the *Snipe* been nothing more than a learned camouflage, a cloak that covered her real self? He studied the woman's cold, dead eyes, searching for anything that could be a spark of emotion. He did not find it.

She walked toward him. "I had hoped we could talk," said Kincade, this newly revealed version of the soldier. "I had questions about your kind. Vulcans and the no-emotions thing."

"A common misconception," Tuvok corrected. "Vulcans possess emotions, but we choose to suppress them in order to attain a more logical state of being."

"So you don't actually know what it is like to feel nothing? Not really?"

He shook his head. "Some of my species seek that state. I do not. To deny or expunge emotion is to deny part of the self. I have learned that through countless years of—"

She waved him to silence. "I didn't ask for a lesson. But let me give you one instead. Feeling nothing? It's very *liberating*."

"I believe you are psychologically impaired," he said flatly.

"That's been said," Kincade replied, handing her sniper rifle to the Elloran. "Time for the next lesson. For the Klingons, this time." She drew a curved blade from a hidden holster in her belt. "They believe I'm a poor warrior because I'm only able to kill from a distance. I'm going to show them they're wrong."

"Kincade, don't do this!" Thomas Riker stepped forward, taking care not to raise his weapon. "You kill a Starfleet officer and there's no going back from that."

"You are right," she said, pausing to consider his words. "So that gives you a choice, then." Kincade nodded at Tuvok and Nog. "Shoot these two, and I'll consider bringing you back into the fold."

He grimaced. "I won't do that."

"You don't owe Starfleet anything!" called Sahde. "They abandoned you, remember? Took away your life, made you into a deserter!"

The human shook his head and threw his stolen gun on the ground. "It was never about the uniform. It's about what is right." He looked up at Kincade. "Something that means nothing to you and the people holding your chain."

"Who do you really work for?" asked Tuvok.

"Not Starfleet or anything like it," she admitted, "not for some time. You could say we didn't share compatible goals." Kincade jutted her chin toward the bodies of the dead Cardassians. "You know we were never going to take them back for trial, right? Too problematic."

"I assumed so," Tuvok noted.

She nodded in agreement. "So. Now I've found someone who can better utilize my skills, and it's working out well for me." Kincade held up the blade. "Speaking of which . . ."

At the back of the group, one of the Klingon mercenaries reacted to a sharp tone from the communicator on his arm, and he muttered into it. The warrior called out urgently to Kincade. "There is a signal—"

"Not now," she barked, never taking her eyes off Tuvok. "Do your kind really bleed green?"

"Yes."

And then, for an instant, Tuvok glimpsed the smallest fragment of an actual emotional response in Kincade's icy manner: a chilling need to harm him. "Show me," she said.

He heard the sound then, and Nog turned as his ears caught it too. From out of nowhere, a heavy, thunderous roar rolled from the ragged clouds above, and an angular shape exploded over the ridgeline, buffeting them with an echoing rumble of downwash and the shriek of phaser bolts.

Tuvok was blown off his feet and he stumbled, landing badly as a black shadow passed over him, leaving chaos in its wake. He rolled, blinking through plumes of disturbed dust to see a wedge-shaped craft perform a hard climbing kick-turn over the roof of the domes and turn back toward them.

It was a Starfleet Type-11 shuttlecraft; more specifically, it was the *Marsalis,* an auxiliary vessel from the complement aboard the *Titan.* Deep in the core of Tuvok's own carefully controlled emotions, there was a momentary flare of relief before he shuttered it away and returned to the matter of staying alive.

The Klingon mercenaries were in disarray, some of them firing wildly at the intruder ship, others shooting in Tuvok's direction. He heard Thomas Riker call out and saw beam fire ripping past him. The air was filled with dust and fire smoke as the *Marsalis* made second and third swooping passes, blasting divots from the landing pad and blowing apart the frames of stalled cargo lifters.

The Vulcan struggled as he tried to get to his feet, but he had landed badly and his ankle was twisted at an unnatural angle. The pain signals from his leg told him he had broken bones there, and with a thought he shut off the signals. "I feel . . . nothing. . . ." he said aloud, righting himself.

"But that's a lie." Kincade emerged from the haze, bloody from cuts on her face where rock chips had scarred her like shrapnel. "I'm disappointed," she told him, coming at his throat with the knife. The shuttle darkened the sky again as she lunged, and Tuvok parried, taking a glancing cut across his forearm to his cost. Dark emerald-hued blood stained Kincade's blade, and she gave it a quizzical look. "Ah. It is true, then."

Then the shot came and she jerked, all animation suddenly fleeing from her body. The woman's face did not change—there was no final moment of agony, no shock or fury. Kincade collapsed to her knees, and then went facedown against the ground.

A few meters distant, Lieutenant Nog stood holding the TR-116 rifle at his hip, the spindly extent of the firearm almost as long as the Ferengi was tall. "Found it," he managed. "Sahde must have dropped it." Shouldering the ungainly weapon, he came forward and took Tuvok's weight. "I have you, Commander."

"Your assistance is greatly appreciated, Mister Nog."

Both of them recoiled as the *Marsalis* completed another low-level attack run, marching streaks of phaser energy down the length of the open landing pad. The mercenaries had scattered, retreating back toward the safety of the mining complex, and the shuttle's pilot dogged them all the way, strafing the ground with pulse-fire.

Tuvok caught sight of movement and pointed. "There, Lieutenant." Sahde was racing across the landing pad toward the *Snipe*'s drop-ramp.

Tuvok's weapon had been lost in the first explosion, and Nog fumbled with the unfamiliar rifle. The Elloran saw them and shouted something that was lost in the noise of the shuttlecraft's engines. She pointed the grenade launcher in their direction, and it fired with a hollow, concussive thud. A glowing blue orb leapt from the mouth of the launcher, describing an arc toward the two Starfleet officers.

"Get down!" Thomas Riker called out to them from behind a crumpled cargo container, and they were within arm's reach of him when the photon grenade detonated somewhere behind them. The shockwave shoved both of them into the side of the module with pitiless force.

His senses briefly deadened by the power of the explosion's overpressure, Tuvok felt—rather than heard—the throaty snarl of the *Snipe*'s engines as the ersatz transport ship took off, the drop ramp closing as it rose away into the clouds.

As the whistling note in his ears began to fade, a gust of thruster gas plucked at Tuvok, and he limped toward the *Marsalis* as the long, low shuttle settled to the ground before them.

Hatches snapped open behind the cockpit and at the stern, disgorging Starfleet security officers equipped with phaser rifles and hazard team gear. A pale but familiar face found his, and he saw a smile of relief. "Commander Tuvok? Are you all right, sir?"

"Crewman N'keytar," he replied, recognizing the Vok'sha woman from *Titan*'s security detail. "Your timing was impeccable."

"I'd have liked it more if it wasn't a nick-of-time rescue," said Nog. "A five-minutes-earlier or even a day-or-so-before rescue would have been much better."

"Ferengi," rumbled a voice with a deeper register, "are never grateful." Lieutenant Commander Ranul Keru dropped down from the shuttle and offered Tuvok his hand. "Good to see you in one piece, sir."

The Trill officer turned to his team. "Fan out; hold the perimeter! We're not stopping here!"

"How did you know where to find us?" asked Nog. "We're in the Klingon outlands, light-years from anywhere . . ."

"We cashed in a favor with the chancellor," Keru told him. "That, and some code-breaking."

"The ship . . . the freighter . . ." Thomas Riker came forward. "We have to get after it. . . ." There was a moment of shocked silence as every member of the squad from the *Titan* halted at what appeared to be the sight of a bloodied and beaten version of their captain. "*I'm not him!*" he snapped angrily. "Tuvok, tell them. We have to go, right now! With Kincade dead, we need what's on the *Snipe*. It's our only proof!"

"Correct," said the commander. He turned to Keru. "These two gentlemen are with me. We must withdraw to the *Titan* immediately."

"Aye, sir." To his credit, Keru didn't query the order even though Tuvok sensed he was brimming with questions. "Everyone on board! We're pulling out!" he called, before shooting the Vulcan a sideways look. "You can explain on the way."

If he was pushed, William Riker might have described the situation on the bridge as *fluid* or *dynamic* or *a damned mess*.

It seemed like he had been suspended here in this same moment ever since they left the Sol system at maximum warp, barely even pausing as they raced over the borderline of the Klingon Empire where the *Titan* gained two new wingmen in the form of ships from Martok's elite brigade. Time had become a blur, shifts merging into nothing but a seemingly endless series of duty watches, one after the other. Without his wife and daughter on board, he had taken to eating in his ready room and catching sleep where he could on the couch in there. The headlong flight of the *Titan* had been broken only by regular complaints from Xin Ra-Havreii that running the vessel fast and hot would damage his precious engines; those, and the increasingly strident subspace messages from Starfleet Command calling them home.

The latter he had turned over to Lieutenant Ssura to deal with, and the Caitian was proving adept at running interference for his admiral. Riker guessed that there were ships out there looking to rein *Titan* back in, but the *Luna*-class vessel was one of the fastest in the fleet; the only cruisers that had a chance of catching them were the *Vesta*-class ships with their slipstream drives, and he had won the gamble that they wouldn't be pulled off their duties for the sake of one errant admiral.

But all those concerns had been burned away in a single moment. Riker wasn't sure what he had expected to find in the Nydak system, but it wasn't open battle.

How wrong I was, he thought.

Approaching Nydak II, a pair of K-22s had decloaked, but the ships sent by Martok didn't even allow them the opportunity for the normal declaration of bluster and threats. The void lit up with disruptor barrages; first one Bird of Prey and then the other fell to the guns of their fellow Klingons.

Riker's demand for an explanation was barely acknowledged. *There will be no traces of this dishonor;* those were the Klingon captain's words. As the two ships systematically obliterated all communications relays in orbit, Riker gave Keru the order to take the

Marsalis and scour the complex below for any traces of Active Four.

Now a ship was coming back up from the surface, but it wasn't the *Titan*'s shuttle. "It's a modified Type-8 freighter," reported Melora from her console. "Transponder identifies it as the *Snipe,* registered out of the Triangle."

"That's a flag of convenience if ever there was one," said Lieutenant Rager, at ops. "What is it doing here?"

Riker sank back in the command chair, and something about the action settled him. Ever since Akaar had pinned that rank sigil to Will's collar, he couldn't escape the fear that the center seat was going to be put beyond his reach. But being here, now, felt right again. All the frustrations of the past days could be put aside, because on the bridge of his ship, he could still do something to influence the moment.

"Let's find out." He nodded toward Ensign Dakal at one of the secondary consoles. "Zurin, throw a deep scan over that craft. Tell me what you see."

"Aye, sir, working . . ." The young Cardassian leaned forward over his panel, his deep-set eyes narrowing. "Getting something. Admiral, there are conflicting readings. Very unusual power curves here. I detect higher-than-normal engine output, what may be military-grade weapons and defense systems . . ."

"Life signs?"

"Several, but difficult to isolate. Humanoid and . . ." He broke off as a new reading scrolled across his display. "Admiral, someone aboard that craft appears to be tagged with a Starfleet personal transponder."

"One of ours?" Aili Lavena, *Titan*'s Pacifican pilot-navigator, asked the question on all of their minds. "It might be Tuvok."

"No," said Ssura, seated behind Riker at a standby panel. He had a paw at one side of his head, holding an earpiece there. "Incoming hail from shuttlecraft *Marsalis*. Lieutenant Commander Keru reports Commander Tuvok and two other individuals were safely recovered from the surface. He also relays a message from the commander. . . . Escape of *Snipe* must be prevented."

"Then who is over there?" Melora pointed at the viewscreen.

"Only one way to be sure," said Riker. He tapped the intercom panel in the arm of his chair. "Bridge to transporter room three. Mister Radowski, you're needed."

"Transporter three here, sir."

"Be ready, Bowen. We may require a snatch-and-grab." Riker turned back to Pazlar. "Melora, can we—"

"Captain!" The cry came from Lieutenant Pava sh'Aqabaa, currently standing Tuvok's post at the tactical station. "I mean *Admiral*! Aspect change on Martok's ships; they're locking onto the *Snipe*, going weapons hot!"

"Confirmed," said Dakal. "The freighter is responding in kind."

Riker didn't stop to consider if that was a foolish or brave thing, and he looked to Ssura. "Lieutenant, warn them off. That's a civilian ship."

The Caitian's whiskers twitched in agitation. "I hear the same reply as before, sir. 'There will be no traces of this dishonor.'"

Riker went to his feet, his jaw hardening. He imagined that the chancellor had given standing orders to eradicate anything that could connect the Klingons to the assassination. He would not risk damaging the

Empire's alliance with the Federation, and he could discredit General Shaniq at the same time. It would be win-win for him.

He turned to Ssura's console and jabbed the transmit key. "Attention, Klingon vessels: This is Admiral William Riker. We need that ship in one piece! Stand down!"

A snarling voice filled the bridge. *"You have no authority here, Riker. Rescue your people and go. This is a Klingon matter now."*

Bright lances of fire stabbed out across the space beyond the viewscreen, connecting the *Snipe* with the warships. "They're engaging," called Rager. "Sir, what do we do? Those are *Qang*-class vessels; we can't go toe-to-toe with a pair of them."

"Take us in closer," Riker ordered. "We'll crowd them."

The *Titan* rocked as a stray disruptor bolt creased the shields, sending a shiver through the vessel's hull.

"Let's not pretend that was an accident," said Pava.

"Do *not* return fire," Riker told her. "We're in enough trouble as it is."

"The *Snipe* is shooting back," said Rager. "They're scoring hits, but that's only going to make the Klingons madder. . . ."

On the screen, Riker saw the slab-shaped transport ship move too fast for a barge of its type and design. Pop-up phaser turrets were lighting up the shields of the Klingon ships, but in return the freighter was taking a beating. A salvo of quantum torpedoes detonated in a chain-fire blast, and the *Snipe* veered away, trailing plasma and pieces of hull.

"*Snipe*'s shields are down, their hull integrity is at sixty percent," said Melora.

"Klingons are coming around," reported Dakal. "Sir, the next pass will finish off the freighter."

Riker tapped his combadge. "Radowski? Now's the time."

"No pressure, then," muttered the lieutenant, peering at his console. "Admiral, those quantum detonations have thrown up a lot of interference. I'll only be able to pull them out one by one. . . ."

"Do your best, mister," came Riker's reply.

"My best, yeah . . ." Bowen's hands danced across the transporter controls, falling onto the main activation switches. "I'm locking onto the Starfleet transponder first, that's the strongest signal . . . And *energizing.*"

He had barely said the words before the deck beneath him rolled, and Radowski almost lost his footing. He snatched at the edge of the console and held on for the half-second before the *Titan*'s inertial dampers could right themselves and resume stability. With his other hand, the transporter chief forced the sliders back up the line, and on the pad, a column of blue-white light started to form.

"Transporter room." The admiral sounded as if he was standing beside him. *"We're right in the crossfire; the* Snipe *is breaking up!"*

Radowski's heart leapt into his mouth. Sensors said there were half a dozen souls on that ship—and he only had his hands around one of them. He knew he could quit the beam cycle and restart the process in a heartbeat, maybe try a broad-spectrum snatch or a skeletal lock in hopes of scooping them all up in one go. . . . But the risk level went through the roof for that. There was a good chance he could lose everyone like that. But if he took this one person all the way, he wouldn't be able to try again. He knew that now; he could see the fading sensor reads on all the others. It was taking all the power from every transport circuit on the *Titan* just to hold on to one decaying signal.

No, he reminded himself, *not a signal. A person. One Starfleet officer.*

Radowski went at the controls with renewed impetus, cross-patching the matter stream to B- and then C-circuits, boosting the gain as he went. Sweat beaded his brow, but finally the pitch of the transport effect shifted, and he knew he had it. He dared to look up.

The white glow faded to reveal a blue-skinned Bolian woman in a threadbare civilian jumpsuit. She was injured, dark cerulean blood forming a patch in her abdomen. Bowen snatched the medkit from behind the console and bounded up onto the pad. "Medical emergency, transporter room three!" he shouted.

He caught her as she fell and saw the nametag on her breast. *Ixxen, Y.* "Hello there," she said, her voice slurred from shock. The Bolian's hand flapped over his tunic. "Hey," she added, "nice uniform. I have one just like it." Her eyes fluttered, and she fell silent.

"Radowski, do you have them?"

"One, sir, injured but alive," he said, gathering up the woman with a low sigh. The weight he felt on him had nothing to do with how heavy she was. "I have her."

"Damn!" Riker looked away from the expanding ball of plasma that was all that remained of the *Snipe.* The Klingon warships broke off and pivoted, heading down toward lower orbits that would put them directly over the surface of Nydak II.

"Confirming, freighter destroyed with all . . ."

Lavena stopped and took a breath. "Destroyed with all hands but one," she corrected.

"Chancellor Martok's ships are taking up geostationary firing positions," added Dakal. "They're targeting the structures on the planet below."

"No traces," Riker repeated gravely.

"Sir . . ." Ssura glanced up at the admiral. "Shuttlecraft *Marsalis* has been safely recovered. No fatalities reported."

Riker turned back to the main viewscreen as fire began to rain down from the Klingon warships, burning into the clouds and whatever lay beneath them. "I think we've worn out our welcome here. Lieutenant Lavena, set a course back across the border to Federation space, best possible speed." He folded his arms across his chest. "I think it's time to go home and face the music."

Fifteen

Deanna Troi halted as she walked along the corridor and crossed to an oval portal in the *Lionheart*'s hull. The orbit of the starship was crossing Andoria's day/night terminator, and as she watched, the star Epsilon Indi rose and bathed the cobalt blue planet with a cool, sharp radiance. Unlike the deep azure of the oceans on the two worlds she thought of as her spiritual homes—Earth and Betazed—Andoria's were the milky color of sea ice or rare blue jade. Beyond the planet, a massive ringed gas giant caught the reflected glow, and if she looked carefully, Troi could see the faint flickers of storm cells deep in the layers of its turbulent atmosphere.

Other motes of light moved in the darkness: starships of the Imperial Guard, martial and swift in their aspect. They resembled swords, daggers, and shields, and the implied threat in their construction wasn't lost on her. *Lionheart* seemed isolated and alone here, shadowed by the ships of a people that should have been thinking of Starfleet as friends and allies.

They don't trust us, she thought, *and who can blame them?* When the Andorians eventually rejoined the United Federation of Planets, even with the cure to their species' reproductive crisis in hand, it would still take a long time for that distrust to fade. *But today is a step in the right direction.*

One of the ships drifted close to the medical cruiser—the ambassadorial courier *Kree-Thai* in the midst of preparations to make the return voyage to Sol, now that its most recent mission was completed. Envoy ch'Nuillen was still needed at the seat of Federation power to make his people's wishes firmly felt. Troi's meager luggage pack hung from her shoulder, and she was eager to board the Andorian ship herself. She missed Tasha desperately and couldn't help but wonder how her daughter was faring in the care of the Togren family back on Earth; she had been left with little choice but to leave her child behind in the Denobulan's safekeeping. Dragging a four-year-old girl along on what had almost become a prison break would not have been an example of good parenting, and she comforted herself with that.

She stepped away and entered a transporter room to find Julian Bashir waiting inside, with Christine Vale and Commander Atia standing with him.

That same troubled expression Troi had seen on him in the briefing room still marred Bashir's features. "Well," he began. "I suppose this is good-bye." He extended a hand to Troi. "Commander, thank you again for all you have done for me. I'm sorry I couldn't reciprocate."

Vale and Atia exchanged looks but said nothing, so Troi ventured a reply as she shook his hand. "I think we all understand the circumstances, Doctor. The important thing is that you have your freedom."

"For now," he corrected. "Lieutenant Commander Darrah brought me up to speed on the political situation back on Earth. . . . I think if Ishan Anjar wins the presidency, my stay on Andor will be quite short-lived."

"*If* he wins," Troi repeated.

"Extradition requests take a while," said Vale. "A lot of things can change in that time."

Troi sensed the frustration in him. "And what are you going to return to?" he asked. "I know you all risked a great deal for me. Please don't think I'm not grateful."

"Gratitude not required," Atia answered for all of them. "The worth of the deed . . . is the deed."

Bashir reached into a pocket in his tunic and removed an isolinear chip. "I'd like to ask for just one more favor, if I may?"

Vale took the chip and examined it. "And this is?"

"There's a message on there, for someone very important to me."

"Sarina Douglas?" asked Troi, sensing the ghost of strong emotions in Bashir's surface thoughts.

He nodded, and Vale handed the chip to Atia. "Not a problem, Doctor. We'll see that she gets it."

Bashir took a step toward the transporter dais but hesitated on the threshold, and Troi sensed his reluctance to take the last few steps. *Once he has left this ship, he's an outcast.* "Don't worry, Julian," she told him. "This won't be permanent. You'll come home again."

"I have no doubt of that," he told her. "It's just under what circumstances that troubles me. I broke the law, there's no getting around it, and it's not that I regret what I have done. I accept it. But it needs to mean something."

"It does," Vale reminded him gently. "You helped save a species from extinction. I'm pretty sure they'll have a parade waiting for you down there."

"Really?" Bashir's lips pulled into a faint smile. "I hadn't thought . . ."

"'Bashir's Miracle,'" said Troi. "That's what they're calling it on Andor."

"I can't take the credit," he insisted. "I didn't do it alone. . . ."

There was a chime from the transporter console, and the thin-faced Edoan officer standing there peered down at it. "Signal from the *Kree-Thai*. Diplomatic team is incoming."

"Bring to place," ordered Atia.

The Edoan's head bobbed on his long neck, and motes of energy gathered on the pad, swiftly forming into the distinct shapes of an Imperial honor guard and an older Andorian woman in elegant robes.

"Doctor Bashir?" she asked. "I am Savaaroa sh'Nuillen, bondmate to the envoy. He has asked me to introduce you to the Parliament Andoria and to our people." The *shen* offered Bashir her hand. "It is my honor to meet you. Please, if you will join us?"

"The honor is mine, madam," he said smoothly, and Troi saw confidence return to his manner as he stepped up onto the pad.

"Coordinates locked for Lor'Vela," said the transporter operator.

Bashir gave them one last smile of farewell before he nodded to the Edoan. "Energize."

The group shimmered into white pillars of light and was gone.

Troi watched the glow fade, musing. "My turn now, then." She stepped up to where Bashir had been standing. "The envoy has graciously offered me a lift."

"Not just you," said Vale. She turned to Atia and straightened, becoming formal in her behavior. "Commander, as much as I regret it, I think this is as far as I can take the *Lionheart* before I risk flying her over the edge. As of now, the ship is yours."

The Magna Romanii woman's normally controlled, careful aspect cracked, and she was genuinely surprised. "You have certainty in this?"

"I do," Vale replied firmly, tapping her combadge. "Computer? Log the date and time. Command of the *Starship Lionheart* is now transferred to Commander Atia, acting captain."

"So noted."

"I . . . relieve you." Atia was hesitant.

"I stand relieved," said Vale. "Very relieved, actually. My first command was a pretty good one. I wish it could have been longer. Captain Ainsworth is going to inherit a fine crew."

"We will fall to purpose," Atia promised. "But question must be asked. Why now? Is there not more to do? With the traitor Maslan in irons and likely others of his ilk still out there upon the field?"

Vale nodded. "True. But you've done more than enough. And I'm not going to put this ship and this crew at greater risk. Like Bashir said, I'm going to have to answer for what I did, for the orders I gave you. . . . But unlike him, I can't outrun it."

"True," noted Atia. "Would it trouble you to know Darrah and I kept orders for arrest from your attention?"

"My arrest?" Vale's eyes widened.

"Aye." Atia smiled. "Orders seemed to have arrived after you left. Inconvenient timing."

Vale walked up to join Troi on the transporter pad. "Lock onto the *Kree-Thai* and send us across," she told the Edoan.

Atia stood at stiff attention and gave them both a nod. "Duty is known clearly now," she told them. "Tell Admiral Riker he need only speak and *Lionheart* will answer call."

"Energize," said Troi, and their journey back into uncertainty began.

The door closed behind him, and Admiral William Riker looked into the haunted eyes of his own ghost, seated there at the far end of the *Titan*'s briefing room.

"William," said the other man, with an incline of the head.

"Thomas," Riker replied, and immediately he flashed a contrite grin. "Tell me something; did that feel as strange to you as it did to me?"

"More so," said Tom. "It's good to see you. You look well. I guess congratulations are in order for the promotion and . . ." His twin gestured around. "Everything else."

Was that a slight edge of jealousy he caught in the other man's tone? Riker decided not to dwell on it and took a seat across from his "brother." "I'm glad you're alive," he said, and he meant it. "After the Dominion War, you just vanished. . . ."

Tom nodded. "I stayed dead for a while. It didn't take."

Riker had a hundred questions he wanted to put to the other man, but so many of them had nothing to do with the matter at hand. He took a breath and pushed those to one side, focusing on what was immediately important. "How did you get pulled into this business with Active Four? I've read Tuvok's report. . . . Soldier of fortune never really seemed your style."

"You'd be surprised what choices you have to

make when the best options are all closed to you." The resentment again, just for a moment. Tom sighed. "The truth is, I was running out of road, and Kincade happened to find me at the right time." He looked away. "Everyone who believes in what the Federation stands for was angry about Nan Bacco's murder. Kincade offered me a chance to regain something and to do some good. I took it."

"What do you know about her?"

"Not much. Rumors that filtered out of the special-ops community. If half of them were true, it's a wonder she hadn't been drummed out of Starfleet before this. Even Section 31 would balk at some of the things laid at her feet. I didn't believe the stories myself; perhaps that was naïve of me. . . . But maybe she had a guardian angel looking out for her, keeping her in uniform." Riker let Tom's implication lie where it fell, and after a moment, he carried on. "At first I didn't look too hard at it. But then when Tuvok and Nog joined the team, and we saw it was Velk calling the shots, that's when I started to wonder about why Kincade had recruited me specifically."

Riker had entertained the same thoughts on learning about his transporter twin's involvement in Active Four, but he let Tom say it for him.

"In the end, I think it was less about my skills, as good as they are, and more about this." He pointed at his face. "Now I know that you're involved, I'm certain of it."

Riker nodded gravely. There was no limit to the number of troubling possibilities for the exploitation of a man who was essentially an exact duplicate of a Starfleet admiral. "Thanks to Martok's warriors and Kincade's actions, all I have is you and three other witnesses to the existence of Active Four and their mission. Every viable piece of proof of the True Way's apparent involvement in the murder of President Bacco is gone, as is anything that could prove that Galif jav Velk was aggressively attempting to manipulate that information. Beyond some circumstantial evidence and partial data, we've lost our chance to blow this open. . . ."

Tom returned the nod. "If word gets out that Cardassians killed Bacco, there will be hell to pay. It won't matter if they're extremists or not. And all the hawks lined up at Ishan Anjar's shoulder won't be happy if they can't pin this on the Typhon Pact." He folded his arms. "And then there's the question of how far it goes. Is Velk at the top of this or not? Did he make it happen?"

The admiral rubbed the bridge of his nose, for now unwilling to answer that particular question. "What a damned mess. How did we come to this? Our own people riding roughshod over the truth, pushing agendas based on fear instead of hope?"

"War does that to people, Will. We've both seen it." Tom gave a bitter chuckle. "Hell, in the last few years there's hardly a man, woman, or child in the Federation who hasn't been affected by it."

"I refuse to accept that." Riker met his gaze, indignation burning in his eyes. "We're better than this, Tom. We have to strive to be, every day. Because backsliding is what gets us undeclared conflicts and the constant threat of interstellar hostility. We're supposed to be explorers not soldiers. If we lose sight of that . . ." He trailed off, shaking his head.

Tom studied him, absently tracing the line of a scar on his face. "You're not about to take the hand that you've been dealt with this," he said. It wasn't a question, rather a prediction from the one man in the galaxy who fully understood Will Riker's character. "I can hazard a good guess as to what you're going to do when *Titan* gets back to Earth." He nodded toward the ports of the briefing room where warp-stretched stars raced past them. "And I am going to do the same. I can help you get to the roots of this thing."

"No offense, but the word of a missing-presumed-dead ex-Maquis with a half-dozen warrants on his head may not carry much weight before the Federation Council."

"None taken. But I wasn't thinking of that." Tom chuckled again and pointed at Riker's uniform. "Once you get out from under the rank and the colors, things change a lot. It's less black and white, more a sea of grays. And there are people out there who won't talk to Starfleet but who will talk to me."

"And what do you propose to do with these . . . less-than-legal contacts?"

He opened his hands. "What do you need, Will?"

The answer to that question took time to assemble, and the two of them talked for another hour, finding ways that both men could work to bring light to truths that were hell-bent on retreating into the shadows, never to be seen again.

By the end of the conversation, the dark pall that had hung over them had dissipated somewhat, and their shared anger and frustration was fueling a renewed sense of purpose. Tom stood up and walked to the ports.

"Can you contact the bridge and order up a minor course change?"

"To where?"

"Delta Leonis. There's a Freeport colony there,

along with some Miradorn who owe me favors. *Titan* can drop me off, and you won't lose much time."

Riker nodded. "I'll see to it, if that's what you want. But you can come back to Earth. You don't have to stay away. . . ." The words felt awkward in his mouth. "That's not what I meant. You know what I mean."

Tom shook his head. "I don't know if that's a good idea."

"Deanna . . ." He hesitated. "She would be pleased to see you, to know you're okay. And I'd like Natasha to meet her uncle."

Unbidden, a grin formed on Tom's face. "*Uncle?* I like the sound of that." But then just as quickly, his twin's good humor went away. "I don't think I'm ready to meet them just yet. Later. When we're done with this."

Part of him wondered if Tom really meant what he said, but Will knew better than to call him on it. Instead, he accepted it with a nod and stood up. "Talk to Keru—he'll get you whatever you require. I'll have Lavena divert to Leonis." He offered Tom his hand. "Thank you."

His brother took it. "Here's to second chances."

"I assure you," Tuvok began, "I am well enough to resume my duties."

With exaggerated care, the Pahkwa-thanh doctor turned his long predator's snout away from the Vulcan's face and down to where his exposed leg lay under the head of a sensor pod. Ree made a show of examining the unpleasant purple bruising around Tuvok's ankle where the joint had dislocated during the melee on Nydak II. He sniffed at the flesh, then the tip of his pink tongue emerged from between rows of needle-sharp teeth and deftly licked Tuvok's epidermis. The Vulcan did not react, even if he found the saurianoid's action slightly alarming.

Ree leaned back, considering what he tasted in the manner of a vintner evaluating the flavor of a wine. "Yes, you are healing swiftly, that Vulcanian physiology at work again. But you are not recertified for duty, Commander. I want you off your feet for another twenty-four hours, not standing a post on the bridge. We'll be back at McKinley Station soon, so there will be little for your attention anyway."

Tuvok maintained a steady tone. "I beg to differ."

"As well you may. However . . . *doctor's orders,*" Ree insisted, stalking away on his taloned feet. "Don't make me confine you to quarters."

"As you wish," Tuvok replied, admitting defeat. He swung his legs off the examination bed and adjusted his uniform, glancing around.

"Here you are," said a voice, and he found Lieutenant Nog at his side, offering up Tuvok's boot.

Tuvok accepted it and pulled it on. "I take it you have been given a clean bill of health?"

Nog rubbed at a fading contusion on his broad forehead. "Some cuts and scrapes, not much else. No lasting damage, thank the Blessed Exchequer. Ferengi are tougher than they look, you know."

He sensed something unsaid in the younger officer's manner and decided to address it without preamble. "Mister Nog, what is it you wish to discuss with me?"

The Ferengi's attempt to maintain a lighter tone faded with his words. "I suppose . . . I'm looking to understand. I though perhaps you might be able to help me."

Tuvok stood, testing the ankle. "I will endeavor to assist if I can."

"Why us, Commander?" The question tumbled from Nog's mouth in a rush. "I mean, Kincade or Velk or whoever it was who set this all in motion, they could have chosen anyone to be part of Active Four. But they specifically selected you and me. And as hard as I try, I can't make my peace with that. *Why us?*" he repeated.

The same uncertainty had been troubling Tuvok's thoughts for some time, and the solutions that he came up with did little to put his mind at ease. "Walk with me, Commander," he said, and together they made their way out into the *Titan*'s corridors.

With each step they took, part of Tuvok's mind was zeroing in on the low, dull pain from his injury, and he was working to nullify it. He found it helped him focus. Nog didn't seem to have the same capacity; the engineer was worrying at his concerns, and his disquiet was evident. "I don't think it was random chance we were recruited for Active Four," he was saying. "And I don't believe it was just for our skills, either."

"I concur in part with your statement," Tuvok replied. "Consider that our individual skill sets are useful to a clandestine action group. Both of us have direct experience of frontline military and covert operations as well as more . . . esoteric mission profiles."

"I suppose so," said Nog glumly. "But I can't help wondering if they chose me because I'm Ferengi. I mean, my people don't exactly have the best standing in terms of trust and reliability."

"You believe they thought they could buy your loyalty, Lieutenant?"

"My people have more privateers and mercenaries out in the galaxy than there are captains in the whole of the Ferengi Alliance flotilla."

Tuvok shook his head. "I have a different theory. I have observed from my interactions with you that you are . . . honest."

Nog gave a snaggletoothed smirk. "Funny. I feel honored and insulted all at once."

"It may be to your detriment," Tuvok went on. "Mister Nog, for a Ferengi, you have very little artifice to your character. I would hazard a guess that you were brought into Active Four not only for your skills, but because you could be manipulated."

Nog's smile fled. "How?"

"You saw President Bacco die, did you not? You were there in person."

"Yes." The engineer's expression stiffened, his emotions beneath the surface running deep and strong.

"Mister Nog, it is my estimation that you are a fine officer with a strong sense of the moral tenets at the heart of our oath to Starfleet. But I also believe Kincade intended to use your outrage at the assassination as a way to make you follow her lead."

"When it happened on DS9 . . . I felt so *powerless*." Nog halted, a faraway look in his eyes. "She died right in front of us, and there was nothing we could do to save her. I was angry, Commander. But then when I got the orders, I thought I had a chance. . . . A way to do something about it." He shook his head. "You're right. I never stopped to think what that could mean until it was too late."

"Do not punish yourself, Mister Nog. Every one of the Active Four recruits was being manipulated in one way or another. I suspect that had events gone according to Kincade's plans, all of us would have eventually suffered because of it." *Or worse,* he added silently.

Nog eyed him. "So what button did they push for you, sir? I thought Vulcans were above that sort of thing."

"No," Tuvok admitted, a frown threatening to mar his features. "We are not." He hesitated, then began to speak; thoughts that he had dismissed over the past few months now rose back to the surface, things he had not spoken of even to his wife T'Pel that he now felt compelled to reveal to Nog. "I have in recent times become withdrawn, Lieutenant. Recent events I have been party to aboard the *Titan* have caused me to question myself. I have experienced much in terms of loss . . . and self-doubt. I have attempted to occupy myself with my work, without a great degree of success."

"So, are you saying you were chosen because, what? They thought you would simply obey orders? Focus on the mission and nothing else?"

"One could make that assumption," Tuvok said with a nod. "But as with you, Lieutenant, they were mistaken. I also suspect that my involvement could have been used to implicate the *Titan* in some way."

Nog rubbed his hands over his ears, wincing. "Wheels turning within wheels. I feel like I'm the cog that looked up for the first time to see the whole machine around him." He scowled. "I don't like being used, sir."

"I concur," offered Tuvok. "But that time is over. We will be entering the Sol system in a few hours, and with diligence, we will learn the reasons why this happened and find those responsible for it."

"You make it sound easy."

Tuvok shook his head. "It will be anything but that, Mister Nog."

Time seemed to play itself over again.

Riker could almost lose himself in the moment. A peculiar déjà vu had crawled over him as the *Titan* swept back into Earth orbit. In just twenty-two days, it seemed like William Riker's life had turned through a complete orbit, coming back to almost the exact spot it had occupied three weeks earlier; emotionally and physically, he was virtually in the same place.

He was worried about his future and the fate of his family and his crew. Concerned about events far beyond his control and fearful of how those things were going to radiate out into the galaxy beyond. And above it all, Riker could see a shadow looming over everything that was dear to him.

Before, that had just been a vague and directionless doubt. Now he was returning home with a reaffirmed purpose alongside the grave disquiet lurking in his heart.

He half-expected to find a master-at-arms detail waiting for him at McKinley Station or an "escort" from Starfleet Security. There was only an order, a summons like the one that had cut short *Titan*'s exploratory mission and brought Riker and his ship back from the Gum Nebula. A command from the office of the Admiral of the Fleet, from Leonard Akaar.

As he stepped onto the transporter pad to answer the call, Riker ran a finger over the rank pin on his collar and closed his eyes as the beam-out began. Perhaps now it would be time to give that up, to be stripped of the brief status it had given him. *I wouldn't resist,* he thought to himself. *I'm not sure I'll ever be able to get used to the weight of it.*

He materialized in familiar surroundings, feeling the warmth of the afternoon sun on his face and the familiar sea-tang of the Presidio's air. Riker automatically knew he was on the Starfleet Command campus before he opened his eyes again, and he stepped down onto Earth.

The ornamental gardens outside the great sculpted curve of the headquarters building stretched out before him, and he started walking. Akaar's orders had not specified where Riker was to go, but now that he was here, he knew exactly how to find the admiral. Threading his way past flower beds, immaculately manicured lawns, and ornamental ponds, at last he came across the small stone lacunae where he had tracked the Capellan admiral before embarking on the journey that had taken him to Klingon space and back again. It seemed like an age had passed since then. With everything Riker had learned—and everything he now *suspected*—that moment felt as if it had happened to another person.

Akaar was waiting there for him, and this time he had eschewed one of his potent cigarillos in deference to the other party seated on the stone bench.

Deanna Troi turned and stood to meet her husband's embrace. For a moment the two of them forgot everything else, briefly losing themselves in the closeness.

Riker basked in her, feeling Deanna in his thoughts, a welcome and calming presence. *Imzadi. I missed you.*

"I know," she whispered. "It's good to be back."

He broke away and studied her. "Tasha?"

"She's with Christine and the Andorians, out at the diplomatic compound in the city."

"You both did well," he told her. "Thank you."

Troi's moment of joy at seeing her husband once again now fell away, as did Riker's emotions at seeing his wife—all put aside for now. There was still the job at hand to be dealt with.

The couple broke their embrace and turned back to Akaar. He stood like a towering sentinel, circumspect as he allowed the brief moment of reunion.

"So when should I expect to be arrested?" Riker began. "I ignored a recall order or two."

"You're an admiral now, remember?" Akaar's reply was dry. "It's only captains and the lower ranks who get dragged away in manacles." He beckoned them to sit near the muttering waters of the nearby fountain. "Rank hath its privileges, and one of those is discretion."

"It *would* be unseemly for Starfleet's newest flag officer to be detained in full view of everyone," said Troi. She nodded over Riker's shoulder, and he turned to see where she was looking.

A pair of security officers was loitering some distance away, making all effort to look anywhere but in their direction. "Are those your men, sir?" asked Riker. "Or someone else's?"

"I forget," Akaar replied, feigning a frown. "I'm sure we'll find out soon enough."

Riker studied the other man. The fatigue he had seen in Akaar before had deepened. He looked more and more like someone waiting out the clock. "Admiral, it appears that I and several of my officers are now one step ahead of an official warning, or worse. After what we found in the Nydak system—"

Akaar cut him off. "I've been doing what I can from here. If the worst happens, I can protect Commander Vale. There could be a demotion, a black mark on her file. It might be a long time before she gets a shot at the center seat again, but she'll have her career." It was telling that he said nothing about Riker or his wife. Akaar eyed him, his tone turning flinty. "What you did with Bashir . . . that was a big risk."

"I acted on my own initiative, just as you told me to," Riker responded, ignoring a flash of irritation at Akaar's reply. "So did Christine. I won't apologize for it, and neither should she."

The Capellan ignored Riker, turning his gaze on Troi. "It was a good gambit, Commander Troi, bringing in ch'Nuillen like that. You forced Velk into a corner." He looked away. "And now we'll see how that shakes out in the long term."

"What do you mean by that?" she asked.

"Bashir didn't give you anything, did he?" Akaar retorted. "We all know why that is. He's afraid to jeopardize the freedom of the other doctors who helped him with the Andorian cure."

"I have faith in Doctor Bashir," Troi replied.

"All well and good. But that doesn't count for anything right now."

"And here we go again." Riker's eyes narrowed. "Everything is playing out the same way it did before. Why is it whenever I talk to you, *sir*, I get the feeling that I am playing catch-up?"

"A lot happened here while you were chasing across the quadrant and back, Admiral Riker. Tensions in the Federation Council are high. This business with the Andorians intervening with Bashir has split them down the middle. Half the representatives are applauding it and want them back in the fold immediately, the other half are calling it reckless and bullheaded. Public support is going back and forth like a pendulum."

"With all due respect, that's not our focus. You told me you brought me here and gave me this rank so together we could look into unsanctioned executive orders from the office of the president. I've done that. Ssura sent you all the data, all the reports on what we found." He took a breath, marshaling his thoughts. "Picard was right, the Cardassians *were* the assassins. The True Way killed Nan Bacco. The Tzenkethi lead on Deep Space Nine was a fake trail, designed to point toward the Typhon Pact. And someone in our government knew about it."

"Galif jav Velk," said Troi. "At the very least."

"Throk openly accused Velk of engineering the whole thing," Riker added.

"Remind me again what proof we have?" Akaar matched his gaze. "The word of a dead man. A corrupted holoprogram. The unverifiable testimony of three Starfleet officers and one convicted criminal, all of whom could be implicated in illegal military actions themselves." He shook his head. "It's not enough. We need cast-iron certainty. . . . We need a knife with blood on the blade."

"Chancellor Martok—" Troi started to speak, but Akaar cut her off.

"The Klingons won't offer any more help. Martok has closed ranks. He has his own problems to deal with right now, purging his government of those working against him. The existence of Nydak II is an embarrassment to the Empire. Martok will expunge all trace of it, and all Klingon connection to this sorry business, for his own sake." Akaar's expression grew stony. "That leaves us with nothing we can take up the line. . . ."

"No!" snapped Riker. "Even with Onar Throk and the others dead, we still have enough evidence to bring this to the Federation Attorney General. It's enough to demand an investigation be opened, this time with Starfleet's full involvement as well as the Federation Security Agency."

"If we can investigate Velk, we have a way to get to the heart of this," added Troi. "We can have him arrested; we can bring him to account!"

Akaar gave Riker a level look. "You were right about playing catch-up, Will." He sighed. "We can't go after Velk because he is *already* in custody."

"What the hell?" Riker shot back, his decorum lost in the reaction. "How?"

"This morning, while you were both racing back here ahead of a reprimand, the president pro tem gave a press conference in Paris. Ishan Anjar went before the Federation Council and the whole quadrant to inform us that his chief of staff had come to him with an admission of guilt."

"Velk . . . *confessed*?" Troi frowned. "Given what I know of him, that doesn't seem realistic."

"It's more like he fell on his sword," Riker replied. "He had to know that *Titan* was at Nydak II. After Julian Bashir was turned over to the Andorians, he knew that his time was running out. . . ."

"The Federation Council has ordered a special board of inquiry for Velk. Evidence about the existence of the Active Four group has come out, and all of it lays right at that Tellarite's feet. He's accepted full responsibility for running an unsanctioned covert operation, subverting the chain of command, illegal rendition . . ."

"But nothing about conspiracy to murder," Deanna said quietly.

A burst of anger pushed Riker to his feet. "This is a

ploy," he snapped. "They're trying to get out in front of us by taking Velk off the board. He takes the fall, and Ishan Anjar sails on, untouched!"

"We don't know that Ishan is involved," warned Akaar.

Riker rounded on him. "*I* know," he snarled. "A man in Ishan Anjar's position is not ignorant of abuse of power on this scale!" The sheer injustice of it all made him furious. "The Federation doesn't work this way. We didn't end the Dominion threat for this. We didn't endure the Borg for this!" He shook his head. "I won't . . . We *can't* accept it!"

A decision formed in his thoughts, and he saw his wife's eyes widen as she sensed his intentions. "Will . . . what are you going to do?"

He gave her a farewell kiss on the cheek. "I have someone to see."

"Riker!" Akaar stood, towering over him. "We lost this round, understand that. But there is still—"

"We haven't lost," he broke in, "not yet." Riker reached up and tapped at the combadge on his tunic. "*Titan*? I need a site-to-site transport. Starfleet Headquarters to the Palais de la Concorde. *Energize*."

Sixteen

Riker always found it hard to estimate the age of Bajorans. They tended to mature at a slower pace than humans, so what one could consider a middle-aged aspect might be more senior in reality. Ishan Anjar inhabited that space, a man of distinguished good looks and a face that could be patrician in the right light. He was in the process of adjusting the sleeves of a dress shirt as Riker marched into the presidential office on the fifteenth floor of the Palais, a jacket of conservative cut folded neatly over a chair near the large, ornate desk.

"Admiral, this is an unexpected pleasure. Please, do come in, take a seat. I'm sorry, I don't have much time to spare." Ishan smiled thinly, nodding in the direction of the window. "There's a meeting in Kyoto tonight, and I have to attend." Behind him, the evening glow of Paris ranged out behind a broad panoramic window, like the light of stars from deep space.

Ishan's practiced attempt at a knowing welcome fell dead as Riker failed to take the offer of a chair, instead choosing to stand at attention. "We need to talk," he replied. "*Sir.*"

"Yes." The president pro tem stopped and exchanged a look with the members of his staff in the room—a younger Grazerite woman and a Vulcan male from his security detail—dismissing them both without a word. "Yes, I rather think we should." Ishan went to a server alcove, and Riker caught the perfume of *cela* tea as he poured himself a cup. The politician didn't make any move to offer any to the admiral.

The oaken door to the office closed and they were alone. Riker had a handle on his anger now, taking the reins of it in the walk across the plaza outside the Federation's seat of power. He was ready to direct it, sharp and unswerving.

Ishan's manner turned in a moment, changing from a kind of fatherly detachment to a stern, uncompromising façade. He was the hawk again, the man Riker remembered from the speech at Bacco's memorial on Luna. "We have a complex situation unfolding here," he began. "I wish you had come to me first. There's division now, Starfleet versus civilian authority. That's bad for all of us."

"You have no idea," Riker told him, and he deliberately made it sound like a threat, throwing down the gauntlet. "It's hard to know where to start with the list of everything that's wrong. And I'm sure it will only get longer."

Ishan sipped his tea. "I want all your reports and debriefings, of course. I'll add that to the materials that Galif provided to me." He gave a slight shake of the head. "It's troubling, Riker, to know that someone so trusted could go so far off the path. But we have to take what we can from this disorder and make the best of it. There are a lot of questions, and there will need to be answers. The *right* answers."

"A Cardassian national named Onar Throk, an aide to former Castellan Rakena Garan of the Cardassian Union, was the shooter who killed Nanietta Bacco." The words tasted ashen in Riker's mouth. "He confessed it to one of my officers. He was part of a terrorist group called the True Way. They committed this act to disrupt the Federation and fracture our alliance with Cardassia—"

"That is a strong possibility," Ishan broke in, showing no sign that any of this was news to him. "It is hard to prove such allegations conclusively without evidence. I'm a son of the Occupation, Riker, and I have no great fondness for the Cardassians. But throwing around accusations that the Cardassian Assembly has sponsored terrorism inside our borders? That's very irresponsible."

"That's not what I said—"

"That's what people will *think*," Ishan countered.

"Just like they *think* the Typhon Pact are responsible for the assassination?" Clasped together behind his back, Riker's fingers tightened. "The discovery of Tzenkethi DNA evidence on Deep Space Nine was supposed to be kept secret, and yet somehow that information made its way into the public domain."

"The truth will out," snapped Ishan. "That's one of your human proverbs, isn't it? Once that was revealed, I had no choice but to comment on it."

What Ishan called a "comment" had only been a shade away from an outright accusation laid at the Typhon Pact's door, but Riker saw no advantage in bringing that up. "And what will you say now, sir? Now we know that it was Onar Throk behind the trigger and possibly your own chief of staff who put him there!"

The Bajoran smiled without warmth. "We do not *know* that, Admiral. You're exaggerating the situation. I had thought you would understand this, as a man who has to deal in certainties every time he stands on the bridge of a starship. Throk is dead. We have only his word that he was poor Nanietta's assassin. And even if that is so, it does not automatically make the Tzenkethi blameless! They are a perfidious people, Riker. I have no doubt a connection will be found between the True Way and the Typhon Pact." He gave an airy shrug. "And as for his ridiculous assertion that Velk somehow masterminded the murder of my predecessor? I won't even dignify that with an answer. Have you seen the media feeds? Suggestions that the True Way was a Pact cat's-paw are already being publicly aired. I only hope we can find some measure of the complete truth in the days ahead. I'm sure the new Cardassian castellan and his cabinet will do all they can to help in that endeavor. If they value their membership in the Khitomer Accords, of course." Before Riker could frame a reply, Ishan went on, putting down the tea. "I know you and Akaar are unhappy about these unsanctioned operations, as am I. . . . I am only just learning the full scope of Velk's activities. But the fact is, no matter what the circumstances are, the Federation captured and dispatched a group of terrorists responsible for a horrific act of aggression against us. I would call that a victory."

"In one breath you say Throk is a liar," Riker shot back. "In the next you take credit for what happened to him. Which is it?"

Ishan waved away his challenge as if it were nothing. "The True Way is made up of terrorists, that is not in doubt. I'll sleep soundly knowing there are fewer of them to threaten the citizens of the galaxy." He eyed Riker coldly. "If death is the justice they received, I will live with that."

"And the law be damned?"

"It was the Cardassians like Throk who taught me law and justice can sometimes be very different things," said the Bajoran. "I haven't forgotten the lesson."

"You approved Velk's actions." Riker threw out the accusation and dared Ishan to deny it.

"Do I approve *of them*?" Ishan replied, refusing to take the bait. "I approve of those who understand that the United Federation of Planets needs strength now, not divisiveness. That is why this business with the Andorians has been so disappointing." He looked away, shaking his head. "I hope the Prophets smile on Galif. He realized too late that he had crossed a line in his zeal to protect the ideals of the Federation. That's why he came to me and told me everything. He knows he has done wrong. He will accept his punishment and seek forgiveness."

"He jumped before he could be pushed?" Riker's tone was acid.

Ishan ignored his words. "It falls to me to salvage this now. I was willing to rise to the call when President Bacco was taken from us, and today I have had to do that again, to stare a painful truth in the eye and not flinch from it. I do this, Riker, because I must. And if the people of the United Federation of Planets wish it, it will be my honor to go on doing that."

Riker took a step closer and placed his hands on the worn, dark surface of the desk, the centuries-old wood cool beneath his fingers. "I don't believe for one second that you were ignorant of what Galif jav Velk was doing." His voice was low and loaded with menace.

"Your opinion is your right," Ishan replied, matching his tone. "No matter how mistaken it may be. But I am your commander in chief, and you will follow my lead. Is that clear, Admiral?"

Slowly, Riker pulled back and returned to parade-ground attention, eyes staring straight ahead and out the window. "Yes," he said after a moment. "But I would be negligent in my duties if I did not make something very clear to you. It's the reason I came here tonight."

Ishan stood up, reaching for the folded jacket. "Really?" He was offhand, concentrating on dressing for his next public appearance. "And here I thought you had barged into the highest office in this government in order to beat your chest." The Bajoran gave him a cursory glance. "If you have more to say, let's have it. Speak freely, while you still have the rank to back it up."

"You talk about advocating strength, but all you project is antagonism. The Federation has never started a war in all the time it has been in existence. A belligerent stance against the Typhon Pact won't defuse tensions, it will only escalate them . . . and then we'll find ourselves back in the bad old days of the twenty-third century. At best, another cold war like the conflicts we fought with the Klingons and the Romulans, full of proxy skirmishes and secret warfare. At worst . . ." He hesitated, sensing that dark shadow looming again. "A battle on a dozen fronts and a Federation that will crack under the strain."

Ishan adjusted his jacket. "You paint a vivid picture, Admiral. Now let me do the same." He took a breath. "We are wounded, Riker, and our enemies smell the blood in the water. Even our allies look at us and wonder how we will stumble on, watching and waiting for the next aggressor to attack. I will change that. Together, *we will change that.*" He walked past the admiral, and the doors opened as he approached. "You would do well to consider which side you wish to be on when that begins."

"I took an oath," Riker said. "To defend the Federation. And that won't be set aside to fuel one man's political ambitions."

But Ishan had already dismissed him from his thoughts, and he left Riker standing alone in the presidential office, the room silent around him.

Along the *Titan*'s longest axis, through the center of the primary hull, there was a single continuous corridor that almost ran the full length of the starship from bow to stern. Wider than normal, big enough that a ground rover could have traveled it with room to spare, the ship's crew called it "Broadway" after a colloquial term from Earth's oceangoing navies, itself a reference to a location in the Terran city of New York.

It reminded Nog a little of the Promenade on the old DS9 but lacking the scrappy and unpredictable nature of the things aboard the aged Cardassian space station. Remembering it gave him a curious flutter of homesickness, and as he walked, Nog wanted to be back there, among the safe and familiar. But that place was gone now, destroyed by a terrorist attack in the midst of a battle with ships of the Typhon Pact.

He pushed away a gloomy mood that threatened to cloud his thoughts. His debriefing regarding the aftermath of the Active Four mission was at an end, and he had been declared free to return to his previous duties. It was, he had to admit, somewhat unexpected; Nog had imagined that he would be kept on Earth for days, perhaps weeks, to come, forced to reiterate the circumstances of his recruitment by Lieutenant Colonel Kincade and his experiences while part of the covert task force. Instead, a dour Betazoid from Starfleet Intelligence and an equally taciturn human from the Federation Security Agency had grilled him for a few hours then cut him loose.

He wasn't about to question his good fortune. All Nog wanted right now was to be away from here, away from all the things that were troubling him. . . .

He halted and sighed. *But going back to the new DS9 won't make that happen. It's not like I can just turn my back on what took place at Iota Nadir and Nydak. I'm involved. I'm part of this now. Like it or not.*

"Lieutenant Commander Nog?" He turned as he heard a woman's voice call his name. "I'm Commander Vale, *Titan's* first officer. Do you have a moment?"

"Yes, sir," Nog replied. He hadn't met Vale before, but something about her reminded him of someone he knew. She studied him, a searching, strong gaze that peered out from under a cut of dark hair with a single striking white highlight. *Odo,* he thought. *She has that same look Odo used to give me when I was a youth.*

"Walk with me." He fell in step with Vale, stealing a glance at her. "So you're heading down to the forward locks to disembark, is that right?"

He nodded. "That's right. There's a runabout waiting on McKinley that'll take me to Bajor."

"Eager to get back?"

Nog gave a halfhearted chuckle. "Does it show?"

"A little." Vale smiled back. "But I'm afraid you're going to be late." She turned off the wider corridor and into one of the smaller radial passages. The commander's body language made it very clear she expected Nog to follow her.

He trailed after her, his brow furrowing. "Uh, sir. The airlocks are *that* way." Nog jerked a thumb over his shoulder.

"Your ride will have to wait," she told him, halting outside a hexagonal double-door hatchway. Vale tapped out a string of numbers into a pad near the hatch and it hissed open. Nog glimpsed the grid-plan deck and walls of a holodeck inside. "After you," said the commander, indicating the entrance.

Nog stepped through warily and found Tuvok waiting within. The Vulcan gave him a curt nod and returned to his observation of two individuals working at a large holographic template construct in the center of the chamber. One of them resembled a tawny-furred grazing mammal but augmented with cybernetic implants and prosthetics, while the other was a humanoid-arachnid form clearly of artificial origins. The spider-like mechanism had an odd, glassy texture to it, and as Nog studied it, he realized it was not actually a physical construct. "That's . . . a holo-program of some kind?"

"A limited definition, sir," said the deer-like being in a piping voice, and now Nog saw the alien wore an ensign's insignia at his throat. "White-Blue is a purely synthetic artificial intelligence matrix acting through a holographic drone-form."

The name rang a bell. "The . . . Sentry? I read a monograph about them in the *Starfleet Journal of Engineering.* . . ."

"Yes!" The ensign bobbed on his clawed feet. "I wrote it! Ensign Torvig Bu-Kar-Nguv, sir."

"Lieutenant Commander Nog," he said by way of reply, before glancing at Tuvok. "This is an interesting ship you have here."

"Technically, my designation is SecondGen White-Blue Iteration Two-Point-Zero," noted the AI. "You are: species identifier: Ferengi."

"That's right . . . but I thought you had been downloaded or something. . . ."

"Affirmative. I have since rebooted and undertaken a system upgrade."

"Okay." He didn't question the reply; it wasn't the most unusual thing he had encountered during his time in Starfleet, not by a long way. Nog walked closer, studying the complex holotemplate floating before them. "This looks like a subspace domain pattern . . . an encrypted field model?"

"What would *your* estimation be, Mister Nog?" asked Tuvok.

He shrugged, but in truth Nog's mind was already caught up by the mystery of the subspace waveforms—not to mention the strange AI. He heard the doors open and close behind him as he went on. "At a guess? A micro-dimensional pocket domain acting as a subspace radio conduit. But deep into the low ranges, hard to find unless you know the exact quantum frequency."

"Tuvok was right, sir," Vale was saying. "He *is* good."

Nog turned to see who the commander was addressing, and he immediately snapped to attention at the sight of a human in an admiral's uniform. At the admiral's side stood another female commander, this one a striking dark-haired Betazoid. Nog was momentarily wrong-footed when he recognized the senior officer. "Tom . . . ?"

"Huh," said the admiral, almost to himself. "Now I know how *he* feels." He shook his head. "No, Mister

Nog, I'm William Riker. You've already met the rest of my people; this is *Titan*'s diplomatic officer, Commander Deanna Troi."

"The daughter of the notorious Lwaxana Troi?" He bowed slightly. "An honor to meet you, Commander."

"*Notorious?*" asked Vale, raising an eyebrow. "Don't you mean *famous?*"

"No," said Deanna wryly, "he doesn't."

Nog felt all eyes on him, and it wasn't comfortable. "Sir . . . why have I been brought here?"

"Let's get to that," said the admiral.

Riker turned to Tuvok and threw him a nod. The Vulcan went to the holodeck's control panel and entered another code string.

"Secured," reported Tuvok. "This compartment is fully isolated from all of *Titan*'s internal systems."

He looked around the compartment, taking them all in, meeting their gazes one by one. "I'll come right to the point. In the past few weeks we have all been forced to cross lines. To make choices that were unpalatable to us, because of circumstances beyond our control. But that ends now." Riker walked into the middle of the chamber, studying the subspace domain Torvig and White-Blue had uncovered. "I am taking back control. Not just for myself, but for my crew, my fleet, and *my* Federation. I need you to help me do it." The room was silent now, and Riker's throat became dry. "In the past, I've sailed close to the wind more times than I should have. Bucked regulations, even downright disobeyed direct orders on occasion. And I've asked a lot of you, taking you with me into harm's way time after time. It is my privilege that you didn't question, that you gave me your trust. I want to thank you all for that . . . and then ask you once more, to do so again." He thought about the others who were not in this room, people like Ssura, Ranul Keru, Melora Pazlar, Y'lira Modan, and other members of the *Titan*'s crew; all of them had already given implicit declarations of their loyalty. Riker found Deanna's warm, steady gaze upon him, and he drew strength from it. "Everyone here senses the shadow that has fallen over the United Federation of Planets since Nan Bacco was assassinated. The laws we stand by are being eroded. The principles we swore to uphold, dismissed. Power . . . abused." He shook his head. "Enough is enough. Our duty is clear-cut and undeniable. We either stand foursquare behind the ideals this uniform represents, or we stand aside and watch others push us to the brink of open war. Our resolve has been tested to the limit by the challenges we have faced, and now a new threat is rising." Riker glanced at Nog. "You've seen it. We all have."

"Aye, sir. . . ." said the Ferengi quietly.

"Here's what I need. I want every one of you to dig deep, to call in *your* favors, to use every ounce of skill and courage you have. I want you to help me get to the heart of what is going on in the shadows before we reach the point of no return." He paused, weighing his next words. "There is a rot at the core of the Federation . . . and we are going to put an end to it."

"You demand much, William-Riker," said White-Blue.

"No one knows that more than I do," he admitted. "I won't question anyone who wants to step away. This road I'm on . . . it could take everything from those who follow me."

"I'm in," Vale said simply.

"Agreed," offered Tuvok.

Riker looked around the holodeck, and he was heartened by the affirmations that surrounded him. *It is my pride and privilege to know these people.*

Nog rubbed a hand over his scalp. "So. Where do we start, sir?"

"It will be difficult," said Deanna. "We're going to be watched closely. It may be hard to know who to fully trust."

"This subspace domain and the holomessenger we intercepted are just parts of a larger covert communications network," said Torvig. "This network is the key to finding evidence of any criminal acts committed under the aegis of the Federation government."

"I'll do what I can from Deep Space Nine," Nog added.

"Somewhere out there, there has to be a trail. An archive," said Vale. "*Proof.*"

"Find it," said Riker.

The group dispersed, and soon Will and Deanna found themselves alone on one of the *Titan*'s observation decks, looking down at the blue-white vista of Earth beneath them.

She reached up a hand and touched his cheek. "This is going to test us all," his wife said quietly. "You know that Tasha and I are here for you, no matter what happens."

"I know," he told her. "You're the reason why I have to do this. More than my oath, more than because it is right. A galaxy controlled by men like Ishan Anjar is not one where I want us to live, and not where I want my daughter to grow up." He met her gaze. "If we look out to the stars and we see only darkness and dread, then we've lost something we will never get back. That fear will spread like poison."

"We'll stop it," she told him.

He gave a solemn nod. "But one ship, one crew, isn't going to be enough. We can't do this alone."

"You're right." Deanna smiled and crossed to an intercom panel. "Bridge?" she called. "This is Commander Troi."

"Go ahead, sir," said Keru. He sounded as if he had been waiting for the call. *"Ready to proceed."*

"I need you to compose a subspace signal, Ranul," she told him. "For immediate dispatch. Route it via civilian comm channels *only*."

"What destination, Commander?"

"Enterprise. Captain Picard."

"Tell him . . ." Riker hesitated, searching for the right words. "Sometimes the enemy hides in plain sight."

Acknowledgments

Thanks to my *Fall* colleagues David R. George III, Una McCormack, David Mack, and Dayton Ward for inspiration and comradeship in good measure; to Stan Goldstein, Fred Goldstein, Rick Sternbach, Michael Okuda, Denise Okuda, Debbie Mirek, David A. McIntee, Diane Duane, Keith R.A. DeCandido, Daniel Dvorkin, David Dvorkin, S. John Ross, Steven S. Long, Adam Dickstein, Forest G. Brown, Harold Apter, Ronald D. Moore, Mike Krohn, John Vornholt, and many more for their works of reference and of fiction; my most patient editor, Margaret Clark; and forever with much love to my own *imzadi*, Mandy Mills.

About the Author

James Swallow, a *New York Times* bestselling author and BAFTA nominee, is proud to be the only British writer to have worked on a *Star Trek* television series, creating the original story concepts for the *Star Trek Voyager* episodes "One" and "Memorial"; his other *Star Trek* writing includes the Scribe award winner *Day of the Vipers, Cast No Shadow, Synthesis,* the novellas *The Stuff of Dreams* and *Myriad Universes: Seeds of Dissent,* the short stories "The Slow Knife," "The Black Flag," "Ordinary Days," and "Closure" for the anthologies *Seven Deadly Sins, Shards and Shadows, The Sky's the Limit,* and *Distant Shores,* scripting the videogame *Star Trek Invasion,* and more than 400 articles for thirteen different *Star Trek* magazines around the world.

As well as nonfiction (*Dark Eye: The Films of David Fincher*), Swallow also wrote the *Sundowners* series of original steampunk westerns, *Jade Dragon, The Butterfly Effect,* and novels in the worlds of *Doctor Who* (*Peacemaker*), *Warhammer 40,000* (*Fear to Tread, Hammer & Anvil, Nemesis, Black Tide, Red Fury, The Flight of the Eisenstein, Faith & Fire, Deus Encarmine,* and *Deus Sanguinius*), *Stargate* (*Halcyon, Relativity, Nightfall,* and *Air*), *Tannhäuser* (*Enigma*), and *2000AD* (*Eclipse, Whiteout,* and *Blood Relative*). His other credits feature scripts for videogames and audio dramas, including *Deus Ex: Human Revolution, Fable: The Journey, Battlestar Galactica, Blake's 7,* and *Space 1889.*

Swallow lives in London and is currently at work on his next book.